FORBIDDEN FRUIT

FORBIDDEN FRUIT

Psalms of a Black Master

WILL KANE

KENSINGTON BOOKS
http://www.kensingtonbooks.com

KENSINGTON BOOKS are published by

Kensington Publishing Corp.
850 Third Avenue
New York, NY 10022

ISBN-13: 978-0-7582-1566-6
ISBN-10: 0-7582-1566-5

First Kensington Trade Paperback Printing: October 2007
10 9 8 7 6 5 4 3 2 1

*For my FireBird,
whose encouragement got me started and
whose inspiration kept me going.*

*For Gene,
the only boy to say "no" (but I ain't mad atcha!) and
whose mounds are my own personal Everest.*

Contents

Introduction

"Oh . . . my . . . God! Is it real?"

"Uh, it's erotica, dawg."

I am often asked if my stories are "real," which is an interesting question in itself, really: Just what IS the fundamental nature of realness? The individual, discreet incidents that are related in the stories that follow are "real," in the sense that they actually happened. To me. Really. The characters described are "real," in that they are based on actual people whom I have interacted with. The contexts of the stories are "real," in that they are set in actual places that I have traveled to, lived in, visited, or otherwise developed some connection to. But are the stories, in and of themselves, "real" as related? Well, the honest answer has to be . . . not really.

In order to protect a very long list of allegedly "innocent" parties, my counsel has advised that discretion is the better part of valor. Thus, I have taken the liberty of mixing things up; taking the plethora of sexy soirees, minor and major indiscretions, sleazy encounters, anonymous gropings, and just out and out damn horny pig debaucheries that have been the story of my life these many years, stuck them in a metaphorical blender, and hit "Whip." Consequently, as I like to say: nothing is as it seems. Frankly, it was the only way to let the guilty off the hook and protect what few genuine innocents there were. So to them, guilty and innocent alike (and you know damn well who you are), I say, with all due respect and much love, "You owe me, nigga!"

After many years of therapy, I have come to accept and acknowledge the fact that I am, in all reality, a crazy mo-fo, but in a nice way. I love sex. I love sex with men. I love sex with Black and Latino and Asian men. I love sex with Black and Latino and Asian men with really hot asses. I am at my absolute happiest when I am deep inside the incredibly hot ass of a totally freaky Black, Latino, or Asian man. These are my truths. And being a fully self-actualizing, highly functioning sentient being, I do my level best to always honor my truths, Every Fucking Day. Hence, the jumble of incidents that have been collected in this present volume. It's not that I'm sexually compulsive, addicted, or just a horn dog. As can be seen from what follows, sex comes up from behind and mugs me while I'm just minding my own business. Really! Now, I do admit to being very good at rolling with the punches, going with the flow, bending like the willow in the face of the hurricane, but if Sex thinks I'm just going to roll over and go down quietly, well, it's got another thing coming!

You see, I may not get up in the morning wondering: How am I going to get off today? But I do make the most of whatever comes my way. That's where the Mastery comes in. In whatever happens, I will find a way to control the situation to my satisfaction. Being a Capricorn (cusp) and Aquarian, with Cancer rising, means that I'm not a shrinking violet by any means. Control, whether that means my active command of events or the subtlety of acting through others, is what I gain in every situation, every time, always. You may surprise me, but in the end, I'll make you my bitch for sure. It's just my nature, and consequently, I am on top of things even when I'm pigging out on the bottom. Just don't call me "versatile."

The stories are also reflective of the fact that I am deeply, heavily, totally into some real kinky shit. Oh, don't worry, you won't be grossed out; I've tamed it down as much as possible (damn lawyers!).

But still . . . there is that Edge, which permeates the background and adds some spice to the mix and "BAM! Kicks it up a notch." My kinky side is a manifestation of the Master-of-the-Universe ethos that is also a deeply ingrained aspect of my character. I have been blessed and extremely fortunate to have been able to obtain a world-class education at some very prestigious institutions, public and private, and to do some incredibly interesting things in my working life. The expectations others have set for me have paled in comparison to the expectations I have set for myself. Overachiever, driven, focused, hard-charging, dedicated, tenacious are just some of the terms that my friends, colleagues, competitors, and, yes, lovers, have used to describe me. Consequently, I have earned some measure of success in all of the worlds in which I have traveled.

The result, I hope, is a rather special and somewhat unique collection of black male erotica. I wanted to write a collection that would be interesting, challenging the conventional notions of what black men, particularly same-gender–loving black men, are about and how we get our freak on. The men in these stories are overachievers, driven, focused, hard-charging, dedicated, and tenacious. They don't get stress, they give it. They are Top Guns, Alpha Dawgs, and *Masters of the Universe.* They are anything but victims of their circumstances. They are the kind of men that it has been my inestimable pleasure to get to know intimately. These are the guys I worked with, played with, fought with, loved, cried over, and, yes, even buried. I'm telling you now, you won't always see a condom or some lube or some other safe-sex stuff in these stories. That's because it's Erotica, and, as such, Erotica is not "real." It goes without saying that in the Real World, you stick a jimmie on it or you just don't stick it.

So, as they say, "Sit back, relax, and enjoy the ride!" But fasten your seat belts, punkin, because turbulence is ahead, fo' sure!

> Will Kane, Master
> On a beach somewhere
> (with some smokin' dude, as usual!)

After Hours

Everything about the day was just fucked up.

My taxi to the airport got into an accident. My plane was late taking off, after standing on the tarmac for hours. The airline lost my luggage, which had my money and credit cards stashed inside. The client that I had flown three thousand miles to see was out of town, thinking that our meeting was next week, even though I had confirmed with his secretary just the day before. And to top it off, it was pouring rain. Naturally, I didn't have an umbrella, and all I had left on me was pocket change, just barely enough to pay for a cab to get me halfway up Market Street, about ten blocks from my hotel. I'd be hoofing it the rest of the way, the steepest part of the fucking way, in the rain. Welcome to San Francisco!

By the time I reached the lobby door, my mood was as foul as the weather, which had whipped itself into such a frenzy that the rain was blowing sideways, like it was being shot from a water cannon, gushing down Twin Peaks, straight into my face. The guy behind the counter was one of those chatty types, always cheerful even when there was nothing to be cheerful about. I could have smacked the cheer right out of his ass but restrained myself when I spotted the familiar silhouette of my lost suitcase propped against the back wall behind the counter. After more forced pleasantries with "Sam, but everyone calls me Sammy, like the singer in the Rat Pack? 'Cause I'm like always singing along with those Sinatra records, ya know?", I collected my wayward bag and mercifully trudged off to my room, thankful that I didn't "know" and, moreover, hopeful that I would never find out.

Beck's Motor Lodge isn't what you would call fancy; in fact, it's downright shabby, in a "gay ghetto chic" kind of way. It was notorious for being something of a gay bathhouse disguised as a legit motel. It was not uncommon for dudes to display themselves in the windows of their rooms, as naked as Dutch prostitutes, to the parade of guys passing by on the exterior walkways that wrapped around each floor. Even guys who weren't staying at the motel would come by, cruise the three different levels in some pornographic game of "Mystery Date," knocking on doors looking for a "friend." I could have stayed downtown, in fact I was originally booked at the Hyatt on Union Square, which was one of my favorites, but after the hell I'd been through, even before the rain, I was in the mood for something a lot less refined. As I opened the door to my room and the strong stench of bleach mixed with the vaguely sweet smell of Crisco settled into my nostrils, my temperament swiftly shifted. I was hungry for some retribution and ready to take it out on somebody's hot, tight ass.

Of course I didn't bother to close the window blinds as I peeled off my soggy clothes and dried my ample dick and balls before stuffing myself into a pair of ripped jeans that barely concealed my then current state of mind. The boner I was sporting was giving those poor threads a real workout. A small group of willing "friends" had by then glued themselves to the window, eyes all wide and mouths slack jawed, too stunned to even bother knocking on the door. Unfortunately for them, I have no time for boys without guts. Give me a real man who knows what he wants and isn't afraid to risk everything to get it. I slipped on a tight black T-shirt and threw a well-worn leather jacket over it, then headed out the door. The awestruck groupies silently shuffled back against the railing to make room for me to pass, and only as I neared the stairwell did one of them finally break his silence to limply ask if I wanted company "or something." I pretended not to hear him and bounded down the stairs to the courtyard and then briskly walked out onto the street. Mercifully, the rain had given way to a heavy mist, which was not unlike being in the fetid confines of the Circle J Theater, hunkered down on a dingy side street not far from the Hyatt, during a lunchtime circle jerk.

The gentle wetness caressing my skin eased some of my tension, and I gradually started to sink into funky, horn-dog cruising mode, discreetly checking out the dudes on Market Street as I window-shopped my way to the Castro. There was a hot-looking, shirtless Latino guy in Image Leather trying on a bar vest, so I ducked inside to get a better look-see. On closer inspection, he was not particularly handsome, but his bare ass practically screamed for release from the leather chaps that exposed their firm, swarthy, bubbliciousness, with a thick mat of black hair sweeping down the crack in luscious curls that reeked of the need for an intense tongue-bathing. "Ummmm," I thought to myself, "me gusto mucho culos calientes." A salesclerk noticed my intense interest in the dude before I could approach him and quickly intercepted me, groping the bulging beast in my pants and asking if he could be of any assistance to me, "*Anything you need, sir, ANYTHING at all!*" Distracted from my main target, I took a good look at this rather cheeky clerk who had the nerve to feel me up so solicitously. He was a stunningly cute Asian bear cub—short, spiky black hair with blond tips, a little bit of a pot belly, finely cropped beard and moustache, with a mass of soft, black fur covering his creamy porcelain chest, stomach, arms, and who knows what else, hidden from view as it was by sleek latex pants that gleamed in the glow of the florescent lights. His coal black eyes were sparkling like obsidian, eagerly anticipating my response. After a moment spent contemplating what fun he might be, given my raging need for man flesh, I made my decision. How could I resist?

"What's your name?" I asked imperiously.

"Derek, sir."

"Der-*ek*," I repeated, playing with the syllables of his name like a cat who's found a new fixation to toy with. "Okay. You got any cock rings?"

"Yes, sir!" Derek responded, twitching like a lapdog ready for his daily walk. He briskly steered me to a small display counter near the dressing rooms, filled with a wide assortment of small leather items, including a copious selection of various and sundry rings to enhance any dick. "Which would you like to see, sir?"

I pointed to a thin rubber number, which came in several sizes and colors: blue, red, yellow, and, of course, black. "Let me see that one." Derek snapped open the case and pulled out three rubber rings in various colors, each a different circumference. Then, after further consideration of my swelled crotch, he pulled out a couple more, one in brass and another in chrome.

"I think you might like these too. Would you like to try them on, sir?" Derek asked, the crotch of his pants getting tighter by the second.

"Yeah, sure," I said, giving Derek a long head-to-toe glance, then added in a low deep voice, "Why don't you give me a hand with this?" as I slid my fingers across the front of my fly.

Derek's face flushed as he smiled ear to ear. "Right this way, sir. I think this dressing room is available," he whispered as he opened the door. We were both a little startled when the half-naked Latino in the chaps suddenly sprang out of the room, his firm, fleshy cheeks marred by coarse, ruddy streaks, and the black hair along his crack freshly slicked with a suspicious oily residue. He blushed when he saw us and hurried out of the store. He was followed a split second later by another guy, larger, darker, and rougher looking, who snapped his belt shut and rearranged his considerable package as he sauntered out after his trick, clearly unmoved by the sudden interruption of their tryst.

"Sorry about that, sir," Derek stammered, a little flustered.

"That's the Castro for you,'" I shrugged. As I slipped past Derek, I felt him up as he had done to me earlier, only with some added tweaking of his nipples, which were like hard, dried raisins. My fingers couldn't resist seeing how much pressure it took to make him squeal. Derek's face was soon twisted in a heady mix of surprise, pain, and lust. "So, you coming or what?" I called from inside the small space, still reeking of its last occupants. Derek, gasping, quickly followed and shut the door behind him. I slowly ran my hand down the front of my jeans, fondling the curve of my stiff prick as it fought the confines of the worn denim. Derek's eyes followed every movement of my hands, as did his little bear-cub dick, stretching the pliant latex and sexily exposing the shape of his fat mushroom knob. I unbuttoned my fly just as slowly, enjoying how he panted like a bitch in heat as each stud came undone. When I finished, I just hooked my thumbs into the belt loops at my side and stared at him, letting the fly gape tantalizingly open but still concealing its dark secrets.

The little room got hot quickly as the eroticism of the moment coursed through and between us. I could smell the pre-come in his rubber pants mixing with the dry breath that he exhaled in staccato bursts as if he was about to hyperventilate, and it was making my dick heavy and stiff. Derek looked into my eyes and then at the yawning blackness of my fly, then back again. I could have toyed with him some more, I suppose, but I was beyond horny, and seeing that other boy's well-fucked ass just made it even worse. I gave Derek a fleeting nod of encouragement, and tenderly, his hands shaking a little, he reached into my pants and took out my fat, pierced dick. Unleashed at last, my dick thrust itself into the air, stretching out every one of its eight dark cinnamon inches and slapping the moist palm of Derek's outstretched hand.

"Damn," he said in a barely audible whisper, "I love big dicks."

"Think you can handle it, boy?" I teasingly replied, shifting a bit so that my dick bobbed against Derek's own hard bulge. I could feel his dick responding in kind. "He won't be able to hold it much longer," I thought.

His face flushed a deep scarlet as Derek dropped to his knees and began working over my dick with his tongue and mouth. Exploring each heavy vein and sucking all around the lip of the meaty, swollen head. He especially seemed to like the two big steel rods that impaled my dick along the underside of the shaft. He lavished attention on them like a dog licking its balls. The boy was talented, that's for sure. I was feeling on the verge of shooting my load, but I wanted to stretch out his throat first, just to make sure he got the full taste of my hard eight. I placed a hand around the back of his head and pulled him deeper onto my dick as he sucked it.

With each stroke, I moved into him more, until I was fully fucking his throat, rubbing his nose in my pubes and slapping my balls against his chin. Poor Derek nearly gagged from the reaming, but he was a game boy and did his best to relax and deep throat my meat as I worked up to a massive explosion. I came so much that juice was leaking out of his nose. I pulled out just enough for him to gulp down on some of the mammoth wad and regain his breath a bit before force-feeding him some more dick. Soon I was shooting yet another load, and I got concerned because I thought I was choking the poor boy with my meat and come as his face started to turn a little blue.

I pulled out and rubbed my dick all over his face and chin, smearing the last few drops of juice into his beard and moustache. As I did so, Derek blew his load into his pants, which I knew had to have felt good, sloshing around inside that latex crotch and slowly dripping down his legs. While relieving a little of my pent-up tension, Derek's blow job only made my dick harder, which meant that slipping on a cock ring was out of the question. As he held the little assortment next to my prick, it was obvious to him too that none of them were big enough to fit me. We looked at each other and then started to laugh.

"Listen," I said, "Why don't we continue this another time?"

"The store closes at eleven," Derek replied confidentially. "I'm closing tonight, so why don't you come back then?"

I checked my watch. It was only nine-thirty. "Okay," I said as I helped Derek to his feet and grabbed his crotch, rubbing it to spread his load around his balls and between his legs. "Stay lubed for me," I quipped as I opened the door and held it for him to exit. He just grinned broadly, wiping some of my juice off his cheek with the back of his hand and then licking it clean. I walked out of the store, and the sudden rush of fresh air urgently reminded me that I hadn't eaten all day. I headed off down Market to Castro and wandered into Without Reservations, one of my favorite reliable and cheap boîtes.

Along the way, there were so many hot-looking guys who caught my eye, ensuring that my dick stayed rock hard and attracting plenty of attention of its own, especially since I had somehow forgotten to button my fly, allowing tantalizing peeks of my rod. There's really nothing like cruising in San Francisco. It's the kind of town where you're always running into someone you know, even if you've only just met them for the first time. Who should be sitting at the table across from mine but the Latino guy with the cute ass in the leather chaps and his dark, hunky "friend," enjoying a post-coital nosh? The hunk spotted me right off and gave a conspiratorial nod of his head, a big shit-eating grin spread across his face. He waved for me to join them, so being neighborly, I did.

"Yo, homes, what up?" the hunk boomed in a deep, sexy baritone. He was a beautiful, olive-skinned brother. I had initially mistaken him for one of those hot, swarthy Italians that San Francisco overflows with. He was stacked solid, with huge guns, the kind that come from serious working out every day for hours. His nose was flat and decidedly crooked, as if broken in a fight, but it suited his features perfectly, actually enhancing his macho sensuality. He moved with the easy grace of a boxer, and I could picture him standing in a ring, stripped down to just some shorts, his sweaty chest gleaming in the lights. But it was those dreamy, heavily lidded bedroom eyes that made me take an immediate liking to him.

"Plenty," I responded, grabbing my throbbing crotch. The hunk laughed heartily and pointed at his cute-ass comrade.

"See there? I told you he'd still have plenty left over for ya." The cute-ass guy didn't say a word, but his eyes never left my crotch. I sat down next to him so he could get his fill.

"The name's Will. What's yours?" I asked of the hunk.

"Rashawn," he replied, extending his hand, "and this is my main man, Lorenzo." I warmly returned Rashawn's greeting and then extended my hand to Lorenzo, who distractedly shook it, still deeply engrossed in staring at my open fly. "Yo, man, you fuck that Asian hottie?"

The way Rashawn's thick, full lips curled around the word "fuck" was off-the-hook sexy, as if his lips were pantomiming the very action implied and literally fucking each letter. Recalling that huge package of his, I started having serious fantasies of a hot foursome with him and his boy. "Naw, that comes later."

"Um, if it was me, I'd a been all up in that phat ass, fo' sure."

"Right, I've seen how you work," I said as I leeringly peered behind Lorenzo to take in his curvaceous ass up close.

We made more small talk for a while, feeling each other out in that indirect, guy-thing way. Talking about marginal subjects of little real interest to us but which served as convenient cover for our real objectives. Speaking in code filled with double entendres and innuendoes, wrapped in a sensual wariness that guys use as they try to figure out the power dynamics between them and determine what possibilities might be on offer. As it turned out, Rashawn was in town for a Hellfire Club conclave, which was a pleasant discovery for me since I had come across relatively few black guys into the dark side of the Force, and that only added to my interest in him. After a little more give and take, it was clear that while Rashawn and I were usually Alpha Males, some heavy-duty, no-holes-barred action with a superfine hot stud was a temptation not to be lightly passed up. We agreed to meet later that evening, with our boys in tow, at Beck's, where, coincidentally, Rashawn was also staying, and really give the voyeurs a show. I checked my watch, and, happily, it was time to head back to the store and see what Derek was up to.

There are few olfactory pleasures that compare to the intoxicating aroma of a good leather store. The walk-in humidor at Nat Sherman's, on Fifth Avenue and 42nd Street, ranks up there, as does the dark-chocolaty, maduro-wrapped Padron Anniversario cigar, which is so smooth it's like holding a piece of heaven in your hand and sucking on an angel's tit. The Dakota leather cabin of a brand new BMW 650i convertible will make you mess your drawers, and I'm also fond of the heady, exotic notes of a Pusser's Painkiller cocktail at sunset on the terrace of the aptly named Veranda Bar at Bermuda's Elbow Beach.

In fact, a Padron and a Pusser's on the beach at sunset is pretty close to achieving Nirvana in this lifetime. The sweetness of the two just wrap you in their languid embrace, and the warmth of their kisses melts away all traces of your mortality, so that when you finally slip behind the wheel of the Bimmer and make that long drive back to the Fairmont Princess Hotel with the top down, as the sultry trade winds blow the otherworldly scent of frangipani in bloom across your face, you *know* that you are the Living God incarnate. Image Leather is a very good leather store, and the earthy musk of the black motorcycle jackets, hats, chaps, pants, vests, and the various and sundry adult playthings on display gets itself deep into your subconscious, unlocking the hidden door of your innermost recesses and allowing the animal within to roam freely in all its untamed splendor. In other words, it'll get your FREAK on, baby.

Derek was busy with the closing rush, caroming from customer to customer like a well-played pinball racking up a top score. He gave me a very big smile when he spied me over by the rack of cock rings. I amused myself while I waited for the last customer to be rung up. I tried on some expensive jackets and struck poses in the three-way mirror, doing my best Brando imitations from *The Wild One*. Finally, I slipped off my clothes and settled into a supersexy ensemble consisting of matching custom-tooled vest, ass-exposing chaps, and dick-enhancing codpiece. It is just amazing how little one can wear and still look dressed to the nines.

At last, Derek walked the last customer to the door and locked it after him. We were alone in the belly of the beast. Derek switched off the exterior lights and dimmed the ones in the store, making for a dusky gloom that was punctuated by the spotlights on various displays, creating a mysterious patchwork of light and dark spaces. As he came toward me, appearing and disappearing like an apparition, I started to feel that familiar tingle running down the length of my prick and under my balls, pulling them tighter to my body. My pulse picked up as he got near enough for me to smell his sweat mingled with the moist leather of his vest. It might not have been a Padron, but I'd lick an angel's sweaty armpits any day.

"So, Daddy, you need a cock ring to complete that hot outfit?" Derek asked in a hoarse whisper, running his hands along the bulging codpiece.

"Yeah," I replied softly, "I want something really special," and unsnapped the codpiece, letting my dick, sporting its full length though soft, but slowly getting harder by the second, flop out of the pouch.

"I think this one might be a good fit," Derek replied as he turned slightly, presenting his firm, pear-shaped ass, and unzipped the rear flap of his latex pants. I reached out and peeled the flap down, exposing his small, tight, hairy, deeply dimpled butt.

"Well," I said, as I slid my fingers across his ass, rubbing my palms along the inside of his crack, massaging the globes of his butt and exposing the coal black button of his hole, hidden beneath a thicket of soft black fur, "let's check it out, shall we?"

I was soon on my knees, digging my tongue deep into his tart little ass, trying to taste as much of his essence as my mouth could grab. His acrid sweat, a little tangy, made my taste buds tingle. I moved from his hole, down the furry glory trail of his crack, to his balls, which were shaved smooth and hung beneath him like two ripe avocados, surprisingly large and very responsive to the full-on assault of my tongue. I had to lift him onto the balls of his feet to accommodate my head and shoulders as I feasted on his delicate sac from behind, which caused Derek to bend far forward, legs spread as wide as the roll of latex around his ankles would allow, his hands flat against the floor in front of him. As I continued to make my way to his hard dick and that fat mushroom head, I jabbed a couple of fingers into his asshole, and he started to buck and gyrate his butt while letting out a low growl. His ass was so hot for a good fucking that I didn't even need to use any lube to open him up. After only a few minutes, it seemed, I was running three and four fingers inside of him, stretching his hole wide and making his dick drip, which I greedily slurped up as I sucked on his thick fleshy head like a straw, eager to drain the juice from his balls.

Before he could come, I forced him to his knees and rammed my dick into his willing hole, deep-dicking him to the point that it felt as if his ass was sucking on my dick like one of those penis pumps, making it expand even bigger so I could fuck him that much deeper and harder. As I reamed him, I reached under and grabbed his nipples, pulling on them as I pinched them until they were full and fat, like tender berries ready for the plucking. Derek exploded. His head snapped up so hard I thought he'd break his neck. His eyes rolled back into their sockets, exposing only the whites. And his whole body quivered so intensely that the vibrations seemed to penetrate my bones as they increased in their frequency until at last it was as if I were riding a wild stallion in the breaking ring. All the while, the powerful suction of his asshole was working my dick until it felt as though he were draining my soul clean out of my body. When I came, I just knew that my balls had been turned inside out and pulled halfway down the shaft of my dick.

After we recovered from that first fuck, we took full advantage of being locked inside the candy store, doing it in every conceivable position and using every toy we could lay our hands on. Derek was one hell of a pig bottom boy. He loved to take dick and anything else I had a hankering to stuff into his butt. It was as if the more he got, the more gluttonous he became. And I was just as much of a pig as he was, eating out his ass, sucking on his dick, balls, and nipples, running my tongue around the world until I had inspected every inch of his naked hairy body. And the more I fucked him, the more I wanted of him. My dick never felt so good being buried to the hilt inside another man's ass.

I slapped his cheeks as I fucked him, making them raw and supersensitive. Then I'd rip my dick out of his hole and slobber my tongue all over those pliant flanks, cooling them down so I could start all over again. I bent his legs back over his head, his knees knocking against his ears, and plowed his sloppy, loose ass with my dick and balls shoved all the way inside him. When he came that time, it took my breath away as his guts squeezed the living hell out of my balls. We fucked standing up and sitting down, on the counter and bent over the stools used in the shoe department. We left a slick trail of come and sweat from one end of the store to another. And the only thing that stopped us from going all night long was the cleaning crew, who came in by the rear entrance only to find Derek and me furiously fucking in their janitorial closet. Boy, what a mess we left for them!

We hurriedly scrambled to find and then grab our clothes amidst the detritus we had amassed during our wanton bacchanalia, managing to pull on just our pants before dashing past the still shell-shocked cleaners and out the rear door, running barefooted at full speed back to Beck's, wildly laughing our heads off in the cool drizzle like two crazy men sharing a secret no one else is privy to. As we neared my room, I noticed a familiar sight just across the way, on the floor below mine. I pointed it out to Derek, and he gave me an eager smile as we headed over to Rashawn's room, where he was working over Lorenzo's bubble-butt with one humongous Mandingo dick. We pushed our way to the front of the crowd standing in front of the window and knocked on the pane. Rashawn peered between his legs, giving us a good view of his hard, high ass and low hangers, dripping sweat profusely, and he flashed a huge smile when he recognized us. He lifted himself off of Lorenzo, leaving his beautiful ass gaping wide open, and walked to the door.

"Yo, peeps, I was hoping you'd show up!" Rashawn boomed, standing in the doorway in all his naked, hard-muscled glory, a condom dangling off the tip of his thick meat, obviously full of more than a few heavy come loads, which I was eager to unburden him of. Now it was going to get real, for real.

But that's a story for another time.

Russian Bath

It sat there on the Lower East Side on a narrow, nondescript
street that was only just beginning to evidence the first signs of
gentrification disease, wherein assholes with money glom on to a
quaint neighborhood with real character and then quickly trans-
form it into just another sterile strip of haute luxury. But for
now, the decrepit-looking building hulking in the middle of the
block, sporting tattered awnings with the simple and direct legend "BATHS" emblazoned along their scalloped edges, exuded
all the character and grace that one would expect from an establishment that claims to have been in continuous operation since
1892. As I made my way up the steep, well-worn steps, I could
feel the ghosts of all those previous patrons who had made that
same climb, seeking a little bit of relief from the chaotic excesses
of the city and hoping to rekindle some of the camaraderie of
their mother country.

A number of my straight friends had told me about this place,
particularly the therapeutic powers of a good Russian bania,
over the years—timeworn stories recalled in hoary reminis-
cences fading into the stuff of mythic legend, as in "Before the
baby was born . . ." or "Once, when I was still in college. . . ."

But I admit I didn't pay much attention to them, since how much fun could a straight bathhouse be, really?! As a gay man, I know bathhouses, especially bathhouses in New York City, from the West Side Club to the Mt. Morris Baths to the Wall Street Sauna and everything in between. I'd even been to Plato's Retreat (after the venerable Bette Midler haunt, the gay Continental Baths, was taken over by the new swingers of the Studio 54 era), so I knew about coed baths too. But a straight, male bathhouse, even if only for a few "men-only" hours in an otherwise sober, straight-laced, legit establishment, fun? Puhleese!

But it was one of those odd, only-in-New-York coincidences that the trick I had picked up at The Cock the night before happened to live a few doors down from the very same baths, and as I was leaving his place early Sunday morning on a bright, warm Indian Summer day in late September, I serendipitously decided to check out the place for myself. Besides, after the hard night of ass-punishing sex I had just meted out, I could use some old-world revitalization. I was inauspiciously greeted at the front counter by a gruff, ancient Soviet cold-warrior who didn't seem to have thawed out even though the Wall had fallen and the Soviet Union had long since given way to the Russian Federation. He barked a series of questions at me, reminding me of my one visit to the old USSR in 1986, to Leningrad then (now St. Petersburg), when a hard-line immigration officer raked my Capitalist American Pig ass over the coals before giving me an entry visa (no doubt the pair of brand-new Levis I discretely slipped him helped ease the process!).

In such situations, I have found it best to smile broadly and act totally clueless. Unless the other person is just a total jerk (or looking for a bigger bribe), they will often take pity on you and wave you through without much additional hassle. My present examiner's thick accent made it nearly impossible for me to comprehend most of what he was asking me anyway, so I just stupidly nodded and bobbed my head, throwing my hands up in the universal gesture of "I have no frigging idea what the fucking hell you're saying!" Realizing that I was beyond hopeless, the old guy shook his head in that other universal gesture of "Jeesh! Stupid Americans!" and pointed wearily at a faded sign on the wall, which basically said to place your valuables in one of the boxes on the counter. I immediately complied, then he handed me two keys and pointed toward the entrance to the men's locker room.

Things surprisingly picked up quite nicely once I made it to the locker room. As I looked at the two keys with some puzzlement, a drop-dead handsome young Arab guy, maybe mid-twenties, with an impossibly skinny, lithe build, beautifully hairy, swarthy complexion, and the most seductive, deep-set brown eyes peeking out from under a unibrow that was actually sexy, wearing only a short, thin towel, approached me warmly.

"Your first time here?" he asked helpfully.

"Yeah. I'm not sure why I have two keys."

"One's for your valuables, and the other is for the locker." He took the keys from my hand, and as he did so, his body brushed lightly against my arm. I loved the softness of his skin, the coarseness of his hair, and the musky scent of his body. Despite a raucous night of heavy-duty ass-digging, my somewhat raw and sensitive dick was not too tired to stir itself in response. He looked at the number imprinted on the keys and then found the locker. "Here it is," he called as I stood back to watch his half-naked, sinewy body from behind, taking special note of the firmness of his ass, tightly bundled in the towel. Perhaps I hesitated a bit too long, because he turned in time to catch my lecherous gaze and gave me a smile that was at once coyly innocent and all-knowing.

"My name is Murad," he said, angling slowly so I could get a better look at his lightly muscled chest and his large, fleshy nipples, a reddish chestnut color that contrasted warmly with his tawny skin tone. "What's yours?"

His question shook me from my lustful reverie and forced me to pull my tongue back into my mouth. "Will," I stammered. "Nice to meet you." I extended my hand to shake his.

Murad had a surprisingly strong grip for such a scrawny guy. I admit, that was a real attraction for me, being somewhat inclined toward skinny guys as it is, since I just love the way a skinny guy's ass spreads itself wide open when he bends over, presenting that come-fuck-me asshole like a vacancy sign on a Motel Six at two AM on I-95—"We'll leave the light on for you" indeed! Murad seemed to sense it, as his hand held mine just a bit longer than a casual greeting required, more in a hoping-to-get-to-know-you-*much*-better kind of way. We held each other's gaze in like fashion, his eyes sparkling in sly amusement. He suddenly broke off and sat on the edge of one of the lounges set out in the middle of the locker room.

A couple of guys were laying on the lounges, one wrapped head to toe in towels and a robe, totally oblivious to anything going on around him. The other had just a towel draped very casually over his privates, oh so nonchalantly putting his meaty, uncut dick on display, one arm covering his face in a way that still allowed him to see if there were any takers. Murad sat, making no effort to obscure his own rather ample endowment as it hung off the edge of the lounge, spreading his legs to ensure that I could get a full view of the long, thin shaft of his dick that ended in his superthick knob, barely peeking out from behind the voluptuous folds of his juicy foreskin, and a gloriously hairy ball-sack dangling its precious contents, swaying slightly from side to side, as Murad continued his orientation on the ins and outs of the place. It seems my timing couldn't have been more perfect, since Sundays before two PM are reserved for "men only."

I listened distractedly, slowly fumbling with my clothes, trying to will my dick to behave while staring at his inviting package. Then it dawned on me that given our relative positions, he was waiting for me to give him an equally interesting show. That sudden realization stirred my dick into seizing control of the situation, and I learned long ago to faithfully listen to my dick. As a consequence, I paused for a moment and looked squarely at Murad, my face a stoic mask that slowly gave way to a seductive gaze. I ran my fingers under the hem of my shirt and pulled it slowly up my torso, keeping my eyes steadily glued on Murad's face. As I pulled it over my head, I paused a bit again, to give him a good look at my hard, muscular abs and powerfully built chest, with its intricate tattoo work and the huge ring piercing my left nipple.

I wanted him to see how my naturally smooth, hairless skin rippled as I moved, the golden brown hue catching the dull light and refracting it into a sheen that made my skin glow like a precious jewel. Then I pulled off the shirt and dropped it casually into the locker, my eyes still fixated on Murad. He licked his lips in anticipation. Next, I unfastened the top button of my jeans, and, after another brief pause, I undid each button in turn until my pants gaped open, exposing the briefest glimpse of the top of my thick, dark brown dick, snuggled in a mass of rich black pubic hair. Murad's dick stiffened slowly until its thin nine inches were pointing straight out in front him, the fat knob, still swathed in its fleshy folds, silently bobbing in the air, keeping time to a rhythm of its own. Even the wise guy on the lounge was sporting a nice fat boner, clearly not "sleeping" as his pose suggested. Encouraged by the audience response, I continued, only this time I bent down and took off my shoes and socks, then placed them in the locker. I knew what they were waiting for, and I was going to make them wait just a bit longer.

When I spied a small jewel of glistening, pearlescent pre-come oozing from the end of Murad's dick, the juices started flowing from my balls up and into my own hard member, causing a wet spot to form on the leg of my jeans. Murad extended the tip of his tongue and licked his full, succulent lips in a long, circular motion that left them wet. The guy on the lounge started to beat off. I placed my hands on the waist of my jeans and then slowly wiggled them down my thighs, exposing the brawny shaft of my stiff prick little by little until at last it was freed from the tight confines of the jeans and could swagger in its full majesty right in Murad's face, just a few inches from those sweet, wet lips. I was dripping thick droplets of juice onto the floor, even as thick beads flowed down the underside of my shaft to hang precariously from my balls before falling at my feet.

Murad's eyes widened in lustful desire; his dick was so hard that even his fat knob finally exposed itself to see mine. He leaned forward as if to wrap his lips around my throbbing dick, but I turned slightly at the last moment, bending down to lock the locker, and as a result, Murad's sweet mouth landed in the crack of my ass. His hot tongue immediately darted into my hole, lapping at it like a man thirsting for water in the desert. His face pressed deeply against my cheeks, and his hands grabbed at me, trying to feel and explore every part of my dick and balls. I ground my hips into his eager face, backing up on his tongue, and rode his sweet lips hard, reaching behind to push his face still deeper into my ass. I could feel the wetness of his pre-come drooling down the backs of my calves and ankles like shards of molten glass etching his desire into my flesh. The grunts of the wise guy on the lounge as he reached his sloppy climax made us seek out more privacy, and Murad led me to a small toilet just off the locker room with a full-length door that could be locked.

Once inside, I returned the favor, firmly grasping his small, fleshy cheeks and stretching them tautly open as I sat on the lone commode and pulled his gaping asshole to my lips, burying my head in his musky, warm crack and unleashing my crazed tongue in a torrent of deep, fevered ass-eating. Murad bent over and grabbed my thighs, both to brace himself from falling and to lift my dick to his mouth so he could deep throat my shaft and suck the living hell out of my balls. It was as if we were in a mad sexy competition to see who could suck harder, deeper, and stuff more into his mouth, as we matched the ferocity of our hunger for the other's juicy parts. I slipped down on the commode so that my back was parallel to the floor, and Murad was able to eat out my ass as I worked my way to his balls, sucking first one into my mouth, then the other, then both at once, running my tongue all over them as I gagged on their hirsute splendor.

Murad's tongue felt so good digging into my tight hole, parting it with a strong circular motion that drove me wild. He ate me out like it was his last meal on earth, and my dick was drooling like a leaky faucet, making a huge, slick mess on my stomach that made his hairy belly sticky as it rubbed against me. I worked my mouth down his long, thin shaft and finally took that fat head of his all the way down my throat as Murad started bucking his hips to fuck my face. I pumped my hips in response when he went down on my dick again and fucked his throat, then upped the ante by sticking my index and middle fingers deep into his asshole. Murad grunted, my dick banging against the back of his throat, and he backed his ass down on my fingers to drive them deeper into his ass. As he did so, he stuffed both of his thumbs into my ass and pulled my hole as far apart as he could, massaging the rim and trying to jam even more fingers into it. I was on the verge of blowing my wad big-time, but I wanted my dick in his ass first.

I lifted Murad's skinny body off my chest and, still firmly grasping his ass cheeks, pushed his butt and hips down my body as I pulled myself into a sitting position on the commode, until my swollen, hard joint was pressed against his sleek, hairy crack. I thrust my meat up and down the crack of his ass to let him know that he was going to get it good. Murad curved his body backward, his head rubbing against the side of my face, moaning, "Fuck me, fuck me hard." I didn't need any lube to get my dick up to the hilt inside him. Murad's ass was like warm butter around my thick, fat dick, and as I ground my prick deep into his sizzling guts, I could feel the juice rising in my shaft. I had just started to get a groove going, pumping my hips in slow, deep thrusts, impaling Murad so deep that his breath skipped its rhythm with each reaming plunge, when there was a sudden loud knock at the door, like a fist being slammed against it.

In a flash, Murad was on his feet, my dick ripping out of his ass just as I erupted, sending thick sorties of come toward the gaping target of his hole. He turned around just as suddenly and thrust his stiff prick all the way down my throat and blew a massive wad that nearly caused me to black out, choking as I was on both his big dick and all that juice. Then he was gone, scurrying out a second doorway that I hadn't noticed when we first entered. I sat there dazed for a few seconds, my mouth filled with his hot, tart load, and rapped my knuckles against the first door to let the person on the other side know that this toilet was occupied. It seemed to satisfy the stranger, since I was able to finish collecting myself enough to leave in peace.

When I exited, there was no sign of either Murad or the mysterious interloper whose damnably poor timing ruined a perfectly good fuck session. The two dudes who had been lounging before were both gone as well, and the locker room was a beehive of activity, with a wide assortment of guys in various states of undress. I'd say the average age was about fifty-five, with maybe half the guys a lot older than that, a big group clustered between forty to forty-five, and a smattering of younger guys between twenty and thirty. There were a lot of older Jewish guys, many still wearing their skullcaps even though nearly naked and clearly headed to the mikvah. A ton of hugely overweight guys, tottering about on delicate feet, gingerly headed toward the succor of the baths in a flotilla of pasty white flesh that had never seen the light of day. Not many guys of color, though the few that I did see were in just okay shape. I considered leaving right then, but I glimpsed the hard, high bubble-butt of a hunky blue-black guy just as he disappeared around the corner and decided that maybe I ought to do some further research before making a final decision. I quickly grabbed a towel and scurried off in the direction that the brother had gone.

To get to the baths, you have to climb down a really steep flight of dingy, dimly lit, slippery, tiled stairs that looked like they led straight to hellfire and damnation. A very noticeable odor percolated upward from the depths, a kind of dirty, wet-dog smell that did nothing to assuage my growing skepticism. At the bottom, I was greeted by a young Russian guy who practically ran into me as he headed in the opposite direction. He was dressed in a T-shirt and warm-up pants that marked him as some kind of attendant. He gave me an appraising glance and then blurted out "You want massage?" in a really thick accent, not so much asking as ordering. "I do sport massage, shiatsu, Dead Sea salt scrub, Black Sea mud bath, anything you like." I was beginning to take a fancy to this strapping blond, who sure looked a damn sight better than the crowd I had just witnessed upstairs. "I'm Tibor," he offered. "I take *special* care of you."

Well, how could I resist that invitation? And there was something about the way Tibor said "special." So I agreed to let the towheaded hunk take care of me, and he led me into the real heart of the baths. On the way to the massage rooms, he pointed out the Swedish and the Turkish saunas and their relative differences (the former is dry, the latter wet), the steam room, the cold plunge (which was kept at a very chilly thirty-six degrees), the showers, aligned in a semicircle, which meant that you were always on display to everyone else, and finally the raison d'être of the place, the Russian sauna or bania. The bania was essentially a huge furnace for heating rocks, which then provided the enclosed room with enough heat to cook meat, if left too long on one of the hard stone benches of the upper tier, where I lasted only five seconds before jumping down and dousing myself with a bucket of ice-cold water that did nothing to stop my meat from smoking. The old Jewish guys, hunched over their well-worn prayer books and sitting as calmly as Sam McGee in his burrow of glowing coal on the marge of Lake LaBarge, cackled under their breaths as I punked out.

Tibor laughed too—"It take a little getting used to"—as he guided me into a smallish cubical with a slab straight out of some old *CSI: Cold Case* rerun in the middle of it. He motioned for me to lie down, "Face up, face down, how ever you like," and I spread out, face down, my towel draped across my butt, the coolness of the slab a welcome relief for my poached dick and balls. Tibor deftly removed the towel with a sharp snap of his wrist and seemed to take great pleasure in examining my naked body. Unhurriedly, he ran his fingers and palms up and down my legs and thighs, massaging my sculpted tokus, rubbing the edge of his palm along my crack, pressing firmly against my asshole in a circular motion that was so relaxing I thought he was going to fist me. His touch was sensuous, gentle, but commanding.

My dick was already in tune with Tibor's rhythm, poking stiffly between my legs, clearly inviting some "special" attention. As he massaged my inner thighs, Tibor would caress my prick as he slid it from side to side, pulling my testicles from underneath and rolling them in his hands like Ben Wa balls. "Chinese exercise," he said as he worked them over. "Good for health." As he manipulated my balls with one hand, Tibor ran the other along my spine, from the base of my skull to my ass and then down my crack again and again, his fingers poking at my tight hole, teasing it, making it beg for his fingers to scratch that suddenly incessant itch deep inside. With each stroke, his fingers would linger just a bit longer on the threshold, driving me insane and causing me to bump and grind my ass like some freakish Venus flytrap hoping to catch a tasty morsel.

"Turn please," Tibor commanded, jarring me from a lustful trance. I rolled over onto my back, feeling like one of the lumbering behemoths beyond the door. My swollen dick slapped hard against my belly and then twitched in deranged spasms, hungry for still more attention. Tibor stepped away from the side of the slab for a few moments, and when he returned, I felt enveloped by a warm, earthy slickness wherever his hands touched me. As he applied the pungent Black Sea mud to my dick and balls, Tibor's hands seemed to lose their restraint and firmly grasped and stroked them until my dick was dripping and my balls felt like they were being unscrewed from my body. He tweaked my nipples as he jacked me, pinching them hard as he stroked my dick, pumping it almost to climax. He worked the head of my dick, polishing it, drawing it between his fingers, spreading the lips of my slit, rubbing the sweet spot just under the head and squeezing out thick droplets of pre-come to mix with the mud and form a slick lube to spread up and down my shaft.

Tibor's frenzied fingers even found their way into my hungry ass at last, deeply probing it, gouging it, stretching it wide as they groped in search of that itch, digging it out, leaving no corner unexcavated, turning it inside out, popping that cherry, making a whore of it, punking it, forcing that bitch to sing for its daddy. And he didn't let up on my dick for a minute either. Jacking it rough, hard, soft and sweet, teasing and caressing, pumping it until the skin felt raw, digging his nails into the soft underside around the lip of my head, pulling my thick eight-inch grower to a hard nine-and-a-half and threatening to break off that chocolate stick at the fucking base. In an act of mercy, Tibor made me come, his fingers thrust deep into my ass and choking my dick as if he was going to wring every last drop of come out of it, allowing me to blow until my balls ran dry. I came for days, like in a bad porno movie where all the guys in the orgy scene spill enough cream to make Elsie the Borden cow jealous, and still Tibor milked my ass and balls. Goddamn "special care" indeed!

I'm not sure how long I lay on the slab after Tibor finally hosed me down and gently dried me off. He gave me a hearty slap on the butt and a strong friendly shake of the shoulder before leaving me to recover. I somehow got to my feet and walked out into the madness of the baths, totally naked, throbbing from head to toe and too utterly unconcerned about anything as provincial as modesty at this point to bother with the farce of a towel. My height, powerful build, copper-colored complexion, and big fucking dick literally stopped traffic. Guys in the showers gawked at me while rubbing their dicks in that universal symbol of "If you want it, show it hard."

As I made my way to the Turkish sauna, passing through a gauntlet of guys sitting on low, tiled benches that put them eye-level with my phine phat bone, other guys licked their lips and gaped their mouths like goldfish; translation: "I want to suck your dick." Once inside the sauna, I pressed my way past slippery mounds of corpulent flesh that only grudgingly moved aside enough for me to reach the upper bench, surreptitiously copping a feel of my ass and dick, translation: "Fuck me, Daddy."

The two guys on either side of me, a rail-thin, young Slavic guy whose glasses were constantly fogging up in the humidity and a superhairy old fat guy with thinning red hair rubbing his belly like an Irish Buddha, got a close-up view of my ass as I turned to sit between them, our ass cheeks rubbing together. They could barely keep their own pricks from rising to salute my impressive meat, displayed in all its splendor for admiring eyes to ogle to their heart's content. I felt the stares of those in the room as if they had lined up to gang-suck my dick. Though not hard, my dick flaunted its superior thickness and length, making most of the stiffening pricks around the room look puny in comparison. There was nothing but silence at first, just the hushed homage of lowly vassals to the Black Dick God in their midst.

The benches were in the shape of a horseshoe, with two wings to my left and right. Guys sitting on the sides were close enough that if they stuck their feet straight out they could play footsies with the guys opposite them. There were three levels that rose stadium-style, and in front of my section there were three shower nozzles dangling from the ceiling, making anyone using them to cool off an instant object of curiosity for the group. Next to the showers, and beside the glass door, there was a large glass window giving those outside a good view of what was happening inside, and vice versa. There were probably twenty or thirty guys in the sauna, making it fairly crowded and very intimate. You couldn't help but rub against the slick, naked flesh of at least four guys, more if you were sitting in the middle row, since you had the legs of the guys on the upper bench pressed against your back and the backs of the guys on the lower bench pressed against your legs.

There was a pretty good-looking papi sitting in the middle of the top bench to my right, his dark honey complexion standing out starkly from the sea of pink around him. And to the right of the Latin guy, on the middle bench, there was a stunningly attractive Asian dude, with a hot, muscular build, killer abs, and thighs that gave me palpitations. Boy, how I wished to have those wrapped tightly around my waist! And damn! That Asian dude was hung sweet! My dick was beginning to firm up as I surveyed the rest of the room for still more interesting sights. Down on the first level, to my left, was the beautiful dark-skinned brother whose hard bubble had started me off on this adventure, his blue-black skin and bald head shining like obsidian. Now I was fully erect and hungry for some hot colored ass, despite being sorely sensitive from Tibor's ministrations.

I caught a glimpse of the Slavic dude out of the corner of my eye, staring at my bone and repetitively licking his lips like the always-hungry Weasel gawking at Foghorn Leghorn and dreaming of what a good meal he'd make (I say, I say, you look a might bit peaked there, son). The pinkish purple head of his short, skinny, uncut dick was mooning from beneath the flap of his foreskin, one hand gripping the underside of his balls, the other furiously pushing his glasses back up his thin nose so he could keep his baleful eyes glued on every slight motion of my dick. I rustled on the bench, making sure to rub my muscular ass and torso against his slight, ninety-eight-pound-weakling frame just to tease him and make his dick hard. All around the room, there was a hushed quiet, interrupted only by the periodic whistling of another blast of hot steam surging into the space and temporarily filling it with a blinding mist that obscured everything but the fuzzy outline of whoever was right next to you. During the moments of clarity, guys darted their eyes around the room with the lean and hungry look of young Cassius sizing up Caesar on the steps of the Senate.

There was a palpable hunger in the room, and it dawned on me that everyone there was acutely aware that time was running out and soon the baths would be open for women to join them. I knew that feeling, well almost, but it wasn't dissimilar from cruising in a gay bar at last call and realizing that you still hadn't settled on a hot trick to pick up and the last thing you wanted to do was go home and jerk off alone. These so-called straight guys were desperate to make a connection, maybe even get off a good nut, before it was back to their dreary, everyday world of the wife and kids, the job they despise with the boss they hate, the apartment that's too small and the reality that life has left them behind and it wasn't supposed to be this way and, oh, how they could have been a contender.

Yeah, I felt their pain, and it was like a jolt of electricity flaring out of my ass and down along the underside of my balls, firing up the shaft of my dick and exploding through every pore of my dick-head, making my dick huge, veins popping and stretching so hard my slit opened up like a bitch in heat. Dudes coughed, snorted, scratched at their pits, sweat dripping off them like roasting pigs over a fire, and all the while their eyes greedily sucked in long, hard stares at dicks and balls. Every guy of color got intense scrutiny, and when the fine Asian dude shimmied down to the front and rinsed himself in the cooling showers, every man in the room was up in his butt, dreaming of licking the sweat off the hair around his asshole.

He knew it too, and he took his time, slowly running his hands all over his taut body, rubbing himself where we wanted to rub, looking at us as he did it, taunting us with his eyes, taking the palms of both hands and grinding them along the inside of his groin, caressing his balls and stroking his firm, hard prick, flicking water from the tip of it onto the feet, knees, and thighs of the horny bastards in the front row. When he finished, he turned and ran his hands down his sides, over his awesome fleshy ass cheeks, and spread them ever so gently, emphasizing the lusciousness of those perfectly round handfuls (I say, I say, don't you want a taste, son?). It was a mass wet dream, everybody twitching, but only the troll on the end of the middle row broke decorum, noisily whack-ing his microscopic weenie and sounding like an asthmatic pug. The Asian guy gave us all one last long look at his beautiful hard dick and then made his exit.

Once outside, in the busy hallway, he took the seat next to a light-skinned brother who was sitting on a single bench, only big enough for two, placed next to what looked to be the foyer of an-other massage room, isolated by a glass door from the bustle of the baths. After a few minutes, two guys came out of the room and exited the foyer by the glass door. The brother got up and went into the foyer, followed a split second later by the Asian guy, and together they disappeared into the lone room. It didn't take much to figure out what was happening. The sexual tension ratcheted up several notches after that, with more guys openly feeling up their stiff dicks as they feverishly hunted for a flash of requited passion. The Slavic guy rubbed up against me, his hand feeling my knee. The hot papi also signaled that he was very interested, stroking up and down his stubby dick with his thumb and forefinger.

There were others too, but I focused on the bald-headed, blue-black brother down front, my stare boring into the side of his head, making him turn and face me. Our eyes locked, and the data flowed between us in a thick torrent, telepathically exchanging name, rank, and serial number, negotiating the terms of our détente, defining the territorial boundaries. I saw his fat, thick dick, its wicked right curve tightly wrapping it over his thigh, swell up and lengthen like an anaconda uncoiling to seek out fresh prey. It was impressive, that's for sure, and the white guy next to him had his tongue halfway out of his head like a bullfrog with a bead on a dragonfly.

There was a hiss of steam, and in the dense fog, the Slavic guy reached out and started jacking my dick, pulling back almost as quickly as the mist began to rise. The black guy got up and rinsed off, still maintaining our eye contact, dragging his large hands over the sharp angles of his chiseled frame with delicate precision, the better to emphasize the erotic dynamism of each perfect line of his body, before turning his beautiful back to us and then bending down to rinse his thighs and legs, those magnificent ass cheeks parting just the way I like them, revealing the most gorgeous asshole my tongue and dick could ever desire. The deal was done.

I watched the black guy exit and sit on the bench, in the exact same seat that the light-skinned brother had occupied. There was another hiss of steam, and this time, I stood up, grabbed the Slavic guy by the back of his head, and forced my dick down the back of his throat, fucking his face hard until the mist began to rise again. He busted a huge wad between my legs that landed all over the back of the guy in front of him. I pulled out and slipped down to the front, making sure to rub my ass and dick against as many guys as I could along the way, feeling voracious fingers poking at my ass and grabbing at my dick.

I rinsed off quickly, my fat prick waving in front of me like a weapon of ass destruction, and wasn't surprised to find the papi beside me, bumping his firm, square ass against me as he bent down low to rinse his feet (I say, I say, you dropped your soap there, son). When I turned, my ramrod-straight dick poked him between his legs, and his thighs clamped down hard as his hips spasmodically jerked it in an unsubtle bit of frottage. The room exploded in pandemonium, a circle-jerking frenzy as guys grabbed dick wildly in the blinding fog, trying to get off before the mist rose. In the confusion, I pulled the papi outside and stood in front of the black guy just as the light-skinned brother and the Asian dude came out of the room beyond the glass door.

There are some things for which mere words are totally inadequate. In the language of desire between men there are infinitesimally more effective means of communication. As the five of us looked at each other longingly, our stiff dicks met in a tight circle, sharing sacred sacraments amongst their drooling slits, obliterating the need for us to say anything. The Asian guy pulled the light-skinned brother back toward the room, and the black guy and I followed quickly on their heels, with the papi, pressing hard against my ass, bringing up the rear.

I say, I say, be careful with that thing, boy!

Mile High

I had gotten the call only a few hours before that the Markham deal was a go and to be in Frankfurt first thing the next morning to start the due diligence. My secretary had to scramble to get me on the four forty-five PM flight, no business-class seats available so it would be the cattle car, but on the aisle, and it was only a minor miracle that I had my passport with me. Since I didn't have time to pack anything, I wound up buying a bunch of stuff at Pink's, across the street from my office, and a carry-on bag and toiletries at some shops in the Lufthansa terminal at JFK. It was outrageously expensive, but what the heck: the client was going to pay for it in the end. My flight was not going to be boarding for a while yet, and I had some time to kill, so I headed to the men's room to take a wicked piss before grabbing something to eat. I saw the two of them standing at the urinals, and I just knew they would be trouble with a capital T. Or at least, I hoped they would.

The taller of the two was a rail-thin skinhead, maybe mid-twenties, sporting a pre-adolescent babyface which stood in stark contrast to his modern-primitive neck tattoo, pierced eyebrows, and double pierced nose, dressed in standard-issue bomber jacket, tight jeans jammed into scuffed-up twenty-hole Ranger boots that came over his calves, and bright red suspenders to keep his pants from falling off his skinny, no-ass frame. The other was almost the polar opposite of the first, plump sliding toward fat, shorter by a head, with an unruly mop of thick, black-dyed hair with purple highlights, a light coat of white powder on his face made more expressive, no doubt, by matching black lipstick and heavy *Clockwork Orange* eyeliner, and dressed in the simple black uniform of confirmed Goths: buckles, chains, and zippers going every which way but useful, bondage cuffs on both wrists, and copious crucifixes dangling upside-down from around his neck. How they ever got through security is a wonder. Picture Laurel and Hardy in a bad acid flashback.

There was a space between them, so I stepped up to the open urinal, pulled my dick out of my pants, and waited for the piss to fly. It's funny how when you know you have to take a leak but you delay it and delay it and then finally go to relieve yourself, nothing happens. It's like your bladder and dick are ganging up on you just to jerk your chain for not giving in to them before. That delay can be embarrassing, especially at a public urinal, with strange guys lurking around, surreptitiously seeking a hookup with some guy looking to get a blow job or, even better, willing to blow them. I mean, there you are with your meat hanging out, catching cold in the breeze, trying to concentrate on doing your business, and before you know it, the guy next to you starts shaking his dick like he's at the Indy 500 waving the checkered flag, trying to get your attention so he can check out your stuff to see if there's any mutual interest. And with me it's even worse, because the longer my dick hangs outside my pants, the greater the likelihood it's going to start sniffing around for something to get into, getting all hard and stiff and giving some guy something to make conversation over.

"Gee, I guess it's true what they say about you black guys, huh?"

It was the fat Goth that got the ball rolling. "Nice," he continued, licking his lips in a way that made me cringe (supposing he thought my dick another tasty morsel to suck down his gut, never to be seen again) and curious (how good a fuck would that fat ass be?). His buddy craned his neck to get a look too and grunted his approval as well. I noticed that the skinny dude was sporting a monster, foot-long Johnson, the bulbous head wrapped tightly around a 0-gage Prince Albert. "Damn," I thought to myself, "not fucking bad for a white boy." The fat one wasn't hung too poorly either, a solid little wedge of a dick, narrow at the head but widening out at the base like a fleshy pink butt plug. I still hadn't pissed, yet my dick put on a good show, getting thick and hard with their rapt attention. I smiled back at the fat boy, "You don't know the half of it," as I stroked my fat dick to a full-on, piss-tight erection.

"Umm," said the fat boy, "I'd like to."

I let the fat boy stroke my dick, his pudgy hands wet with perspiration and eager to feel a hot black dick. His humid, slimy, but delicate touch was a real turn-on, his fingers greedily exploring every inch and bulging vein of my long, smooth, caramel dick, running back and forth over the piercings along my frenum, surprised that a black guy in a suit would be a member of the tribe. After watching the fat dude for a while, the skinny guy, not wanting to be left out, reached over to cop a feel as well, his bony hand competing with the fat dude for my meat, and between their hungry hands they jacked it up real good. To maintain my balance as they pulled and tugged on my dick, I held on to both of their asses, enjoying the pleasant contrast between the doughboy softness of the fat guy's ample cheeks and the sinewy hardness of the skinny dude's bony rump, digging my fingers into their cracks and trying to steal a read on how tight their buttholes might be.

When the fat boy started to kneel down to wrap his thick lips around my dick, I suggested we move to an empty stall, not wanting to push our luck and get caught in flagrante delicto by an uptight janitor or something. Fortunately, the doors on the stalls in the international terminal come almost to the floor, just like in Europe, making it difficult if not impossible for prying eyes to see what might be happening inside. Once our strange little threesome was securely ensconced, the fat guy and the skinny dude raced to be the first to scarf my juicy dickhead down their throat, with the skinny dude proving to be the more agile of the two. Man, could that boy suck dick! The fat boy settled for licking my shaft until he could work my balls out of my fly, at which point I lost them to his velvety-smooth and delectably hot orifice. I was suspended between their two insatiable mouths, their tongues slurping and sliding in delirious ecstasy, triggering every pleasure receptor in my dick and balls. As I slowly gyrated my hips, humping their faces, I felt their hands unbuckle my belt, pull down my pants, and begin to explore my muscular thighs and firm, round ass. The fat boy, his head between my legs, worked his hot tongue from my balls and deep into my asshole, leaving the skinny dude unfettered access to my crotch.

Now it was hot! There's nothing like having a piss hard-on and getting sucked and eaten out at the same time. A warm wave of carnal energy pulsated out of my ass and through my whole body, turning on all of my senses and driving me slowly wild with lust. I was sweating up a storm, dressed in a new Valentino suit, Armani shirt with Asprey cufflinks, and Turnbull & Asser tie. The smell of damp virgin wool, wet balls, and tongued-out ass mixed with dirty white boys face deep in black funk created a heady *eau de perfume* that flooded the stall and worked itself deep into our nostrils, acting like an aphrodisiac and making all three of us lose all inhibition. In no time, the fat boy and the skinny dude were naked from the waist down, and the fat boy was pressed up against the wall, spreading his fleshy ass cheeks to take my huge bone, while the skinny dude was furiously fingering my ass to get it ready for his big albino anaconda dick. As my dick drove deep into the fat boy's soft, creamy ass, the skinny dude jammed his full length into mine, his massive Prince Albert hitting that spot inside my ass reserved for mad crazy muthafuckas packing large. We fucked like dogs in heat, pounding ass like it was the last we would ever see, fast, hard, feverishly, and just as it was slamming, the loudspeaker announced my flight was starting to board. Damn!

Extricating myself from the center of that human sandwich proved difficult: the skinny dude's fucking huge dick felt like it was stuck in my hole, and the fat boy's ass was like a vacuum cleaner, sucking my dick inside and not wanting to give it up. Not that I was eager to leave that sweet, hot vise either, truth be told. But I pried myself off the snake in my ass, certain that my guts were going to drip out of my gaping hole, and literally ripped my dick out of the deep recesses of the fat boy's ass, making a loud popping sound, and hurriedly tried to pull my pants up before exiting the stall, only to get my piss-hard dick stuck in the fly and exposing myself to some old guy wringing his hands under the dryer. He was either really shocked or very interested, because he didn't flinch as I wrestled my unruly dick, still rock hard, coated in ass slime and dying for a good piss, back into my pants, straightened my shirt, and smoothed my tie before leaving the bathroom and running to the gate.

It was a full flight. The first-class section was filled with older, heavy-set men in Hickey-Freeman suits wearily settling themselves into their seats and sipping on the first of many cocktails to get them through to their final destinations. Business class was loaded with younger guys in Italian designer suits, busy pecking away at their laptops, making last-minute revisions to Powerpoint presentations and going over spreadsheets one more time, making sure they didn't miss some obscure error in a cell formula. The cattle car was just its usual nightmare, filled with too many overweight people, with too much stuff, acting like they've never flown before and taking up way too much room. All I wished for was that there would be no whining babies or rambunctious rugrats anywhere near me. My seat was 30C, on the aisle in the first row of the last section of economy, just after the lavatories. As I was stowing my bag in the overhead compartment, I noticed what looked like a row of three vacant seats at the absolute rear of the cabin. I crossed my fingers and hoped for a shot at getting at least two seats to stretch out in. Frankfurt was eight hours away, and it would certainly be great if I could arrive somewhat alert and rested.

The flight attendant was making the final boarding announcement, and I was feeling better about being able to make a seat switch, when, to my surprise, the last two passengers to board were my two fuck buddies from the men's room, who smiled like cats who had just eaten the canary when they passed by me on their way back to the last row. They reeked to high heaven of stale sex funk, and it dawned on me that I must be pretty ripe myself, which was confirmed when the woman next to me held a moist towelette in her hand as she covered her nose and gave me a disapproving look. I fastened my seat belt tightly, my ass trying to pull itself together while my still-swollen dick made a slick mess down my thigh, knowing that it was going to be a very bumpy ride. I craned my neck to look behind me and saw the fat dude sitting on the aisle, grinning at me while rubbing his crotch. Yeah, they knew it too. I settled back in my seat and waited for the games to begin.

Experienced international travelers pretty much know when the chaos in economy will settle down to a minor pain in the butt: generally right after takeoff, as the plane gains cruising altitude, it's reasonably sane, as people get over their pre-flight jitters and are feeling lucky to have survived thus far; then it gets calm once again after the first pass of the drink cart, as the alcohol and light snacks hold the attention of the hoi polloi; and it gets quiet again for about two hours after the dinner service, before everybody realizes they have to pee at the same time; and then there's one last period, of about an hour, before the breakfast cart makes its way down the aisle signaling the waning ninety minutes of our forced confinement before landing. Four periods, roughly three hours and forty-five minutes, where, if one has a mind for it, they can get into some nasty mile-high shit relatively undisturbed. I personally think the designers of the Airbus A340 were seriously into in-flight sex, since the plane is made for getting it on. The seats are wide, the legroom spacious, and the lavatories very, very accommodating for some serious Kama Sutra. Speaking from experience, it's a damn sight better than anything Boeing's got.

We were still climbing when the captain turned off the Fasten Seat Belt sign, and, finally thinking that I could take that long-delayed piss, I got up and waited outside the lavatory just on the other side of the bulkhead from my seat. I turned and faced down the aisle, looking for Stan and Ollie. They were still grinning like the Cheshire cat, and it made me break out in a shit-eating grin too. After a brief discussion between themselves, the skinny dude crawled over the fat guy and sauntered up the aisle toward me. My ass began twitching, the memory of the reaming from that massive trouser snake still freshly seared into the walls of my anus, and that got my dick hard, damn it!, with no way to hide the fact from every nosy busybody peeking up the aisle at me. Soon the skinny guy and I stood face-to-face, secretly communicating in leering glances what was up and how it was going to go down. Before either of us could say a word, the door to the lavatory opened and this elderly fraulein stepped between us, gave us both a good once-over, and then dismissed us with a flick of her hand as she tottered back to her seat. The skinny dude dashes into the lavatory and locks the door. A few minutes later, the door unlocks from inside, but he doesn't come out.

I made furtive glances all around to see if anyone was paying attention to what was happening, but thankfully no one was. I slipped inside to find the skinny dude butt nekkid, perched on the lip of the sink, one long, thin leg propped against the wall of the lavatory while the other was resting on the floor. He was working his dick, trying to get that bad boy stiff, and that's when I made my move. I dropped my pants, lifted his leg over my shoulder, and rammed my thick, mean fucking machine right up his ass, straight up to my balls. That boy turned beet red from head to toe, and the shocked expression on his face made it all worthwhile. I knew it hurt; my dick can stretch a tight hole real good, and without lube it's like being hosed out with sandpaper. But I soon fixed that as, at long last, I took that piss I had been holding, right in that bony skank of an ass, sending a hot golden shower deep into the skinny dude's guts with every twisted thrust of my hard eight. God, I do love to give piss enemas to boys with tight asses. He didn't lose a drop as I fucked him hard, pulling his hips toward me and impaling him on my dick, throwing a blistering combination of punishing blows at his hole that reverberated all along his spine, making his head jerk like a bobblehead doll. The skinny dude just rolled his eyes into his head and leaned back against the mirror, giving his ass up to me for my total domination.

If that boy's big meat was good, man, his ass was even better, and he could take dick like a real pig bottom. And being surprisingly well trained, he didn't even make much noise as I drilled his butt deep, pushing that load of piss all up in his ass, turning his hot pink hole inside out like a rose, banging his bony white buns black and blue. It made me fuck harder to watch my smooth, thick black dick ream in and out of his ever-widening hole. I was determined that he was going to feel this fucking for a long time afterward and ripped into his butt with renewed abandon. Given that we were kind of making up for the previous coital interruption, it didn't take too long for us to get our balls to the busting point. I tried to hold it, but when that skinny dude's asshole tightened around my joint so hard I thought he was going to break it off as he blew his hot load over my shoulder, I lost it big-time, coming so hard my legs were shaking as stars circled around my head. And I just kept on coming, like a foam machine at a Fire Island tea dance, until that boy's asshole was ringed with a thick, slimy sludge of come, piss, and shit. My balls were throbbing, and I felt weak in the pit of my stomach, but I kept thrusting my dick into that hot, sloppy hole, forcing that skinny boy to bust one more nut after another until his balls were purple and his dick was an ugly scarlet color. He collapsed against the mirror, smeared in sweat and soaked with come, while my limp dick slipped out of his rent chasm with a heavy thud as it slapped against his thighs. I reached down and picked up his boxer shorts and wiped myself off as best I could before pulling up my pants. My shirt was soaked with perspiration, but somehow I had no stains from other bodily fluids.

When I came out, the drink carts were just starting their march down the aisle, dispensing cocktails, beverages, and snacks. I didn't need to look at the lady next to me to know that I was reeking really badly now, so bad that people were whispering about "that smell" three rows back and across the aisle. Frankly, I didn't care; all I could focus on was what a hellacious fuck I just had. The skinny dude came out of the lavatory walking so bowlegged you would have thought he was a professional rodeo rider. He gave me a big thumbs up as he passed slowly back to his seat, and I knew he'd have quite the report for the fat dude. As the cabin settled down after the drinks were served, I leaned back in my seat, closed my eyes, and happily replayed that fuck scene in my head as I grabbed a few winks. I was rudely awakened by a sudden weight dropping onto my lap. It seems the fat boy was making his way to the lavatory when we hit some turbulence, and he just happened to fall in my lap, will wonders never cease?

I had very fond remembrances of how good that fat ass felt sliding up and down my fat, stiff joint. And the lap dance the fat boy was giving me only served to sharpen the memory. With a little difficulty, he got back to his feet and stood outside one of the lavatories. He waited until he had my undivided attention, then silently mouthed something (like I'm supposed to be able to read lips) before disappearing inside. I sat in my seat for a respectable few minutes before nonchalantly following after him. People in the cabin were too busy getting a good buzz on to pay any attention to me as I entered. Once inside, the fat boy, pants around his ankles and that little pink fireplug of his waving in front of him like a baton, was all over me like white on rice. It seems we were going to flip the script, and since I had done a number on his buddy's ass, he was going to extract payback on mine. Now that, I thought, was a novel idea, not really expecting much from his small dick, especially since I was pretty well loosened up from before. I couldn't have been more hopelessly wrong.

That fat boy's prick was a lethal weapon. Its narrow head teased my hole into a false sense of security while that thick base split my ass open like a log. By the time I regained my breath, fat boy was whupping my butt with his heavy thighs, practically knocking me off my feet with every stroke, my poor butt battered senseless to the point where it couldn't remember how to close itself shut. All I could do was brace myself against the lavatory wall and pray that it was strong enough to hold up against fat boy's assault. Mercifully, fat boy was getting tuckered out from the exertion, his strokes labored and uneven. Soon he popped a big, wet load all over my ass and lower back, smearing it around and between my legs with his dick, and then he collapsed onto the commode, spent.

I grabbed his head by the ears and jammed my eight inches all the way down his throat, choking him with my dark meat, making him gag for air. His beady little eyes looked scared. I made him suck my dick good and deep, wearing the black lipstick from around his mouth and causing his eyeliner to run from the tears that rolled nonstop down his cheeks. I pulled out and started bitch-slapping his face with my dick, beating it hard enough to bring a rosy color to his pale cheeks. Then I force-fed him another load of thick, dark meat, jamming it so far down his throat that I was practically sitting on top of his face, stuffing my balls into his mouth, making his face turn blue around the edges, before pulling out and blowing a nice fat wad of thick white come right between his eyes. I smeared my come all over his face, washing off his makeup, and then made him suck my dick clean. When he was done, I turned and jammed my ass in his face, making him clean up after himself. My hole was supersensitive, and I was on the verge of tears myself as his tongue scoured it out. I grabbed some towels and wiped myself dry, then grabbed several sanitary napkins to stuff into my butt crack as an extra precaution against any "accidents."

I left fat boy spread-eagled on the commode, wheezing frightfully, and went back to my seat. I caught a glimpse of the skinny guy before I sat down, his eyes big as saucers, wondering what happened to his buddy and flashing me a dopey grin like he couldn't wait for his next at bat. "There are six hours left before landing," I thought to myself as I eased my sore ass down on the pillow I had placed under me. "How the fuck am I going to make it through this flight!?" Even as the thought crossed my mind, I knew how. "Bring it on, baby! Bring it ON!!"

A Stranger's Smile

Okay, this is the truth.

For real.

Now, it's a fact that when I'm out, and some pretty sistah starts flirting with me, I know she's checking my shit out. Not my package, that comes later, but she's looking for any obvious signs that some other woman might have some claim on me, you know, like a wedding ring (or the tan line of a ring that's "fallen off"), smelling for perfume, and shit like that. She's also looking to see if, you know, I swing *that* way, you know what I mean, that DL shit? I mean, with me it's impossible to tell, because I'm one straight-up dude. For real, homes, I'm not lying. I'm a 100 percent true outdoorsman (hiking, mountain climbing, winter mountaineering) and wild-azz nature boy (yeah, that's right, I hike, swim, snorkel, and run butt nekkid and dare you not to notice). I'm a serious saltwater sport fisherman, going way offshore to the deep canyons in search of marlin, swords, sailfish: the Grand Slam, baby. I love a good cigar almost as much as I love a smooth ass, and I've been known to chase both with a sip of fine single-barrel Kentucky bourbon. I'm tall, dark, and handsome, with a thick head full of "good hair." And yeah, I be packin' it thick, yo. Man, when a sistah sees me, she gets wet thinking about how pretty our babies are going to look. And *because* I swing **THAT** way, a guy like me has got to be careful lest shorty gets the wrong idea and starts planning that big June wedding too soon.

So anyway, there was a time when I did curry favor with the ladies and was a regular stud at it, no lie. I was young, confused I admit, and still trying to sort out what I liked and what I wanted. It wasn't that I was on the DL or trying to lead the ladies on or even living a lie. Back in the day, I found it pretty exhilarating just to fuck, boys AND girls, sometimes on the same nights and sometimes at the same time. Sometimes I still do, even now. But there was one girl in particular, if there was ever the possibility of someone becoming Mrs. Kane, who still brings a smile to my face and puts a bone in my drawers at just the memory of her. Yeah, man, she could have been the one, maybe, if she hadn't brought me fully into the Life. Yeah, she was special, all right.

The dance was going full blast when I arrived; people were already drunk and starting to pair up as I cruised the edges of the dance floor looking for an easy lay. I wasn't in any hurry, since I usually found what I was looking for the later it got. Suddenly there was a big commotion across the room, and the crowd seemed to be scrambling away from something. My curiosity was piqued, so I pressed my way over through the tightly packed throng to see what the fuss was all about. There, in the middle of a circle of gawking guys and girls, stood this tall, statuesque Amazon of a black woman, wearing cats-eye glasses with flashing rhinestones bouncing sparkles of light off the walls, a white silk blouse without a bra, and leopard-print lycra riding pants tucked into black boots that came up to her knees, cracking a bullwhip over the heads of the crowd as she danced by herself. I dropped my beer and got an instant hard-on.

In college, in Western Massachusetts, I had not found many

women of color in my wanderings through the "bush," so to speak, and to find this goddess, 'cause she was ALL that, in her glory being the center of attention and giving no quarter to anyone who tried to approach her, in fact keeping people at bay with that whip, made me feel so deeply that this was my soul mate that a lump welled up in my throat that threatened to choke me right there. I just watched her moving to her own rhythm with a smooth litheness that was sexy, seductive, and entrancing. When she twirled around in synch with the music, she caught my eye, and she faced me for a moment and smiled back at me, then slowly nodded her head as if giving me, alone of all the people on that dance floor, permission to approach her. She was still cracking the whip to the beat of the music as I shimmied up to her, put my large, rough hands lightly around her delicate waist, and matched her footsteps as she danced. She didn't say anything, but she wrapped the whip around my neck and pulled me off the dance floor like I was her kill for the evening. I didn't know where she was taking me, and I didn't care; I was just happy that I was with her. She smelled of lilac and gardenias. Her light brown arms were covered in downy soft black hair that was such a turn-on for me that I could feel the first faint moisture forming at the tip of my dick. Her long ebony locks were pulled tautly into a serpentine coil, like the deadly viper that she was.

When we got to her room, she shoved me to the floor in front of her bed and, standing over me, cracked her whip all around me, expertly brushing me with its tip, just hard enough to sting but not enough to break the skin. She cracked the whip at me until I had taken off all my clothes and was lying naked on the floor, and then she whipped my big hard dick and fat balls, the sharp sting of the hard leather raising hot welts on the inside of my thighs, making my skin raw, hurting so bad I could have screamed if I wasn't also enjoying the sensation of being totally dominated by this fierce African Queen whipping my balls and dick until I came, shooting gobs of thick white come that landed all over her knee-high black boots. She wrapped the whip around my neck again and forced my head down so I could lick my come off of them. When I was finished, she rolled me onto my back, dropped her pants, and rode my stiff, bruised, raw dick like a mad crazy succubus until she was totally satisfied, dripping her hot pussy juice down my shaft and onto my balls and making my thighs frothy with sweat and funk, whipping me from time to time to make me buck my hips faster or shift my position.

Through it all she didn't say a word, letting that big black bull-whip do all the talking for her. When she had finally had her fill of my dick, she stood up, ripping her tight pussy from around my dick and leaving it quivering in the cool air, and put a foot on my balls as she watched me jack off, streaming long, thick globs of juice straight up into the air that landed sloppily on my chest and face, as I stared up at her, looking into her eyes. When I was done, she stepped to the door, opened it, and then finally spoke: "Get out." As I gathered up my clothes and crawled toward the door, I begged her for her phone number, and she thought about it for a moment, then grabbed a marking pen and wrote her name and number on my ass. It was around four in the morning as I stood naked in the hallway, covered in my own come, crying like a baby in front of her door.

In Rachael I found a woman who was as sexually voracious, self-confident, driven, smart, and totally unpredictable as I was. Moreover, she was funny and vivacious and enjoyed being alone as much as she loved the company of others. She was also an outdoorsy type, liked to hike, and was an Olympic hopeful in dressage. She was a senior and planning to go to law school after graduation, in keeping with her family tradition, given that her mother was a judge and her dad was a partner in a prestigious Wall Street law firm. I was enthralled with her because she allowed me to be the tough guy in public while indulging my fantasies of being a kept man in private. I liked that she was a strong personality and could take as good as she gave. We played the most elaborate games, and she introduced me to the many hidden adult sex stores that dotted Western Massachusetts, where we would buy toys and accessories, and occasionally pick up some lucky guy or girl, to add some extra spice to our inspired sexual escapades.

But in all of our intimate sexual play, Rachael had one rule: she was on top, always. Once, I made the mistake of getting too feisty and suddenly flipping her onto her back and fucking the shit out of her really hard. She dug her nails into my back with such force that she drew blood with all ten fingers, and she just gouged the wounds even after I rolled over so she was on top again, all the while looking deeply into my eyes with a look that made it clear that I was never to even remotely try that stunt again. I was HER boy toy, and there was no reciprocity in our relationship. Needless to say, I let Mistress have her way. And as long as Rachael was happy, she could be unusually generous, pampering me with new clothes, taking me on trips to her family's place in Oak Bluffs, bringing me to orgasms that left me practically unconscious. It is because of Rachael that I learned to accept the fact that I liked fucking guys.

One January, Rachael surprised me by taking me to New York City for the long holiday weekend of my birthday. She came to my dorm in her battered BMW 2002 coupe, backfiring like a machine gun, and honked like a mad woman until I came outside. I had been shaving, getting ready to take a shower, and I hadn't expected to see her since she had told me she was going to Boston for the weekend. When I heard the noise downstairs, I really didn't think anything of it until a group of my housemates paraded into the bathroom, ripped my towel off, and started flicking at my ass and dick with it while teasing me about being pussywhipped. After reclaiming my towel, I took the precaution of throwing on some jeans and a sweatshirt before rushing downstairs to see Rachael.

Just a few weekends before, she had pulled a similar surprise, only that time I ran out in just my towel, thinking it was another of our sex games in the making, and Rachael wound up driving nearly to Albany, to a seedy little motel in Troy, just off Route 2, where she proceeded to screw my brains out wearing an extra-large strap-on dildo while I was handcuffed spread-eagle to the bed, my ankles bound to my wrists, as she pumped quarters into the slot on the nightstand that made the bed vibrate like a drunken bastard. I couldn't go anywhere even if I wasn't other-wise restrained since I didn't have anything to wear, and Rachael was always fond of leaving me in such a position for hours only to come back with one or two skanky people to share me with. The drive to Troy took almost two hours, and my balls nearly froze off since the heater in Rachael's car wasn't working. Now she was downstairs again, honking the horn, impatiently waiting to spring something new on me. Understandably, I wanted to be accommo-dating since I always enjoyed her wicked delights, but not blindly so.

Rachael looked ravishing, wearing a blue fox-fur coat with matching pill-box hat that had a veil which covered half her face. She reminded me of Lady Di in *Lady Sings the Blues*. She rolled down the window and blew kisses at me while the look on her face said she had something really special planned. I slid into the passenger seat, and before I could even close the door, Rachael stepped on the gas, wheels throwing up gravel in our wake as she gunned it down the highway. When I asked where we were headed, Rachael just stroked my chin and smiled, letting her hand fall casually into my lap, stroking my crotch and making my dick stiff. We drove down Route 7 and picked up the Massachusetts Turnpike, which took us over to the Taconic Parkway and then down to New York with Rachael giving me the longest hand job I've ever had. Just as we pulled up to the entrance to the Plaza Hotel, I busted a huge nut all over my pants, the dashboard, and the windshield. Rachael laughed as she licked my come off her hand while I searched desperately for something to clean myself off with before the valet reached the door.

We swept through the lobby like we owned the place. All eyes were on us as she registered us as Mrs. & Mr. Smith. I had nothing but the clothes I was wearing. Rachael had an expensive and very large trunk that the bellman wheeled behind us as we went up to our suite, which overlooked Central Park. The bellman was an old black man, in his early sixties maybe, and I could tell from the look he gave me that he most certainly didn't approve of Rachael and me, thinking we were up to no good and trying to figure out which of us had the lower moral character. Being the man, nevertheless, the old bellman looked to me for his tip and sucked his teeth in disgust when Rachael reached over and tipped him as I just shrugged my shoulders in the sudden realization that I had no wallet or money with me. I guess I was the 'ho in his eyes, since Rachael paid for everything. It was the first time I had been to New York City, and I came as the boy toy of a very strong-willed and dominant woman who had still more surprises in store for me.

At first I thought that she was just going to keep me naked the whole weekend, since soon after we christened the room with an intense fuck that badly soiled the chintz sofa and loveseat with stains that housekeeping would be talking about for months, Rachael suddenly left, taking my clothes and the room keys and locking the door behind her. When she returned a while later, she surprised me with a whole new wardrobe, having picked out what she wanted to see me in that weekend, which turned out to be tight-fitting jeans that sat low on my hips, exposing the top of my butt crack, and which had a flap at the crotch with buttons all around, like sailor pants, which had the effect of giving particular emphasis to my dick, since it barely fit inside. She had chosen white for the jeans because that color showed off my assets very well. Even though it was January, Rachael had bought me some equally tight-fitting T-shirts without sleeves that exposed my hard abs as I moved. She had also bought some black Frye boots with a stirrup-like buckle on the sides. To top it off, she gave me a black leather motorcycle jacket, with matching hat, which I had to admit made a pretty sexy outfit.

But Rachael wasn't done. She reached into her purse and pulled out a heavy silver cock ring and then began to undo the buttons on my jeans, releasing my hardening dick, and tried to stuff it into the cock ring. I told her that I was too hard to get the ring on, so she made me masturbate until my dick was spent enough for the cock ring to fit over it. Once it was in place, she stroked my tingling dick until it was hard again and then stuffed it back into the jeans and buttoned them up, making a bulge in my pants that left little to the imagination. Satisfied with her handiwork, Rachael grabbed me by the hand and then took me out into the streets. If we had caused a sensation with our entrance, the sight of my huge dick and tight ass threatening to explode out of those white jeans and that black leather jacket over the tight T-shirt made everyone in the lobby of the hotel take a deep breath. I got surreptitious winks from men and women alike who found me extremely desirable, and, taking note of the interest I was garnering, Rachael whispered to me that she was going to make a lot of money with me that weekend. I didn't understand what she meant at the time.

We took the subway downtown to Christopher Street, which was the heart of the gay ghetto then, and strolled arm in arm through the Village, window-shopping and carrying on, putting on a show for the crowds that passed us by. The sexual energy on the street was palpable, and the sight of all those hot men, dressed surprisingly similar to me, I noted, made me hard to the point that my cock looked like it was ten inches and almost as big around with that cock ring pumping it up. Rachael felt it too, and she seemed to be looking for men as much as I was, pointing out every guy that she found especially attractive and asking me what I thought. The more I got into the game with her, the more piqued I was to bust a nut. I was hungry for sex, and Rachael was keeping me on a tight leash. I just knew that whatever was going to happen, it was going to be the bomb.

Since I looked older than my age, getting into the bars wasn't that difficult, and Rachael seemed to know which ones to go to, and she was accepted as my fag hag. There weren't many blacks in those bars and, besides Rachael, absolutely no women. I didn't feel uncomfortable being in a gay bar since I took it in stride as part of the performance Rachael and I were engaged in. I couldn't really imagine myself ever going into such a place on my own. I felt too butch for most of the places we visited, flaming bar queens and cabaret music not being my cup of tea, as it were. In one club, Rachael went over to this drop-dead beautiful Latin hunk, tall and olive skinned, and spent some time talking with him, leaving me sitting at the bar, where one dude after another hit on me unmercifully. Whenever I looked in Rachael's direction, the Latin guy flashed a thousand-kilowatt smile that dazzled me as she spoke into his ear, but I had no idea what they were talking about. After a while, they both came over to me, and Rachael made the introductions.

Rafael had an apartment nearby, and he invited us back to his place for a drink. It was a large studio, spacious by New York standards, and I thought it was so sophisticated, with its rows of books and tasteful artwork, male nudes in various poses, on the walls. We drank Manhattans, which were a specialty of Rafael's, listened to some soft jazz, and then Rachael blurted out, "So, how do two guys fuck?", which must have been some secret code she had worked out with Rafael, since he started giving her the clinical explanation and then asked her if she wanted to see for herself. She eagerly said yes and then looked at me, as did Rafael. I was more than a little drunk and not quite following what was transpiring and just sat on the sofa with what must have been a comical look, because they both burst out laughing. Rafael reached over and touched my face before planting a deep tongue kiss on my mouth. I liked the way he smelled and tasted, and I loved the feel of his strong hands on me. He was older, late twenties–early thirties, and had an incredible body. He said he was a dancer, and his firm butt, big thighs, powerful arms, and sleek, muscular chest certainly affirmed his vocation. I hadn't been touched by a man with as much tenderness as he touched me, and despite the fact that my girlfriend was seated nearby, I melted into Rafael's arms as he gently tugged at my nipples while kissing me. He reached up under my T-shirt and rubbed his hands over my chest, which made my dick start dripping so much that it soaked though my pants.

Soon I felt myself being pushed backward onto the sofa and Rafael's strong hands squeezing my throbbing crotch and rubbing my balls. I was panting slightly as he undid my pants and circled the tip of my dick with his thumb, rubbing the sensitive spot just under my dickhead and milking the juice out of it. He never moved hurriedly, taking his time and feeling my body as if reading my soul with his fingertips. At some point he had removed my shirt and gotten my pants off, but all I felt were his powerful lips and tongue exploring my mouth and his musky scent filling my nostrils. Then he started to kiss and nibble my chin, neck, nipples, and stomach before he began to suck my dick and balls while fingering my ass. I stole a glimpse toward Rachael, and she was masturbating with both hands between her legs, her mouth slightly open, eyes riveted on Rafael as he slowly ate out my willing ass. I closed my eyes and gasped as he worked three fingers into my hole, opening my quivering sphincter while sucking my dick all the way down to my balls.

This was all new for me, gentleness and tenderness with another man, not like the rough-and-tumble quickies in a restroom or cramped rumbles in the backseat of a car or the skanky tricks that Rachael would bring back during some of our trysts that I had experienced up to that point. And in my view, Rafael was a real man, masculine, butch, a man's man just like me, which made my willingness to submit to him and give him whatever he wanted all the more emotional for me, since this is what I had most wanted sexually, my relationship with Rachael notwithstanding. I was making a real mess of his sofa, though, what with my pre-come liberally flowing all over the place, but he didn't seem to mind, using it to lube my asshole and then to rub on his huge uncut dick, way bigger than Rachael's strap-on. As he started to fuck my ass, his hard, thick dick stretching my hole wider than I had ever experienced before, Rachael let out a low moan as she bucked her hips in orgasmic spasms, her eyes bugging out of her head. She shifted her position, sitting down near the sofa so that her head was just inches from my dick as she watched Rafael's dick deep-stroke my ass. I reached up and stroked her soaking-wet pussy with my hand, but she moved it to her ass, rubbing my fingers against her own asshole in rhythm with Rafael's strokes into mine. I fingered her ass, stuffing three fingers inside of her, while she watched my ass get reamed out good.

Rafael was a really good fucker, and his big dick pumping deep into my ass felt so good that I just buried my head into the soft pillows of the sofa and floated out of my body, rising up to watch him work every inch of his dick all up and down my ass, twisting my legs from side to side so as to make certain that he fucked every part of my butt. Rachael stripped off her clothes and grabbed my dick, steadying herself with a hand on my chest as she slid first her pussy for a while and then her asshole down on my dick, riding it with wild abandon as Rafael nibbled on her nipples. It was the incredible sensation of the orgasm seeming to flow from the center of my chest down into my balls that pulled me back into myself just as Rafael and Rachael reached their peaks as well. It was as if there was a bolt of lightning exploding out of Rafael's dick into my ass and out my dick into Rachael's pussy that had all three of us jerking and bucking in serious seizures. The orgasm passed through us like a sexual circuit had been connected, looping between us until we collapsed, dazed and spent, unable to move, and so we just laid there, still connected, soaked in come and sweat and grinding our hips until it happened all over again, and again and again, until we dozed off, only to do it some more when we woke, all night long and into the next morning.

Rachael and I rode in silence in the back of the cab as we made our way uptown to the hotel. She had a sly smile on her lips, and I was still in a state of confusion over what had just transpired. Back at the room, I immersed myself in a long, hot shower, and when I finished, Rachael was nowhere to be found. Her clothes were still there, but she had left without even a note telling me where she had gone or when she would return. I carefully washed the stains out of my jeans and dried them with the hair dryer in the bathroom, then dressed and headed out to get something to eat, since it dawned on me that I hadn't eaten anything since the day before our impromptu tryst with Rafael. When I returned to the room, Rachael was there with another woman, deeply engrossed in eating out the woman's pussy. I was stunned to find her like that, given what we had just been through, and just as I was turning to leave, the woman motioned for me to stay, so I took a seat across from the bed and watched, figuring it would be my turn to enjoy Rachael's fantasy.

I have to admit that it was pretty hot watching the two of them go at each other. The woman, a pretty, petite blonde with small, pale, perky breasts that had huge dark brown nipples, seemed to be putting on a show for my benefit while Rachael seemed totally oblivious to my presence. My joint begged for attention, and when I couldn't hold it off anymore, I unleashed my fat brown beast and stroked it just inches away from the white girl's lips. Her eyes were like saucers as she flailed her tongue at my meat, trying to get a taste, but I teased her, keeping my dick just beyond her reach while Rachael's mouth twisted her pussy in knots. She was panting heavily, and I finally relented, stuffing my fat dick down her throat until she could take it without gagging. And boy could she suck dick! As she got into my dick, her body was heaving as Rachael bored into her pussy. Then Rachael twisted her body so that her pussy was in the woman's face, and I pulled out my dick so the woman could eat out Rachael. As she did so, I moved down and lifted her legs, then fucked her ass while Rachael stayed busy with her cunt. It didn't take long for the woman to explode, and I guess Rachael also busted it, because they were both choking on each other's muff. And that got me off, pumping a couple of hot nuts deep inside the woman's ass as Rachael spread her cheeks wide. After that, I felt in need of some fresh air, so after I washed off in the bathroom, I headed for the door, leaving Rachael and her friend still entwined and going in for seconds.

It was early in the afternoon on a brilliantly sunny January day as I strolled aimlessly through the park, wandering along the footpaths, eventually finding myself in a heavily wooded area with many small hills. Though the trees were bare, the area still retained an overgrown remoteness that was different from the rest of the park. Whereas before, the footpaths were filled with joggers and people pushing strollers, in this area the paths were sparsely populated by men walking alone, eyes keenly evaluating strangers as they passed by each other. My dick told me what was happening even before my brain put the puzzle together. I had wandered into a gay cruising area, and I decided to check it out a bit. Lots of guys looked hungrily at me, eyes drifting furtively to my crotch and widening at the bulge in my pants. The men were quite diverse, young and old, handsome and trolls, fit and fat, tall and short, mostly white but with a smattering of Asian dudes and a healthy number of Black and Latino guys as well.

One, a well-dressed white guy in his late forties, still blessed with a boyish handsomeness, took an especially keen interest in me, following not far behind me as I roamed along the various paths in the Rambles. Out of curiosity, I stopped, sat on a bench, and waited for him to come up to me, which he soon did. We made small talk, about the weather, the Yankees, and he suggested that we find a more private place. I told him I was new to the city, and he said that he knew of a place nearby that might do. I followed him to a nearby bridle path, the gravel crunching under our feet, as he headed toward a dark tunnel. I stopped warily at the tunnel entrance, and he turned and motioned for me to join him. With some reluctance, I walked into the shadows after him. The tunnel was empty, and we walked to the middle of it, where it was darkest, and the man turned suddenly and roughly grabbed my crotch, feeling my dick getting hard. He asked me "How much?" and I was so taken aback by the question that I stammered, "What do you think?" He said twenty dollars, and quickly getting into the role of a hustler, which was a new game to me, I said, "Forty for a fuck." The man grunted his approval and dropped to his knees as I undid my pants and rubbed my dick against his face.

He sucked my dick in short, fast bursts, like a greedy pig trying to get as much slop as possible, his teeth roughly scraping my shaft, fingering my still-tender ass with his sharp nails in an effort to make me shoot my load in his mouth. I wasn't ready to come, and the man's total lack of sensitivity to my needs made me angry, so I pulled my dick out of his mouth and forced him down on all fours, roughly pulling his pants down. He pushed his underwear down then spread his pale, flabby butt cheeks in anticipation of taking my big black dick up his ass. As I rubbed the thick head of my dick against his hole, he asked if I had any lube, which I didn't, and he reached into his coat pocket and opened a small dark brown vial that he sniffed deeply from, then tightened and replaced in his pocket. The stench from the vial was so powerful that I felt my head spinning as well, and I hadn't even gotten a good sniff of whatever it had contained. It was a warm feeling that ran like a hot river of molten lava straight into the tip of my dick. I spit on his ass and then rammed my meat into him mercilessly, wanting to hurt him with the thickness and length of it, and the man only moaned deeply. I fucked him really hard, wailing on his ass, but he just held his butt cheeks as far apart as they could go with his eyes tightly clenched, grunting with each sharp thrust of my dick inside him.

In what seemed like only a few minutes, the man's asshole contracted around my dick, and I felt his whole body shuddering underneath me before going limp, his head resting on the gravel path. I didn't stop pumping until I was on the verge of coming, which took much longer, and I could see the man was on the threshold of passing out just as I pulled my dick out of him, his asshole fluttering open and shut like a big blinking eye. I grabbed the collar of his jacket and pulled his face to my dick as I shot my load into it. He licked my dick clean, hungrily lapping up my come and his own ass juice, then fished out his wallet and gave me sixty dollars, a tip he said for the best fuck of his life, and I felt a little guilty about my earlier desire to hurt him. I departed from one end of the tunnel as he left by the other, and headed back to the hotel, feeling really proud of myself for having turned a trick in a public park as if I were an experienced whore.

I couldn't wait to tell Rachael about it, college honor student to gay hustler in two days, and then I remembered her comment about how she was going to make a lot of money off me this weekend. I grinned like a mad fool as I bounded into the lobby of the hotel and headed for the elevators, eager to give my pimp her cut. As I waited for the doors to open, the old black bellman came over with a barely concealed smile turning at the corners of his mouth as he sneered at me. "She's checked out," he said. I looked at him in disbelief, but he continued, "She and some white woman checked out, with all their stuff. I put the bags in her car myself. She said she left something for you at the front desk." Then he folded his arms, satisfied at himself for obviously having been the first to inform me. I inquired at the front desk and found that Rachael had indeed left me an envelope. Inside, there was a note and one hundred dollars. The note said that she was happy that I had finally found myself and that she and Veronica had hit it off so well that they decided to spend the rest of the weekend together at Veronica's family's place in the Hamptons. She said the one hundred dollars was my share of the money that Rafael had paid her to fuck me. She said that some other guys had offered her more, but she felt that he was the best one to turn me out. She ended the note by wishing me happy birthday.

I stood there in shock as it sunk into me that I had been pimped and abandoned on my first visit to New York City. I was dressed like a hustler, had no wallet or identification, and the only money I had was from turning tricks with strangers. How had I come to this? I wondered. How would I get back to school? It was over four hours away by car. Being the resourceful, self-sufficient, world-wise stud muffin that I am, I roused myself to action. It was only Saturday, and I didn't have any classes until Tuesday morning. I could take a bus back to campus as late as Monday. That gave me at least two more nights in New York City. I headed out of the hotel not knowing how I would pull it off but secure in the knowledge that I had a great dick, a hot ass, and a whole city filled with guys willing to pay for a chance to taste my sweet chocolate.

One Front Street

DAMN! DAMN! DAMN! DAMN! DAMN!

Four fucking A.M. and I done lost the boy! Damn!

He was a phyne bro too: not too tall, not too short; thin build, broad shouldered, caramel complexion; tight locks sprouting like a crown on his otherwise shaved head; thick black eyelashes, long and curled like fans, shading his hazel-colored, bedroom eyes, giving him that "just woke up" look; thick, luscious, wet cherry lips begging to be kissed for days; smooth muscular arms displayed to perfection by a taut wifebeater; sharply cut abs descending to a perfectly small waist, barely bigger than two hands clasped around his tight hips; full, round, hard, phat booty, like two cassavas bound together in freshly pressed 501s, squeezed so tightly that just the barest hint of his silky black down-covered crack peeked over the top. Tyrone or Byron or Kenyon, the beats were too loud to hear his name for sure. He was the stuff that wet dreams are made of.

And I lost the fucking boy. DAMN!

I'd been cruising around the city, aimlessly hitting one scene after another: toking on a blunt with a superhot boricua papi on the roof garden at Paradise Garage, chilling between Larry's blistering sets on the turntables, watching in dazed amusement as two stoners fumbled with each other, trying to find a warm hole to fuck; later, rubbing up against the sweaty torsos of half-naked leathermen begging to drink the piss from my dick and trying to unzip my pants as I ordered a beer upstairs at Crisco Disco, while Frank, presiding like Mephistopheles come to get his pound of flesh from atop a giant can of Crisco, turned up the heat on the dance floor and got everybody into a cool acid groove; then later still, hooking up with a fierce Blatino drag queen hopped-up on X, Esmeralda, hell-bent on spreading "da wuv, baby" to every male body, at the Ice Palace. She dared me to show it hard on the dance floor while Frank H. was spinning a sizzling set that made people lose all inhibition (and sense) as the rush hit everyone at once and was so taken by it that she grabbed hold of it and dragged me around by my dick all night.

It was Esmeralda who got me to Brooklyn in the first place, batting those glitter-coated false eyelashes at me while cooing "Sweetums, Mummy's going to find a red-hot culo for this big ol' man meat" as we hopped the last car on the #2 at Columbus Circle just before three 3 AM, titillating the rubes as she jacked me off. Yeah, man, the good, bad old days in the Big Apple, when LEE, Futura 2000, Dondi, and Fab-5 were painting the town and shit like that happened, uptown, downtown, all around the town. It was nasty. And tough too. If you had a heart attack and fell down in the middle of the sidewalk, nobody would give you a second look; they'd step over your dead ass like climbing the curb. A *nikka* being dragged around by the dick and jacked on the subway by a giant Blatino drag queen? No big deal, been there, done that, seen it before. Yeah, New York was a helluva town, back in the day. Hallelujah! "Mummy" knew the DJ at this club on Front Street, down under the Brooklyn Bridge, and she said that only the "hottest of the hot" papis, b-boys, ruffnecks, and cuchifritos turned out to get a serious groove on. It sounded good to me, and besides, how can one say "No" to a six-foot eight-inch, two hundred thirty-five pounds-of-pure-muscle drag queen who has your dick in a vise grip wearing two-inch-long Lee Press-On Nails? I mean, I have a little bit of a masochistic streak in me, but I'm not crazy enough to risk having my Johnson shredded by an angry queen in a bitchy mood.

Downtown Brooklyn wasn't the boring, upscale, yuppie haven it is today, and when we got off at Clark Street, the first thing we were greeted by was a pimp screaming at the top of his lungs, "BITCH, gimme my money!" We squeezed past the lovely couple as they proceeded to trade vicious blows that would have staggered even Smokin' Joe Frazier in his prime and picked our way past the winos sleeping in their own piss and other assorted denizens of the nether regions down the three or four blocks to Front Street. A cold fog was just rolling up the East River, under a waning moon already worn out from the debauched antics of her children and eagerly anticipating the changing of the guard at dawn, as we arrived at the club, where a scraggly line of zombied-out club kids waited their turn to impress the diesel-sized hood rat standing guard over the door, seeking one last chance to score before sunrise, when the "regular folk" reclaimed the streets of the Emerald City once more. I glanced around at the decrepit warehouses and nodded my head: "We sure as hell aren't in Kansas anymore, Toto!"

Esmeralda wasn't fond of lines, and she stomped up to the bouncer, threatening to attack him like the 50-Foot-Tall Woman. *A drag colossus! Her mountainous torso! Skyscraper limbs! Giant desires!* Some bro's prick in her hand!? Before she could get one word out, to his credit, the bullet-headed wise guy unclipped the velvet rope and waved us through. From the street, the building didn't look like anything much was happening, but once inside the front door, BAM! It was Alice stepping through the looking-glass into another world. The joint was hoppin', and the crowd was so fine my eyes hurt. Some HOT! muthafuckas was up in here! Breakin' half naked in groups of two, five, seven all over the joint, sinewy bodies whirling like messengers from the Source, carrying the enlightenment of the Dervishes to those ready to receive it in the muscular gymnasticism of their artful syncopation. And the music! Man, it was jamming off da hook, and my feet were already into it before the sound hit my eardrums. Mummy done all right!

We'd only gotten a foot into the dancing melee when, from stage right, two huge drag queens and their motley entourage, preceding and trailing them like the imperial court of the Red Queen, encircled us. "There goes the neighborhood!" the stouter of the two gushed as she vigorously greeted Esmeralda, throwing enough air kisses to float even the Weather Girls, whom the two queens rather resembled from my drug-impacted perspective. "And look what the bitch done dragged in!" the other screeched as she pawed my dick and displayed it for her entire retinue to admire. "Mine's bigger," the first queen sniffed, snapping her fingers to call forth this blue-black brotha packing some real heat. "Well, mine's thicker," the second queen countered as she reached over and pulled a strapping Latino hunk from the edge of the circle sporting a nice fat piece.

Esmeralda sucked her teeth dismissively and stroked my shoulder as she replied, "Mine is a grower, watch." She pulled my balls out of my pants and gently stroked them, circling her fingers underneath, just the way I like it, and my dick responded like a trooper under fire. While I fell a few inches shy of the brother with the snake, I did manage to dwarf both him and the papi in girth and thickness. It seems that I had been corralled into some strange game of drag-queen Treasure Hunt, and even though I liked the attention, I had to take a wicked piss. Not waiting to see what the grand prize was, I excused myself and pushed my way out of the circle and headed for the john.

That's where I first laid eyes on the boy.

He was standing at a trough that passed for the urinal, a convenient arrangement I'd always thought for checking out other guys' stuff, cupping his skinny, uncut dick in his right hand and gushing like a fountain. I sidled up beside him, my fat hose already streaming as I held it in my left hand, crossing his trail of piss in the trough. "Sorry, bro," I casually said as my shoulder lightly brushed against his, "didn't mean to splash you." He was steadily watching my dick unload, between brief glances to look me in the face. "*No problem, hombre,*" he replied in heavily accented English with a deep island lilt. "*Tu boricua?*" I replied. "*Soy Dominicano, y tu?*" he rejoined, his eyes brightly lit in hopes of having found a fellow traveler. "Harlem, yo, in da house," I said as I shook my head negatively but with what I had hoped was a sexy smile and noted that he had long ago finished pissing but stood at the trough with his dick out, decidedly longer now, stroking it ever so gently. He caught me looking, and since my dick was getting pretty hard at that point, there wasn't much left to do but state the obvious.

"You like?" he asked, displaying his hard, curved nine-incher. I moved a little closer to him, my dick just barely separated from his, my shoulder now more firmly in contact with his. "Yeah, it looks real good," I responded, "real good," glancing around to see if there were more-private places to continue this budding conversation, as well as to see if there were witnesses to what was going down. A little exhibitionism is always good to get the blood flowing, but sometimes a dude just wants to keep it on the low, if you know what I mean. He moved his dick so it touched mine, and rubbed its cloaked head along my thick shaft. The contrast between his long, thin, caramel prick, smooth and sharply bent to the right, and my big, fat, cinnamon sausage, with its prominent veins and hard-edged straightness, got us both wet. We smiled into each other's eyes conspiratorially, me falling hard for those dreamy lashes of his. Our dicks got to be pretty good friends as we stood there grinding our bodies closer together. I jerked my head toward the stalls, and he smiled broadly, nodding affirmatively, flashing a perfect row of pearly whites with just a flash of bling from a lone silver-and-diamond-encrusted cap. After he went inside, I waited a second, making sure that no one was paying attention to us, and then followed behind him, in breathless anticipation of the pleasures that might lie behind that black metal door.

He had the wifebeater pulled up over his neck, exposing his hard, flat abs, covered by a light coating of soft, curly black hair, and his pants were drooping halfway down his slight thighs, his overgrown bush looking like a wreath around his long, hard dick and totally obscuring his balls. He smiled at me as I undid my pants, pulled up my shirt, and rubbed my stiff dick against his, rustling its fat head in his wiry bush. He leaned into me and kissed me full on the lips, and I couldn't restrain myself from driving my tongue into his mouth, which he didn't object to; in fact, he encouraged it, and we got into some deep oral probing that had us swapping spit (and gum) for days. I felt his hands on my dick, exploring it, stroking it, rubbing the traces of slick pre-come around the head, making it raw and sensitive to the touch, hungry for more. I ran my hands along his sleek flanks, feeling up his deeply dimpled, melonlike cheeks, so round, so firm, so hairy, so hot to the touch, flicking my fingers toward his crack, following the trail of silky black fur to the edge of his butthole, rubbing my palms up and down the cleft of his cheeks, teasing his hole before wedging my thumb into his chute.

Whoa! Was it hot in there! The boy's hole put a lock on my thumb, and I felt it getting scorched from the heat inside his ass. As my finger melted, I broke off from the boy's mouth and started slobbering kisses down his chin and throat, sucking hard on his neck with the wicked intent of covering him in hickies from head to toe. He responded by squeezing and pulling on my dick like he was milking it, milking the nut right out of my balls, milking it down my shaft, milking it until it was all over his own dick and balls. And I didn't disappoint him, shooting a thick wad of cream into his bush and then poking my slimy dick between his legs, humping his moist thighs and rubbing it up under his balls while I finger-fucked his hole with my thumb. His dick was pressed tightly against my flat belly, lathering us both with sweat and my come and his own pre-come. I worked my mouth to his nipples and sucked the shit out of them, half expecting to taste his man milk. He liked that, I could tell, because his asshole spasmodically bit down on my thumb like it was chewing it off, and his balls started to dance up and down on my dick, still grinding between his legs. He shot a hellacious wad that covered my chest and stomach, and I could feel some of it dripping from my chin too.

With my thumb still in his hole, I licked his chest and then knelt down to taste the commingled fruits of our passion, mixing his come and mine with my tongue, languidly lapping at his silky bush and burying my face in its moist confines. Then I substituted my index and forefinger in his ass, driving them hard and deep inside him as he gasped. But his butt responded like I had pressed the secret spot to unlock all of its hidden treasures and sucked my fingers deeper inside him until I had all but my thumb reaming his ass. I wrapped my lips around his still-rock-hard shaft and sucked his dick clean of my come, working my tongue around the inside of his foreskin and picking out any errant drops that I might have missed. I licked the slit of his wedge-shaped head, darting the tip of my tongue as far inside it as I could manage. I loved the smoky taste of his dick, the warm muskiness of his bush, the sweetness of his juice. I sucked that boy's dick hard, drawing it deep down my throat as my hands pressed up into his ass, pushing on his prostate and forcing him to give up still more of that precious, hot juice. Yeah, I made a pig of myself, sucking on that boy's dick until he was shooting blanks, and him being a young guy that took a lot of sucking! But his thin dick was so easy to swallow, despite its length, and I felt like just eating it until there wasn't anything left.

My jaws were aching, and my fingers were starting to cramp, so I decided to come up for air, sliding my tongue along the boy's sweaty body until I had retraced my tracks back to his juicy, thick lips and equally hungry tongue. We kissed passionately, as if our mouths couldn't get enough of each other. Then the boy slipped down to lick my nipples, biting them tenderly and making them stiff and pointed. He lapped his way through the slime on my chest and stomach until he was at the base of my dick, and then, instead of taking it into his mouth, he licked underneath the shaft and sucked on my balls like he was going to rip the hair right off them, each one separately and then together, until they were so hard I could have fucked his ass with them like Al Parker. He was talented, this boy. By the time he got around to my dick, I had dripped a huge slick of pre-come all in his hair. He grabbed the base of my dick and teased it, flicking his tongue around the slit, drawing long, gossamer ribbons of silky juice that he'd spread around his lips, then make little love bites around the edges of the head, the sharp unexpectedness of the momentary pain drowned out by a full-on deep swallow, taking it up to the balls and sucking it like a Hoover.

What's good for the goose is good for the gander, I guess, because the boy got into a deep suck on my joint that made it clear he was going to milk me like I had milked him. There was nothing to do but sit back, relax, and enjoy the ride. And enjoy I did. Grabbing the back of his head and driving my dick into his beautiful face, with those high cheekbones, that broad, pert nose, the razor-traced line of hair from his small diamond-studded ears down to his goatee. Fucking that fine face, stuffing every inch of big, ugly dick as far down his throat as his gag reflex would allow and withdrawing it slowly so he could catch his breath, slapping his pretty face with it, only to stuff it down him again, training him to take even more, fucking it slow, fucking it firm, fucking it so he knew he was being fucked by a real man. And the boy sucked that dick like a man who knows what he wants and will settle for nothing less, no ambivalence, no equivocation, no substitutes allowed. The boy wanted meat, and he wanted it hard, he wanted it strong, and he wanted it not to give out until his hunger was satisfied. And judging by the way the boy took my dick, he must have been starving. I blew one load after another. It felt like I was eighteen again, my balls heavy with come, each successive explosion merely drawing in fresh reserves ready to fire again and again.

While I was drowning the boy in come, he was soaking my pants and boots in it as well. Thankfully, they used black lights in the club, so nothing was going to show up on my black jeans. And feeling his wet come slowly drying against my crotch would be an exquisite experience. At last, the boy released his grip on my dick after one last gusher that drained me so bad I felt light-headed. I slumped against the back of the stall as the boy rested in a crouch against the stall door. We gazed at each other in a stupor, almost in disbelief at how good the last hour or so had felt and not wanting to break the connection just yet. I reached out my hand, and he gripped my forearm as I pulled him to his feet and brought him into my body, enveloping him with my muscular arms and holding his skinny body tightly, feeling the fluttering of his heart against my chest and running my hands up and down his naked, bony spine, nuzzling his neck, biting his earlobes, planting sweet kisses against his soft lips. We held each other like lovers reunited after a long absence, thankful to have found each other again, quite by an accident of fate, in a place we'd never have imagined could have held such good fortune.

But isn't it always like that? Two guys meet, hook up, and find a spark, a connection, which seems to transcend their carnal urges. Fresh in the afterglow of heated passions, having exchanged the most sacred of intimacies, the question rises like a familiar specter, overshadowing them both: Is he the one? We could hardly speak, as if talking would somehow break the spell that gripped us in its woozy embrace. Couldn't we just let our bodies speak for us? To communicate the desires of our hearts when our tongues would surely fail us? Looking into his eyes, I could see the fire beginning to burn from that spark, and I felt it too. But having been singed by those flames so many times before, how could I be certain that this wasn't just a passing fling that would fade into a distant memory only too soon? So we just kissed and hugged and gazed into each other's eyes until it was no longer possible to stay hidden in that stall. The party was blazing, and there was a steady stream of guys coming and going, snorting lines off the sink, dropping acid, exchanging pills, shooting up, blowing chow, pissing everywhere. It was crowded, and there was a long queue of agitated hipsters checking their watches and wanting to take care of business as quickly as possible so as to not miss a chance to find that warm hunk who was going to take them to Funky-town. "Buy you a beer?" I finally blurted out. "Yeah," the boy responded breathily.

Back on the dance floor, the bass thundered in my chest, resetting my heartbeat as Gloria brought the children to their feet, reassuring them that they too would survive. The boy held on to my hand as we threaded our way past the frenzied bodies lost in the music, trying not to lose one another. But the sweat, the come, the jostling crowd were too much, and somewhere near the middle of the madness, I lost him. I lost the boy. Frantically, I turned around just in time to see him swallowed up in a sea of crazed fan dancers *locking* in synch on the dance floor. The power of the fans blew me in the opposite direction as the troupe cleared a large swath in which to regale the adoring crowd with their inspired play. I worked myself around the outer edge of the floor, searching in vain for the boy. I made my way to all of the bars, on all of the multiple levels of the place, but there was no sign of the boy. As if to add mockery to the pain of my loss, I found myself fending off the clawing attentions of blissed-out horn-dogs as I desperately searched for him everywhere I went.

"Damn! I fucking lost the boy!"

As I stood at the edge of the balcony overlooking the dance floor, Esmeralda caught up with me, like a big, hairy fairy godmother.

"Oooh, what da matter, punkin?" she cooed, pinching my cheeks and trying to raise my lips into a smile.

I told her about the boy. Not everything, (I don't drop dime like that) just the losing him part. And she pulled herself up to her full height, leaned far out over the railing as she surveyed the scene below, then bellowed, "Is that him?" as she pointed toward a beautiful thin boy shyly hugging the edge of the dance floor, dancing in a tight circle by himself, as if in a trance. And damn if it wasn't! Never underestimate the power of a drag queen. They have magic, you know. I hugged her tight, patted her on the butt for good luck, and then dashed off to hook up with the boy. As I ran, Esmeralda's voice chased after me. "See! Mummy's always there to make t'ings right, uh-huh."

The club was morphing into a serious rave, the drugs were flowing, the highs kicking in, and people were grooving to the jams like waves lapping the shore of a long stretch of white sandy beach. Even though my feet were moving, it felt like I was swimming against a strong tide. I seemed to barely move, and yet eventually I found myself within sight of the boy once again. His eyes opened briefly as I neared, and he smiled at me, the blaze still alight from our previous encounter. But before I could get to him, I was body-slammed by an impromptu chorus line that pulled me back into the melee of the dancing throngs, losing sight of the boy once more. As the wave of people crashed over me, I heard, above the din, Esmeralda's voice yelling directions at me. "Right!" "Left!" "Back!" Guiding me once again toward the boy. Thank heaven for drag queens! And once more I was in sight of the boy, close enough to reach out and touch him.

This time, fate was on my side, and the surging crowd pushed us together, intertwining our limbs and bringing us face-to-face. We held tightly to each other, and then, as if to rekindle the flame, we kissed deeply, merging our tongues and seeking out the traces of the other. The sparks ignited an inferno. His hands rubbed my crotch, hungry for more of my dick. I slid my hands along his ass cheeks, eager to satiate his desire. As our bodies spoke the secret language of unbridled passion, the crowd swept us into its wake, carrying us along like flotsam, and gently deposited us into a quiet eddy near the door. Drenched in the fire of an all-consuming flame, we smiled conspiratorially as we headed out of the club and into the crisp morning air of the deserted streets, the sun merely a forlorn glow in the billowing fog that cloaked the bridge hulking above us. Down by the water, only a few blocks from the club, there was a derelict warehouse, cordoned off by a decrepit chain-link fence that merely suggested at the notion of No Trespassing. We shimmied through one of the larger gaps and found a half-rotted door along one side of the building that came off its hinges just as a subway train rumbled overhead. Open Sesame! The boy quickly disappeared inside the pitch-black opening.

The cavernous space echoed from the fluttering wings and scrambling feet of a million startled denizens at our entrance. As long as I didn't feel any of them underfoot or dripping shit on me, I was cool with the scene. There was just enough light filtering in from sections of collapsed roof that I could make out the boy, illuminated from the neck down against the wall farthest from me like a piece of living sculpture, his shirt pulled over his head, his pants down around his ankles, long, skinny dick arcing in front of him, pinching his nipples, feeling his heavy, furry balls, his lean torso like polished bronze, glowing, a beacon in the darkness, like a siren calling me to the rocks of eternal damnation. Fuck, he was phyne! My mouth watered, remembering the taste of his come and the velvety smoothness of his meat crammed down my throat, his prickly bush tickling my nose. My dick was so stiff that it made walking difficult, so I unzipped my fly and let the dawg run free, pulling my ass toward the boy like a hound on the scent.

My body careened into the boy, knocking him up against the wall, my dick parting his legs and snaking into the crack of his ass. His dick pulsated against my belly as our lips locked and our hands flew over all the chakras, searching for that hidden sequence, that code, which separated this existence from the bliss of the everlasting light. We were like two hungry cannibals, consuming each other, breathing each other in, sucking the life out of one another, desperate to merge our essences into one. We couldn't kiss deep enough, couldn't hold each other tight enough, couldn't touch each other, couldn't feel each other, enough to slake the hunger that drove us into a mad sexy frenzy. I remember grabbing the boy's legs and throwing them over my shoulders, bracing my arms against the wall and pinning the boy with my dick, drilling out his ass. I dicked the boy down, man, ramming my piece into his sweet ass so deep my balls were beat to shit, yo. The boy's ass was so fine, it was like a hot apple pie right out the oven. American Pie was no lie. Soft like velvet, smooth like honey, tight as a vise, and hotter than hell. My dick burned, and I didn't care. If fucking that boy was tantamount to going to hell, then move over Satan.

I rammed my hips in hard, sharp thrusts, beating out a rhythm that reverberated all up the boy's spine, making his head twitch like a bobbleheaded doll. Eyes squeezed, mouth agape, the boy reached his hands down and spread his ass cheeks wide, his slippery hole sucking my well-greased dick deeper with each stroke, hungry to feed on my meat. And I drilled his ass, man, digging it deep like an insane wildcatter looking to strike gold, black gold, Texas crude. I pounded it good too, hitting paydirt. The boy's eyes snapped open, and he looked at me, startled by the power streaming through him as his butt clamped down around my dick, his balls bouncing as his dick spouted one massive gusher after another, flinging fat white globules of pearlescent cream all up into both our faces, chests, arms. Man, the more his ass bit down on my dick, the deeper I pumped it, driving him to close his eyes once again and rest his head against the wall as he surrendered his ass to the tender mercy of my prick, surrendered his body to the mercy of my will, surrendered his heart to the mercy of my soul.

I'm not sure who was master of whom. The more I fucked him, the more I felt powerless to stop, as if the boy's desire was controlling my dick, instructing me how to pleasure him and not allowing me any rest until he was sated. Then too, I wanted it bad, and I wasn't in any mood to slow down even if he said to. So we got it on, got down, got nasty and fucked, man, just fucked ourselves stupid. We fucked in a circle of light that radiated with our body heat and made us glow like torches in the darkened cavern. And the only sounds that could be heard were the cries of our passions, grunting and moaning at the top of our lungs, without care or concern about who or what might hear us. It was some crazy shit, man, I'll tell you what. And even after my legs and arms gave out, forcing us to slink down onto the slimy concrete floor, we kept it up, fucking the shit out of each other, trying to penetrate each other heart-to-heart, merging right down to the cellular level, not certain where one person's body ended and the other's began. I couldn't feel my balls anymore, lost them in the fray, man, and didn't even give a damn about it. I was *IN* this boy, and that was all that mattered.

There was a loud scream from somewhere in the darkness of

the building that shattered the spell we had cloaked ourselves with, scaring the shit out of me so bad I leapt up off the boy, ripping my dick clean out of his ass. I was in a crouch, arms raised, fists ready to beat down whatever came near us, to protect my boy, my heart pounding so hard I thought it was going to bust out of my chest. I could hear more sounds coming from somewhere to my right, gasping sounds, deep and raspylike, and the thought crossed my mind that somebody was blowing a big wad, and while it eased my senses somewhat to think that it was just another amorous couple, it nonetheless unnerved me to know that my boy and I had not been alone all this time. There were shuffling sounds, and that's when I called out, "Who's there? Show yourself!" After a little while, I could hear footsteps coming toward me, and I straightened up, though still ready to fight if need be. And to my surprise, there, in the glimmer of the light which surrounded the boy and me, stood Esmeralda, smoothing her dress and straightening her hair, mascara streaking one cheek and her lipstick smeared like the Joker.

"Esmeralda!" I cried. "What are you doing here?" She reared up and finally got a good look at who was talking to her, and then let out a loud laugh.

"Aiii! It's my wittle papito wit da pinga grande!" she cooed as she hugged me against her firm breasts, kissing the top of my head. Then she suddenly stopped and clasped her hands together in front of her as she screamed, "And see! You got a good culo, chico!" as she surveyed the boy lying naked on the floor, looking up at her with his bedroom eyes and a big shit-eating grin on his beautiful face. "What did Mummy tell you?" she said, bending down to plant a sloppy wet kiss on the boy's cheek. "You said I'd find the man of my dreams," the boy responded, and then looking at me, "and I did."

"Oh, Mummy is so very, very happy!" Esmeralda cried, wiping her eyes with the backs of her hands and smearing the remnants of her eyeliner. From out of the darkness there was another sound, a loud grunting, and Esmeralda turned quickly and disappeared into the shadows once more. "Oh, I almost forgot." When she returned, she was pulling the bullet-headed wise guy by the arm, looking as if the brotha had had a damn fine time himself and barely able to keep it together. He surveyed the boy and me, naked and covered in sweat and come, and just shook his head approvingly. So I had to ask, "Were you guys watching us the whole time?" And Esmeralda said, "Sweetums, you two where so hot, even the rats were humping each other!" The boy laughed as he got to his feet, grabbed me around the waist and kissed me so deeply that it was as if time stood still. I was pulled back into reality when the bouncer, looking even bigger than I remembered him to be and sporting a bulge to match, barked, "Yo, hon, can we eat now?" Esmeralda, enchanted by the boy and me in our reverie, shook herself and grabbed the bouncer's hand, slapped me hard on the butt, and commanded, "Come along, children, we're going to Junior's to celebrate!"

Like I said, drag queens have power, magic even, and it's always best to do as Mummy says, because "Mummy's always there to make t'ings right, uh-huh."

New York Blues

"Damn it, Bruce, will you just keep your shirt on for a second?! I told you I'm on my way up there, and I'll get to the bottom of it, okay?! Franklin is a stand-up guy. . . . He's not going to fuck us over. . . . He's my frat brother, an Alpha, we've been best friends since freshman year, and I trust the guy with my life. . . . I'll call you later, yeah . . . after I get up there and check things out. . . . Yeah, I just crossed the bridge. . . . 'Bye."

"GOD DAMN IT ALL TO HELL, FRANKLIN, WHAT THE FUCK KIND OF SHIT GAME YOU PLAYING, NIGGA?" I yelled at the top of my lungs as I finally got free of the bumper-to-bumper traffic just after the Whitestone tolls and barreled up the Hutch at high speed. "MOTHERFUCKER, I'M NOT GOING TO LET YOU RUIN THIS!"

Franklin Anthony Botrell Lathrop V, of Oak Park and Oak Bluffs, "Man, we were going to Oak Bluffs before there was even an Oak Bluffs to go to," darling of the Sunday Styles' **Bold Face Names,** one of the Talented Tenth, scion of an extremely wealthy black family, "I think my people might have owned your people, bro," bon vivant and man about town, always squiring the most sought-after models and starlets to the most exclusive clubs, the man no velvet rope is ever closed to, aka "FAB Frankie" in the Adams Morgan for the over-the-top parties he threw every weekend while we were supposed to be studying, aka "Fabrice" at a certain guest house in Key West that "we'll just keep this to ourselves, no reason for mother to know about that unfortunate incident down at the Dick Dock."

I'd been cleaning up after his high-yellow ass since he nearly got us thrown out of school over yet another "unfortunate incident," that time with the dean's nephew. Now, nearly twenty years later, I'm still cleaning up after the guy. There were a whole host of reasons NOT to do this deal, not the least of which was the fact that Franklin was not CEO-of-a-Fortune-500-company material, which this deal would certainly make him. But on the flip side, he did have an uncanny knack for attracting good talent under him and amazing luck in owning the rights to a very promising, newly patented technology that could really revolutionize the B2B-commerce space. Of all of the bankers trying to get in on the action, Franklin chose me because we go way back, and now, with the IPO just weeks away and the road show in full swing, the dumb fuck chooses THIS moment to flake out.

Damn, things were going so well too! He'd recently hooked up with a great girl, Allwynn, whom he seemed to really be in love with. I mean, for as long as I've known Franklin, the man has been a serious playa, but Allwynn seems to have gotten his wandering eye to focus on just her. Truth be told, she's a fox, the kind of woman I could see myself settling down with, if circumstances were different. She likes the same small-batch Kentucky bourbons I'm partial to, and I swear the woman even gets into the occasional maduro-wrapped Padrons that I can't seem to ever get enough of. Personally, I think she's packing some meat between those firm thighs of hers, and it ain't Franklin's. And I wouldn't put it past Franklin to pull some sneaky *Crying Game* shit like that, either. A number of guys I know like to feel some tits on their backs while they're getting fucked in the ass, and Franklin was just kinky enough for it. I extended an invitation to Allwynn and him to come down to my place in St. Barth's after the deal closes. I can't wait to get them out to Grande Saline to see if my suspicions are correct.

Franklin and I had spent only part of the weekend together, going over the final details of presentations for some analysts and fund managers. He had come up to my place in Garrison that Friday night. We worked a little, made some minor adjustments, and reviewed some hot-button issues that had come up in previous meetings with them. Later, I grilled up some ahi tuna steaks, and we threw back a few beers and reminisced about the wild times we'd shared. It got late; he felt tired and spent the night in the guest house. The next morning, I gave him a briefing packet, and he headed up to his place in Dover Plains to prepare for the upcoming meetings. He looked fine to me at the time.

It wasn't until this past Tuesday morning, when he didn't show up at my office like we had agreed, that things started going downhill. I called his apartment in the city, but his housekeeper said he hadn't come back from the country house. I rang the house in Dover Plains, but there was no answer. I even called Allwynn on her cell, but she was in London on a shoot and hadn't spoken with Franklin since late Sunday afternoon. My first clue that there might be something deeper to the mystery was when she said that he sounded "strange," and when she pressed him, he said it was nothing, "Just a cold."

Franklin didn't get colds. Never, not in all the years I'd known him, not what you might typically think of as a cold. No, the only time he got "sick" was when he let the blow that he was sometimes fond of get too tight a grip on him. So I was steeling myself for the worst as I finally turned onto High View Road and started down the rutted gravel driveway that led to Franklin's manicured nine-acre retreat, nestled deep in the rolling hills about two and a half hours north of Manhattan. As I pulled up to the house, I grew apprehensive when I noticed that the front door was wide open. I began looking around the grounds for any sign of him. The swimming pool was a short walk from the house, set on the banks of a natural pond, with an infinity edge that created a small waterfall that ran down to the pond. I headed to the water first, calling out his name and praying that I wouldn't find the fool floating in either the pool or the pond. Thankfully, he wasn't there, though I did find one of his slippers abandoned on the pool deck.

Heading toward the house, still calling out his name, I noticed what looked like the bottom of a set of pajamas dangling over a hedge near the sport court. I retrieved them, thinking that he might be somewhere close by, but all I found was his other slipper. Damn, the nigga was wandering around barefoot, half-naked and with a lot of acreage out there, most of it heavily wooded. "Please don't make me have to go tramping around looking for your fool self," I pleaded. Once again, I headed back to the main house, looking for any more signs of his passage. Just inside the front door, I was stunned by the stench that greeted me, a putrid odor that mugged my nostrils and brought tears to my eyes. "God, please don't be dead, nigga." I held my handkerchief over my mouth and nose, trying to provide some small relief as I began searching the house.

It was a mess too, like the aftermath of a kick-ass frat party that had devolved into a wild orgy at some point. Empty bottles of booze, cigarette butts, and roaches smoked down to a nub were littered about. The floors were sticky, and there were empty packets of lube everywhere. Curiously, no used condoms were anywhere to be seen, but there were plenty of come stains in various states of desiccation all over the place. "It must have been a heck of a party," I thought to myself. At one point, I wiped my finger over traces of a fine powder that covered a glass side table in the den and sampled it. It was the best damn coke I'd tasted in a long while. That was it then. Franklin was on a bender for sure.

Some guys do that when they're on the verge of great success; the sudden realization of what will be expected of them drives them into a panic, and they sabotage themselves, pulling defeat out of the jaws of an otherwise certain victory. Funny thing, though, Franklin never had to worry about succeeding. It was as if success was just handed to him, first by his dad, who left him a very successful company, then by his mother, who was such a fearsome battle-ax that she would have given Attila the Hun nightmares. Whatever he wanted, Franklin's mother made sure he got it. And whatever SHE wanted, Franklin damn well made sure she didn't have to ask twice.

A rush of thoughts were going through my head, trying to calculate the next steps, figure out the best damage control, juggle the loose ends and keep the deal on track. I'd already decided on a plan to get Franklin clean and sober enough to gracefully bow out, citing a "family matter," so I could get Gerry DiBartoni, Franklin's Chief Operating Officer and by far the man with the best skills to run the company, to go through with a revised road-show schedule and still get down to the closing as planned, when I heard a sound coming up from the basement. It nearly made me shit my pants, sounding like something rising up from the dead and giving birth to some demon child. I grabbed a big knife from the kitchen before heading to the stairs that led down into the basement. For some reason, the light switch at the top of the stairs wasn't working, and I hesitated a long time before taking the first few steps down, yelling Franklin's name but getting no answer, just those blood-curdling wails coming up from the depths of the darkness.

It was cold down there, and, to make matters worse, there was a draft that blew uncomfortably on the back of my neck, like something was close behind me and breathing heavily. The wailing grew louder as I felt my way slowly to the bottom of the staircase. Just as my fingers found the light switch, I felt something brush my face, and I screamed like a banshee in heat as I flipped the switch, knife drawn up, ready to slash the shit out of whatever it was. Well, if I was frightened out of my skin, it was nothing compared to Franklin's face as he stood there, naked except for a ratty robe clinging precariously to one shoulder, screaming. His eyes were as big as saucers and fixated on that big old knife in my hand. We must have looked like Abbott & Costello Meet Frankenstein, screaming our heads off at each other for a good five minutes, before either one of us got a lick of sense back into us.

"NIGGA!" I yelled. "YOU MADE ME MESS MY DRAWERS!"

"FUCK YOU, BASTARD, YOU NEARLY KILLED ME!" Franklin yelled back.

At that, I dropped the knife and clutched my chest to calm my beating heart. Franklin backed away and rested his hands on his knees, his head dangling against his skinny chest, trying to regain his breath. After a few minutes recovery, though, I grew angry again and marched over to Franklin and grabbed him by his narrow shoulders.

"WHAT THE FUCK!" I yelled, shaking his thin frame violently. "WHAT THE FUCK DO YOU THINK YOU'RE DOING?" Franklin just looked at me, his mouth slowly opening as if he was going to speak, but no words came out, only a low, deep moan, like the wailing sound I had heard before. "WHAT?" I yelled, shaking him for emphasis. "WHAT'S GOING ON!?"

At that moment, Franklin's eyes rolled back into his sockets, flashing me just the whites, and I got really scared again, thinking he was going into some kind of shock or something from an overdose. But then I heard something crash to the floor, followed by a sputtering sound, like something running out of juice. I looked down, and there, in the space between Franklin's feet, was a fucking massive, realistic-looking, vibrating dick, only it wasn't vibrating anymore. I was too shocked for words. No, I was stunned out of my fucking mind. All I could do was stare, slack-jawed and dribbling spit like some backwoods hick out of *Deliverance*, at this huge fucking dildo that had just fallen out of my best friend's fucking asshole. I guess that explained the orgy scene upstairs.

My eyes were blinking like strobe lights as my mind threw out every plan that I had just made, revising my strategy to take in this sudden turn of events. Franklin, still in a dumbfounded stupor, just looked at the ass-slime–covered monster on the floor, dripping thick blobs of come from the end of his dick into a puddle beside the thing. That's when I noticed the sensation of wetness on my leg. I broke my gaze from the plastic prick to look at my thigh and, to further confound my shock, saw a huge, thick wad of Franklin's spunk congealed to my pant leg, making it look like the back of a buddy booth in a Times Square adult-book store. I had never seen so much come in a single wad before in my life. I shook my head to clear out any revised notions of what I had to do next and began to settle on the only logical course a guy could take under the circumstances. I had to call EVERYBODY that Franklin and I knew and tell them what had happened.

"Ah, okay then . . . ." I began, nodding my head as I tried not to look Franklin in the face, "I see . . . um, ah . . . that . . . ah . . . ."

"Oh . . . oh . . . oh . . . no . . . no . . . no, nigga," Franklin started, trying to grab my arms as I kept waving them to keep him from getting a grip.

". . . you have things under . . . ah, control, yeah . . . ." I continued.

"No . . . no . . . nigga, no . . . I can't let you go, nigga . . ." Franklin said, shaking his head vigorously, a wild, crazy look creeping into his eyes, as if he had read my mind.

"Yeah, ah, I'll just, ah, yeah . . ." I stammered as I began backing up toward the stairway.

"No, nigga, don't make me have to cut you, now," Franklin barked, stomping his bare feet for emphasis.

I reached the steps, still fending off Franklin's attempts to grab me. "Gotta go now!" I said sharply as I pushed Franklin away and began to back hurriedly up the staircase, never once showing my back to him, just in case he meant what he said.

"Nigga! Don't you dare tell nooobody about this!" Franklin yelled. "Where the fuck is that knife? I'm a have to cut that nigga for sure!"

As Franklin wheeled around to look for the knife, I turned tail and stormed up the stairs, taking three and four steps at a time. I slammed the door at the top closed and then booked toward the front door, flying over a sofa and knocking over several tables and chairs along the way. When I hit the front porch, I caught Franklin out of the corner of my eye, running from around the side of the house. Damn those walkout basements! He was totally naked now, nothing to hinder his full-out run toward me, his toes digging into the soft turf, clutching that big knife. My car was maybe sixty yards away. It was going to be close, but I took off running like Jerry Rice on fourth and goal, cursing my new Ferragamos, as they were slow to gain traction on the grass.

Franklin was getting closer, but now I was only twenty yards from the car. I had the keys in my hand and clicked the automatic start-engine button and unlocked the doors, figuring that I would jump in from the passenger side and lock the doors again before Franklin could open the driver's side. Ten yards, and Franklin was reaching out with his long, skinny arm trying to make a fingertip grab of my shirt. My legs were pumping so hard my knees were slapping me in the face. Just as I was within reach of the car, Franklin so hot on my heels that I could feel his sweat on my back, God came to my rescue! Right then, the automatic sprinklers came on, and Franklin stubbed his toe on one of the pop-up sprinkler heads, dropping the knife. I made a zig and a zag, changing my plan at the last minute, figuring that I could just make it to the driver's side of the car instead and be home free. That proved to be an unfortunate miscalculation on my part.

I had failed to take into account Franklin's forward momentum when he hit the sprinkler head, and as I got my hand on the car door, the nigga flew into me with enough force that he was able to get a solid hold of my pants and tackle me to the ground by pulling my pants and drawers clear down around my ankles, causing me to trip and fall just at the finish line. We struggled on the wet ground, the sprinklers making my clothing a total drag on my ability to fend Franklin off. He was trying to crawl his way on top of me, and I was trying to roll to either side to keep him from pinning me down. Somehow, in the ensuing confusion, I felt Franklin's dick knocking on my ass, and to my sudden surprise, my Benedict Asshole let the motherfucker's skinny snake in!

"NIGGA!" I screamed. "Are you FUCKING me? Are you FUCKING my ASS!?"

Franklin was struggling hard to stay on top of me, keeping his dick buried in my butt in the process. I'm not sure even he knew what he was doing, but he seemed to know he liked it. For such a skinny fucker, I was even more surprised at how much upper-body strength he had, threading his arms under my armpits, making it next to impossible for me to twist my shoulders to break his grip. But that wasn't even the half of it; I was also kind of getting into his fucking me.

"Damn, Franklin, you fuck good!"

He was starting to work up a good rhythm, his skinny dick rocking my hard bubble butt in all the right places, and I was beginning to lessen my attempts to shake him off.

"Oh, fuck, Franklin . . . yeah . . . yeah, that's it . . . yeah . . ."

I was into it, now, feeling his hard, bony body slamming my

hole, his hairy balls banging between my legs. It was as if a mouse was fucking an elephant, but sometimes it can be a good thing to just reverse roles and go with the sexual flow of an all-out reaming from an unlikely suitor. Yeah, Franklin fucked r . . e . . a . . l good.

"Shit, nigga, why didn't we ever do this before?" I moaned, backing my ass up to get all the dick Franklin could give.

The downside of being a sometime coke fiend is that one's stamina is severely impaired. After a short while, Franklin started pumping his dick in deep bursts, and soon I felt my ass fill up with his load. Damn, I have to get his secret for big fucking wads of come! He filled me with so much juice it was like getting an enema. When he was done, he collapsed on top of me, spent, the full weight of his body feeling like a heavy blanket on my back. I rolled out from under him and then spread his legs, lifting them over my shoulders as I drove my overexcited bone into his well-abused asshole. I was further surprised to find that his butt was still tight enough to put some good suction on my dick, even after burning out the batteries in a King Kong–sized dildo.

Damn, Franklin had a good ass. Always had. I never got tired of seeing my honey-colored dick ripping into his butter crème buns. I dicked Franklin's ass out, making the nigga's eyes solid white and taking his breath away. That's what it's like when a real man is working out your hole, instead of some piece of plastic. It fucking takes your breath away and makes your eyes roll up into your head. It was just like old times now, back in the day, a long, long time ago, when we were just two crazy kids experimenting in the backseat of his car on a dark turnout in Rock Creek Park, taking the long way home through the bushes in Meridian Hill Park, and getting freaky under the 23rd Street Bridge, at the end of P Street, after closing the Fireplace.

"Yeah," Franklin whispered. "Yeah . . . Fuck me, Daddy . . . Fuck your boy."

I rolled Franklin onto his shoulders and tucked his legs against his chest, raising his ass so I could fuck it deeper, harder, tenderly, wildly, losing all my senses in its hot embrace of my dick, feeling the velvety smoothness of his small frame against my larger, rougher edges, kissing those plump, thick lips that were always eager to share their secrets with mine. There had been the occasional fucks for old time's sake over the years since we had graduated. I guess we had gotten under each other's skin, and because it felt so good, so right, when we were together, it scared us, and we would make fumbling excuses after the fact and beat hasty retreats to some airport to catch a flight to anywhere the other wasn't. Then, after long absences and deafening silence, out of the blue, there one of us would be, standing on the other's doorstep or dropping into the office for a quick shout, a cold beer and a familiar embrace, another drink, and then another and then wake up disoriented in a strange bed, listening to muffled voices explain a history that was etched in the dried sperm that pasted our balls to the inside of our thighs.

Life is filled with complications, and sometimes it seems that all a man does is stumble from one confusing situation into another, never able to get his bearings, unsure of his feelings, afraid to face the cold realities. All he's got is his dick and ass, and sometimes it's just easier to let them do what they are wont to do than let his heart or his mind get in the way, making matters even more confused, more complicated, more difficult to comprehend. Here I was, naked from the waist down, fucking my best buddy in the middle of his driveway in front of all creation, under a steady drizzle, and not wanting it to stop, not wanting to have to get up yet again and bury my feelings for him while someone else got to be by his side. And yet knowing full well that that was indeed what I was going to do, again, because there were the expectations of others, because there was Allwynn, because there was Franklin's mother, because there was my position in the firm, because there was his social prominence, because there was a world that could not comprehend two black men with feelings for each other. Chalk it up as just another unfortunate incident.

I watched Franklin's face, lost in ecstasy, as I drove my dick deep into his ass and just held it there, pumping the base of it against his asshole, massaging his G-spot. That handsome, boyish face, with the high cheekbones, the delicate flair of his strong nostrils, the ruddy color of his lips, those deep, widely spaced eyes. Damn, he was a fine man, with his golden-hued skin, a downy coating of fine black hair in just the right places to give him a masculine edge that contrasted with his slender frame. Only a few stray flecks of gray peeking from his temples, giving him an air of distinction.

My head was pounding as the orgasm welling up from my balls began to work itself into every part of my body. Franklin seemed to feel it too, as he opened his hazel-colored eyes and stared right into my naked soul, laid open before him, revealing truths that could not be voiced, his body trembling in concert with mine. We came together with such force that it was as if our bodies had merged into a single entity, vibrating in synchronicity and allowing our souls to migrate between us in the spaces between our atoms. Our foreheads touched as we tried to hold the moment for as long as possible, cradling each other tightly, not wanting to let go.

"This is all your fault, you know," Franklin said softly at last, as he brushed some stray grass from the side of my face.

"What's my fault?" I asked incredulously, raising myself up on my outstretched arms.

"You've made me love you, mothafucka," Franklin responded, only half in jest, "and now you're going to have to deal with Mother."

"And what about Allwynn?" I said, mimicking his tone.

"Yeah, and her too!"

"Wait a minute, what's this 'You made me love you' shit?" I said, rolling onto my side and getting my legs under Franklin so he was propped up into a seated position, squatting on my dick, as I rested on my back, supported by my elbows.

"You know," Franklin said. "You know how you do, with that big old fat dick you got in my ass!" He was still wiggling his butt and working my still-hard joint.

"Whoa, now, nigga! I only fucked you because you fucked me, and since you got off before me, I had to do you to finish what you started!"

"Well, I wouldn't have fucked your fine bubble butt if you hadn't driven me insane last Friday night, teasing me and shit, making me all wet and shit."

"Last Friday night? We didn't do anything! I never touched you!"

"That's my point! You always did those other times we got together. I was expecting it."

"You're confusing me, nigga, talking all this shit. What's love got to do with it?"

"You know how I feel about you, and the way you fucked me just now, I know you feel it too. Why keep on denying what our dicks already know?"

I had to admit Franklin touched a nerve with that one. As soon as he spoke, my dick was responding like an old dog that's just heard his name called at feeding time. "Damn, Franklin, I didn't know you felt the same way."

"Hell, nigga, I felt it that first time we did it! I've been waiting twenty years for your retarded ass to come around to the same conclusion!"

"Now hold on there," I said, rising up to look him square in the face, his bony ass rocking from side to side, squeezing my dick. "You never said a word about any of this shit before, nigga!"

We bickered back and forth like an old married couple, and then, when the passion was too much to ignore, we fucked ourselves stupid again. That's how it went, fucking and figuring, fucking and strategizing, fucking and planning, fucking, fucking, fucking, and more fucking. Thank God Franklin's property is surrounded by dense forest and is isolated on a bend off a country road that doesn't have any other neighbors. We fucked by the pool, on the sport court, on the deck, in the woods; we crisscrossed the whole damn nine acres. We were caked in mud and just didn't care as we fucked inside the house, all over the place, leaving a trail of come and dirt everywhere we went. Later, in the twilight's last gleaming, as we lay on the bed in the master bedroom, after sharing a hot bath, we circled back around to those old complications.

"So tell me again," I started. "What about you and Allwynn?"

"Hey, she's all right, man; she likes you too."

"You think she's going to go for this threesome business?"

"Ah, hell, man, she's the one who suggested it, I told you."

"I still can't believe that. Though you know, I kind of had this crazy notion about her being some kind of special woman."

"Oh she is, man, she is!" Franklin enthused. "And let me tell you, sex with her will blow your ass away!"

I let that image settle into my mind, though I'm sure Franklin was going off in a different direction, since I had still not broached *The Crying Game* thing to him. We had decided on a number of things, and though the way forward would be difficult, what in life isn't? Carving out one's happiness in a world where the odds are heavily against you, regardless of who you are, what race you are, or how much money you have, is the crux of the human condition. We've been dealing with those complications since we woke up in the Garden of Eden and found that snake in there. So even though it might be difficult for the world to comprehend, the fact is Franklin and I were game to make it work for us, and as long as we had each other, were looking out for each other, then we had the strength to deal with whatever life threw our way. The deal would go forward; Franklin would become non-executive chairman of the company; he, Allwynn, and I would go to St. Barth's, and together, the three of us would work out the next steps of life's great adventure.

"But there is one thing that I sure don't envy you, bro," Franklin said in all seriousness.

"What's that?" I said, rubbing the curve of his beautiful ass.

"Mother's going to be furious at you!"

I smiled, shaking my head. "Naw, man, I got that all figured out. I'll tell her it's just another unfortunate incident. Just like all the other times." And with that, we both cracked up laughing, entwining our arms and legs together in a deep embrace.

Midnight Showing

The only saving grace was the fact that, as a last-minute traveler, all they had available was first class. At full fare. I could just hear the client screaming about the bill when he got it, but it was his own damn fault. He was the one in such a rush to have this meeting, even though I tried to tell him that there wasn't anything worth getting into a panic over. Target companies always went for the poison pill when faced with a hostile offer, especially one that way undervalued them. My colleagues and I had advised him that his bid was too low and that he'd have to raise it substantially if he really wanted this acquisition. All he'd accomplished now was to piss off the target and put it firmly in play. There was no telling what other suitors would come crawling out of the woodwork as a result. But hey, London is great anytime, even now, on the cusp of winter. And to top it off, my favorite hotel on a quiet Lancaster Gate cul-de-sac across from Hyde Park still had room for one more.

What should have been a relatively uneventful flight turned into a nightmare when one of the passengers from the cattle car, a young woman, pretty face but showing signs of great wear and tear, with a screaming infant in her arms and a fidgety two-year-old running circles around her, was shown to a couple of empty seats in first class. The seats in the row behind my seat, in fact. It seems that her baby had a bad case of the colic, and the brat was being a supreme pest just after the meal service and as the movie began. In the interest of preventing a general riot amongst the hoi polloi, the flight attendant thought it might be less troublesome to place her somewhere else. Of course, my trip went straight to hell after that.

I arrived at Heathrow at the crack of dawn, feeling a deep kinship with W. C. Fields. I was a wreck as I dragged myself through customs and dreaded taking the tube to Paddington Station during rush hour so I headed for the express train. As the woman and her brood passed by in a sullen, embarrassed silence, also heading for the Heathrow Express, I couldn't help but agree with Fields that *"Anyone who hates children and dogs can't be all bad."* I think my seatmate certainly claimed allegiance to that notion; he was cursing a barely audible blue streak under his breath as he too passed the woman and her ankle-biters, all going in the same direction. Since she was heading toward the trains, I decided it was time to take a cab, despite the fact that rush-hour traffic would certainly make a mess of the M4.

The brisk air jolted me wide awake as I left the warm confines of Terminal 3. A cab rolled up just as I reached the curb, and the courtly Sikh driver was already holding open the passenger door and barraging me with pleasantries. His attitude certainly helped ease the sting of a miserable flight. Himmat was tall, slender, a golden wheat color, and exceedingly handsome. He was young, just celebrated his twenty-fourth birthday the week before in fact, working on his degree at night, in theater and performing arts, against the wishes of his father, who wanted him to become a doctor or engineer. He was quite articulate and had an informed opinion on everything. I suppose it could have been a bit much, a motormouth cabby at six AM after a sleepless night, but there was a certain chemistry, bordering on an attraction, that seemed to bond us together in mutual camaraderie.

I watched his face in the reflection of the rearview mirror as he drove, mesmerized for some reason. Maybe it was that beard that seemed so unbecoming for his narrow face and big brown eyes filled with a childlike mirth and innocence. I liked his eyes, large, round orbs that seemed to see through things. His hands were nice too, long, straight fingers, tapering delicately at the tips, and they moved in a quick, precise, yet subtle way. I liked the way they moved. I liked his thick, full, kissable lips, juicy and moist like a succulent peach. I liked the way he smelled, of patchouli and cardamom. I was digging his thick, bushy eyebrows that ever so slightly overlapped above his prominent, leonine nose in a slight unibrow. I like hairy guys with unibrows; there's something, I don't know, primal about them. Maybe it was that primal urge that was making my dick stiffen in my pants as I rapturously gazed at his pulchritude.

"Yar, you okay?" Himmat asked inquisitively.

"Huh?" I replied, somewhat still in a stupor and a little surprised by his question.

"You are looking at me kind of strangely," he said. "I was just wondering if everything is okay? If you are feeling well?"

"Oh." I exhaled a short breath, just a little embarrassed at having been caught in the act of fantasizing about this fine, phine, phyne young man. "I was just admiring your handsome face." A big smile erupted on my own face as I shamelessly flirted with him.

"You like my face?" Himmat responded, now also grinning broadly, a glitteringly white smile that seemed to spread sunshine into the backseat even as it bleakly drizzled outside under an overcast sky. "Yar, that's good, that's good. I think you are very good-looking man as well."

There is nothing like a Sikh's directness; they cut right to the chase. But don't underestimate the bluntness of a horny ass-pig with a boner, either. "So, you wanna fuck?" I rejoined, grinning like the Cheshire cat. What the hell? I was only following a gut instinct. At worst, I'd get a wall of welcome silence for the rest of the drive into London; and at best, I'd get this jones wrung out of my pants.

After a lightning-quick pause, Himmat, still smiling that "you're making me wet between my legs" smile, jovially responded. "Yar sure! Why not? Maybe by then this traffic will have thinned out." He made a sharp turn across two lanes of near bumper-to-bumper traffic onto a small gravel road, little more than a driveway, really, just past a large farm. After driving a short distance, basically putting us in the middle of an empty field, Himmat stopped and turned off the ignition. He leaned over the driver's seat and looked me square in the face. "Do you have any disease?" he asked earnestly.

"No. I'm clean. No drugs, no diseases, no smoking except for the occasional cigar, no drinking except for a sip of bourbon every now and then."

"Good. Protection?"

"Yeah, I have some in my briefcase, right here."

"Very good. Because I am eager to feel a big black penis in my bunghole."

Happily, I do have a big black penis, and happier still, fucking Himmat's hirsute butt in the commodious backseat of the cab was off the meter. Literally. In long, deep strokes, I dug out his ass with meticulous care, making sure to grind the base of my dick hard against the rim of his hole until he was moaning like a lone wolf at a full moon. Being the good Sikh, Himmat kept his Five Ks[1] at all times, even during a dicked-down fuck session. So you

---

[1]The Five Ks of Sikhism are: Kesh—Uncut Hair; Kanga—Comb; Karra—Circular Bracelet; Kachera—Shorts; and Kirpan—Small Sword.

know I was going to be as respectful as possible, since you never screw around with a guy wearing a kirpan around his waist. His butt was sweet. Solid, firm cheeks that made fucking his ass like pounding my dick into a fat rubber bumper. And it was tight too, despite being whooped like Duran in his second fight with Leonard. My dick threw a blistering set of combinations at his hole, and the fucker just stood there begging for more. Damn, it was a good fuck.

We started with Himmat on his knees, one knee on the floorboard, the other on the rear seat, while I mounted him from behind, doggie-style. When I reached up under his shirt and started to play with his big, rigid, protruding nipples, I thought he was going to come out of his skin. His body shuddered so hard I felt like a professional bull rider on Old Killer. I rode his ass like a wild man, holding onto his tits for dear life as he bucked and shook under me to a massive climax that had his spunk splattered all over the seat and half the passenger-side window. As he heaved in long, labored breaths, I flipped him onto his back and raised his legs over my shoulders, then moved down on him so that his skinny thighs were pressed against his chest as I used my full body weight to just ream the crap out of his ass.

I piston-fucked him until his butt was smoking and then pulled out to let him cool off while I turned him onto his side to work him from a different angle. By the time I finally emptied my balls, his asshole was turned inside out, looking like a beautiful red rose. After Himmat dropped me at my hotel, I couldn't help but wonder which of Sikhism's Five Evils[2] was responsible for our fuck fest in the field. Personally, I was leaning toward Kam as the guilty party. Even so, the dirty fun contributed to at least a couple

[2]The Five Evils are: Homai—ego; Krodh—anger, rage; Lobh—greed; Moh—attachment; and Kam—lust.

of the Five Virtues[3] wrapping themselves around our spent forms
to help defeat the evildoer. With his offer to be my personal driver
during my stay, at least I'd be able to ask Himmat about it next
time we met.

The day was jammed with meetings from the moment I hit my
firm's offices in The City at eight-thirty AM until about ten PM that
evening in the East End. I'd gone full tilt on less than an hour's
sleep and with balls bluer than the Blue Sapphire martinis that my
pub-crawling client insisted on buying for me in partial gratitude
for saving his ass and keeping his bid alive. We drank ourselves
from Liquid Lab to the Aquarium to Katabatic to Cantaloupe to
Barley Mow to the Bricklayers Arms to Cargo to 333 to Shore-
ditch Electricity Showrooms before finally landing at Home. By
then, I was a friggin' zombie, a friggin' hungry zombie too, and a
friggin' hungry, horny zombie to boot. After thanking my host for
the pub tour and his hospitality, I exited into a soft, fleeting drizzle that bitch-slapped a modest degree of sobriety into me, as I
made the long march to Old Street station, where I grabbed the
Northern Line for the trip to Soho.

The tube was packed with City lads in various states of inebri-
ation, so I felt in good company as I nursed the steady onset of a
massive hangover to be. When the train arrived, I had to squeeze
between a tall, auburn-haired hunk who could have been the latest Ralph Lauren/Polo model and a short, dark-haired South Asian
man wearing glasses that made his stunning brown eyes look like
Mr. Magoo's, with an intense expression that contorted his boy-
ishly handsome face into a frightening grimace. I was attracted to
the South Asian dude kind of like people are attracted to accident
scenes looking for the gore.

[3]The Five Virtues, which are used to combat the Five Evils, are: Contentment,
Charity, Kindness, Positive Thinking, and Humility.

In my then current state, I stared at the man with what must have bordered on the obsessive, because I noticed a woman across the aisle staring at me and trying to figure out if I was stalking the South Asian dude or something. But the South Asian dude didn't seem to notice, and I just kept on staring at him until we came to Leicester Square, which was my stop and, it turned out, the South Asian dude's as well. I followed him off the train, keeping a respectful distance between us as he headed up Charing Cross Road, toward Soho proper. The weather had cleared slightly, and the wind was kicking up in light gusts, blowing the man's trench coat and giving him the general appearance of a dashing foreign correspondent on the trail of some great story. I, on the other hand, might have been mistaken for a thinner Harry Lime with a better tan.

There wasn't anything particularly remarkable about the South Asian dude. He looked to be in his thirties, well dressed, carrying a slim briefcase, with a copy of the *Financial Times* rolled up under his arm. He walked with an easygoing stride, as if he didn't know quite where he was going and wasn't in any hurry to get there. I found that intriguing because it belied the severe expression on his face, which indicated some great pain or burden was weighing heavily on him. He had a smallish frame, well proportioned, and I did note how the cut of his trousers seemed to emphasize the small round cheeks of his ass, one nice-sized globe for each hand, since I was a friggin' horny zombie fuck, after all.

As he crossed the boulevard and headed down Old Compton Street, my heart skipped a beat. Could it be? Was he heading toward the gay village too? My dick stiffened even more, which I didn't think was possible since it was already difficult to walk with that bone crawling down my leg. My mind began to race with new calculations, as the game was definitely heating up now. When my quarry stopped in front of Balans and reached for the door, I was relieved on two counts: first, I could finally satisfy the rumbling in my stomach; and second, I could plot my next move toward satisfying my rabid libido. My mystery man quickly stepped up to the bar. Balans was crowded as usual given its prime Soho location and large picture windows overlooking the hipster scene on the street outside, not to mention the drop-dead gorgeous waiters who gave a whole new meaning to "eye candy." Fortunately, I was able to find a seat at a small side table along the wall opposite the bar, the better to watch my man's every move.

The man ordered a double old-fashioned of scotch, neat, with a water chaser. As it was placed in front of him, he picked up the scotch and threw it down in one mammoth gulp, snapping his head back to guzzle every last drop. When he was done, he slammed the glass on the counter and ordered another, followed in quick succession by another, and then yet another, never once touching the water. Clearly, our man had a hankering to drown his sorrows, and he was wasting no time getting as shit-faced as possible. I estimated that given his small frame and thin build, it wouldn't be long before his defenses could be breached. After he had downed a few more shots, I decided to make my move.

"Whoa, take 'er easy there, Pilgrim," I drawled in my best imitation of the Duke as I sidled up beside the now visibly tipsy young South Asian man.

"Huh?" he replied, seemingly unable to focus on my face as he held onto the bar to keep from falling down.

"Here, let me get you to a seat before you fall face first into that old chap's supper," I offered cheerfully as I guided him to the empty chair at my table. He sat heavily, like the whole weight of the world was resting on him.

"So, there are faster ways to get to Hell, you know." He gave me a quizzical look, so I continued. "At the bar? I just assumed you were on a mission." I was smiling my softest and most friendly smile, staring flirtatiously into his eyes, my knees touching his under the tiny table. He took off his glasses, which made him look even more beautiful, and shook himself.

"Who are you?" he asked at last, the drink slurring his speech.

"Beelzebub," I replied, snappily extending my hand to shake his. "The name's Beelzebub. At your service, squire." He limply shook my hand with a confused expression on his handsome, darkly featured face, but I welcomed the opportunity to feel his soft skin, the delicateness of his smooth palms, the coarseness of the hair on the back of his hands, the heat that his body was emitting, and the moist sweat that made his palms clammy. My body was like a live wire, crackling with current and sending sparks flashing in all directions. When we touched, it was as if I had been grounded, discharging a fraction of the forces flowing through me into the South Asian man. He jerked a little, like he felt the current flowing too, then squinted at me to make out my face, his glasses still on the table.

"What kind of a name is Beelzebub? You Pakistani?"

"No," I said, chuckling, "I'm a citizen of the world and dark places. You? You're from Pakistan?"

"My dad's from Karachi, and my mum's from Bristol, so I'm kind of half and half," he explained in a soft voice.

"That's covering quite a lot of territory. How did they meet?"

"At university. My dad came to London to study business, and Mum was in one of his classes. You know how it goes; they hit it off, and nine months later, here I am," he said, laughing slightly, easing some of the pain that still clung around his gentle dark eyes.

"And what did they name you?" I asked in good-natured jest, since he hadn't told me his name yet.

He smiled, slightly embarrassed. "I'm sorry, please forgive my lack of manners. I'm Jameel." He extended his hand, and we shook once more, only this time I held his hand just a little longer, just ever so slightly, lingering over the experience of touching him even briefly. I liked the way he felt.

"But you, what about you?" he continued, the puzzled expression returning to his face. "What kind of name is Beelzebub?"

I started to laugh heartily as I began to explain. "Let's just say it's a convenient moniker for a guy who has been stalking you since Old Street with the evil intent of getting into your pants."

Jameel's mouth dropped open as puzzlement gave way to shock. I'm not sure which disturbed him more, the fact that he had been so closely followed or that anyone would be interested enough in him to bother. "You've been following me?" he asked at last, a plaintive tone in his voice.

"Yeah, I liked the way you look, and it seemed that something was bothering you. I just wanted a chance to make your acquaintance and see if I could take away the hurt."

After a long silence, Jameel's head sank low into his chest as tears began welling up in his eyes. He began to sob uncontrollably, and I did my best to comfort him, even going so far as to put my arm around his narrow shoulders and hold him closer to me. I felt bad for him, and besides wanting to get into his pants I did want to ease whatever was troubling him, if I could. Jameel seemed to appreciate my efforts, and before long he regained enough composure to tell me that he had just lost his job as an analyst at a bank in The City. "General redundancies" was the reason given. His parents had been so proud to have their son working in a prestigious position at one of London's most venerable institutions that Jameel didn't know how he could face them with the news of his sacking. He felt ashamed and thought he had failed both them and himself.

"So, because you lose your job, you come to a gay pub in Soho to drown your sorrows?" I teased good-naturedly, trying to lighten his mood.

"Why not?" he replied. "I have no reason to hide it anymore."

I smiled as he spoke, happy that the stars were aligning in my favor. I ordered some strong coffee and an assortment of appetizers for us as Jameel and I passed the time in pleasant conversation, getting to know one another better and allowing him a chance to regain his senses. I must admit, I was totally smitten by Jameel. My dick was starting to leak in my pants, and it was all I could do to cover up both my hard-on and the telltale wetness that threatened to betray my thoughts. Fortunately, under the circumstances, I was given a very clever ruse when a noisy and energetic trio, a guy and two girls, dressed to a tee as Riff Raff, Magenta, and Columbia, knocked over the bottle of water on our table as they passed by, spilling its contents into my lap. The icy water helped suppress my bone and washed out the damn spot to boot.

It was about five minutes to midnight. Since not many people parade around in costumes like the trio of revelers, it could only mean one thing: *The Rocky Horror Picture Show* was playing nearby, and the revelers were part of the audience participation that always accompanies the show. I quickly paid the bill and dragged Jameel in hot pursuit of the merry trio. They led us to a theater not far away where it seemed like everyone in the crowd was dressed as their favorite character. Jameel and I, being dressed in suits, were roundly greeted by shouts of "Brad! Brad!" as we took our place in the queue. Jameel was still a little dazed by it all, but I was glad to see his face lightening into a megawatt smile as he got into the flow of the raucous throngs.

Once inside the old, ornate theater, a little dowdy and showing signs of fatigue, I took advantage of the fact that they still had an upstairs balcony and steered Jameel to a pair of seats deep in its darker recesses. The stage and the screen were clearly visible, but we couldn't be seen from below, and there were no working lights where we were sitting. A number of other folks, various pairings of guys with guys, guys with girls, girls with girls, and some couples of uncertain gender, no doubt with similar thoughts on their minds, also chose refuge in the balcony. Fortunately, however, there weren't so many nasty and evil-minded souls as to compromise a modicum of anonymity and privacy between the various parties. As I watched them enter and find just the right seats, I wondered how many of them would actually remember anything of the movie, to say nothing of the live entertainment that followed the action on the screen.

The house lights dimmed, and as the curtain went up and the impromptu actors took their places on the improvised stage, I was tingling from the sensation of feeling Jameel's hand on top of mine on the armrest. He made no effort to move it, so I took that as an indication that the attraction that was developing between us was mutual. In short order, the bone in my pants returned with a vengeance, and I spent the opening scenes contemplating my next move. As usual, fate had a way of intervening on my behalf. Jameel had purchased some sweets at the concession stand and was trying to open the box with one hand, since his other was occupied, stroking the back of mine. Somehow the box managed to flip out of his hand and land in my lap. He moved his hand from mine to retrieve the box and found the throbbing bone in my pants instead. It was a find that he seemed to rather enjoy, since not only did he hold on to it, but he rubbed his hand up and down to explore its length and girth.

I reached my hand into Jameel's crotch and found his dick was also rock hard. I stroked him just as he stroked me, and both of us got even harder with the mutual attention. Around us, I could make out the sounds of zippers being lowered, the gentle rustling of clothes being removed, stifled gasps and muffled slurping of lips on private parts. That added to the heightening passion enveloping Jameel and me. He reached for my zipper at the same time I was undoing his, letting the dawgs run free. It was on now, baby, and where it went from here, well, *"It's astounding, time is fleeting, madness takes its toll. . . . With a bit of a mind flip . . . you're into a time slip . . . and nothing can ever be the same. You're spaced out on sensation. . . . HAH! Like you're under sedation. . . . Let's do the Time Warp again!"*

Jameel wrapped his lips around the head of my dick and nuzzled it, licking his tongue around it and exploring the sensitive slit, pushing the tip of his tongue into it and lapping at the silky juices welling out of it. I could feel his dick getting slick as well, his long foreskin creating a pool of pre-come that overflowed onto my hand. His balls were shaved, and the thick bush of his pubic hair was surprisingly fine, like velvet. As Jameel slid down on my dick, sucking it to the base, I took my wet, slick hand and probed between his legs, feeling under his shaved balls, sliming them with his own juice, searching out the moist, tender, pliant embrace of his asshole, eager to feel its tight grip around my fingers. He spread his legs and slumped down in his seat to ease my journey. Just as I neared the precious object of my quest, I pulled out my hand and stuffed it down the back of his pants, caressing his solid, hairy cheeks and furry crack, now sweaty in anticipation of the violation that was so close at hand.

My fingers were on the verge of his hole now, and the intensity of the heat that was radiating from it felt like fire, like his hole was a roaring furnace eager for fresh kindling. As the heat of his hole made my hand moist with sweat, I felt hot all over, and that's when I heard it. *"Give yourself over to absolute pleasure. Swim the warm waters of sins of the flesh—erotic nightmares beyond any measure, and sensual daydreams to treasure forever. Can't you just see it? Don't dream it, be it."* Dr. Frank-N-Furter was absolutely so right-on. And give myself over I did, in spades. I gently jammed my fingers into Jameel's asshole, which willingly opened to accommodate all the stretching and probing I gave it. That led me to shoving his pants down around his thighs and encouraging him to sit on my stiff, fat dick, lubed up by his spit and the pre-come flowing like a fountain from his slender dick.

Oh man, was Jameel's ass hot! He was grinding his butt deep and hard on my dick, clamping his hole around it and choking the fucker with every stroke of his ass. I slipped my hands under his shirt and teased his soft, round nipples, which only made him a fucking satyr, gyrating his hips and pumping his cheeks like a human milking machine. My dick was on fire in his ass, melting against the ribbed walls of his rigid chute, and I was bucking my hips fast to try and come sooner so I could cool it down in there. But the heat also made me want to fuck him long and deep: damn the blisters, just give me more of this man's ass! I could feel my balls turning into molten puddles beneath Jameel's butt cheeks, and the sensation was so thrilling that my ass started burning in anticipation of the fiery love lava flowing its way.

As the heat intensified, Jameel began stripping off clothes until he was nearly naked, riding my dick like a man who hadn't been fed a good piece of meat in a long time and, now that he finally had one, wasn't going to give it up easily. He jacked his dick as he rode me, sending a shower of come flying into the seats in front of us. With his first nut out of the way, it just made him hungry for more and bigger ones. The more he rode my fat dick, the bigger it got, stretching out to its full length and getting a good hosing down by Jameel's insatiable ass. All I could do, pinned to the seat, was lick the sweat off Jameel's back and nibble on his neck and earlobes as I fed his hungry hole and rubbed his nipples raw.

I loved fucking his taut ass, feeling his athletic body straining to take more dick and eager to give up another nut. When he came, it was as if he was pulling the nut out of my balls too, which would have been good since I was building up a load of pressure that just wouldn't let fly because of the heat of his ass. Jameel was a greedy, piggish fuck, just the way I like it. The more dick he got, the more dick he wanted. I swear, I could have fucked him the whole night right there, but the end credits were starting to roll and the house lights were coming up, bathing our little corner in a dull, reflected glow of flagrante-delicto shadows plainly visible to the casual observer. But that wasn't enough reason for Jameel to get off my dick. When a couple of guys stood and watched for a moment, squinting to see more clearly into the shadows, Jameel was like a Dutch whore in the Walletjes putting on a show for potential clients in her picture window. The man was a fucking freak!

As I slipped deeper into the warm waters of sins of the flesh, I felt a welcome tingling in my balls and ass that signaled at long last my nut was about to break. Jameel worked his ass even harder, as if he could feel it too and he wanted nothing more than to have that volcano erupt deep inside his ass. The circle of voyeurs grew a little larger, until we were actually surrounded by a mob of people whose features we could no more make out than they could clearly see us, but the electricity of the erotic current bound everyone into a tight-knit coven. The nut slowly moved into my balls, filling them to bursting, loading up the chambers that would find release through my dick with a thick, hard cream that I could feel even though it was still inside me.

Jameel's ass stroked all up and down my dick, stretching it, pulling at my dick like it was trying to break the sucker off, hungry to feel that big load fill his hole. Then, with a rush that made me light-headed, and a searing pain like my insides were ripping open, I shot that nut, pumping so much come that it overflowed Jameel's ass and soaked the seat so bad my butt was swimming in my own juice. I was pumping and creaming and shooting one massive load that just didn't want to stop, cramming it all up in Jameel's ass until his head snapped back and he shot another massive nut of his own. From various points in the circle around us, I could hear others creaming too, a couple of guys even showered Jameel and me with come.

Soon, every guy in the circle was shooting big honking loads all over us too, until we were soaked in sweat and come from all sides. And still I was pumping juice into Jameel's ass, so much so that he must have felt like he was going to burst. He squirmed like a stuck pig, trying to get off my dick, but it was too tightly jammed up inside for him to squeeze off it. It was a dog fuck, man; we were stuck together like fucking dogs. As the last guy spent himself all over Jameel and me, my balls finally emptied the last of their thick contents. Only then could my dick find sufficient relief to soften just enough for it to slip out of Jameel's sloppy crater of a hole.

We made our way down the stairs and out into the misty pre-dawn gloom of Soho, shivering in come-soaked clothes beneath our stained trench coats, arm-in-arm, walking toward the Tottenham Court station to pick up the Central line back to my hotel. Jameel rested his head on my shoulder, a blissful expression replacing the deep furrows from earlier. I felt like I was walking on clouds. I told Jameel that I'd make some introductions for him at my firm. I knew they were looking for some good analysts, and from what I'd seen, he was very good indeed. He laughed and pulled me closer to huddle against a sudden gust of wind. The moon was still hanging full in the western sky, and the good burghers of London were fast asleep, preparing for a new day.

"Jameel," I said, "I think this is the beginning of a beautiful friendship."

What the Broker Knew

My first real apartment (as in: my own place, without room-mates, where I could walk around naked and jerk off in the living room while watching porno on my big-screen, flat-panel TV without having to put some stupid handkerchief on the door to let some other person know they should come back later) was a duplex on 35th Street, across from a small park where lithe, tall, super–well-endowed (judging by the humpy outlines in their flimsy jams) Black and Puerto Rican guys played basketball, shirts versus skins, outside the large picture window in the dining area. Murray Hill was a great neighborhood, a quiet island unto itself with leafy streets and quaint townhouses interspersed with the occasional high-rise. But what made it a perfect neighborhood to me were the secret sex clubs that plied their trade behind the smug, cozy exteriors of elegant doorman buildings and nondescript apartment blocks. One of the brokers who worked on my account clued me in to them.

Back in the day, before there was the Euro, I was a foreign-exchange trader on Wall Street, and my bank had relationships with dozens of money brokers around the world. I handled the

Scandinavian currencies, buying and selling Swedish, Danish, and Norwegian kroner for corporate customers and the bank's own account. The US dollar was freely floating against the world's currencies, which created opportunities for currency speculators to make huge fortunes by correctly guessing the direction of the dollar versus other currencies. Currency traders like me were fast becoming the new stars in finance as we moved tens of billions of dollars a day through our trading books, making one-sixteenth of a tick here and there to reap many millions in profits for our institutions. Because my bank was a major player, we always had to have a bid (buy) or offer (sell) price in the market, which was handled by brokers who matched up sellers and buyers, for a vig, naturally.

Being a broker was supercompetitive, because a trader like me had thirty phone lines, at least, dedicated just to brokers, which meant that brokers tried very hard to ingratiate themselves with a trader to gain more of his business. Volume meant profits for brokers, and the more trades a trader put with a given broker, the more money the broker made. Brokers had a variety of methods for earning favored status with their trader clients, the most common of which involved tickets to Yankees games, with seats just behind home plate or above the home-team dugout. But there were other ways as well, such as expensive three-martini lunches at Peter Luger or visits to high-class gentlemen's clubs where there was no name superexpensive champagne, scotch, and gin, and the hostess took you to small rooms in back and suggested that you make yourself comfortable, do a few lines of coke, take off your tie, and one thing leads to another, and you've just had the best fuck of your life and still have time to get back to the office and square up your positions before the New York market closes, all courtesy of your helpful full-service currency broker.

Paolo was one of the brokers assigned to cover my account; his firm was relatively new, and he genuinely wanted to earn my business. He was tall, about six feet, thin but muscular, as befits a world-class swimmer, and very handsome, with dark curly hair that kept dropping into his hazel-colored eyes in a sexy sort of way. His thick, pouting lips were always slightly parted, his tongue darting out to moisten them every so often. He had a classic aquiline nose that combined with his olive complexion to give him the look of a Roman centurion. While having an introductory lunch, we discovered that we both lived in Murray Hill, not too far apart, and as I was still a relative newcomer to the neighborhood, Paolo offered to introduce me to some of the area's hidden charms. We set a date to meet later in the week, a Friday evening, after work.

A trading desk is a hypermacho, racist, sexist, homophobic environment, in today's lexicon, where in addition to making a good profit for the bank, traders go into the arena like gladiators and fight fiercely to become a BSD (Big Swinging Dick), which signifies that they have taken the biggest risks, correctly intuited the next major trend, and put it all on the line—their careers, their balls, at times even the solvency of their institution—and won, big. You have to have extremely thick skin to survive in such an environment.

As the only black guy on the desk, I took my full ration of jokes whose punch lines invariably dealt with black dick size, black sex drive, white women, and Cadillacs. I never really took any of the ribbing seriously or to heart, since the guys on the desk, nice Italian gumbas all, originally from Brooklyn but now in the 'burbs on Staten Island, ex-altar boys and still good Catholics, mass twice a week, dished more shit on each other than they did on anyone else. In fact, tossing shit around was a form of endearment for them, like calling each other "faggot" and "pussy," and complaining of getting their asses "punked" whenever they were jammed with an unwanted position. On the whole, the sweetest bunch of fucking misanthropic misogynists you could ever hope to meet.

Besides, I was just as much a terror as any of them, giving it back as good as I got, laughing just as hard as they did when I got off a good stinger of a reply, and when I scored a huge win on a complex arbitrage I had set up, everyone on the desk stood up, applauded, and gave me a fat Macanudo cigar, signifying that I was a Big Swinging Dick and had the balls of a bull. It wasn't really mean or hurtful, just the kind of trash talk that a close-knit group of professionals engages in to keep their collective sanity and who respect each other and have each other's back in a high-stress, pressure-packed job that carries huge risks and even bigger responsibilities, since the daily profits and losses of the trading desk were directly reported to a Vice Chairman of the bank. I was just one of the boys, and being part of the camaraderie on the desk made the difficult times pass quicker and the good times that much sweeter.

Most of my fellow traders had been clerks and gradually shifted to the trading desk as a form of upward promotion; many didn't even have college degrees. When they were hired, the world existed in a fixed-exchange-rate environment, with the currency values set each morning by conference calls among the governors of the world's major central banks. But after the move to floating exchange rates, that staid gentility was swept away by the raucous rough and tumble of market-driven forces. The trading desks took on new importance, and the banks gradually started to add staff with more education but not necessarily more trading skill. I was among the first group of new traders to join the trading desk who had ever been through the bank's formal management-training program, a test case of sorts for the new guard that was to eventually take over most trading positions. The guys on the desk nicknamed me "Joe College" and razzed me mercilessly.

Under the circumstances, then, I wasn't going to wear my sexuality on my sleeve. I wanted the gumbas to like me and to teach me how to be a good trader. I wanted to be a BSD. It just didn't seem necessary for my colleagues to know that I actually had a big swinging dick and a fondness for guys. Hence, I made myself available to socialize with my fellow traders after work, even if that meant taking in the strip clubs in Hoboken and getting wasted on Rusty Nails. I went out with the brokers, even if that meant getting laid at fancy gentlemen's clubs. Come the weekend, I lived out my sexual fantasies my way, and in the process even came to an accommodation with the dual worlds in which I traveled. I thought of myself as truly bisexual, having the best of both worlds and able to enjoy hot, steamy, no-questions-asked, no-strings-attached, "dick it down until it don't come up" sex regardless of the gender of my partner(s).

Thus, when Paolo came along, I was ready for anything, finding him extremely attractive but also willing to fuck women with him as long as he was buying. While I felt that he might have experienced a similar attraction, neither of us broached the subject when we got together that Friday. We met at the Doral, a boutique hotel on Park Avenue South that catered to Japanese businessmen, for happy hour at the bar. Paolo lived nearby, and this was his favorite hangout. He said it was because they poured the best drinks at cheap prices, but the stirring in my pants as I watched a handsome young salaryman nearby who matched my stare with a sultry intensity told me that more than a cheap drink might be had there.

Paolo was impeccably dressed in a fine, lightweight wool suit that sleekly hung on his taut body. He was packing a pretty good bulge in his pants too, I noticed. He had evidently been checking me out as well, because he pointed to my crotch and exclaimed in that brusque Italian directness that it must be tough for me to find pants with enough room for my equipment. I replied that finding underwear that fit was my biggest problem, and he agreed and said that he had stopped wearing it years ago because he could never find any that were comfortable. We laughed, eyeing each other just a bit more closely.

After a few more cocktails, by now joined by Yoshi, my Asian voyeur, the three of us headed out for Paolo's expert guided tour of Murray Hill. Our first stop was two blocks away, just off Madison near the Morgan Library, in front of an elegant limestone townhouse. Paolo went up the steps to the parlor floor and buzzed the intercom. After a few moments, he bounded back down the steps and led us to the garden-level entrance. We were buzzed inside a richly appointed foyer, all white marble and gold gilt, with a fountain splashing in one corner. A butler came and took our coats and pointed us to the drawing room, where about three dozen well-dressed, elegant people were chatting quietly over drinks. They were a mixed group, ranging in age from late twenties to early forties, mostly white with a smattering of Blacks, Latinos, and Asians, with men just slightly outnumbering the women.

More people were ushered in as the evening wore on, until the room was quite full and uncomfortably hot. By then, everyone was pretty well liquored up and the heat was starting to cause some interesting reactions. One young blonde got the ball rolling by slipping out of her dress and wandering around in just her bra and panties. A man followed suit, stripping down to his underwear. I went next, getting into the spirit of things, followed by Yoshi, who followed me closely all evening and who had a great body, well proportioned and lightly muscled, just the way I like and surprisingly furry. Paolo stripped down next, without any underwear to hide his huge, uncut dick, fully erect, and he playfully grabbed the young blond woman in the bra and panties and kissed her on the lips, his hands unbuckling her bra straps. That set the place on fire, and folks started getting naked real fast.

Before long, people were groping and sucking and fucking everywhere, in all sorts of combinations. I found myself fucking this gorgeous black woman with a shaved pussy right behind Paolo, who was busy with the blonde, our butts bumping with each thrust of our hips. At first it was accidental, but then it seemed to get very intentional, as we rubbed our sweaty cheeks together, grinding our asses as we fucked our respective partners. Yoshi's furry ass squeezed into the mix and wound up rubbing against Paolo's and mine, and the three of us enjoyed a little extra-special connection that soon overwhelmed any interest we had in the women we were with.

Paolo finished first, and he stuck his thumbs in both Yoshi's ass and mine while we fucked our respective ladies, making us both come faster than we intended. As we disengaged from the women, Paolo, still with his fingers in our asses, maneuvered us to a sofa in an alcove that had just been vacated by another couple. There he worked us both over to the point of blowing another load, getting almost four fingers inside us. Just as it seemed we couldn't take any more, Paolo then fucked us both with his thick ten-inch rod, switching from my ass to Yoshi's and back again after a few good, deep thrusts, really getting the two of us red hot and crazy sexy.

When Paolo stuck his big dick in my ass again, I grabbed Yoshi and rolled him under me, deep-dicking his wet furry hole as I took Paolo up to his balls. It didn't take too long for us all to just explode, Paolo filling my ass with his hot juice, Yoshi's ass overflowing with mine while he covered the sofa with his. I pulled out of Yoshi's ass and then bent Paolo over, knocking him onto all fours as I shoved my dick into his tight, square ass. The force of my hard, fat eight inches suddenly reaming him took his breath away, and I didn't let him recover quickly. Yoshi moved around in front of Paolo and stuffed his dick down Paolo's throat, matching my strokes to his ass, and together we fucked him until we had filled him with come at both ends. After we wiped ourselves down after the serious hosing we had given each other, Paolo suggested that there was an even better party going on not far away, so we got dressed and headed for yet another orgy.

The second place was in a fifth-floor walkup. After being buzzed in, we climbed the narrow stairs up to the landing on the fifth floor, where we were greeted by a stunning redhead, with the greenest eyes, manning a small table. She collected the rather hefty entry fee, for single males, one hundred dollars each, while women entered free and couples paid only fifty, which was a relatively common method for trying to regulate the ratio of dick to pussy in such places. The redhead's other role was to screen out undercover cops, and for that, she made us whip out our dicks, knowing that police rules forbade cops from exposing themselves. After we complied, she then asked us to give each other head, which I think was just her way of having some fun, since having put our meat on the table she already knew we weren't likely to bust the joint, at least not in that manner. We decided to give her more than she bargained for, and so we took turns fucking each other, each of us getting to spend time in the middle position, fucking and getting fucked at the same time.

Her mouth just dropped as we got into it; then she started playing with her tits and fingering her pussy, never taking her eyes off of us. At that, Paolo reached over and pulled her up from the table, laid her on her back, and slid his big dick into her, while Yoshi stuffed his balls in her mouth and I fucked Paolo's ass. After Paolo came, I took his place and fucked her with my thick dick while Yoshi fucked me and Paolo fucked her throat. After I blew my wad, Yoshi took his ride on her while I fucked his ass and Paolo worked himself under her and fucked her ass. After that, the woman gave us our money back, and we entered the apartment orgy for free. It was already a mad scene, this orgy having twice the number of people in about half the space as the first place. Walking into it naked, it didn't take long for our dicks to find some new holes to fill, and we were pulled in different directions.

As if by some secret sexual compass, however, the three of us found ourselves fucking side-by-side sometime later, which led to another round of heavy ass play between Paolo, Yoshi, and me. Yoshi got the action going by slipping his beautiful, superthick uncut dick into Paolo's loose hole and fucking the holy shit out of him as if Paolo were a bitch in heat and Yoshi a mad dog with a serious bone that just HAD to be buried. Now! Paolo was totally engrossed in giving a hot Russian dude with a deep tan that made his snowy white cheeks look like two soft pillows a good dicking with that fat prick of his when Yoshi just went off on his butt. The Russian was bent over and spreading his ass with his big hairy arms. I went up to him and lifted his chest so he was resting his back against Paolo. Then, while Paolo's dick was still buried in the Russian's ass, I lifted the Russian guy's legs as Paolo held him tightly under his armpits and shoved my big black dick up in his snowy white ass alongside Paolo's. Man, that Russian dude turned beet red despite his tan as both of our big dicks ripped his hole wide open and fucked his eyes into the back of his head. He blew a wad so thick and hard into my face, I thought for sure I'd need a skin-peel just to get it off.

Yoshi must have drained his balls inside out because the gri-mace on his face as he came was so tortured that I felt his pain, to the point that I let loose inside the Russian's ass with a load that was so hot it made the skin on my dick smoke. Paolo was so turned on by the hot juices coming at him from the front and rear that he nearly dropped the Russian dude when he finally threw it down. That scene only made the three of us so off-the-hook horny that we played together the rest of the night, fucking the mess out of each other and making the occasional foursome with some guy or woman just to spice it up. By the time I finally dragged myself out of the second orgy, leaving Paolo and Yoshi double-fucking some woman's ass and pussy while they were being fucked by a line of guys taking their turn in a gang bang on their asses, it was almost one-thirty on Saturday afternoon. The following week, Paolo never mentioned the activities of the previous Friday, but we established a very special bond between us, hooking up regu-larly on the pretext of checking out new finds in the neighbor-hood. I also threw a good chunk of my business his way, making him a star at his brokerage firm. Yoshi went back to Tokyo soon after our evening of debauchery, but we managed to hook up whenever business brought him back to New York, even after he got married and his wife was pregnant with his first child, my god-son.

As I got into the rhythm of New York—long, boozy lunches, late dinners before the Tokyo markets opened, after-dinner enter-tainment lasting well into the wee hours of the morning, getting up and into the office by seven AM to catch the end of the London trading day, nursing hangovers and runny noses from all the coke, showing up in the office wearing the same clothes from the day before, several days in a row—I was literally gagging on the cor-nucopia of it all, gorging myself on the booze, sex, drugs, and discos like every day was my last day on earth. The food and drink were the best that money could buy, the people were gorgeous, sexy, smart, and tough as nails, the pace was so fast that I began to appreciate Nick Romano's line from *Knock On Any Door*: "Live fast, die young, and leave a good-looking corpse."

A.M.—Griffith Park—P.M.

Even at this early hour of the morning, the sun seared my bare shoulders, making the marrow sizzle clear down in my bones. God, it felt good to move. Long, lean strides propelled me along the river bank, a light Santa Ana wind at my back helping to push me forward at a blistering gait. I felt like a gazelle, power in motion, built for speed, my muscular legs and thighs carved from stone but supple and agile, my body tanned by the unrelenting sun a deep, reddish bronze. Against the faded backdrop of the sandy-colored slopes, I was a streak of red lightning blazing along the trail, my gossamer-thin shorts in bright yellow beaming my imminent approach to any passersby like a warning beacon: "CAUTION! LOCOMOTIVE APPROACHING! CLEAR THE WAY!"

I know the lonely commuters on the slow-as-molasses Golden State Freeway wished they could move as fast as I clipped down the main trail which ran parallel to the highway. They would look up from their weary drudgery and stare at my nearly naked body as I cruised past. Some honked their horn, as if trying to get my attention so I would pause for just a brief moment, the better to soak in the magnificence of my taut muscles, pierced nipples, and intricate tattoos. Yeah, I know I looked good; hell, I had to, as much as I worked out every week. As I sped down Crystal Springs Drive, heading toward the zoo, two women jogging briskly behind a high-tech stroller that looked like something fit for an Apollo moon walk matched my stride and just stared at me in wide-eyed amazement. Moments before I peeled off at the horse trail, one of them said to the other, "Damn, I'd do him right here in the middle of the fucking street!" I smiled broadly, disappearing in a cloud of dust. God, it felt good to move.

No matter where I travel, I always make it a point to be located as close as possible to something natural, with trees or water or just something other than endless concrete canyons to help relieve the stress of my high-powered job. So when I'm in London, I like to stay in Bayswater, near the Lancaster Gate tube, so I can go jogging in Hyde Park. In Toronto, I prefer the Rosedale area, around the Castle Frank station, next to the Don River Valley and a maze of trails winding through the forests along the riverbank. When I'm in Los Angeles, I head for sleepy little Atwater Village, nestled beside the last wild stretch of the LA river and close to Griffith Park but without the pretentiousness of its more affluent neighbors. It is way more convenient for my downtown appointments than being stuck out by the ocean, even though running along the beach is usually high on my list of To Dos. And then there are the "fringe" benefits of being close to the park. Like taking the Skyline Trail in the early morning on a hot day in the making and stripping just past the water tower, running au naturel. There's nothing better than that. Well, maybe there's one thing better.

I was making good time, hitting the Patterson Tunnels, just north of the zoo, at around six-fifteen AM. There had been a light rain the night before, so the horse trail was a little sloppier than its usual sandy firmness. Hopefully, the ridge trails would be in better shape. I prefer running on anything other than concrete or asphalt, so the equestrian trails became my favorite haunts, especially given the extensive network of routes through the hills and valleys of the park. I could piece together any kind of a run I wanted, from an easy, mostly level jaunt to a tough, strenuous hill climb. The park can get up to nearly 1,700 feet in elevation, and there are still some pretty remote and treacherous places where the unwary can find a heap of trouble. And despite the fact that it is surrounded by densely urbanized development, you can still surprise some coyote, and even the occasional deer, deep in the park's interior sections. The main trail forks at the tunnels, and I took the path to the left, which would take me up behind the zoo and wind along a broad crest providing good views off toward Burbank, Glendale, and the valley beyond, if the smog and wind cooperated, providing the "skyline" in Skyline Trail.

The first time I did it, I was still horny from an intense fuck session the night before with this cute twink from WeHo who had been slumming at one of my favorite hangs, the Detour, a notorious dive bar out on Sunset and Santa Monica that served the coldest beer and the hottest men in LA, or at least that's what they printed on their bar napkins. My dick was so hard that it rubbed uncomfortably inside my running shorts, so at first I just slipped it out through the leg hole and let the sucker run free. But then it was banging against my thighs as I ran, like a shuttlecock in a wicked badminton game, getting the piercings caught on the fabric and causing nothing short of holy hell. So that's when I just said to heck with it, pulled off my shorts, and just started running buck nekkid. At the very least, my piercings weren't going to get caught on anything I'd rather they not. I didn't come across anyone and had the best 10k run in a long time. Before too long, I admit, I kind of got into the habit of picking out remote stretches of trail and just going bare. Running naked is a gas, and for a horny guy like me, it sure burns up some excess energy, shall we say.

So far, it was a pretty typical run. I steamed up the zigzagging switchbacks, busting out in a major sweat, working up a good burn in my legs, and rose swiftly to the undulating trail on the crest. LA is not exactly a morning town, and my only companions so far were numerous squirrels, a couple of mangy coyotes, and some hawks circling high overhead. The water tower was less than a quarter mile away, where the manzanita, scrub oak, and sagebrush form a thick screen along the edges of the trail, but I was feeling so into it that I stripped off my shorts a little earlier than I normally might, figuring that if someone creeping along the freeway down below could see my naked ass, why deny them the sight of something that could give them a lift on an otherwise boring commute. Ironically, this stretch of the trail looks down on the gay cruising spots east of Traveltown and Live Steamers, in an area called Pecan Grove. It's a fitting name, actually, since a lot of the guys there are young cholos, with creamy, café-au-lait skin tones and luscious pecan-colored pingas. A tasty combination for sure!

The trail is usually blessed with good views into the rugged hills behind the zoo, on the left, and just enough shade from the welcome oaks and patches of eucalyptus to blunt the sun's intensity. It's a good three-quarters of a mile from the top of the switchbacks to the point where the Condor Trail splits off. If I was going to run into anybody, it would be after the split, and since I had a clear view down the trail from the water tower, I would have time to cover up if need be. For the past few weeks of my indulgence in wilderness streaking, I never saw anybody on any of the ridge trails. So it was a little startling, to say the least, when I rounded the bend just past the split and nearly collided head on with this guy coming up the Condor Trail. He was a tall, thin Asian dude, with a great body, six packs on top of six packs, small waist, broad shoulders, well-muscled pecs, a light coating of silky black hair underlining the curves of his chest, dark chocolate nipples pointing straight out in front, like Hershey's Kisses, and those legs! Long, hairy, and powerfully built, like a dancer's, with a light, almost delicate quality that belied their robustness.

Fortunately, he wasn't going nearly as fast as I was, due to the moderately steep slope at that point. So since I had the momentum going downhill, I wound up slamming into him, scooping him up in my arms, and carrying him until I could come to a complete stop. He felt really good, my arms wrapped tightly around his hard torso, my rogue dick firmly planted between his thighs. He was beyond flustered. I mean, how would you feel being body-slammed and carried off like the Sabines by a big, brawny, naked black dude? After making sure he was okay, and after effusive mutual apologies, it was if we settled down enough to take a really good second look at each other. He clearly liked what he saw, judging by the stiff lump in his tight shorts. And to me, he was absolute perfection, my own private Mr. Sulu. My dick was off-the-chart hard.

"So, dude, we've got to stop meeting like this," I offered cheerfully, a crooked grin slyly breaking across my face.

"Yeah, I guess so," he replied, staring keenly at my dick, which was so hard now it was bobbing to a rhythm all its own. "It can be somewhat difficult."

"I'm Will," I said, extending my hand toward him.

"Russell," he replied, shaking my hand vigorously, with a firm grip. "Uh, do you run naked often?" he asked, his eyes boring hard on my bone.

I smiled, pausing sheepishly, "Ah, yep, I reckon I do," I answered, then laughed out loud. "It's a riot; you ought to give it a whirl."

"Ah, no, I don't think . . ." Russell started, then paused for a moment, still staring at my gyrating dick like it was some snake rising out of a charmer's basket casting hypnotic spells.

"Oh, sure you could," I offered helpfully. "Come on, take off those shorts; they look like they're kind of tight anyway."

I approached Russell and pulled suggestively on his shorts, rubbing my fingers inside the waistband, just lightly brushing the top of his stiff dick with my fingertips. "Come on, let me see you naked," I whispered, my eyes boring straight into his. We held each other's gaze for what seemed like an eternity, signaling our desires in a subtle Morse code of darting tongues to moisten suddenly dry lips, heavy-lidded blinks of eyelashes, and intense dilation of pupils. Our breathing was curiously synchronized, in short, staccato pants. I tugged on the shorts again, with just the slightest force, easing them down enough to expose one of his surprisingly smooth bubble cheeks. Russell pushed the rest down with both hands, until the shorts were around his hairy thighs, still holding my gaze. I leaned into him, wrapping my arm around his waist and pulling him close against me, then kissed his full, plump lips, lightly at first, then losing myself in their sweet embrace.

Russell's powerful arms and hands explored my muscular body, feeling my ass, massaging my back, as we kissed like the world was about to end. Our rigid dicks rubbed against each other, his trapped between our chiseled abs, mine locked tightly in that space below his balls, where his thighs joined his torso, dazzled by the moist, furry heat and the pounding of the blood coursing through his veins. We were dripping slicks of clear juice when Russell slid down my body and took my dick into his mouth, sucking on my dick like precious fruit from a forbidden tree, savoring the illicit delicacy as if it would be his last taste of the pleasures of the garden. My tongue reeling from the absence of his lips, his scent permeating my brain, I reached down and

lifted Russell by the legs, twisting him so that as he sucked feverishly on my dick, I could bury my tongue and face in his ass, digging out his hole with my tongue, feeling his shaved balls and
uncut dick against my throat, feeling his hot juice drip down my
chest.

It didn't take long for either of us to bust it, and before we
could recover our senses, Russell was down on all fours, backing
down on my dick as I fucked the shit out of his ass, my fingers
having a field day with those nipples of his. We dicked it down,
man, tore it up, stomped it, and then got a serious freak on. His
beautiful round bubblicious ass was beet red from the sun and
the palms of my hands; I couldn't help it—they looked so good
shining in the daylight, I just had to beat out my tune on them
skins. Since we had already gotten the easy nuts out of the way, it
was mad crazy shit to see who could get off last, and Russell,
damn, Russell was a good fuck. I shot a hell of a bomb, man; I
came so hard my balls felt like they were retreating back inside
my groin. That's when Russell pulled off my dick, got his shorts
off, and started to race down the Condor Trail, yelling, "Last one
to the point gets it up the ass!" Shit, mothafucka, if ass is on the
line, especially my ass, I'm smoking Michael Johnson, Carl Lewis,
AND Jesse Owens.

Russell had a good ninety seconds on me as I got myself together and started off after him. I closed fast, but he was a hell of
a runner too, and one good kick put him in front to win the race.
With his hands on his hips, the bright red knob of his dick poking
out from his foreskin, pointing straight at me, Russell barked,
"You loose, I'm a fuck you now, bend over!" Damn, he sounded
so sexy, with that shit-eating grin on his face, I just got down and
served it up. Shit, if Russell's ass was good, his dick was even better. He worked my butt out good. And that kind of became our
little game, sprinting in a mad rush to some imaginary finish line
and then the loser getting fucked stupid. It was so much fun, I'll

admit, there were more than a few times I kind of let Russell win just to feel his smooth prick find new erogenous zones in my ass. No, really, I had to keep it fair? Honest!

Anyway, that morning in particular, we ran and fucked our way over to the Mineral Wells trail, west to the Toyon, around the old landfill, and then down the Hollywood trail back to the Mineral Wells, looping onto the Condor and back to the scene of our initial perversion, where I fucked Russell so hard he almost passed out when he came. I was a little late for my appointments later that morning, but boy, was I one happy camper. I had a smile on my face that you couldn't slap off, just grinning like a damn fool from ear to ear. People kept asking me all during the day, "What's got into you?" And all I could tell them was, "God, it felt good to move."

My last meeting finished up late; the sun was an angry blaze, with ribbons of fire streaking across the cloud-filled skies, as it sank beneath a heavy blanket of smog and haze out in the distance. As I climbed into my rented car, loosening my tie and undoing the collar button on my shirt, I was still beaming. I let the windows down and opened the sunroof, cranking up the stereo just in time to hear Human League sing my adopted anthem, "Tainted Love." Easing into the heavy traffic heading down Sunset Boulevard toward home, I was even beginning to feel a special kindred with the Big Enchilada: yeah, I could learn to love LA. At least as long as it served up such hot takeout food!

In typical LA fashion, though, what ought to have been a twenty-minute commute morphed into a nightmare. An unexpected road closure, an accident, some nitwits behind the wheel, the usual assortment of drivers training for the demolition derby, and the tension was working my nerves. I felt my right eyelid twitching, and I just knew that my blood pressure was heading for the red zone. I needed release, and I needed it now. What to do?

I made a reckless right turn across two lanes of traffic and buzzed up Silver Lake Boulevard, passed the reservoir, made a left on Glendale, and took it past the split with Rowena down to Riverside Drive. Another left, and I was soon cruising back in familiar territory, back onto Crystal Springs Drive, back in my hunting grounds of Griffith Park. I had a load of tension making the veins in my temples pound. *I needed release, and I needed it now.*

After dark, the park takes on a whole other persona: darker, more menacing. New fauna slowly replace the innocent children babbling noisily as they wait to enter the zoo. The sounds of the merry-go-round give way to different tunes, more primitive, guttural, and incoherent. There won't be any joggers breezing effortlessly through the hills at this hour. Being LA, the action moves to car-cruising on darkened lanes, furtive assignations in equestrian tunnels under the freeway, glory holes in desolate restrooms that dot the park's circumference, quick fucks on empty picnic tables in remote groves far off the beaten paths, each location attracting its own special clientele, but all accessible by automobile.

Older married men looking to suck some juicy Mexican dick before going home to their wives and kids in some bucolic subdivision sit in their expensive cars out on Zoo Drive and watch hustlers parade by for their approval. Athletic types hang out near the soccer fields down by the bend in the river, scoring goals with straight Central American guys whose girlfriends wait for them in the grandstands. Young twinks troll in the bushes next to Live Steamers, playing hide the salami. Serious fucks, like me, head for Mineral Wells and climb the short path toward Amir's Garden, where we can get it on like we are wont to do, far from the madding crowds cruising on the trails by the dam below. Because the path starts out very steep, it tends to separate the men from the boys, making the pickings up on top extra fine.

Don't get me wrong, I like boys, with their awesomely tight assholes that suck your dick like a penis pump. After a night with a boy like that, my dick often gets up to nine, nine and a half inches, easy. But boys are like tiramisu: tasty all right, but you can't live just on cake, Marie. You need meat, protein, and that's when it's time for a man, a real man, scruffy, a little ripe, experienced in the ways of the world, a man who knows what he's got, what he wants, and what he's willing to do to get it. A boy is like taking aspirin when you've got a headache; a man is like doing shots of Wild Turkey with beer chasers to forget you even have a head.

There were no lights as I pulled into the small turn-out across from the parking area at the picnic grounds: crazy kids shooting out the streetlamps again. But the light glow in LA never really allows anywhere to get pitch-black dark, so there was visibility enough, at least for what mattered. It was crowded tonight. Most of the guys parked here would be heading west, toward the small dam and the paths beaten amongst the thickets of bamboo and pussy willows. After a short stroll along the stream bed, there is a natural depression, like a bowl, covered in trees, making a fertile playground for men seeking a good draining or a heavy reaming or both. As a precaution, I left my watch, wallet, and loose change in the glove box and locked it. Then, straightening my tie, I started the climb up the gravel path toward the top of the ridge. The soles of my dress shoes slipped ever so slightly on the loose rocks and sand, so I walked slowly, firmly planting each foot to maintain traction.

It probably seems a little incongruous to be wearing a shirt and tie and dress pants in a place better suited for jeans and work boots. But that's kind of the point when one is cruising for a quick pickup, isn't it, after all? To call attention to oneself, stand out from the crowd, make people curious to know your story. Besides, I was wearing my power tie, a deep red color, and a crisp white shirt, and even if they couldn't see it in the darkness, believe me, the men I was seeking would know that I was a badass Master of the Universe just by the mere fact that I had a tie at all. What a turn on: some blue-collar guy down on his knees, servicing the thick black dick of a white-collar executive. What a hot scene: an ordinary workman stripped naked and being fucked by his fully dressed superior. Yeah, trust me; I was dressed perfectly for what I had in mind and for the man I had in mind to do it to.

About halfway up, at the end of the steepest part of the path, there is a small level spot dominated by a large water tank and a dilapidated old shack tucked about three-quarters of the way behind the tower. Now, when you're fishing, it pays to read the water if you want to catch game fish. See, bait fish like cover, which can be anything with some structure to it, like plants, logs, trees, water towers, or shacks. So when you see some likely cover, you can just about figure that there are bait fish lurking under it. Bait fish are important, of course, because predators go after them. All game fish are predators, and they're the ones you're after. So when you see some good cover, it pays to flip your lure in that direction and jig it a bit as you reel it back in, to simulate the action of the bait fish and hopefully entice a game fish to bite. Once they bite, you snap your line hard to set the hook, and then it's you and the game fish in a fight to the finish.

I walked toward the old shack, where I saw some shadows moving back and forth through the busted-out windows. About ten yards from the shack, I stopped and rubbed my crotch, massaging my dick until it was hard. The shadows were motionless as I did so, a good sign. Slowly, I unzipped my fly and then waited. One of the larger shadows started to move toward the opening. I reached a hand inside my pants and felt my stiff dick, jacking it inside my pant leg. Before the shadow could come out of the shack, I suddenly turned and began walking up the path, now much more moderate in slope, heading toward the saddle where the path intersected the trail on top of the ridge. I could hear footsteps crunching behind me, a very good sign. *Ése, ése chico, ése.*

At the intersection, the main part of the trail goes down to the left, where Amir's Garden is. To the right, the trail goes uphill to a fork, where to the left of the fork is a short path to a large sunken field with another dilapidated old building at the far edge of it. I've had some pretty wild times down in that field. It attracts really hot Mexican guys who sling some mean dick and serve up some of the sweetest ass you'll ever find. But it tends to be a gang-bangers' ball, and I wasn't in the mood for a crowd tonight. So before the footsteps behind caught up with me, I walked straight ahead, toward a tiny opening in a wall of evergreen shrubs, where old Amir had created some terraces of succulents and juniper, with lots of night-blooming jasmine and fragrant hibiscus. *Ése, ése chico, ése.*

There was a flight of steps carefully cut into the hillside that ultimately led to a rugged trail that looped and switchbacked its way down to the upper parking lot of the golf course. But I only needed to go about a quarter of the way down, to a well-worn path out along one of the terraces, where a sturdy park bench, made of rolled steel and solid wood planks, was set into a banquette of jade plants and pine trees, a hidden oasis amidst the decadent splendors. Seated on the bench, I once again reached into my still-open fly and retrieved my throbbing dick and heavy balls and let it stand at attention in the still, night air as I took in the view of the lights at the old boy-scout camp across the valley and waited. *Ése, ése chico, ése.*

A few moments later, the footsteps came crunching down the stairs, overshooting by several steps before retracing themselves and ambling slowly along the terrace path. He was a big Mexican guy, looked to be over six feet, with a thick build, not fat, but muscular in a beefy, hard-hat kind of way. He was wearing a wifebeater and baggy dark jeans, with a bandana tied around his head in the style of an East LA cholo. *Ése, ése chico, ése.* He sat down on the bench next to me.

"*Ay, cómo estás, jefe?*" he grunted in a strong, deep baritone. "*Tienes un pene muy grande, jefe.*"

I stroked my dick and shook it in his direction.

"*Me gusta su pene, jefe.*"

He bent over and took it into his mouth, the sharp bristles of his beard scratching my balls in a pleasant way as he sucked my fat dick all the way down to the balls, my knob deep down his throat. *Ése, ése chico, ése.* I placed my hand on the back of his head, letting my fingers get a firm grip on his slick hair, and forced him down on my dick, choking him with my thick, fat knob of hard black dick deep down his throat. He struggled only a little bit before giving in to my rhythm as I fucked his face. He was hooked now, and the fight didn't last very long at all.

He was a good cock-sucker, and after a short while, I took my hand away from his head and he kept up the rhythm, just the way I like it. He grabbed my balls and started to squeeze them, kneading them between his fingers. I moved my hand down his back, feeling the hard mass of muscles from his shoulders down to the haunches of his ass. There wasn't an ounce of flesh on him that didn't have its place. I liked the way he felt. He felt the way a man's supposed to feel, brawny, strong, powerful, seething with the capacity for great violence, but restrained, disciplined, stoic. This was a man, and he was sucking my meat as if it were his own, teasing my dick with the kind of knowledge that only a man has of how to make a thick black pipe tingle from the tip of its fat knob all the way down into the heavy, low-hanging balls underneath.

I slipped my fingers inside the waistband of his jeans, no underwear, the way a man wears jeans, nothing to get in the way of exploring his hard bubble butt and the furry crack that holds a man's Achilles' heel. I don't care how much a man's dick craves pussy, once his ass cherry is popped, he's a slave to that feeling for the rest of his life, even if he never does it with another man again. It's a sinful pleasure that is beyond a man's weak nature to ever wean himself away from. That's why guys come to places like the park, sneaking out on their wives and girlfriends, to get that voodoo that only we do so well. As my fingers felt their way down the crack of his ass, his butt squirmed in anticipation, and as they found what they were looking for, that soft, delicate depression that gives way with the slightest force, revealing a furnace of carnal desire that only a man's dick can stoke until it reaches its maximal intensity, his hole pulled my fingers inside it, licking them, sucking on them with as much gusto as he sucked my fat dick.

Yeah, he was hungry for it, and I was eager to give it to him. I slipped his belt off his pants and made a slipknot of it, then placed it on one of his wrists and tightened it, hard, causing him to flinch ever so slightly, then tied the loose end around one of the steel poles that held the wooden slats of the bench. After making sure that the restraint was fast, I slipped my belt off as he sucked on my dick, then moved out from under him and fastened his other wrist the same as the first. He was now bent low over the back of the bench, his arms outstretched and his knees placed against the seat to keep his neck from rubbing uncomfortably against the top of the backrest. I reached around and undid his pants, then pulled them down around his ankles. His beautiful, hairy ass was helpless and exposed to me. He moaned softly as I massaged his cheeks and rubbed his asshole in slow circles, opening its lips, making it loosen its resistance, until it became pliant, like putty in my hand. Then I knelt down and licked the soft, curly hairs of his crack until my tongue was firmly embedded in his funky manhole, making him moan deeper as I tossed his salad, slobbering his funk all over my face.

My dick was in a mad, raging boil now, dripping like a broken faucet and thrusting up and down, fucking the air. I pulled a condom and a pillow of lube from my pocket and got ready to get down to business. Soon my dick was probing the hot depths of his hole like a poker in a fire. Damn, his cholo ass was fine. He groaned as I deep-stroked it right up to my balls and then pulled clear out of his hole before plunging all the way back in. In and out, in and out, in and out, the strokes just went on, and on, and on, as I reamed his ass out. We both worked up a light sweat, but the cool night air only made me fuck harder to ward off any chill. The deeper I pounded his ass, the lower he dipped his back, serving that ass up real pretty, making sure he got every inch of that good black dick up in there. I reached up under his T-shirt and grabbed his stiff nipples, pinching them with such force that as he let out a long, deep moan, his asshole opened up so wide that my balls slipped inside him as I deep-dicked his butt.

Yeah, he was almost ready now. I could feel his nut moving up out of his meaty balls and starting to make its way down his thick, uncut chorizo. It had a long way to travel before it could find release, though. But I didn't want him to come just yet, so I slowed down, changed pace, really worked on loosening up his hole, making it a sloppy whore as my dick bitch-slapped it into submission. When it was nice and ripe, I pulled my dick out and started to feed him something a little more challenging. He seemed to know what I wanted, and he took the fingers of my hand like a man who had been there before.

As the palm of my hand slipped inside him, mi hombre strained against the ties that bound him prostrate before me, groaning in a low, guttural rumble that reverberated along the bones of my arm. It was if his ass were calling my body to take him to that place, that El Dorado of the senses, where a man gets close enough with his profane fingers to touch the face of the sacred once again, to walk again in that garden from which he fell from grace. And as my elbow nudged firmly into place, his hole gripping me tightly, my chest emptied of air as he exhaled deeply, and when he breathed in, my lungs exploded along with his. We were one, now, joined at the soul, *hermanos de la sangre. Padre, perdonamos, por favor, nos tenemos la enfermedad muy mal. Ese chico y yo.*

Later that night, driving back to my place, reeking of my hot cholo's ass, drenched in sweat and come, I felt relieved, calmed, satisfied. The tensions of earlier were not even a distant memory; it was as if nothing else had existed prior to my arriving at the park, climbing up that hill, and burying myself in that fine, hot, Mexican ass. Just the thought of what had transpired was enough to get my dick squirting one more time. As the hot juice spread into a puddle on my thigh, a smile broke out across my face. God, it felt good to move!

Mac's Redux

With a serious head fake that had Jerome spinning around chasing his own ass, Ricardo glided up to the boards as if going for the dunk but made a quick behind-the-back pass to his brother Tomás, on the edge of the key, who sank a wicked three-pointer that ended the game and gave the locals a slim come-from-behind victory. The final score: San Juan—92, Brooklyn—91. It was utterly depressing man, getting our butts kicked three out of five games by a bunch of short dudes, two of whom were in wheelchairs. Charles, our best forward, was so through he asked Willie if he would show him how to play ball on wheels. What a trip! You should have seen the nigga, all seven-plus feet of him, cramped up in a tiny chair, his knees nearly striking his chin, trying to do spins and wheelies while dribbling up court. The brotha flipped over twice and nearly broke his damn fool neck for real!

Jerome, Charles, Stan, Nelson, and I were in San Juan for the annual Memorial Day soirée that brings together blatino brothas from all over for a little Caribbean spice and island heat. While most of the events and activities take place in and around the

Condado, we opted to stay in nearby Ocean Park, with its laid-back charm, instead of the glittering bustle of the gauche resort palaces. Moreover, our quiet little guest house was on a much less crowded beach and had the best local eye candy. We found the ballers hanging out at Parque Barbosa one afternoon and got into a friendly pick-up game with a great group of Taíno dudes. One thing led to another, and soon we were playing every afternoon, skins vs. skins, until the sun sat low over the ocean. Jerome and Stan had been scouted by the pros, and Charles was a pro, so even with Nelson, an ophthalmologist who was a pretty fair college baller, and me, a fish out of water on a B-ball court for sure, we still felt pretty high on our game. But Ricardo, his brother Tomás, and their friends Eduardo, Juan, and Willie sure taught us a thing or two.

Tomás had broken his back while trying to impress this girl on the boardwalk at Coney Island some years ago. He and his homies had been doing crazy shit all day, showing off their fine, cut bodies and fearless derring-do to a group of honeys they had been eyeing. Tomás decided to do a back flip off the railing and land in front of this girl named Layla to startle her. He'd already done the trick a few times before, so he didn't think anything of doing it again, only shirtless. But instead of making a perfect landing, the shirt he had looped through the belt of his pants got caught on the rail during his takeoff and wrapped itself around his ankle, so he didn't really get the height he needed and BAM! At least, that's how his brother Ricardo told the story, and he was there. Tomás's version had him taking a bullet trying to protect his elderly abuela during a shoot-out between rival drug gangs as they walked home from mass on the streets of their neighborhood in the Brownsville section of Brooklyn. With Tomás, the truth was always a little shaded around the edges.

But he was a cool dude, still swaggering like the Big Swinging

Dick he was before the accident and a veritable chick magnet back on the streets of Santurce, with his fine black hair, smooth cooper-colored skin, and dark green eyes set in a face that could stop traffic when he smiled. Those Taíno dudes were real fly hotties; all that native Indian blood mixed with a touch of Carib warrior and a dash of Euro suaveness. That's what was so cool about being around him and Willie, who lost the use of his legs after a bad car accident driving back from visiting his parents in Utuado. They were just regular cats, smooth talkers, S.E.X.X.X.Y. as Hell and with spirits that made you happy to be in their company. Tomás and Willie exuded a deep, sensuous carnality that was so scorching you felt overdressed even when you were half-naked. It was easy to forget that they used wheelchairs, and the way they got around, it seemed as if we were the ones with the handicaps.

Usually after a game, we would go back to the guest house and chill, drinking a little and smoking a little until everybody was so wrecked you kind of forgot who you were fucking as long as it felt good and you got off. Juan and Tomás maintained they were bisexual and could swing it for the right dude from time to time. Charles, Jerome, and Stan seconded that, though I had to slap Charles, since I knew he was having a torrid affair with a mutual friend. Willie admitted he was just keen to fuck, since being in a chair severely cramped his style and he didn't get nearly as much pussy or ass as he could handle. Eduardo, Ricardo, Nelson, and me admitted we had all fooled around with women back in the day, but guys were our first, last, and primary choice. But this time, "to raise the stakes" he said, Jerome declared that the losers had to straight out give it up to the winners, no holes barred and no alcohol or dope as an excuse. It was going to be gang-bang style, each loser getting it from all five of the winners.

I think the fool was still out of his mind from the San Juan Brothas party the night before, where things got a whole lot crazy, and somewhere in the confusion four hundred brothas "lost" their clothes and just went buck wild, skinny-dipping, freaking, and sipping Cristál as it poured off a go-go boy's dick. Jerome was one of the baddest of the bad, even without all the X he was doing. I had never seen the cat so off the hook before. Later, in the dawn's early light, as we ushered out the last of our Boricuas de noche after a slamming four-way freak fest, Jerome leaned over conspiratorially and said, "Dude, what's done in San Juan, stays in San fucking Juan!" That wasn't as big a deal for me as it was for Jerome, since I know for a fact that his dad, who's still chairman of the company that Jerome is CEO of, wouldn't be too approving of what all Jerome was into down in San Juan.

Anyway, I think the Taínos were as supermotivated at the thought of getting some phat nigga azz as we were about banging some freak papi culos. Ricardo was drop-dead gorgeous, a sometime model for Nono Maldonado, the hottest fashion designer on the island, when he wasn't plying his trade as a high-priced escort. He was rico suave all the way, right down to the Ricardo Montalban voice and his penchant for fine Corinthian leather. He had the same copper complexion and stunning green eyes as his brother and a thick round booty to die for. He also packed so much heat it looked like he had three legs. Eduardo worked as a lifeguard at one of the fancier resort hotels, which meant that when he wasn't flexing his perfect gymnast's physique under the watchful eyes of every woman planted around the pool, he was screwing their husbands and boyfriends in the men's room. It was his way of boosting his tips, he said, though it smelled more like hush money to not spill their secrets to their womenfolk. With deep, black, bedroom eyes, thick lips, a tousle of fine black hair brushing his shoulders, and that body, it was easy to see why Eduardo was so prized.

But Juan was the bomb, man; shorter than the rest of the PR

crew, built to perfection, with a body by God and a dick almost as big as he was tall. That papito's shit hung so low he swore he had to shove most of it in his ass just to keep from stepping on it while he walked. Personally, I think the dude was so horny he had to fuck himself just to keep his balls from exploding. Juan was a dawg, jack! If he wasn't fucking, he was thinking about fucking, and if he couldn't fuck, well then, he'd get fucked, damn it, as long as he could get off. The boy just reeked of fresh hot sex all the time. Juan was a jive-talking hustler too, no lie, with a perpetual shit-eating grin that signaled in flashing red letters the boy was up to no good, but you went along with it just to be able to stare close up at that muy guapo mug of his. I had my eye on Juan from the get-go, and since he was the one guarding me most of the time, we got real physical on and off the court. If there had been a ref for our games, both of us would have fouled out in the first two minutes.

As soon as Tomás's three-pointer swished the net for the win, Juan was pointing his stubby finger right in my face, leaving no doubt about what he wanted and giving me a fierce boner in the process. All that was going through my mind, however, was, "Damn, Jerome, why *this* game?!" Because Juan had a bubble ass that I was mad crazy to smack down; he mooned me in the restroom at the parque once when he caught me staring at it a little too hard while he took a piss. I jacked a honking load every time the mere thought of his ass crossed my filthy mind. Now we had lost, and the Taínos were hungry to make good on their win. Ricardo was rubbing his crotch and laughing while Jerome walked around in circles, dazed and confused. Charles was hunched up in a ball in the middle of the court with his head buried between his legs while Willie did wheelies around him. Meanwhile, Eduardo and Tomás debated the relative merits of Stan and Nelson as they tried to make up their minds about whose butt they wanted to fuck first.

The long walk back to the guest house gave us all plenty of time for the gravity of the situation to clearly settle in deep.

"Shit, Will," Nelson whispered in my ear as we strolled slowly under the watchful eyes of the Taínos bunched tightly along our flanks and rear, like they were herding cattle or something, "I'm too tight to take these dudes, they're all hung like fucking bulls!"

"Trust me, bro, in an hour they'll be able to park a 747 in your ass with room to spare!" I laughed in reply, which only made the sour expression on Nelson's face look even more ragged.

Up in front, Jerome and Charles were leaning together, speaking conspiratorially, or so it seemed to me. I saw Charles bobbing his head as Jerome spoke. Those two were up to something, but I was too far back to overhear them. Stan was closer, and when they paused at the corner, waiting for the traffic to clear, they brought him into whatever it was they were scheming to do. The Taínos seemed oblivious, still carrying on in high spirits and taunting us with how hard they were going to fuck us and making predictions as to who was going to scream most like a girl. As our motley crew reached the entrance to the gates that separated Ocean Park from the rest of the hoi polloi, Stan, Charles, and Jerome broke into a balls-out sprint and rushed to the gatehouse. Sadly, as the outlines of the scheme became clearer, it was evident that Nelson and I were getting the shaft in more ways than one.

Willie, Tomás, and Juan grabbed Nelson and me by the wrists and arms to keep us from making a break for it too as Ricardo and Eduardo dashed after our punk "friends." The guard at the gatehouse made it clear that there would be no further efforts to follow, as Stan, Charles, and Jerome kept running, laughing and hollering at the top of their lungs, stealing an occasional glance backward to wag their fingers at me and Nelson. This was not going to go well, I thought, thinking of the terrible gang-banging that lay ahead, especially since Ricardo and Eduardo would want to take some revenge for being dissed. With the Taínos pressed in a circle around us, Nelson and I were led deeper into the gritty environs of Santurce. On the whole, I must admit I wasn't really all that concerned, since these were some damn fine Boriqua dudes. No, it was Nelson I felt sorry for, with his phat "come fuck me" butt and soulful eyes that just begged you to drive your dick deep down his throat so you could watch him suffer. That boy was going to get the stuffing of his life.

Juan, Ricardo, and Eduardo were in a deep discussion about where exactly to take us, which was particularly vexing since most of the guys still lived with las familias. Finally it was decided to head to a local sauna where Eduardo knew the owner and could virtually guarantee getting some free accommodation, especially if the owner were allowed to watch or better yet participate. To say we were off the tourist grid by the time we came to the derelict old building sitting hard between Calle Carrion Maduro and Calle del Parque, off the expressway, would be too kind. We weren't even in the same hemisphere. From the outside, the life-less-looking hulk carried only the faintest vestige of its former glory from back in the day, circa 1600-something, when it was probably a stylish emporium carrying the finest mercantile goods from the Continent for the well-heeled patrons of the landed gen-try.

But once inside, it was unmistakably the most hip, modern, and luxurious men's bathhouse on the island, complete with a sleek Euro-style décor and ambient techno wafting out of the extensive sound system and playing the latest bootlegged Enrique Cruz and Latino Fan Club pornos on the monitors. It bore a strong resemblance, in fact, to my favorite club in LA, the old Mac's on Hyperion in Silverlake. And by the looks of it, the place was "Locals Only," no foreigners in sight other than Nelson and me, but with all the luscious coffee, mocha, caramel, café con leche, almond, chocolate, lemon, and vanilla bean swirling around us, we could easily be mistaken for the local flava too. And fine? Good Golly, Miss Molly! There wasn't a single dude in the joint, and they ranged in age from barely legal to old grand-dads, that I wouldn't have done it with on first sight! Seeing as how my thick bone practically put his eye out as it popped to attention, Tomás playfully grabbed it and started trying to pimp me out to guys passing by.

As Eduardo and Juan herded Nelson and me into a small room equipped with a couple of slings set side-by-side, a St. Andrew's Cross, a wooden fuck bench, and some mean-looking manacles hanging from the ceiling that clearly were meant to suspend some hapless victim by the wrists and ankles, it was evident that the real game was about to get started in earnest. It is absolutely vital for self-preservation under such circumstances to identify the Alpha Dawg and take him down so you earn respect from the rest of the pack. I had only a matter of seconds to make my move before my ass was in a world of hurt. Now, there was no way I was going to get out of getting banged, but at least I could determine the circumstances. Personally, I preferred to go down fighting. Being outnumbered in the first place already meant that I was going to suffer some nasty consequences, but that's the difference between a punk and a warrior. A punk is too afraid to take the bullet, while a warrior knows he can take a lot of hits as long as none of them is instantly fatal.

The Taínos were all sporting major-league hard-ons, and Nelson was already stripped naked and being placed in the manacles. Who was the Alpha? Eduardo, the pretty-boy enforcer? Perhaps Ricardo, the suave-tongued mouthpiece? Maybe Juan, the calculating hustler? Was it Tomás, Mr. Personality? Or Willie, quiet, always alert, constantly moving his eyes, missing nothing, man of few words? As Juan and Tomás came over to me, I exploded, throwing a Flying Crane that even Mr. Miyagi would have been proud of, that sent Juan careening across the room and slamming up against the far wall, where he slumped to the floor. With a quick arcing sweep of my legs as I landed, I caught Tomás hard across his windpipe, sending him spinning backward in his chair and crashing into Eduardo and Ricardo, knocking them all to the ground. That left me and Willie staring face-to-face. Of all the dudes in that room, Willie was the most dangerous ... other than me.

You know a man who spends half his life pushing a wheelchair around has got hellacious upper-body strength. Willie had all that and more. In a flash he was driving into me with his chair and grabbing me with his powerful arms. The pain in my legs was intense, but that was nothing compared to the viselike grip Willie had on my throat. Feint, parry, and thrust: the only way to deal with superior force. I poked at Willie's eyes with my fingers, which got him to release one of his hands from my throat so he could swat wildly at mine. That gave me just enough of an opening to twist my neck and then put a wicked bite on the papi's privates that had him whooping, hollering, and beating on my head and shoulders trying to dislodge me. But I hung tough as a pit bull and grabbed the dude around his waist, lifted him from his chair and wrestled him into one of the slings, then bound him tightly in the restraints.

Only after Willie was secured could I turn my attention to the rest of the crew, who by now were charging toward me. With a Jackie Chan run up the wall, I did a back flip and landed behind them, then rushed them, slamming them all face-first into the wall. I pulled Tomás from the heap and strapped him down in the second sling. Now, it was three to one, and I was starting to like those odds a little better. Still dazed, Juan had no idea what hit him when I put him in a headlock and hurled his ass, spread-eagled and facedown, on the fuck bench. But just as I got him securely fastened to it, Ricardo and Eduardo were furiously punching at me from all sides. Want to stop a pretty gay boy dead in his tracks? Hit him in the face; he'll be so absorbed by the possibility of having his looks ruined that you can count him out of the fight from that point on. With a quick backhand, I bitch-slapped Ricardo across the nose and mouth and he was gone, squealing and shrieking. And then there was one.

Just as I had figured, Eduardo was the muscle of the group, and he put the hurt on me. But with Willie out of the way, muscles without brains are just overdeveloped meat. I head-butted Eduardo right into the Cross and was able to clamp the shackles on his wrists before he could resume his fusillade to my guts. After a devastating struggle, the time of major combat was finally over. With blood trickling from my nose, mouth, and God knows where else, I stood in the middle of the carnage, heart racing, with the fattest boner I ever had in my life. My inner sadomasochist was in full glory, and I was so horny I could have fucked grizzly bears without a condom. Nelson was just in awe, hanging in the middle of the room from the ceiling, his phat booty right at crotch level, clearly impressed with my close-quarters combat skills. Poor sucker, he didn't see it coming. I was Kane the Conqueror, favored by Ptah, son of Amun-Ra, brother of Ogun, and that meant only one thing . . . RAPE & PILLAGE! It started with Nelson.

I piston-fucked the brotha as he dangled in midair, my dick drilling him so hard he didn't even have time to lose his breath. His eyes were bugged out and his mouth was open, but he couldn't make a sound. I know the brotha said he was tight, and damn if it wasn't the truth. Nelson's ass was so tight even his farts needed a password before they could escape. But it didn't matter to me: my long, thick dick pried that bad boy open like a can of sardines and dug him out so deep daylight was peeking through from his nose. I loved fucking Nelson's phat ass. Once it was opened up, he was just the sweetest 'ho, putting out the welcome mat and making my dick feel right at home. Tight-ass niggas surely have the best pussy holes. Keeping all that sweetness locked up like that makes a hole real hungry, and when it finally gets a taste of good dick, it goes plum wild. You want some freak sex? Fuck a nigga who says his ass is tight.

This was a whole new fairy tale in the making, "Big Red Bone and the Six Phat Bootays." I went around testing one sweet Taíno hole after another: Oh, this one's too tight!; Oh, that one's too loose!; Oh, this one's too short!; Oh, that one's too rough!; Oh, that one's too deep!; Oh, oh, oh, fuck yeah, this one's juuussst riiiight! Juan's cunty hole was just as juicy and hot as he was, and it was my favorite by far. I knew it would be, because I'm an ass man and I know azz. The longer and harder I fucked that cuchi frito, the longer and thicker my mean dick got.

Dayum! I understood now why he liked to fuck himself. Man, if they ever bottled that boy's ass, it'd put every other penis enlarger out of business. The tight papito just screamed curses at me as I slipped my ever-growing fatty between his perfectly round, smooth cheeks, sliding clear up to my balls in thrust after thrust. His hole was so accommodating I could feel it massaging my dick from the head all the way down to the base, squeezing my joint in a good firm grip and then kneading the fuck out of it as it milked that sucker dry. He was backing that ass up too, despite his protestations to the contrary, trying to get every last inch up in his shit, just riding that good hard bone until he was squirting one huge wad after another.

Tomás, Ricardo, and Eduardo also gave some good ass, especially Tomás, who not only loved taking dick but bounced so good on my thick meat all I had to do was just stand there pressing it into him while he did the rest, using his arms to rock the sling every which way. As he fucked himself into a blissful stupor, I sucked on his beautiful uncut joint as he rode mine, licking his thick, cheesy foreskin until his dick was slimy with the tastiest pre-come, a salty-sweet mixture that I just couldn't get enough of. I must have swallowed three or four loads before he was heaving blanks. Then I moved on to Willie. Willie knew he was going to get deep-dicked, and, being the Alpha Dawg, he was gracious enough to accept his fate with honor and class. His cheeks were hairy, with a thick, curly black furrow covering his crack that made his tawny brown mounds stand out by contrast. It was looking so good I had to eat out that ass until the boy blew a load all over my back. Only after I had it all wet and sloppy did I slip my hungry joint into Willie's deep-dish pussy hole.

I was so impressed with Willie's total submission to my dick, that after I reamed him out, to the point that he and I both were plumb out of come, I felt compelled to honor the code of the warrior. I undid the restraints on all of the Taínos and then climbed up onto Willie's sling and straddled his still-hard meat, taking it deep inside me, which, given its size, was damn deep. The others gathered around us and took turns double-dicking my insatiable ass as Willie's thick, hooded monster gouged me out. It was insane! As much as I loved those copper-toned bubbles, I have to say those superthick, long, deep brown Taíno dicks were even better. The Taínos finally got the satisfaction they had earned by dint of their victory on the court and fucked the mothafuckin' shit out of Nelson and me. Nelson hardly seemed to mind, since each successive dick that fucked him was bigger than the one before it and just scratched that itch a little deeper until he was begging for more.

It was the mother of all gang-bangs, and it got even wilder as the other patrons of the sauna came in to watch and then got swept up in the madness. Even the owner got his fill of hot nigga ass while Nelson and I were sixty-nining in one of the slings as our asses got reamed from both sides. Willie and Tomás didn't need their chairs as they slipped from one hot dick stuffing their butts onto another hot ass opening wide to take their willing meat. Ricardo, Juan, and Eduardo were interspersed in a daisy chain of guys fucking that stretched from wall to wall, clear across the room. We fucked and sucked until every soldier in the room was down for good. Shit, bodies were piled up all over the place, dicks dripping come, assholes dripping lube, well-used condoms littering the floor, dudes buried in ass and dick, getting off until there was just no more ammunition to shoot or, like me, skin on their dicks. Poor Nelson could barely stand up by the time we finally stumbled outside into the blazing heat of the humid midday sun. On the ride back to the guest house, Nelson forgave me for fucking the shit out of his ass, acknowledging that if I hadn't opened him up, he might not have made it.

It was around midnight when I was finally recovered enough to rouse my sore ass out of bed. There was a note on the floor that had been slipped under the door of my room, from Jerome. It read:

> Dear Freak,
>   You must have been slammin' last night! Not one of the Taínos showed up to play ball this afternoon! I knew you'd know how to show them a good time!
>   J.
>   P.S. The Farewell Party is at Eros if you still got change in your moneymaker!

I called Nelson's extension to check on him, but there was no answer. Somehow I didn't think he would be in any shape to shake his moneymaker tonight, or any night for the next six months. As I stepped into a hot, steaming shower, letting it rain down soothingly on my aching dick and nearly raw ass, a deep, cold shiver spilled out of my very core, making my legs all wobbly. I had to hold on to the wall just to keep from falling. Who was it that said "Revenge is a dish best served cold?" Kahn quoting a Klingon proverb in that second *Star Trek* movie? No, it was the French dude, de Laclos, in *Les Liaisons Dangereuses: "La vengeance est un plat qui se mange froid."* Yeah, it was going to get damn *froid* tonight, the shower notwithstanding. As the blazing water slowly revived me, each searing drop lancing a dull pain on some part of my anatomy, I quietly meditated on the most exquisite forms of *la vengeance*.

The party was in full swing by the time I arrived. Brothas were already jamming in various states of undress on the sweaty dance floor and making moves on their chosen hottie for the night. It was a Black Party theme, with lots of leather, latex, rubber, feather boas, and bare skin in so many flavors of chocolate and cinnamon that I was getting hungry just watching. I was able to survey the entire scene from a quiet vantage point up on the second level, having spent the last hour casing the club. Below me, completely oblivious to my presence, Charles, Stan, and Jerome were getting their freaks on with some really hot papi chulos. They had been drinking heavily all the while I was observing, and, knowing my punk friends, they had been hitting it pretty hard even before that, along with some weed and a little blow, most probably. And since it was also our last night in San Juan, I figured they'd want to make it memorable. I was certainly going to do my part to help them. It was just in the timing, that's all.

Charles made the first move. He headed toward the restrooms, and I quickly followed, leaving a safe distance between us so he wouldn't know I was there. The urinals were all taken, and Charles couldn't wait for an opening; he was dancing some funky jig as he hopped and stepped into one of the stalls. In his hurry to relieve himself, he even left the door open. Bad mistake, homes. I rushed up behind him and violently jerked his pants and drawers all the way down to his ankles while he was in the middle of taking a piss, throwing him off balance and causing him to smack his head against the back of the stall. The alcohol and drugs had a good grip on the brotha, because the only sound he could make was a high-pitched squeal that sounded like a wounded pig. He was so freaked out he couldn't make up his mind whether to finish pissing or pull up his pants. Flailing his hands limply against his thighs as he tried to crouch down to retrieve his drawers, he wound up doing a little of both and pissed everywhere.

In that momentary panic, I was also able to pull Charles's shirt up over his head, blinding him, and then push him far enough over the urinal to handcuff his hands together under the pipes that fed the bowl. They were his own handcuffs, part of his Black Party ensemble, no doubt intended for the cute papi he was schmoozing. For his sake I hoped he had the key on him as well. Meanwhile, I stuffed a wad of toilet paper in the depression where his mouth was screaming bloody murder and then wrapped duct tape, which I had brought with me for just this purpose, several times around his head to hold the makeshift gag in place.

It was a stellar sight, Charles's naked caramel ass bouncing frantically in the stall trying to figure out how to get loose without smashing his head into the wall behind the urinal. If I could have gotten a boner at that moment, I'd have fucked his phat ass but good. Sadly, last night's orgy was still crimping my style. I quickly stepped out of the stall, pretending to pull up my zipper as this big diesel brotha came up to take his turn. Smiling a big shit-eating grin, I said "Man, that's some good ass in there!" while jerking my thumb in the direction of the stall. The brotha looked at me rubbing my crotch and then flashed a wicked little smile as he disappeared inside. The brotha's loud exclamation of "Shit!" was music to my ears. I returned to my perch, eagerly anticipating the next move.

Jerome and Stan hadn't strayed too far from their spot next to the bar, their cute compañeros long gone, as they nursed yet another pretty cocktail. A really smokin' brotha, tall, thin, dark cocoa complexion, with silky black hair pulled back into a long Stevie Wonder braid, packing large, brushed past them, bumping Stan slightly as he headed toward the bottom of the stairs. Stan was stunned into action, believing that the bump was a none-too-subtle hint of mutual lust, and he took off after the guy. The area near the bottom of the staircase was particularly dark and consequently was a favorite place for guys sliding into second base and hoping to steal third. There was also a narrow shelf that ran along the wall of the lower staircase for guys to rest their drinks while they ran the bases. But it was the foot rail that ran under the shelf that was of keen interest for my purposes.

As Stan walked into the shadows, becoming disoriented by the sudden darkness, I pinned his arm tightly behind his back and shoved him around the corner of the stairs into the belly of the beast. Putting my foot across one of his ankles, I managed to trip him to the ground, where I planted my knee in the middle of his back to hold him there. I love duct tape. The best kinds have a toughness to them that can be even better than handcuffs. I was using a thick tape that had a grid of reinforced nylon fibers under the heavy outer coating. It was flexible and molded well to the contours of Stan's skinny arms and wrists as I wound it up to his armpits. There was no way the boy was getting out of that without a pair of scissors. I removed the belt from his jeans and fastened it around his neck, cinching the buckle tightly against his throat. Looping the other end around the foot rail and then threading it back through the buckle and fastening it, I made sure that Stan could breathe easily but still not be able to wiggle his head free of the restraint.

Satisfied by my handiwork, I pulled off Stan's pants and gagged him with his sweat-soaked BVDs, wrapping more duct tape around his head to make it fast. In an inspired bit of deviltry, I placed one end of duct tape in Stan's superhairy butt crack, looped it around his waist, and then fastened the other end back in his crack. I did it a few times, effectively spreading his ass cheeks wide open and taping down his dick at the same time. I fingered his defenseless hole. Stan had been a busy boy! He was so loose I had four fingers inside him without needing any lube. Good, I thought to myself as I pulled him to his knees so his ass was better positioned. In the darkness, evil eyes see everything that goes down. Unzipping my pants, I pretended to hump Stan's butt, drawing a crowd of curious onlookers. Faking a wicked orgasm, I pulled myself to my feet and declared loudly, "Damn, *papi, tu culo es muy bien!*" Zipping up, I walked away, grabbing my dick as if it was still in shock from a good piece of ass. Like hyenas to a fresh kill, a swarm of shadows quickly engulfed Stan's sweet bubble. And then there was one.

Jerome was starting to feel a bit lonely, I noticed, as he bobbed and weaved his head, straining to see if Charles or Stan was anywhere in sight. After draining his latest cocktail, he set out in search of them, taking a few hesitant steps first in one direction, then turning around and taking a few steps in another. It was a pitiful sight, just a damn shame, but the nigga only had himself to blame. Public humiliation was the thing Jerome feared more than anything else, even more than his overbearing father. Away from the pampered and privileged nest, he was the world's biggest slut, but when daddy was around, the boy was so straight and narrow even the curve in his dick tried to right itself. Another cute papi strolled by, flashing Jerome a smile to die for, making my sore dick take notice even from my vantage point. Jerome was instantly hooked and followed after the papi with newfound purpose. By the way his pants cupped his ass, I knew Jerome's dick was leading the way toward new hills to conquer.

It couldn't have been a more perfect setup even if I had planned it in advance. As it was, the papi, knowing he had a big one on the line, made a winding circuit through the main floor, stopping every so often to make sure his quarry was in hot pursuit. To set the hook, he bent over at one point, flashing just the tops of his round, creamy mounds, set off by a deep cocoa tan. Dayum! The papi had me and Jerome both frothing at the mouth as he wandered into a back room hidden away at the extreme rear of the club, not far from the staircase. Jerome was so fixated on the papi he totally ignored the commotion off to his right, where Stan was being fucked by only the latest in a long line of horny suitors. The papi was just faintly visible in the vestibule of the room, obviously waiting for his Nubian king to follow. Jerome cruised up beside him, and together they went deeper into the murky darkness.

There were a lot of guys in the back room, getting all sweaty, hot, and bothered. The funky smell of sex permeated the air in the place, which was so thick with lustful carnality that just breathing was tantamount to getting fucked stupid. Finding Jerome would have been all but impossible but for his girlish falsetto giggling, which only happened when he was excited as hell and his dick was on the verge of penetrating something really good. In all the years we'd known each other, Jerome and I had never fucked. We'd been in the same room getting it on with other people, so I knew that giggle well. But we never knocked boots, which was another shame, because Jerome was a real fine dude, with a nice high ass and thick bubble cheeks. Between my lust for the sweet papi that Jerome was by now fucking with his long, fat monster dick and the mental image of Jerome's tight butt, my sore dick was hard at attention, straining for release from the confines of my jeans.

I moved toward the sound of the infectious giggle, quickly slipping a jimmie over my joint and fishing a pillow of lube from my pocket. My dick homed in on Jerome's smooth cheeks as if it were receiving signals from some F.R.E.A.K. Mission Control, being guided to a perfect landing smack in the middle of his hot hole. Jerome was so busy screwing the papi that he didn't stop even when my dick was pressing up against his hole. As he bucked his hips, his ass just sucked my dick deeper inside him as I leaned closer. Soon I was riding a magic carpet, next stop Wonderland, as Jerome took control, stroking my dick so good I thought the skin on my dick was coming off, as he rammed his big joint in his sweet papi's culo. I was enjoying the ride so much I almost forgot why I was there. *La vengeance.*

There was no way Jerome could have known it was me fucking his fine booty so sweetly. So with growing assertiveness, I really started to ream his shit out, roughly grabbing his cheeks and spreading them as far apart as I could force them. Jerome seemed to like a good, rough fuck. The more aggressive I got, the more he backed that bad boy up. He was talking all kinds of shit—"Ohh! Yeah, baby, right there!"and "Ahhhiiight now! Hit it, papi! Hit ya boi!"—as he got into being sandwiched between my thick dick and the papi boy's hot ass. When I taped his eyes closed, he was still unsuspecting, saying "Okay! Some of that kinky stuff, yeah!" in the same falsetto voice, easily the loudest of the freaks getting their groove on in the room. I bound Jerome's hands behind his back and pushed him forward as I really slammed his butt, driving so hard that I changed his rhythm and even the papi was dancing to my fucking tune. With my feet I pried Jerome's pants completely off from around his ankles, making it easier to wedge my body between his legs and dick his ass down solid.

La vengeance. Jerome swooned as he and the papi both blew their nuts at the same time, resting his body heavily against the papi's sweaty back. It didn't take long before my nut followed, and as I ripped Jerome's phat cheeks to dig out every last drop, I fastened some tape across his mouth. *La vengeance.* I pulled out of Jerome's ass just as roughly as I had fucked it, and I could hear his booty lips smacking after my dick. Grabbing his shoulders, I then pulled Jerome off the papi chulo and dragged him half-naked back out of the room and into the semidarkness near the bottom of the staircase. Stan was still being serviced by a good crowd of dudes anxious to get some booty. I figured they would appreciate some fresh meat, not to mention another hole so the wait wouldn't be so long. Quickly securing Jerome in place beside Stan, I warmed up his cheeks a bit with a good bare-ass spanking before letting nature take its course. Ringing wet with sweat, I finally stood up and motioned for one of the papis nearest in line to step right up and take his turn.

"Where are those guys?" Nelson asked for the umpteenth time as I settled into my seat and fastened the seat belt. The row in front of us was still empty as the flight attendants made their last announcements before closing the cabin doors and readying for departure.

"I dunno," I replied calmly, looking Nelson in the face. "I saw them in the club last night. They looked like they were having a great time with the locals."

Nelson squinted his eyes as he looked searchingly at me, parsing every word I spoke, the inflection of my voice and the slightest movement of my face, hands, and body. "Are you sure? It's not like them to miss the flight."

La vengeance. "I'm just telling you what I know, Nelson."

"You didn't *do* anything to them, did you?"

"Oh, come, on Nelson, you know me better than that."

"Yeah, Will, I do. That's why I'm asking."

The cabin door was finally secured, and as the tug pushed us back from the gate, I replied calmly, "Nelson, what happens in San Juan, stays in San Juan. Now shut up and let me try to catch a few z's. I'm still recovering."

"Will Kane, you're going straight to hell," Nelson responded, shaking his head. "Straight to hell for sure!"

Bankers' Hours

The click-clacking sound is the second thing you notice. Once you enter the Dragon Gates, inscribed with the words "All under heaven is for the good of the people," and mount the crest of the steep promontory that rises above the austere fortresses of glass and steel, granite and marble, with their clamoring armies of suited knights in shades of gray, black, dark blue, and ladies of court in sensible heels, single strands of pearls, and tailored vestments, projecting images of power and prestige that befit their outsized ambitions, it is another world. Up here, where the throngs are thick and the accents as varied as Hunan, Sichuan, Jiangxi, and Guangdong, where store windows proudly display bright reddish orange ducks fresh from the roaster and merchants still value a good haggle with each sale, it's the sound of ivory tiles being slapped on wooden boards by well-skilled hands in smoke-filled dens hidden in the myriad warrens that dot the side streets and alleyways which radiate in all directions.

Once, brothels and opium dens were as densely concentrated in these hoary blocks as systems engineers and investment bankers are now, contemporary equivalents sequestered in newly reno-vated apartments, with a modern style lifted wholesale from the pages of *Dwell,* by way of West Elm and IKEA, the value of which rises and falls with the shifting fortunes of dot-coms, venture-funding rounds, and proximity to IPO dates. Though the new im-migrants are largely absent during the day and only barely perceptible in the evenings, it is the old immigrants, the old tri-ads, the old doors without numbers where words without sounds are the only means of gaining admittance, the old secrets buried in the gnarled flesh of wizened old heads moving stealthily amidst the shadows of the near-ancient past that give the place its soul, that provide its center, that are the very substance which grounds it, along with the incessant click-clacking of the tiles.

Click-clack, click-clack, click-clack, like a restless tide sweep-ing against the shore, as ceaseless as the wind that carries the click-clacking down dusty lanes with names still pronounced in the mother tongue to swirl out into busy streets with foreign names and then bears it aloft to mix with the cacophonous din that reverberates against the panes of the shimmering castles on the plain far below. The monotonous melody is relentless in its in-fectiousness, penetrating even the most tone-deaf tourist the longer they wander the narrow passageways in search of some ex-otic memory with which to regale the folks back home. It was al-ready a part of me as I searched carefully for the red door set in a black wrought-iron frame in the middle of a nondescript stone wall, hidden down a blind alley in a chaotic quadrant bounded by Stockton, Jackson, Grant, and Washington.

His directions were meticulous, which was hardly surprising given the well-ordered state of his affairs. Everything about him was punctilious in its absolute conformity to the old ways: the ways of discipline and piety to the ancestors; honor and respect; loyalty and sacrifice for a higher good. In a precise and elegant script, he had written the details for me personally, signed with his informal name and carefully sealed with a fine red wax, imprinted by the signet ring that had belonged to a distant relation, a courtier in the service of an emperor of a long-dead dynasty. He had sent it by courier to my hotel, to be delivered only to me, in person, and vouchsafed as being in my possession, with my reply an already-forgone conclusion. It was not in the nature of a request being asked of me as much as an invocation of an obligation to be performed by me.

We had spoken of this day on numerous occasions, when the formal might become the familiar. Now, without warning or hint of its imminence, the familiar was dissolving into uncharted terrain, incongruent worlds rubbing shoulder-to-shoulder and barely taking note of one another. I was utterly lost, and that was as it was meant to be, with only the click-clacking of the tiles to provide a touchstone of certainty in my quest. At exactly three PM, when the lobby doors of the bank were closed to the public, I had risen from my desk, gathered my briefcase, which contained his document, and my backpack, with the essentials I would need, and signed out with the guard, who made a perfunctory gesture of checking my bags for some ethical indiscretion. It was a familiar routine between us, he making the joking accusation, me fumbling for excuses as I pulled out my pockets feigning innocence. Maybe one day there would be cause for concern, but not in the manner he might suspect.

I arrived in front of the red door at the stroke of seven, having crisscrossed the whole of Chinatown, including every street, every alley, every passageway, in preparation. Precisely as instructed. Receding in anticipation of my presence, the heavy wooden door creaked on its iron hinges as it opened, permitting a glimpse into the tranquil rectitude of the cloistered garden beyond. I entered, and as I walked along a well-worn path of crushed bark to the right of the garden, the big red door groaned as it once more shut out the unwanted tumult of the other world. Of course there was no point in looking behind me for evidence of unseen retainers well versed in their duties, since there would be none. Instead, I noted how, even here in the garden, the omnipresent click-clack, click-clack, click-clack of the tiles ticked off the passage of time, providing the only constant in an otherwise parallel universe that moved to rhythms beyond the known precepts of the world on the other side of the wooden door.

Somewhat hidden by the luxuriant foliage, a small, well-maintained building of aged limestone and worn granite rose into view as I continued along the short path. Four stories tall, four large windows on each floor, except the first, which only had two, on either side of another large, wooden door, also painted red, its modesty worn with a simple elegance that bespoke the immensity of the fortune within, self-assured, without the need to make declarative statements as to its provenance. To the left of the entrance, where the slope gave way to partially reveal the basement, another path led to a set of large double doors, made of hammered black metal and studded with sharp spikes set in the form of a radiant sunburst rising over a polished-steel horizon, with delicate gold points on the tips to highlight the relief. Once again, as I stood before them, the heavy doors opened to admit me into a vestibule with a solid concrete floor and smooth walls, which was plunged into pitch blackness as they closed silently behind me.

"Did you have a pleasant walk?" a disembodied voice, close at hand, asked amicably from within the inky darkness.

"Yes," I responded softly. "Most enjoyable, thank you."

"It was not so hot today, but still . . ."The voice trailed off in pleasant tones. "May I offer you some cool refreshments?"

"Thank you, maybe later."

"I presume you are eager to begin?"

"Yes, very much."

"Good. So am I."

"How shall we proceed?"

"Please, if you would be so kind as to place your clothes on the bench that is against the wall, to the right of the door."

My eyes struggled to become acclimated to the darkness of the room, but there was little with which to work. I couldn't see my own hand as I held it in front of me to feel for the presence of the wall. In my mind's eye, I was aware of both my hand and the wall but was completely incapable of seeing them. It was somewhat disorienting to be so completely devoid of light so quickly after having spent much of the day in the full glare of a blazing afternoon sun. I found the bench, which sat very low to the ground, and removed my clothes as requested. The air in the room was cool at first, though as I stood at last in all my nakedness, the temperature was rising quickly. Sweat was beginning to moisten my underarms and chest as I turned and walked back to what I supposed was the middle of the room. My dick was already thickening and enlarging to its full length, as if the darkness and the heat were communicating with my libido on another frequency.

"Are you hard?" the voice asked.

"Almost, yeah," I responded somewhat startled, wondering how my host could have known about the tumescence of my dick, which was now completely engorged and rigid, sticking out in front of me with a slight curvature to the right, the heavy, bulbous head bouncing lugubriously as the stiff shaft constantly recalibrated itself to keep its upward tilt.

"My dick is so hard I'm feeling faint," the voice continued in a low register, almost purring.

"You've got me dripping now."

"Shall we start then?"

"I'm ready"

"Good. Please, come this way."

I stepped cautiously in the direction of his voice, my bare feet brushing against the cool slab of the floor, wary of unseen obstructions. After walking a little with my eyes open, utterly useless, I found it more comfortable just to close them. My nose detected a pleasant musky aroma coming from the general direction of my host. As I proceeded to follow the prodding of his voice, the scent grew stronger at times and then faded to just a faint trace at others. I presumed that when he was closer to me the scent was more pronounced than when he was farther away. I found that comforting as I negotiated the darkness, feeling that I could be certain of my host's proximity at the very least. He led me along a narrow corridor, my broad, square shoulders rubbing frequently against the walls, to be closed off from the vestibule no doubt after our passage. The corridor wasn't terribly long, and shortly we entered another space, as pitch black as the ones we had left but with a more expansive feel, as if the ceiling was somewhat higher and the dimensions slightly larger.

This new space was moist and very hot; even the floor was radiating heat and just barely bearable to walk on. My host was silent for a few moments, as if giving me time to get used to this new environment. My skin felt flushed; the heat was making rivulets of sweat form in the small of my back that trickled lazily down the crack of my ass and pooled into heavy globules that dripped off the back of my freshly shaved balls. I turned my head in slight circles, trying to locate a source of the heat, which was quickly bringing on a good, roiling sweat, as if we were in some kind of sauna, but it seemed to come from all directions pretty equally. My heart was beating so loudly it pounded in my eardrums. Could my host hear it too, I wondered.

"Are you ready?" my host's voice rang from some distant part of the room.

"Yes," I answered somewhat tentatively, vaguely unsure of what it was I was supposedly ready for.

"Good. *En garde!!*" my host exclaimed almost giddily, his feet making scurrying sounds as he clambered about the room, sometimes approaching me but always keeping some distance from where I stood.

Standing as still as I could, I let my wet skin feel for his movements in the air, but there were suddenly none. After a few silent minutes passed, a slight trickle of a breeze blew by and then quickly evaporated. Had my host just moved? His scent was somewhat stronger now also, and coming from somewhere behind and to my right. Instinctively, my body slumped into a light crouch, my weight resting on the balls of my feet, equally distributed, ready to instantly leap in any direction. The pounding in my chest sounded as if it were reverberating off the walls of the chamber, practically obscuring any other sounds in the room. With adrenaline fueling my muscles, I nervously prepared for the worst. Straining with all my senses, I tried to discern any warning of an impending assault. But the pulsating thunder in my ears made that all but impossible.

Without warning, hands began squeezing my nipples as if they were zits. My nipples are pierced with 4-gauge, surgical stainless-steel barbells, so the pain was excruciating, radiating all down my arms and making my fingers tingle. Involuntarily I began to scream, but by an act of will stifled it so as not to give my unseen aggressor the satisfaction of knowing my pain. Instead, I groaned in a loud moan that erupted from deep in my diaphragm and completely drowned out the sound of my pounding heart. To him, it could have been a groan of agony or ecstasy, but for me it was both, since as my tormentor drove his fingernails into my nipples, drawing me further into a crouch, I felt him using his face as a wedge to spread my firm, hairless butt cheeks so his ravenous lips could greedily attack my ass. As he drove his tongue into my hole, gnawed on the edges of my sphincter and dug his chin into the soft tissues around it until it began to open, my balls tugged tighter to my body as my long, pierced dick expanded to its full length, the heavy, thick head so engorged with blood that the taut skin made the slit gape open as my ass was soundly devoured.

It was a position my attacker and I held for some time, his face buried in my hole driving me delirious with the pleasure of his flicking tongue, while I was half bent over in sheer agony from the pain inflicted on my nipples. Pain and pleasure mixed liked oil and water, one not completely dissolving in the other, remaining distinctive yet giving way to some third reality that almost craved the necessity of riding the razor's edge between the two. Meanwhile, the temperature felt even more hot and humid than before, adding a sultry texture to the mix. My dick was dripping, but I don't know whether it was sweat or come. My balls were churning in their heavy sack, the pleasure spiraling outward from my asshole as the insatiable mouth of my assailant sucked on my marinating balls, pulling on the loose, silky skin with his teeth until it hurt, then retreating to work over my hole some more. I bent over low, letting my ass spread wide open, giving up my hole to his torments with masochistic relish.

I suppose I could have shaken him off, but if truth be told, then I must admit to my complicity in my afflictions. I took as much pleasure in receiving them as he did in giving them, the pain and pleasure both. I wanted to take everything he had, and thus I made no effort to stop him. I became like the willow that bends in the force of the wind, remaining strong even as other trees are snapped off at their roots. Crouching lower to the ground, on bended knees, I drew him deeper into me, smothering his face between my slippery cheeks with my hands firmly clutching his head by his ears. He responded by madly digging his tongue into my hole, sucking on it, biting it, making my hole a swollen whore eager to feel his abusiveness. He abruptly freed my nipples to my indescribable relief, only to twist and pull my stiff dick and meaty balls between my legs and force my dick in and out of my own ass. As I rode his face, grinding my butt up and down, he would suck on my pierced dick, letting his teeth rub against the ladder of steel rods that line my frenum while sadistically twisting my balls before reaming out my ass again with my own dick.

Only when I felt the white-hot nut rising up out of my balls did I turn the tables and force my will upon him. Grabbing him by his coarse, curly hair, I shoved my rigid fat dick down his hungry throat and fucked his face hard until I erupted in dense, viscous streams of molten sperm that made him choke. With my balls violently slapping against his chin, I drove my dick as far into his piggish mouth as I could, flooding his throat, drowning him in my juice, replacing the air he breathed with my essence. And he did not resist. Instead, he stuffed his long, bony fingers into my puckered hole and tried to milk every last drop of precious fluid from my heavily laden balls, forcing my dick even farther down his throat, as he choked and gagged on my torrent of come. I slid one of my hands along his slimy and sweaty body until I found his quivering dick, still hooded despite its rigidity, and profusely gushing sticky tributaries of his own that overflowed the cone of his foreskin and dribbled down his corpulent shaft.

Returning the favor, I sank down on top of him with the full weight of my muscular body and buried his dick in my mouth, feasting on his fleshy cowl and sucking his bone dry. His body was thinner than mine, but his limbs were long and sinewy and surprisingly well muscled. Our torsos were roughly the same length, his washboard abs fitting snuggly into the ridges between mine, solidly joining us together. As I sucked on his empty bone, his body squirmed under me as if in some deranged ecstasy made almost unbearable by my unceasing stimulation of his sensitive meat. I heard his anguished moans as my tongue gouged out the crevices between his foreskin and the head of his dick in steady circular rhythms that matched his gyrating hips. His mouth matched my rhythm as he sucked my still-hard dick with equal passion. I dug my fingers deep into his soft, shaved ass and stretched his tight hole as I worked my mouth up and down his dick. He reamed out my ass with his fingers as he again scratched a toothy rhythm on my pierced shaft.

The more aggressively he sucked my dick and punched at my hole, I returned his endearments threefold, biting and sucking and ripping at his soft flesh with a gusto only matched by his. Soon, I felt another load rising up out of my balls, and I knew that this time I wanted him to really suffer as my come overflowed his mouth and throat. Jamming my knees hard against the sides of his neck and locking my ankles across the top of his head, I humped his throat deep. When I came, my dick was all the way down his throat with my balls half-way to joining it. I felt the contraction of his neck muscles as he struggled to deal with the onslaught of juice. Nearly suffocating, his dick was suddenly harder and thicker than before, so much so that it was difficult for me to get my mouth around it. He came with a force that took my breath away and had me gagging on his thick, mushroom-shaped head as his salty come shot out of my nose and stopped up my ears.

His fingers were making my ass hurt as I came, the force of my ejaculation causing my hole to clamp down tightly as he dug and ground them into me. The only consolation was feeling the anguished resistance his wide-open hole was putting up as I splayed my strong fingers as far apart as I could while he blew his chunky load into my mouth. I wound my arms tightly around his waist and began to lift his hips off the floor as I crawled up onto my knees, his head dragging between my legs as my swollen dick slipped out of his mouth. I lurched to my feet, carrying him with his dick in my mouth and my nose in his ass, his legs dangling over my shoulders, and staggered forward in the total darkness, hoping to find some solid surface against which to pin his sagging dead weight. Instead, from out of the inky murkiness I tripped against the unexpected base of a low stone bench, the pain screaming from my bruised shins being severe enough to cause me to drop my heavy burden, head first, onto a slick, foamlike surface that gently and surprisingly cushioned our fall.

With his back resting on the forgiving surface of the cushion, my tormentor assaulted me with renewed vigor. He was able to get on top of me and sit with his full weight on my shoulder blades as he grabbed my ass with his hands, spread my cheeks, and resumed his voracious consumption of my hole. Despite my attempts to twist and turn to shake him off, he surfed my body expertly, shifting with my movements while maintaining his steady excavation of my ass. The feeling was luxuriant, hedonistic, and scrumptious beyond words as I lay there in the sweltering darkness and let him eat out my ass until my balls heaved up yet another huge load, soaking my belly in a sticky mix of sweat and come. I felt his furry balls scraping and dripping on the back of my neck, his come-swollen dick slapping against my back as he worked himself up to a thundering climax that shot streams of his come down my back to cascade in warm rivulets along the crack of my ass and into my sloppy hole.

His energy momentarily spent, I flipped him onto his back and raised his legs into the air, pinning his thighs to his chest and making his smooth butt vulnerable to lecherous defilement by my inflamed dick. Fucking his abused hole and feeling the submissiveness of his body to the capricious demands of my meat as it wantonly reamed him only made me mad with lust. Rising up and using my full weight, I leveraged my body into a massive battering ram, unleashing a fusillade of gut-wrenching slams up his hole that made it whither and capitulate to the fury of my big swinging dick. His ass cheeks clenched themselves against my onslaught even as his tender hole lost its senses and impotently sucked on the stout shaft of my victorious dick.

"WHO'S YOUR DADDY, BITCH?!" I screamed as I fucked his ass until my balls felt like they would burst from being slammed so hard against his butt. "WHO'S YOUR DADDY NOW?!"

I don't know what his reply was, if there was one, because my ears were filled with the pulsating thumping and slapping of my crotch and balls against his wet ass. I smelled the funk rising out of him and mixing with my musky sweat. My nostrils breathed it in as an aphrodisiac, throwing more fuel onto the raging fire that drove me to just dick his motherfucking ass down. I wanted him to lose control of his bowels because of the fucking pounding I was heaping on him. I wanted him to piss and come all over himself, his body so twisted by the reaming I was meting out. In my quest for total domination of his ass, his body, his soul, with the power of my dick, I became oblivious to anything and everything other than the feeling of my dick fucking his ass.

"WHO'S YOUR DADDY, BITCH?!"

The glaring brightness of the strong lights dazzled me into a stunned silence even as my words rang loudly in the air, hanging there for what seemed like an eternity before dissolving into the background din of white noise. It took me a few minutes to orient myself to my surroundings and realize where I was. Shocked faces stared at me as if I were some rabid dog or, worse, one of those crazy drunken derelicts that always gravitate to the end of the subway car, where I was sprawled on my side, the front of my shirt drenched in vomit and with a slimy white stain oozing from my crotch down the dark navy wool of my pants leg. I was on the number 6 train, which had stopped in a tunnel somewhere on its journey downtown, the lights flickering on and off, but which was now moving again. I had been at lunch with a client at Cipriani's, marked by copious rounds of Grey Goose martinis, interspersed with shots of Stoli, topped off by a bottle of 1987 Chateau Margaux Premier Grand Cru Classe that his attorney had ordered on a whim, celebrating a favorable court ruling which allowed our transaction to proceed. Feeling faint from too much booze and too horrific a mixture of spirits, I excused myself, which was around three PM. At least I stuck the lawyer with the tab, the cheap bastard.

I stumbled down the steps at Grand Central to get to the subway feeling sick to my stomach. The cute Jamaican brotha across the aisle I was staring at, with the high yellow skin, that hard high ass which his spandex bicycle shorts only succeeded in making look simply irresistible, with the loose-fitting tank top deeply stained with sweat, showing off his finely sculpted arms, muscled chest, and big cinnamon-colored nipples that begged to be suckled until they just fell the hell off his body, with the serpentine bulge in his shorts that wrapped almost around his damn thigh and got me so hot and bothered I threw a bone so big and hard I thought my dick was exploding in my pants, and it scared the piss out of me, just like it's doing now, goddamnit! The boy with those soft, almond-shaped eyes the color of a Caribbean sunset and just as warm and inviting. With the long chestnut dreds that would have fallen clear down to his perfectly square, deeply-dimpled butt cheeks if he hadn't bunched them up under his helmet. The boy who made me mess my pants when he smiled, laughingly no doubt, at the disheveled bum in the expensive suit who was jerking himself off as he stared slack-jawed and crossed-eyed at those full, pouty, "come fuck me, hard" lips that parted to reveal a smile so bright that it could make a blind man see.

Shit! As the train click-clack, click-clack, click-clacked its way down the tracks, the first thing I noticed was the look of fear in the eyes of everyone in the car, crowded into a tight pack as far from me as they could move, not wanting to become part of my drama. I was a fucking mess, and not only were there two more clients waiting for me back at the office, but I was expecting a car service to pick me up for the trip to Newark-Liberty so I could catch a seven PM flight. Shit! As soon as the train pulled into the station, it nearly emptied out in a mad rush as passengers beat hasty exits, many with handkerchiefs covering their nose and mouth as tears welled up in their eyes. Moreover, when new riders began to enter the car and either smelled or saw me sitting in my puddle of debauchery, they headed for the next car. When the doors finally closed, only the unfortunate few who had made a blind rush to catch the car at the last second were stuck in transit hell with a crazy black man dressed in a dark blue suit and reeking to high heaven of piss, vomit, come, and God knows what else. Shit!

Stripping off my soiled coat, shirt, and tie, I made the executive decision to jettison the shirt and tie, try to salvage the suit jacket, and get off at the next stop and make it over to Century 21 before they closed and do a makeover. Fortunately, no one could see my huge bone draining itself of yet another load of hot, sticky come as I climbed the stairs up to street level and the fleeting memory of the Jamaican dude passed from my short-term consciousness. Once more back in the noisy cacophony of the downtown hustle, I fished my cell phone out of my pocket and hit the speed dial.

"Hi, Carol? It's me. Look, I had a little wardrobe malfunction. Tell Chad and Dennis I'll be a few minutes late, but I still want to meet with them before I head out for the Coast. Huh? Yeah, it went fine. Just a little too much to drink, as usual. You know how Ted is. Yeah, that's right! I'll see ya soon, gotta run, 'bye."

Folsom Street Blues

WHACK!

"UHHA!"

WHACK!

"UHHHHAAahh!"

WHACK!

"UHHHHHHAAAaahhhhh!"

A beautiful herringbone pattern, my trademark, slowly came to life on the broad expanse of the Latino guy's smooth, muscular back, extending from his shoulders down across the rump of his firm, plump, freshly shaved ass. Small, perfectly aligned rows etched their way painstakingly along his flanks with a minimal amount of blood, the skin raised in neat, purple welts that flowed seamlessly, one into the next, in a tapestry of the most exquisite artistry.

I have always felt that the cane was a most underappreciated instrument. Not as burly as the flogger, with its exaggerated machismo and the delicacy of a cleaver, nor as heavy as the paddle, such a blunt, gross tool; the cane is light, which belies its stunning power to act as an extension of the master's will, putting thought into action with surgical precision, by turns merciful and merciless. There is nothing in the least bit feminine about the cane, unless its mercurial temperament could be considered such. With a flick of the wrist, the cane can tease playfully, lightly, delicately in one moment, and in the next open the flesh to the bone. It is all in the skill of the master, it is all in the mind of the master, which face of the cane will be made manifest.

The Latino guy was eager to expand his limits and was excited to find a Black Master, for a change, at the dungeon party being thrown in honor of the start of the Folsom Street Fair by The 15 Association, San Francisco's premier SM social club. I had been invited by one of the Fraternal Members, whom I had met the previous year at a "meat 'n' greet" before a Chicago Hellfire Club gathering, in the downstairs darkroom of DEEK'S. The scene between the Latino guy and me was so intense that the monitors stayed close by, ensuring that we both remained in the safe, sane, and consensual zone. Nonetheless, everyone in the dungeon playroom was feeling our erotic vibe, and the air was thick with an acute sensuality that excited the libido and made the balls tingle. As I placed the last finishing stokes of my will on the Latino guy's back, a small circle of devotees had surrounded us, some jacking their dicks as they jockeyed for position to get the best possible view of a Master at work.

Unless you have been in an intense sadomasochistic play scene, it is difficult to describe the emotional bond that unites the top and his bottom. I can tell you that for me, it is as if I am a high priest in an ancient temple, approaching the sacred altar at the summit of a long flight of steps in the innermost sanctum sanctorum, making the ultimate offering of one who has willingly accepted the honor of being sacrificed in homage to a supreme deity. The spiritual euphoria that I feel is not dissimilar to the godlike omnipotence that a topflight surgeon feels after a long and difficult surgical procedure. Drenched in sweat, my body taut with total concentration, I was only vaguely aware of the others in the room, as if they were specters of my imagination and not inhabiting the same plane of existence that the Latino guy and I were on.

As the scene came to its climax, with me rubbing down the Latino guy's freshly embossed back with comforting unguents and gentle strokes of my bare hands, massaging his raised wounds to take away the harsh memory of the cane's sharp sting with a daddy's healing reiki touch, I could sense the presence of someone very close, as if eager to get my attention. After ensuring that the Latino guy was safely and happily cocooned in his own warm state of rapture, I began the process of coming back into myself, back into the plane of reality, to confront this intruding presence before me.

"Hi! Ah, sorry to intrude," the stranger stammered hesitantly as I gazed down at him with haughty disdain. "I just wanted to tell you that was some scene!" he continued, smiling nervously. "My balls feel like they just exploded in my pants, see?" he said, pointing to the dark wet stain that spread over his whole crotch. I remained silent, still recovering from what had transpired with the Latino guy, but the stranger kept on babbling, so a response from me didn't actually seem necessary. I couldn't remember what he said, lost in my own reveries, though I did like the sound of his slightly accented voice. It had a mellifluous quality that was pleasant and peacefully reassuring at that moment. I think that's what made me smile and led me to take a closer look at my interlocutor.

He was a handsome South Asian man, in his mid-thirties, average height, slim build, but it was obvious that he spent a lot of time in the gym; he had great pecs, broad shoulders, and really nice arms. I liked Desi muscle dudes . . . a lot. He wore khaki fatigues, jungle boots, an olive green, military-issue tank top, black leather Sam Browne, and a leather kepi slung low on his broad forehead. His wide-set eyes, high cheekbones, broad, flat nose, dimpled cheeks, and strong, cleft chin were a major turn-on, enhanced by his earnest, sparkling black eyes. I liked the dark cocoa-butter tones of his smooth skin and the way the dark hair on his forearms trickled in delicate ringlets from his elbows to his wrists. My dick was stirring in my pants as I imagined how good his chocolaty cakes might taste if I were rimming his hole right that second. My ears picked up at the word "play," and I was suddenly present, snapped into full and compete attention, focused on his every word, even as my nostrils strained to sniff his intoxicating funk.

"Excuse me," I interrupted, "I didn't catch your name."

"Uh? Oh, Satrajit, my name's Satrajit, but everyone calls me Raj, and like I was saying, I'd really love to play with you sometime, with my boy, the both of us; we could make a hot threesome!"

"Yeah," I responded, still dazzled by Raj's handsome features and fantasizing about his ass, "that sounds like a lot of fun. Why not now?"

"Oh, can't tonight, but I'd sure love to! How about tomorrow? Are you going to the fair?"

"Yeah, I'll be there. It's a shame about tonight, though; you look like you'd be really fun to play with."

"Oh, I know, I know, even though I'm a top, I'd sure bottom for you. You're a hot man."

"Well, I could give you a little taste to hold you over?" I said, rubbing my crotch to emphasize the bulging monster struggling to get loose. Raj hesitated as he eyed my package. I could tell he wanted it; his own dick was betraying him. "Come on," I said, unbuttoning the fly and pulling out my throbbing dick, displaying it for his admiration. Raj licked his lips like a snake flicks its tongue to check the air for signs of prey. "Come on, just a little taste before you run."

Raj reached out his arm and cupped the bronze snake in the palm of his hand, his eyes wide as he marveled at the contrasting sizes of his small hand and my fat dick. It was more than a handful for him. But the challenge that dick represented made it all the more difficult for him to resist. Raj knelt down in front of me and licked my dick with his tongue, bathing it in his warm spit, teasing it until it started to leak little droplets of clear pre-come, which he savored before gorging himself on the beefy head, trying desperately to swallow as much of the rigid shaft as could fit into his mouth.

I held a hand on the back of his head to help him take it down his throat, enjoying the sensation of slowly fucking his face, getting him used to the thickness of my meat, pulling it out and smacking him with it, bringing a little color to his cheeks, then slamming it back down his throat until he gagged. Raj learned quickly, always a welcome quality when breaking in a new boy. After a while, I felt that familiar fullness in the base of my balls, the surging heat rolling down my shaft, the tingling in the head, that sudden pause, then the pulsating electricity of the release, pumping wad after wad of thick cream deep down Raj's throat, choking him with my seed, smearing it all over his face and hair, rubbing it into his pores. I could feel Raj's body vibrating now as he rubbed his crotch and shot his load inside his pants even while still sucking the last precious drops of come from the end of my dick.

"Whew," Raj sighed, finally surfacing. "Man, you got a hot dick."

"That was pretty good."

"Wow! You got some good shit there, man!" Raj continued, in a post-dick-slapped daze. Chuckling slightly, I reached down and grabbed Raj under his arm as he tried to stand up, still a little wobbly on his feet. "Fuck, I can't wait to take that up my ass."

"And I can't wait to put it there!" I said, feeling his small, tight butt as I steadied him. "That's going to be real hot, for sure!" We made plans to hook up during the fair, and Raj took his leave. By then, I was ready to dive into the madness of the dungeon party once again, my dance card surprisingly full with eager new acolytes desperately seeking my benediction. The bacchanalia was in full swing, and as the High Priest of the debauched rites, my special ministrations were sorely needed. Thus, it would have been terribly impolite, as an invited guest, to deny my hosts the pleasures which they so richly deserved. Okay, okay, to put it bluntly, I was a pig in shit, and tomorrow I'd be in hog heaven with a hot Desi daddy and his boy toy. Does it get any better than that?

I awoke the next morning in a totally unfamiliar place: it was a nice room, with good light, a cat purring contentedly in the space between my feet, a warm, moist body snoring deeply next to me. I rolled over slowly, trying not to disturb either of the sleeping creatures, to ascertain whom my bedmate might be. It was the Latino guy. At that moment, my mind was flooded with all of the details of the previous night's festivities, between the time I finished his markings and now, waking up in his bed. As the sinfully delicious memories re-seared themselves into my brain, my dick erupted like Vesuvius, causing me to let out a long, deep moan that woke both the cat and the man, sending everyone scurrying in search of fresh milk to start their day. Breakfast of Champions, indeed!

Jorge lived in the Tenderloin, only a few blocks from South of the Slot, the old nickname for the rugged precinct south of Market Street that had become the nesting ground for Baghdad by the Bay's fiercest denizens and the purveyors who catered to their special requirements. Unlike the genteel Castro District or the now decidedly upscale Polk Street, SoMa still attracted a dangerous crowd who sometimes overindulged their penchant for blood sport. And then there were the queers. SoMa is the last bastion of the Old Guard, the queer leather equivalent of the OGs in the 'hood. There you can find the extreme fetish clubs, the ones that believe it's not really a party unless there is at least one sling hanging from the rafters. Naturally, the more hardcore leather bars and the kinkier sex clubs reside there. And it is in this cauldron of depravity that the annual Folsom Street Fair is held, to the delight of dedicated edge players and voyeurs alike, gay and straight and everything in between. Especially the in between!

The marks on Jorge's back had deepened to a beautiful red hue, which sexily contrasted with his swarthy skin. Their residual tenderness made his whole back one massive erogenous zone; just a light touch, and the man's dick did back flips in his pants. And if your dick was fortunate enough to be stuck in his ass when that happened, man, it was fucking awesome! He was really proud to be carrying the Mark of Kane on him, and as we strolled down Larkin, crossed Market, and proceeded south on 9th, heading toward the fair, he beamed from ear to ear, wearing a "collar" unlike any other. Everyone we passed wanted to stop and marvel at his back, snapping photos and asking him for all the details on his experience in obtaining them. From time to time, an elder of the Leatheratti Tribe looked at Jorge's back and would nod approvingly at me, admiring the old-skool style and craftsmanship.

The Folsom Street Fair is, in a way, just one big tribal family reunion, where folk come out to admire the wide range and diversity of our people, catch up with distant relations, gossip, trade stories, and pass down the wisdom from one generation to the next. Consequently, the feeling of instant camaraderie between strangers is genuine and borders on the brotherly, which makes the temptation toward incest utterly unavoidable. There were so very many temptations spread along my path that day, it was only by a Herculean act of will that I overlooked all of them as Jorge and I made our way to the Eagle, on Harrison at 12th Street, to keep the rendezvous with Raj and his boy. Even though we had talked about a threesome, I didn't think Raj would have any problem with my bringing Jorge, who not only packed one fine piece between his legs but whose phat booty could make a grown ass man cry.

As a favorite gathering place of the tribe at almost any time of year, especially for their Sunday Beer Busts, the Eagle was particularly packed now, with all the family in town. Jorge and I had to squeeze our way inside, and even then it was wall-to-wall flesh in practically every direction, even outside on the patio. But I spied a small pocket of space up on the stage and, taking Jorge by the hand, plowed through the throngs to reach it. We climbed up and found ourselves with a prime perch to see and be seen by everyone in the place. Jorge—shirtless and wearing skin-tight latex pants that showed off his considerable assets and tall, black Rangers—and me—shirtless, with a Y-shaped leather harness that wrapped around my body, front to back, ending in a heavy stainless-steel cock ring, which pumped my package to almost busting out of the custom leather codpiece that was specially attached by a row of snaps to my tight, faded jeans, topped off by sleek leather chaps and Carolina loggers—stopped hearts and created quite the buzz.

It was a terrific late September day in San Francisco: bright sun, no wind, Technicolor blue sky; and the crowds looked great: guys half naked in their leathers, latex, and rubber, some naked dudes who still got it going on, biker girrls looking fierce, and then I spotted Raj. Garam Jism! There along the side of the patio, dressed in tight black leather chaps, with just a matching leather thong underneath, a simple chain-link harness crisscrossing his awesome chest, shiny silver studs in both nipples sparkling in the sunlight, and kepi cap, was the most gorgeous dark-skinned hunk I had ever seen, his color so saturated that it looked like chocolate porcelain. God, give me a Kerala man!

He held a chain-link leash in one hand that led to a spiked collar around an equally gorgeous blond hunk with a deep tan that made the downy blond hair that covered his body look like spun gold in the sunlight. His boy was naked except for Wesco Boss Engineer boots and a black leather posing strap with a red stripe down the center (yum yum!), which looked stuffed to overflowing with the precious contents it held. And that bubble! Dayum! And Raj's super-hairy-fucking-luscious bootay! Double Dayum! Is it any wonder than my favorite beer is a Black 'n' Tan?

Raj was already pointing Jorge and me out to his boy, and both of them had the most wicked grins on their faces, the kind that only bad boys up to no good wear. Like the one that covered the lower part of my face. I pulled Jorge closer to me and held up one hand with four fingers showing. Raj's eyes widened, and his head vigorously nodded as he waved us over. Sensing that something momentous was about to happen, the crowd in front of the stage parted like the Red Sea to allow Jorge and me to make our way over to Raj and his boy.

As the four of us stood together in mutual admiration at what fucking hot, sexy studs we were, the crowd went ballistic. Guys held up cameras and started snapping photos like we were on the red carpet with a pack of paparazzi. The sun felt especially hot at that moment, as if the reflected heat of Raj, his boy, Jorge, and I had created a solar flare that was scorching everything in its path. My dick was burning up in my leather codpiece, and the hotter it felt, the harder my dick got, so much so that several of the snaps burst, leaving the codpiece dangling by just a few snaps.

"Looks like you got something in the oven," Raj said, pointing to my bulging crotch.

"Yeah, it's almost done, want a taste?" I replied salaciously.

His face broke out in a lascivious smile. "I'm still digesting the one from last night! But my boy might want some." Raj looked at the beautiful blond stud. "How about it, boy, you want some fresh, hot daddy meat?"

The blond boy was instantly on his knees, sniffing my crotch, begging like an eager pup and licking my boots, craving to please both his master and me. By then I could feel the crowd behind me breathing down my neck in anticipation of my popping my fat dick out and letting the boy suck it for all he was worth. Uncharacteristically for me, however, I suddenly decided that I'd rather tease the boy, and the crowd, and leaned over to quietly whisper in Raj's ear that maybe we could find a more suitable place to continue our business. He readily assented and suggested that we all go back to his place, which was not far away. To the utter disappointment of the crowd at the Eagle, the four of us headed back to the front door and dove into the multitudes milling around SoMa for the fair.

It turned out that Raj was one of the new pioneers in the neighborhood, having bought a small loft apartment in what was fast becoming known as Multimedia Gulch. The area was attracting new dot-com firms and software professionals, part of the wave of forces quickly gentrifying the old raunchy haunts that made SoMa so much fun. As we made our grand promenade down Folsom to admiring smiles and numerous offers to join us for whatever wretched nastiness we were about to get into, the signs of the coming transformation were already noticeable. Raj's place was in a converted warehouse on Howard, between 8th and 9th, conveniently just a block over from Dore Street, at the end of which is the site of another rude street fair, and only about three blocks, give or take, in any direction from serious depravity. One of my favorite sling clubs was just around the corner, in fact. Lucky dog!

The large first floor was divided between his work space, filled with enough computers and monitors to rival Mission Control in Houston, and his main living area. Upstairs, though, was a leather man's paradise. Raj had painted the walls, ceiling, and floor of the cozy single room that comprised the top floor of his loft a glossy jet black. He had also installed steel cyclone fencing along the walls and ceiling, making the entire room one giant cage. He had a St. Andrew's Cross in one corner and a variety of padded fuck benches and old pommel horses scattered about. Toward the back, there was a chaise lounge, and by the front there was a large, steel-framed, four-poster canopy bed, with D-rings placed all along the posts and a sling dangling from chains attached to the overhead rails. The place had a musky smell that reeked of leather, stale sweat, Crisco, and poppers. It was the perfect place for a down-and-dirty four-man orgy.

"So, this is my place," Raj said, proudly beaming. "Make yourselves at home."

"Thanks," I responded. "This is a great pad. How do you get

any work done with all these pretty playthings running about?" I said, looking lecherously at his hunky boy toy, whose crystal blue eyes and lopsided grin hinted at just what a distraction he could be.

"Oh, it's a challenge," Raj said, stroking his boy's head as the boy nuzzled Raj's crotch. "Yes, a big challenge!" Then, as if suddenly remembering, he continued, "Hey, do you want something to drink? Maybe a bite to eat or something?"

I was seated on the narrow leather chaise, dangling a leg on either side, clasping my hands behind my neck. "Well, now that you mention it, I am a bit famished. And poor Jorge here hasn't had anything solid since this morning," I said, giving Jorge a conspiratorial wink.

"I've got some stuff to make sandwiches, and maybe, I think, there might be some leftover takeout from last night, or maybe—"

"Actually," I said sharply, cutting Raj off in mid-sentence, "I've got a hankering for some cakes."

Raj gave me a quizzical look as he repeated, "Cakes?"

"Yeah, some chocolate cakes," I continued in a softer tone. "Some hot, hairy, chocolate Desi cakes."

"Ooh," Raj smiled, "like these Desi cakes?" He turned and flashed me his naked brown butt, ran a hand over his wooly cheek and then licked one finger and placed it in the crack of his ass.

"Yeah, just like those Desi coco cakes right there," I replied, reaching out toward his butt with one hand.

Raj pulled his finger from his crack, making a popping sound with his lips. "You're in luck! They're done!" Then he proceeded to straddle the chaise and set his full, round, perfect Desi chocolate cakes right down on my face. I reached up under him and grabbed his pierced nipples, pulling his full weight down on my face as I buried my tongue in his moist hole and licked it like it was the chocolate cake mix left in the bottom of the mixing bowl.

I got all up in that ass, chewing on the edges of his hole, slobbering all up and down that furry crack, trying to soak in his sweet Desi funk with my face and mouth, making Raj groan with pleasure. I teased those pierced nipples too, pinching them, feeling the hard steel rod beneath the tips of his erect tits, stroking them in rhythm to the digging out of his ass with my tongue. Raj's nipples were hardwired to his ass: stoke them just so, and his hole was wide open; pinch them just this way, and his hole clamped down hard on whatever was in the way. Damn, and I made sure there was always something in the way too!

Not to be left out of the opening action, Jorge reached over and pulled Raj's thick Desi lund out of the leather thong, then swallowed it deep down his throat in one big gulp, squeezing Raj's balls in his hands and making him twitch and grind his ass deeper into my face like a stripper at the Bada Bing Lounge. Meanwhile, Raj's boy snatched the codpiece off my jeans and started chowing down on my stiff dick like he hadn't eaten for days. If anyone had walked into the room at that point, all they would have heard was the sound of squealing pigs deep in slop at the trough, slurping, sucking, gagging, and moaning like a Michelin chef holding a plate of fresh black truffles. The four of us gorged ourselves until the collective pressure was just too much. As if our DNA were inextricably linked, we all began to speed toward a massive climax, our balls heaving as they loaded up on sperm, our dicks starting to jerk spasmodically, pumping that heavy cream down those long, hard shafts.

I was smothered in Raj's hot Desi ass, oxygen-deprived in fact, which I'm sure accounted for the totally primal way I ate out his hole. I was a fucking cannibal, man; not even Hannibal Lecter could touch me. I had Raj's hole leaking some kind of tasty juice and so loose I could almost feel my face disappearing up inside his ass. I felt Raj losing it, and as he shot his load, I just blasted his boy a big one that gagged him and blew out his nose all over my stomach. Then one whole side of my chest was soaked as Jorge blew his load, followed by the other side of my chest being sprayed by Raj's boy. And it wasn't just your run-of-the-mill "busting a nut," either; it was the "bust it so hard you feel like you just broke something" nut, followed by a sudden swoon and dis-orientation that leaves you not knowing your own name. After that, it just got mad crazy.

Raj's boy tried to mount his skinny ass on my dick, but I pushed Raj's body forward, knocking his boy off balance and into Jorge's arms. Then I slammed Raj's ass down on my throbbing shaft, hard, ramming my dick all the way inside him in one thrust, making his ass squirm as he squatted, trying to get used to that big ass snake up in there. Meanwhile, his boy had his legs wrapped around Jorge's torso as Jorge impaled the boy's tanned butt with his thick uncut whopper, making him lose his grip on Jorge's shoulders and fall backward on the chaise. The boy's head landed just inches away from Raj's fat Desi lund, and he turned slightly to suck it into his mouth. Raj then fell forward on top of his boy and sucked on the boy's heavy tool. As I power-pumped Raj's ass ragged, I could feel the shockwaves from the thumping Jorge was giving his boy right down in my balls. So that made me fuck Raj harder, just to try and send some of that love back to Jorge and see what kind of tune we could beat out of these butts. Man, we made some kind of hellified racket up in that joint!

After being eaten out like a fat man at an all-you-can-eat buffet, Raj's hole was as loose as a two dollar 'ho on Super Bowl Sunday. As I rammed my hard dick in and out of his ass, I found my strokes getting longer as my dick jammed deeper the more I fucked him. My balls were getting sucked inside with my dick on each stroke until I just jammed it all into him, grinding it as deep as the motherfucker could take it, trying to find the bottom of his hole. But Raj had a fucking abyss down there, and the more I shoved into his ass, the more his ass begged to take. And it felt so good, man, like fucking warm Jello. My shit was in so deep it got hard to pull out, so I just kept jamming it and grinding my hips into his hairy cheeks, grabbing a firm handful in each hand and spreading them as wide as they would go, just to get more leverage to shove my dick down into that fucking bottomless pit. I didn't find the end of it, but I did dig a nut out of Raj's ass that nearly castrated me as I played those nipples to a tee.

Jorge must have had a great time fucking Raj's boy, because he came so hard, he left his body and floated above the rest of us, cheering us on as we each crossed over to the other side right after him. It was some surreal fucking after that. A fucking mixed marsala. Up on the Cross, bent over the benches, hanging from the ceiling, we smeared every surface in Raj's playroom with spunk and sweat, lube and piss, and God only knows what else. At one point, Jorge and me took turns double-dicking Raj and his boy, who were strapped down side-by-side on a pommel horse with spreader bars between their legs to keep their asses open wide. I'd straddle Raj, driving my dick into him, then Jorge would stand between my legs and shove his pinga grande in, rubbing up against the piercings on the underside of my dick and making me senseless as our dicks stuffed Raj's hole to the brim. After Raj blew another big load, we'd rip our dicks out of his ass and then fuck his boy the same way. We went back and forth like that for a long time, until I could barely keep it up and Jorge's dick was raw.

After a much-deserved break to regain our stamina, down a few beers, have a bite of real food, we went right back at it. I caned Raj's boy, making tribal marks all over his ass, while Jorge introduced Raj to the finer points of rope bondage, turning Raj into one hot Desi piñata. While he dangled from the overhead rail of the bed, his legs tied to his arms, leaving his sloppy ass vulnerable, I couldn't resist working his hole with one big fat dildo after another. Raj had a huge assortment, in every size and shape imaginable, and I wanted to find the one that could fill his hungry ass. Meanwhile, Jorge took real delight in fucking Raj's boy, especially after he bound the boy's arms behind his back with duct tape, leaving his freshly caned ass open for a good over-the-knee spanking to tighten up his loose hole. At about the same time, I finally found the perfect dildo for Raj's ass just as Jorge found the boy's G-spot. They both started jerking so hard, as they got that good vibration going deep down in that ass, that it looked like we might have to call 911.

The sexual vibe that erupted was so strong that I felt that old familiar feeling come over me, and once again I was the High Priest officiating at an ancient rite. I was so overcome that I pulled the massive dildo out of Raj's subjugated hole and then pushed Jorge into the sling next to Raj, sliding his latex pants down around his ankles as I did so. I then grabbed Raj's boy and threw him down on the bed between Raj and Jorge, with his ass sticking up in the air. I shoved my dick into the boy's wrecked ass and then proceeded to work both my hands and arms into Raj's and Jorge's willing holes. The deeper I fisted them, the harder I fucked the boy. The marks on Jorge's back and boy's butt sent them both over the edge, causing their butt holes to bite hard on my arm and dick. It was a heady feeling, being gummed by their toothless maws and powerless to resist. Raj's ass seized on my arm with equal gusto, as if the monster dildo was just a warm-up for the real deal, literally driving me into another realm.

It was like I was suspended between the sacred and the profane, one foot in Nirvana, the other firmly rooted in the earthiness of the here and now. I lost all sense of time, and before long it was as if I had become the sacrificial lamb, the willing offering to the most fearsome deity. The last thing I remember, before I lost myself in the brilliance of the ethereal light, as I stood there with my dick in the boy's welcome hole and my two arms up to the elbow inside Raj and Jorge, pinned as it were like a moth in a collector's case, was the intense rush of energy speeding down my arms and through my dick like an express train, steaming toward my heart and running flat out into my head, then exploding in a brilliant white light. I heard the fucking angels calling out my name. If this be Heaven, I thought to myself, then God, give me a Kerala man, a hot Latino, and one tight white boy! For ever and ever, amen!

Coral Sands Blues

Damn, he was a big boy! Next to him, Moby Dick was just a guppy. And pale? Shit, Casper the Friendly Ghost was a sunburned Jamaican compared to that heifer. He was the only one lounging in the six-man hot tub, but there was barely room for Joon-ho, the twenty-something son of the motel's owners, and me to squeeze in for a post-coital soak. There weren't many attractions to the decrepit hulk of a motel that stubbornly clung to the seedy underbelly of a little corner of Hollywood which defied gentrification. Joon-ho's smooth, soft, creamy Korean globes rising impressively from his muscular, hirsute legs, his gym-cut body, so well defined he sported a full case of abs instead of a six-pack, and thick black nipples that could put an eye out if you weren't careful certainly qualified as the star reasons for venturing to this forsaken wasteland. I'd met him at Flex Complex, while sitting by the pool. He was impressed by my pierced dick, and I was enamored of his shaved balls, which were blacker than mine and just overflowing with the sweetest juice. We helped "relieve" each other of our respective curiosities and did more than our part to heal the cultural divide between our respective races.

After screwing our brains out for the better part of the day, Joon-ho invited me back to his place, where he was the night and weekend manager. His parents usually worked the day shift, but on the weekends they went on church-sponsored outings all over the southland. That particular weekend they were at the Vasquez Rocks. One of Joon-ho's marketing innovations was to make the hot tub and sundeck clothing-optional during his shifts, which encouraged a rather large and diverse clientele to call the motel home when they came slumming for a little of that ol' Skool flava that LA was once rife in. The Fat Man was a case in point; though he lived in the Valley, barely an hour away, he preferred staying at the motel when the urge to merge sent him searching for a chubby chaser with a Johnson big enough to pork him in all the right places. Murray was actually a very pleasant chap, and while regaling us with his uproarious running commentary on the action taking place in the rooms just off the courtyard surrounding the hot tub, he recognized one of his extra-special fuck-buddies on the balcony upstairs and took his leave.

Murray also took most of the water in the hot tub with him when he got out, which left Joon-ho and me no choice but to go back to the room and find ways to ward off the chill of the night air. I was feeling in an ol' skool mood myself for some reason, from back in the day when we wore alligators on our polo shirts, Stan Smiths on our feet because we were too cool for stripes, and PC stood for Pierre Cardin, which we liberally applied because we thought it enhanced our sex appeal and had more class than Hai Karate or Dad's Old Spice. You feelin' me? When Teddy Prendergast and Al Green and Marvin Gaye mellowed us out quicker than those Phillies Cheroots we puffed between sips of Hennessy and Johnny Walker Black. When Lou Rawls found us At Last and Roberta Flack Saw Our Face and Evelyn "Champagne" King, well, every thang is every thang when Miss King's in da house. And for those times we just wanted to funk, Sylvester and Donna and Chaka brought it on home. It was probably just the weather, a gray cloudy day that left a whiff of nostalgia clinging to everything. Or it could have been Joon-ho's selection of music to fuck by, mostly classic Motown, mixed with some Wes Montgomery, Etta James, and Little Jimmy Scott.

We freaked the light fantastic well into dawn. I'll tell you one thing, those Korean bros got it goin' on, jack! The last thing I remember before passing out after I blew a massive nut was feeling Joon-ho's freak ass milking my dick for more. And the first thing I felt when I woke up in the morning was Joon-ho's freak ass still wrapped around my joint and riding that piss-boner until I almost emptied my bladder all up inside him. I had to really dick the bro down after that, slappin' the mess outta that freak nigga's ass just to get out of bed. Later, as I took a long-delayed leak, I noticed how the skin on my dick looked all discolored and shriveled, as if it had been stuck in some wet, slimy asshole all night long. Shit, no wonder my balls felt as if they had been sucked dry, turned inside out, and wrapped in sandpaper. Fortunately, that last fuck fest put Joon-ho's lights out for good, and he was curled up in the fetal position, lightly snoring, with a deeply satisfied grin on his face as I got dressed and quietly tiptoed into another gray day in LA. I pulled out of the motel parking lot and made my way back down Western Avenue toward the Holiday Inn I was staying at during my latest sojourn to the City of Angels, my dick thumping my thigh in some kind of nervous withdrawal shit from its encounter with the divine Joon-ho.

It was just past noon, and I got a sudden ol' skool hankering for Roscoe's Chicken & Waffles, with some cheese grits and home fries and buttermilk biscuits on the side. There was one over on Gower, so I took a right on Franklin and headed west to "Hollyweird" proper. No sooner had I pulled into the parking lot than I found myself in the no man's land between a transvestite prostitute, agitated to the brink of hysteria, and her equally raving-mad, iced-out pimp, viciously yelling at each other over the hood of my car. My only prayer was that I would be long gone and deep into a stack of gravy-smothered chicken and waffles by the time the whole brouhaha escalated into a shooting war. Sadly, such was not to be, and when the pimp lunged over the hood to tackle Miss Thang, knocking her and me both to the ground, while she pummeled his greasy Jeri curl with the heel of her five-inch platform stilettos, I reluctantly found myself playing the Fool Hero to Miss Thang's Dulcinea until the police and paramedics arrived to take the profusely bleeding pimp away. And just to prove Fate can be a bitch, Miss Thang was so thankful she pressed herself to me tighter than one of her Lee Press-on Nails.

Shaynia was really a beautiful, dark ebony-skinned girl underneath her five o'clock shadow and pancake foundation. With, sweet, wide-set eyes the color of copper, high cheekbones, full, thick lips with deep dimples on either side of her mouth when she smiled, and a cute cleft in her chin. She stood a good six feet nine inches tall in her nylons, was built brick-house solid, and must have had size 13EEE feet. Big hands too. I could only imagine what she must have packed between her legs with markers like those. Seeing the curious expression on my face, she generously offered me a special rate to find out, though, since I had saved her from that "crazy-ass bastard" pimp of hers. When I declined, she pestered me constantly, between generous shovelfuls of smothered chicken and grits that she ate with the gusto of an NBA rookie at training camp. I conceded she had a very nice booty, really fine in fact, after she raised her skirt to flash her bare, thong-sheathed butt in my face in the middle of the restaurant, which only resulted in her being even more insistent in her nagging afterward.

"Why not!?" she whined. "You like to fuck guys in the ass, what's wrong with mine?"

"But you're not a 'guy,'" I weakly offered in defense.

"Honey, don't let these tits fool you. I'm more 'guy' than most men can handle. Come on, feel between Mommy's legs, and I'll show you!"

It went on like that all throughout brunch, and if it had been any place other than Hollywood, we surely would have been the highlight of the day's entertainment. But as it was, we were tame compared to the other contestants in attendance, the most motley collection of cattle-call rejects and reality-show wannabes who ever vied for a shot at *The Springer Show*. I offered to give Shaynia a lift since her crib was on the way to my hotel, and just to keep her quiet during the ride I let her suck my sore but always eager dick as payment in full for everything, brunch included. Girl-friend went out of her mind worshipping that fat dick, slobbering and carrying on so much I thought she half expected it to part the Red Sea, walk on water, and feed the multitudes. That said, Shay-nia was one dick-sucking pro, and she had my joint wound around my bruised balls and busting nuts on my ass by the time she was done.

Dayum! It felt so good, I was of half a mind to give her the head-over-heels ass banging she had so desperately begged for. Instead, she screamed for me to pull over when she spotted one of her homegirls standing on the corner of Western and Santa Monica, near the Blacklight. She left me bone out and balls dry and would have left me stone broke if I hadn't stopped her from rip-ping off my wallet as she slid her sneaky booty out of my ride. With a shy smile she said if I ever wanted some really good ass, I could find her at the Blacklight, and as she exited the car, she made sure to let her dress ride way up her perfectly round butt to tease me just a little more as she strolled up to throw air-kisses to her friend. As I pulled back into traffic, heading south on West-ern, I had to keep one hand on my stiff bone to keep it from banging against the steering wheel as I watched Shaynia's image slowly disappear in the rearview mirror, another ol' skool memory in the making.

BZZZZZZZZZZZ! SLAP!
Six-ten PM. The damned alarm would go off again in another ten minutes. And instead of doing the right thing, just turning it off and pulling the covers up over my head and continuing my well-deserved romp with Mr. Sandman, I was actually going to get up, get dressed, and get some fucking ass. Shit, leave it to Roscoe's to bring out the freak-nigga in me—get a belly full of some down-home cookin' and a good long nap and wake up with a raging, nasty ol' bone. It was still kind of early to hit my usual haunts, like the Faultline or Cuffs. But it was prime time to catch up with the brothas for happy hour at the Study. So once more I headed out into the dusky gloam of the Naked City in search of a little hooch, a little smoke, and a whole lotta shagging. I even stopped at the corner store and bought a pack of Cheroots and a pint of Hennessy, just like old times.

There are two kinds of bars: ones for drinking and ones for preening. The Study is a drinkers' bar, old heads and young heads sitting in the dark with straight-up booze, no fancy-named, funny-colored, froufrou cocktails here, carrying a world of burdens on their hunched shoulders and putting up a good front despite the butt-kicking beat-down the daily struggle sculpts into their weary faces, creating an intricate landscape of bemusement, bewilderment, and desperation between sparse oases of surprising tenderness, sweetness, and calm. The Study is the kind of bar you find yourself in when you suddenly realize that you have finally run out of places to run away to, where the next stop is some restless, undefined state between being and nothingness, like a Green Room for Heaven, Earth, and Hell. It is a smoky, dank chamber kept permanently chilled as if to keep the patrons on ice so they won't spoil before their final homecoming. And despite, or maybe because of, its resemblance to a morgue, it is a welcome respite nonetheless for those men who crave its sanctuary.

Coltrane was pouring out of the jukebox as Sammy refreshed my drink with another stiff double shot of bourbon. I was trying to work the edge off that bone in my pants but without much success. The alcohol was just washing right through me and building up to a mean piss, so I drained the glass and went to the restroom to relieve myself for the umpteenth time. A tall, skinny bro walked in and stood at the urinal next to me, fumbling with his zipper before unleashing one thick mother of a dick that made the beer can in his free hand look puny. While we both waited for the piss to get up enough pressure to drain our veins, we checked out each other's shit, stepping back just enough to keep from splashing on our pants but also to give the other a better look at what we were packing. We were both about the same length, but the contrast was as stark as Fat Albert and Weird Harold. Judging by the relative quickness of both our joints to get stiff, it seemed we each liked what we saw too.

Curtis was a screenwriter, which sounded impressive but meant absolutely nothing in LA since everybody here has at least one script looking for coverage. He was a pretty fine dude though, with a golden honey complexion and cinnamon-colored hair that he wore in a tight Afro with *ol'* skool chops that came clear down to the edges of his jaw and gave him more than a slight resemblance to John Shaft. He had granny glasses sliding down his long, fleshy nose, which gave him a retro vibe that played well with the randy ol' skool skank I was giving. We hit it off right away, and he suggested taking it somewhere more private, like his room in the motel across the street. That's another thing I liked about the Study: dudes there don't play. They see something they like, they go for it balls out, no jive. With the promise of relief at last, it was a fucking struggle to get my bone back in my pants, and seeing how difficult that was proving to be, Curtis graciously bent down and sucked on my joint just enough to get it flexible so I could zip it for the short walk to his place. It was sweet, man, his thick lips and soft tongue working my bone in all the right places.

It had been a long while since I was last in the Coral Sands Hotel, whose dissolute shabbiness was the sine qua non of dive motels with pretensions of grandeur. I had gone there for a handball party with some cats up from San Diego and this rude cabal of locals that hung out at the Faultline. The scene was so mad crazy that just the memory of it had my dick so hard I could feel the inseam of my pants starting to pop. By the time we got to Curtis's room on the second floor, in the back, I had a trail of pre-come all the way down to my boots. To say I was eager to get my freak on was an understatement. No sooner had Curtis turned the key in the lock than I had that boy pinned up against the inside wall nearest the door, my body pressing tight against his and my tongue halfway down the back of his throat. As we swapped spit, my fingers were already twisting his thick nipples until they were poking out his thin T-shirt. His glasses got steamed up from the heat of the body-slamming foreplay we engaged in as I pulled him down to the floor, pushing his legs apart while grinding my crotch into his, still with our clothes on.

Brotha man was on his game too, with a hard, cut body that gave as good as it got. This was going to be some tough man-to-man freaking here, for sure. As we wrestled on the floor, Curtis made it clear by his resistance bordering on aggression that if I wanted his ass, I was going to have to earn it, because he wasn't giving it up without a struggle. That challenge made me hornier than hell, and I went at him with everything I had, a massive full-frontal assault with overwhelming force applied all across the lines of engagement. In our rough-and-tumble grappling, clothes quickly became both casualties as well as spoils of war, ripped and torn from the body of the loser and paraded in triumph by the victor. And each of us got more than our share of spoils. But when I succeeded in pulling Curtis's pants down around his ankles, exposing his big bull balls and perfect ass, I upped the ante. Using his pant legs to bind one of his arms to one of his legs, I put a death grip on his heavy balls that had the boy screaming and turned him so I could slap the shit out of his round, caramel cheeks until they were crimson. Curtis was in trouble, and he knew it.

I wailed on his butt, raising long red welts on each cheek from my fingers. The boy howled with the pain of the spanking and from the crushing his balls were getting. Curtis bucked his hips and flailed at me with his loose hand and leg, trying to deflect the blows falling on his butt with ever-increasing severity.

"Say UNCLE!" I yelled at him. "Say it, nigga! UNCLE! Say UNCLE, damn it! Or I'll beat your yellow ass so black your momma won't recognize it!"

Curtis was crying and hollering; tears were streaming down his face, but the brotha hung tough, man, and started twisting his body something fierce. He landed a good fist upside my head, though, which knocked me off balance just enough for him to get loose. But I was on his ass before he could wiggle free of the tight binding I had made of his pants. I got hold of his balls again and really squeezed them, making him squeal. Instead of beating on his reddened ass, I jammed my tongue in his hole and ate the brotha out until he was moaning more than he was screaming.

"Uncle! Uncle! Ohhhh God! Uncle!" Curtis began moaning and groaning as his ass wiggled in my face, trying to get more of my tongue up in there. I had the nigga now, and I wasn't about to let up on him. I started digging my tongue all up in his shit, pushing my face into his butt crack. In response, Curtis's dick got so hard that the weight of that bad boy pressing against my knuckles made me loosen the grip on his balls. That's when he finally got his chance to make the move he must have been planning for some time. With his balls free, Curtis whirled around and tackled me with his free arm, shoving me onto my back, and painfully pinned my shoulders with his sharp, knobby knees. He started to beat my face with his thick, fat dick, slamming it hard and bitch-slapping me until my head was swiveling from side to side like a bobblehead doll on the dashboard of a tricked-out ride balancing on two wheels. As Curtis got into his little power moment, glee-fully taunting me, I was gradually preparing the coup de grace.

"How you like this dick, nigga?" Curtis maniacally chuckled as he slapped my face again and again and again. "Come on, playa, let me hear you say UNCLE!"

I whipped my legs up and caught Curtis around the neck with my ankles, then slammed his body backward, surprising the shit out of him as his head banged against the floor with a loud thud. I raised myself up and grabbed Curtis by the thighs, bending him over so his dick was aimed at his face and spreading his legs real wide and then brought his sweet asshole up to my mouth. I tore into his watermelon red butt, just eating him out while keeping him pinned with my legs. Brotha man went crazy. You ever eat a man out until he blows a nut so hard it makes him fart? Curtis cut the cheese big-time, stinking up the whole room while his balls just unloaded, repeatedly, all over his chest and face and my legs. I had a mouthful of the most foul-tasting funk, but that wasn't enough to stop me from claiming my prize. While Curtis was still recovering from dumping that big wad, I raised myself up and slapped my dick against his hole, beating his pussy ass with my meat until it opened up, and then I shoved it slowly inside his soft, sweet hole, keeping his body bent over so his feet were pinned against his ears.

Damn, Curtis had a good ass! My dick slid in and out of his hole in a nice, smooth rhythm, slow enough to feel every volup-tuous caress of his tight hole around my long, thick, juicy dick.

His hole puckered as the head of my joint slid almost all the way out, not wanting to give up one tasty inch of my meat, sucking on it to keep it from leaving. But I pulled that bad boy out until the lips of his hole were smacking at my dick like a toothless granny trying to plant big, wet, sloppy kisses on all her grandkids. I made that hole beg to get more of my sweet dick, and then I fed it in slow, shoving it all the way into that hole in one smooth motion. When my balls slapped against his butt, I ground my hips hard into his ass, making my dick work his hole in big circles, widening that sucker and taking the brotha's breath away and making his toes curl up. I kept bending Curtis over until his dick was pointed straight at his mouth, and pumped his hole hard, just freaking on his ass, as the boy began making all sorts of strange, crazy sounds. I hit it, man; I hit that azz from side to side and front to back and all around the town, yo, until I could feel that nut rising up inside Curtis's butt.

Brotha man was in the zone too, working his ass to get the most out of the sweet dicking he was getting. Squeezing his cheeks to pull my dick in deep and wiggling his hole to make sure my joint hit all the right keys to unlock his inner 'ho. And all the while, that huge nut was just working its way out of Curtis's balls and down his big fatty, driving the boy out of his cotton-picking mind and making him bounce that ass better than a jiggy girl in a JayZ video. His legs started dancing, and I knew the boy wasn't going to be able to hold that nut much longer. I jammed my dick hard into his ass, digging it out deep and grinding my fat knob so tight the brotha's eyes popped open and bugged out so far I thought he was seeing the devil behind me or something. Curtis opened his mouth wide and started gagging for breath, and I felt that nut just explode out of his dick, pumping so much come into his gaping mouth that the boy was drowning in his own juice. It was so amazing to watch, my balls started heaving, and I pulled out of Curtis's ass and slipped off the jimmie just in time to add my jizz to the mix and keep the boy sucking on come until he was red in the face. If he'd died, it sure would have made an interesting case for *CSI*.

We hit it a few more times before Curtis just got wore out. I rode that boy hard and put him away wet; shit, steam was rising off his ass, and a thick froth of foam was dripping all down the back of his legs. Curtis started moaning "Fuck yeah, fuck me" and just wouldn't stop. It was kind of creepy, as a matter of fact, sending shivers up my spine and all as if the dude was playing me for some kind of fucking exorcist or something. I tried to get him to speak, but all the boy could seem to muster was a deep, low moan that had the water in the glass on the table by the bed vibrating. I quickly dressed, still dripping with sweat and slime myself, and beat a hasty exit as Curtis just lay on the bed, shaking, eyes closed, legs akimbo, fat dick squirting thick droplets of clear juice, moaning "Fuck yeah, fuck me" as if he were possessed by something.

In my haste to leave, I nearly knocked over this thugged-out brotha who was carrying a big bucket of chicken from the Colonel and all the fixings. It was wack, with chicken flying everywhere and the brotha cursing, stomping his feet and carrying on. I tried to give him some money to cover the damages, but the nigga wasn't having it. He was another fine Nubian prince, and even though he was mad and shit, I found him really attractive.

"So how we gonna solve this, bro?" I said, rubbing my crotch slowly for added emphasis. "You don't want money, so what do you want exactly?"

The fine mocha-hued brotha stopped in mid-tirade, and his big almond-shaped eyes followed every slight movement of my hands, raising deep creases in his forehead as they traced the outline of the big bone in my jeans. He had a slightly puzzled expression on his face, as if he couldn't quite make up his mind about something.

"Yo, bro, I'm willing to make it up to you," I continued, moving closer, only a few inches away from him in fact, near enough to feel the irregular panting of his breath. "Come on, homes, let's settle this quietly, man to man. I know we can find a way to make this situation satisfactory for the both of us. What do you say?" I could tell the brotha was interested: his nipples were hard and erect, like his dick, and both were making a statement about their intentions, even if the dude hadn't said a word.

"Yeah, well, maybe, okay, okay," he finally stuttered in a chocolate-melting baritone that dripped into my ears, slid down my chest, and flowed right out my dick in a thick, wet drizzle.

With a friendly smile, I extended my hand, and he shook it in a firm grip that left no doubt about his workout regimen. I matched his grip, and we stood there for what seemed an eternity but that only lasted a few seconds in real time, testing each other, our eyes locked in deep concentration, electrons exchanging information between us at the subatomic level, sending billions of data bytes streaming into a myriad of complex calculations as we each gauged what our next steps would be, neither one of us willing to be the first to break the connection. By a subtle mutual consent, we both let go at the same time, and then, as if on cue, we each bent down to pick up the mess of chicken littering the ground around us. We made small talk and even shared a good laugh or two as we recovered it all and then stood up, nearly bumping our foreheads together. I liked the way he felt, exuding a powerful, magnetic presence that was as compelling to me as the smell of Hai Karate on those passersby in the old TV Land commercials. I certainly felt drawn to his orbit and made no effort to resist his strong attractions.

Once inside his small room, I grabbed the bucket of chicken and took it into the bathroom to rinse off. The Original Recipe made out pretty good, but the Extra Crispy was a total loss. Fortunately, the sides were all right, so all in all, about three quarters of the brotha's dinner was still good enough to eat. While I cleaned up, Derryck stood in the doorway, directing and passing judgment on what pieces to keep and which to throw away. As I passed him the bucket, I couldn't help myself from reaching over and pinching the hell out of the big fat nipple protruding prominently through his thin wifebeater. Derryck yelped and almost dropped the chicken again, but in kneeling down to save it he also exposed the tops of his firm black butt, veritable mounds of dark chocolate that just screamed for a sticky coating of thick, creamy topping to put Almond Joy to shame. I definitely felt like a nut peeping those luscious cheeks. My hands were all over them, feeling deep inside his drawers and pushing his jeans down to his ankles before he knew what hit him.

I spread those meaty bubbles and licked his crack, circling my tongue around the edges of his hole and getting a full taste of his exquisite funkiness. By the time my tongue was buried in his ass, Derryck was using both hands to spread his cheeks extra wide, making sure I could get up in it all I wanted. Now, this was some finger-licking goooood eating! Derryck was grooving to the mojo and riding my tongue hard, working up a good sweat, when a loud banging on the door intruded on our flow.

"Damn!" I blurted out, lifting my slime-covered face from Derryck's moist crack.

"Yo, dawg, I almost forgot," Derryck replied apologetically as he righted himself and shuffled to the door, his drawers still around his ankles. "I invited this hot chick to knock some boots this evening." He bent down and pulled up his pants. "You wanna join us? We could make it an ill three-way?"

The pounding on the door was getting more insistent, and before I could reply, there, standing behind Door Number 3, was Shaynia, definitely looking the booby prize to the hot number already in my grasp. Damn, I wasn't expecting this to be *Let's Make A Deal,* and I certainly wasn't feeling Derryck's impersonation of a thugged-out Monty Hall in dreds.

"Oooh!" Shaynia giggled, her eyes wide as she took in the tableau of Derryck with his T-shirt pulled over his head exposing his solid abs, the bucket of chicken on the floor in the middle of the room, and me standing with one wicked mother of a bone protruding from my fly. "This looks like a fun game, can I play too?"

Shaynia waltzed straight up to me and stroked my dick, petting it fondly as it stiffened in response to her touch. "Ummm, I figured you'd know where to find the hot bois."

"You two know each other?" Derryck stuttered, his forehead scrunched up again in mild confusion.

"Yeah, we've met," I replied suavely, then looked at Shaynia, "and you can play as long as you follow the rules."

"Rules? What rules?" Shaynia asked, giggling as she jacked my dick.

"All players must be naked from the waist down."

"Oh? Well, in that case, I better get ready, huh?"

"Yeah, let's see what you got going on under that skirt, fly girl."

Shaynia let go of my throbbing member and then stood seductively in the middle of the room, swiveling her hips and throwing dramatic sexy poses at Derryck and me while accompanying herself to the tune of "Hey Big Spender." She shimmied out of her short skirt and then rolled the thong down her long legs and flipped it at me, landing a ringer on my bone.

"Oooh! What do I win!?" Shaynia screamed, jumping up and down and shaking her petite 34Bs and a big ole Bam dick, but way harder, that slapped against her thighs and stomach as she bounced. Derryck saw that meat swinging between her legs and lost his mind. That boy was on his knees and slurping so loud on that joint you'd have thought he was eating the Colonel's wings. Shaynia was surprised at first, but he must have hit the spot because girlfriend rolled her eyes shut and grabbed Derryck's head to push it down on her dick, fucking his face in deep, short thrusts. He undid his jeans so he could jack his meat while she pumped his face, and that really got me in action. I lifted Derryck up and pulled those pants off while he sucked Shaynia's dick. Then I greased up his flaky biscuit of an ass with some of the Colonel's honey and stuck my mean, hungry dick up his butt. To say it was sweet would be an understatement. It was off the hook. There was so much love in the room, it felt like church. Derryck was worshiping Shaynia's fat monster dick and I was worshiping Derryck's bubblicious booty and Shaynia was testifying at the top of her lungs as she was moved by the spirit.

It got so hot in that little room that the three of us were butt naked and sweating up a storm. Flipping it every which way that three horny fucks can get off by, knocking over furniture, breaking shit, just trashing the whole damn room in one full-on orgy of bodacious, balls-out freaking. Shaynia let me have some of that hard, tight ass of hers, and it was even better than she said it was. I could have hit that shit all day everyday for a month and never get enough of it. While I sat in the lone side chair, a big, ugly, stuffed monstrosity whose only value was as a platform for fucking, Shaynia slipped her deep ebony cheeks, with their firm dimples, over my dick and rode it up and down, playing elevator operator and stroking my dick until every vein was bulging to the point of bursting. Watching her ass work my joint was some sight, that smooth hole curling up around the edges as it went up my shaft and then flipping into a deep, insatiable ring as it slid down was turning me on big time. Shit, when she finally twisted herself around so she was facing me, telling me that was enough foreplay, girlfriend had stretched my dick to a good nine inches.

Now, sitting on my dick with her thirteen inches slapping against my belly while she smothered my face in her firm titties, Shaynia worked herself into a mind-numbing frenzy. Meanwhile, Derryck came up behind and sat on the back of the chair, his big balls resting on the top of my head as he fed Shaynia his eleven inch anaconda. We worked out that position for a long time, long enough for my chest and belly to be covered by a deep layer of Shaynia's thick, gooey pre-come and for my head to become soaked with a mixture of sweat from Derryck's balls and the excess nut he blew into Shaynia's mouth that she couldn't quite handle. Being the tit freak I am, I consoled myself with sucking on Shaynia's fat, stubby nipples until I thought I could taste the silicone from her implants. When I mentioned it to her later, she bitch-slapped me, screaming that I ruined her tits, until I could explain it was just a joke. Shit, I forgot girlfriend didn't have a funny bone.

Things went way over the top when both Derryck and Shaynia lifted me by the arms, carried me to the sofa and then proceeded to double-dick my ass, stuffing my butt with over a good two foot of meat. It was the most creative use of mashed potatoes I ever did see. It felt so damn good (the dick, not the Colonel's lumpy tots), I had to wonder why I didn't give it up more often. God knows how I took all that, since it's not something I do very much. Derryck slipped his big joint in first as he lay under me, then Shaynia stuffed her massive Johnson into what little space was left, and together they pried opened my hole so wide I swear if you had shined a light up in there it would have flashed right out my eyes. But the way the three of us worked each other over that night, I guess I was just thankful to be able to keep my guts from falling out of my ass by the time we finally collapsed from utter exhaustion. Derryck though got the worst of it, or maybe the best of it depending on your perspective. That boy's ass was dogged like a piñata on Cinco de Mayo; shit, it could have been mistaken for a manhole that lost its cover.

The next morning, as I stumbled out of Derryck's room while he and Shaynia were still fast asleep, her dick stuck deep in his ass, my dick dripping from one last sweet ride of Shaynia's man-pussy, I felt a powerful rumbling in my stomach that had me bent double as I trekked to my car. As I slid behind the wheel, wincing painfully as my sore ass settled into the seat, it dawned on me that I was hellified hungry. "Ummm," I thought while pulling out into traffic on another cloudy, gray day in LA, still sleepily rousing itself from the previous night's dreams of ol' skool debauchery, "some Roscoe's sure would be good right now; I think there's one over on Gower."

Men Out of Uniform

Somewhere up there in the cloudless, cerulean-and-mauve-tinted sky, God must be smiling, since the stunning fireball rising in all its majestic glory over the eastern horizon in front of me can only be described as the act of a contented divinity. As the four-hundred-and-twenty-five horses of the vintage red '67 Dodge Charger, with a big block 426 Hemi and 4-speed manual, rocketed over the Coronado Bay Bridge into San Diego proper, I was filled with an indescribable joy as I put on my shades and cranked up the radio, blasting Prince's "Little Red Corvette" at full volume. Maybe it was being surrounded by all the hunky men in Navy whites that seemed to spill out of every nook and cranny on Coronado Island. It was, after all, headquarters for two military bases, North Island and Coronado, home of the Navy SEALS. But then again, it might have been the hunky NCO I banged in the cockpit of his thirty-six-foot Grady-White Express, who had offered to take me fishing for big game the afternoon before.

If you can imagine slicing off a choice piece of the Mediterranean Coast, say that little area by St. Tropez, and plunking it down on the Pacific Ocean, then you have an idea of just how blessed is San Diego de Alcala. It's always beautiful outside and thus always a real drag to be stuck inside a hotel conference room listening to another in a long series of boring speakers droning on about whatever. I was staying at the Loews Coronado Bay Resort for a three-day workshop, but the lure of blue skies and deep-sea fishing were just too much to keep me sequestered in such refined, genteel luxury. At the lunch break on the first day, I bailed and, armed with the concierge's recommendation of a good skipper, went in search of Big Blues.

Charles, the captain, was a dark-skinned, good-looking, good-natured, big, diesel brotha, originally from Gatlinburg. He joined the Navy partly because it was a family tradition but mostly to get as far the hell away from the backwoods kitsch of Eastern Tennessee as humanly possible. He had traveled around the world on his various tours of duty, including the Gulf twice. Now he was looking forward to retiring soon to run a six-pack charter business, hauling refugees from suburban hell and conference-room gulags out on the *Bounding Main* for a few precious hours of sanctuary (at $750 a day, $500 a half-day, each, tips for the mate *not* included). For now, it was a part-time gig, and I was lucky to find him at the docks, since he had been told he might be called up for duty sometime that week. It was a bit of a shakedown cruise too, since Charles had only taken delivery of the late-model Grady-White just a couple of days before, so I got a *very* substantial discount off the regular fare despite being the sole passenger.

The Big Blues were said to be running about an hour or so offshore. Giant bluefin tuna are the largest of the tuna species, getting up to ten feet in length and weighing as much as 1,400 pounds. They are fast too, reaching speeds of twenty-five mph. When you have one on the line, you're in for the fight of your life because a Big Blue is the strongest fish in the world and he won't be punked by nobody. As we left Glorietta Bay and the dock behind, passed under the bridge, and rounded the horn of the island, Charles pointed out the various sights, including his ship, one of the Navy's fastest and most powerful aircraft carriers, sitting tranquilly against the bucolic backdrop of sleepy little Coronado. Soon we were in the open ocean, and Charles throttled up the three 250 Yamaha four-stroke engines, sending us booming over the light chop. It felt good to be out on the water, with the sun creeping just past its zenith, spreading a warm blanket of contentedness over all God's creatures.

We passed the time bullshitting, like guys do when they're in the company of other guys. We talked about boats, fishing, cars—Charles likes restoring old muscle cars from bygone eras—politics, religion, and "stuff." But not a word was said about the fair sex, since every fisherman knows it's bad luck to do so while fishing. You'll get skunked for sure. So that left room for a lot of dirty dick jokes along the lines of "An Irish guy, a Black guy, and an Indian guy go into a . . ." The cooler was stocked with beer, Colt 45 and Michelob being the choices, so we threw back a few brews to celebrate just being two cats able to enjoy such a magnificent day. Charles let me know he had some splits of Cold Duck if we got a good catch and some VSOP if we had a great catch. As it was, between the heat and the fresh salt air, the beers were doing a good job of keeping us loose.

Up ahead, to starboard, there was a big gathering of gulls and some frigate birds, which usually meant that bait fish were present. The birds were diving too, another good sign, so Charles eased back on the throttle and brought us in closer as I got the spinning rods ready. We were going to lay out some trolling lines and downriggers for the Big Blues once we got to the secret spot Charles had programmed into his GPS, but when the Fish Gods give you a freebie, you gotta seize it while you can. As Charles expertly maneuvered into position, it was a sight to behold: the sea was like a carpet of metallic blue, deep gold, emerald green, and fine silver for as far as the eye could see. You could have walked on the water. The surface was literally churning in frothy tumult as a huge school of herring, swimming for their very lives, was being attacked from below and on the flanks by voracious dorado and picked off from above by the aerial bombardment of the insatiable birds.

With the first cast of the spinning rod, I had a twenty-pound bull dolphin on the line (no, not Flipper: dorado is also known as dolphinfish and mahimahi). What a blast! The spinning rod only had ten-pound test, so it took some real skill to keep that sucker on the line and bring it in close enough for Charles to gaff and haul it on board. Dorado are a good fighting fish too, and they don't go down easy, so I really had my hands full working the spinners as we drifted with the feeding frenzy and made a number of good catches. We hauled in enough fish to fill nearly half the aft-deck fishbox: lots of popcorn (five to eight pounders), several hefty twenty to forty pounders, and a bunch in between. Charles was especially happy since he'd be able to pay for the day's fuel and then some with what he'd make selling the catch to local restaurants around Coronado. It was enough of an occasion for him to break out the VSOP early. For my part, I was kind of glad it was over, since my arms were nearly played out and the Big Blues were still in front of us, hopefully.

As we neared the secret hunting grounds, the GPS let out a soft bleeping sound, signaling that it was time to set the lines and get ready. We had two outriggers, two stern lines, and the two downriggers, giving us six chances at our quarry. Six infinitesimally small strands of clear nylon monofilament, with plastic feathered lures dangling at the ends of wire leaders in simulation of bait fish, dropped into the vastness of a big, deep, dark blue sea stretching from our little white boat uninterrupted to the far horizon in every direction. I guess if you looked at it rationally, deep-sea fishing is the irrational act of damn fools with more money than brains. All that ocean, six tiny lures and two guys half lit on beer and Courvoisier against a fish that weighs three-quarters of a ton, swims as fast as a Greyhound bus on the 405 at rush hour, and has a real attitude when stuck in the mouth by a sharp hook. Yeah, it may be a bit much, but hell is it fun.

With the lines set, all we could do was just sit and wait for the fish. Charles throttled the *Bounding Main* down to trolling speed, and we puttered along with the gentle swells, watching and waiting. A few more beers, a little more of the VSOP, a lot of sun, the rocking motion of the waves, the heat, and things got a little crazy out there.

"Man, I'm burning up!" Charles yelled out of the clear blue as I was just beginning to fade into a nice, deep slumber, stretched out full length on the cockpit bench. I jumped up, startled, just in time to see Charles strip off his clothes and jump buck nekkid into the water. Being an old hand at this game, I wasn't panicked about the captain abandoning ship in the middle of fucking nowhere. I could handle the boat, no problem. The only thing I was worried about was whether the nigga would foul up our lines just as a fucking big-ass muthafuckin' blue decided that this might be a good time to check out this here lure. Then I'd have to choose between that sorry-ass nigga and that damn fuckin' fish! It just wasn't fair to put a man in that position, you know what I'm saying?

As if underscoring my thought, one of the outrigger lines went zinging out of its clip and started spooling out fast and furious. "FISH ON!" I yelled frantically as Charles swam in lazy circles off to port. "Damn it! Get your ass back up here, nigga!" I ran and grabbed the line, plunking the butt of the rod into my fighting belt, and braced myself against the edge of the bench, waiting for just that split second when the fish pauses in its run to set the hook. With a forceful snap, I jerked the line back and could feel that we had something really hooked up good. The fight was soon on as Charles scrambled aboard and jumped into the helm, slowly reversing engines as I began to wind in the reel. It was big, but it didn't feel like a blue; nonetheless that fish whooped my ass good as it dived and then ran back at us, then darted first to one side of the boat and then the other, making me dodge the other lines as I walked all around the dickpit trying to keep it on the line. After a brutal twenty minutes of hand-to-hand combat that felt like six hours, I finally got it in close enough to make out that it was a four-or five-foot wahoo, maybe weighing close to fifty or sixty pounds.

Sadly, as we got the fish within gaffing range, Charles, still wet from his impromptu swim, dropped the gaff into the sea just as the wahoo made one last desperate lunge, breaking the line and swimming free. I was pissed. No, I was beyond pissed. I went fucking berserk. Now, Charles as I said was a big diesel brotha, 6-6, 6-8, maybe 245, 250 pounds, not fat but beefy. By contrast, I'm a little fuck, 5-11 and 175. My whole head could fit in just one of Charles's mitts, and for him it would have been no more of a challenge than holding a basketball with his fingertips. But that didn't stop me from hauling off and slamming my fist into his slippery, smooth, coal black chest, knocking the wind out of him so hard he dropped to the bench, stunned. I don't know why, it could have been the VSOP, but when I get mad like that, for some reason I get one mean hard-on, and seeing that big naked brute sitting down with his face at my crotch, well, I did what I do. I whipped out my fat dick and jammed it down his fucking throat. I pinched his wide, flat nose closed, making him open his mouth wider, and stuffed my dick all the way down his neck as he tried to breathe.

Whoa! Could brotha man take some dick, yo! I was cursing him out a new asshole and slapping poor Charles upside his bald, bullet-shaped head while fucking the shit out of his face. It felt so freaking good, it didn't even dawn on me to ask him if he was in the life, you know, don't ask don't tell. He calmly reached up, ignoring my pummeling as if it were just some minor annoyance, and put his massive hand inside my pants, throttled my balls until they were squealing, and pulled my long, hard dick even deeper into his mouth. Before long, Charles was in charge, stroking my dick so sweet with those thick, pink lips of his, making my dick a straw to suck the juice straight out of my balls.

He punched and probed the crack of my ass with his short, stubby fingers until I started to sing a different tune. I reached down and began softly stroking the big nipples on the tips of his floppy tits, and his monster anaconda dick snapped to full attention, the foreskin pulled tightly back from the bulbous light-skinned head. Shit, the nigga's dick was so big the damn color ran out before it got to the end. I was working his nipples hard, pinching and squeezing them to the point that Charles's heart was skipping a beat here and there, while bucking my hips between the warm, velvety smoothness of his mouth and his hard, bony fingers in my ass.

It felt so good getting my joint worked out by a man who knew how to suck a dick right that the heat just got so unbearable I had to strip down too. Charles's fingers were digging me out something fierce, trying to bust my nut, but I wanted some of his phat, diesel black ass before I gave up the juice. I pushed him onto his back on the bench and raised his tree-trunk legs into the air, spreading them to expose the sweetest-looking man-pussy. His hole was silky smooth, big, puckered, and when my dick just brushed up against it, it popped open wide and sucked that bone inside like a grouper snatching shad. His ass clamped tight around my dick and rode it hard and fast until we were both covered in foamy sweat. We were so deep into a smooth, nasty groove that the snapping of one of the downrigger lines went almost unnoticed. If the reel hadn't been clipped to the gunwale, a thousand dollars in tackle would have ended up in Davy Jones's locker along with the gaff.

I ripped my hard dick out of Charles's ass just in time to save the line and started frantically reeling it back in, trying to cut the slack enough to set the hook. Charles scrambled to the helm, and we were one hellacious team as we brought the situation under control. With a quick jerk, the hook was set, and, baby, this time we had ourselves a monster blue on the line. It was a serious thrill ride with more twists and turns and sudden drops and loop-de-loops than "Batman the Ride" at Six Flags. As I fought around the dickpit, Charles was running back and forth between the helm and the other lines, clearing them so as not to get us fouled up while also backing down on the fish and keeping us in the fight. It can be dicey working lines in a crowded dickpit, with sharp hooks flying about. But fighting a big-ass fish in the buff with a full-on boner just made the whole experience that much more titillating.

The Big Blue came around the port side close enough for us to get a good look at him. He was huge, not a record but about seven to eight feet long and well over six hundred pounds, and I looked at Charles as if to say, "How the fuck are we gonna manage this, bro?!" The blue seemed to sense our dilemma, because after fighting us for what felt like days, he started playing like he wanted to be caught, as if he was saying "Come and get me now, niggas!" while waving his fins in our faces. Even if we had a gaff big enough, bringing that much fish up over the transom with just the two of us could have swamped the boat or given us a hernia or some nasty combination of the two. As eager as I was to catch a giant bluefin tuna, reluctantly we had to face the fact that there was no way in hell we could get that big-ass fish into the cockpit. And forget about trying to stash it in the fishbox. So with one last mighty heave on the rod, I brought our prize alongside of the boat while Charles reached out and cut the line, setting the Big Blue free to fight another day.

As Charles watched the lucky bastard swim away, I took note of his well-proportioned ebony cheeks, deeply dimpled and scrunched into a big phat shiny ole bubble. My randy dick was instantly eager to finish the business it had started. Charles caught me looking at his naked ass, saw that no-nonsense bone, and just gripped the back of the boat and spread his legs, giving me an impish grin. Without a word, I just tore into his devil's food cakes something fierce. Ummm, ummm! I might not have gotten the big fish, but I was happier than a pig in slop nonetheless. By the time we pulled up to the dock back in Glorietta Bay, my backside was burned to a crisp and my dick was so raw I had to let it hang outside my shorts, draping my shirt to cover it up. Even though my hotel was only a short walk away, I readily agreed to take Charles up on his offer of a soothing rubdown with aloe vera and cocoa butter in the v-berth of the Grady-White's cozy cabin. It didn't hurt that my wicked sweet tooth would be able to get some more satisfaction, either. And besides, I always loved the taste of caramel and dark chocolate together.

The next morning, after a mostly sleepless night of knocking boots, Charles was called in for duty. It's a good thing he wouldn't be sitting at a desk, because I don't think the man could have done that for more than a few minutes at a time without messing his pants. As it was, Charles had to wear a jimmie just to keep from leaking down the front of his drawers every time his butt cheeks rubbed together. Oh, Charles got some payback, though, with that wicked snake of his, taking advantage of me while I was in the shower and all. Yeah, HE dropped the soap, and like a damn fool I bent over to pick it up, and he fucked me up. He said it was just to let me know that he wasn't a total bottom. Shit, if he'd known how many big-dicked brothas I've fucked who were total, 1,000 percent, down, punk, pig-ass bottoms and so quick to give it up they nearly broke their necks swinging those legs up into the air, he might have forgiven me for being a little bit confused and surprised when he began playing with my ass. At least I didn't slap the mess out of him too bad, and I did have to admit, brotha man knew how to throw that bad boy down.

Charles let me borrow one of his favorite rides so I could do some exploring of San Diego's hidden charms. He had even given me directions to one of his secluded hangs, a natural hot springs up in the Cleveland National Forest, just this side of the Anza-Borrego Desert, after he found out how much I love wilderness trekking. I sure was in need of a good, soothing soak, since all that fucking had every muscle in my body worked into a mass of confusion. Hopefully, the volcanic minerals in the piping-hot water would lessen the swelling from the beating I got by Charles's weapon of ass destruction too. I couldn't see how I'd deal with the flight home otherwise. The Dodge sure lived up to its name as it charged out Interstate 8 and then sliced through the curvaceous twists of Highway 79, up past Lake Cuyamaca, and glided into a soft landing in Julian worthy of a NASA space shuttle. I had heard that Julian was known for its apple pies and thought it might be a good place to stock up on some tasty treats.

As I pulled into the sleepy hamlet of Julian, so rustic in its charms I half expected to see little Laura Ingalls walking barefoot down the street, I could smell the sinfully delicious scent of fresh-baked pies wafting in the cool mountain air. My stomach rumbled in dour humor, reminding me that all I had eaten in the last twenty-four hours was some tangy hot ass and big black dick. They were sure good, but not exactly the kind of protein I'd need for the arduous hike in front of me. I parked the car and went in search of real food. Now, if you want to find the best, I mean the absolutely most perfect, apple pie, find yourself a Big Mama church lady and follow where she goes. It's easy enough to do in Julian, since it attracts a lot of Black visitors because of its historical importance. Blacks started settling the area probably as early as the end of the War Between the States. Frederick Coleman, a former slave, started San Diego's gold rush when he struck gold there in 1869, some twenty years after the famous gold strike at Sutter's Mill. Thus, lots of Black church groups and tour buses flock to Julian to see the spot where a freed slave struck gold.

It wasn't too long before I spotted a Real BIG Mama, leisurely perambulating in regal procession with her retainers in tow, sashaying along the quaint covered sidewalks, sniffing the air for just the right combination of cinnamon, brown sugar, apples, and crust. She came to rest in front of a small shop in an alley just off Main Street. The way she closed her eyes, flared her nose, and breathed in the heavenly aroma of warm, fresh-out-da-oven pie said all that needed to be said. As Big Mama and her retinue entered the store, I was hard on their heels. While the ladies took their time deciding what tasty morsels to sample, I took note of the hunky Latino dude sweeping up in the back of the shop. He was about medium height, slim, but with nice muscular arms, a deep cocoa color, shiny black hair, a scruffy goatee that gave him that dreamy, just-woke-up vibe, and stunning gray eyes that sparkled like silver. "Seems Big Mama has a nose for more than just pie," I thought to myself.

The guy flashed me a knowing smile that made my pants wet. My mouth watered as I gazed longingly at the Latino dude's tight, round ass, perfectly framed by the opening of the long white apron he wore. My sore dick was furtively poking hard at the edges of my shorts as if it wanted a better view of the guy too. I was so lost in impure thoughts that I was startled out of my skin when from behind me a deep baritone, Barry White–voice whispered sultrily into my ear:

"You like dat? You ain't had nutin' 'til you had mine."

I whipped my head around to see a tall, trim, gorgeous black guy in olive fatigues flashing his pearly whites and batting his long, thick eyelashes at me. Damn! Is this Heaven or what? Out of the corner of my eye, I also saw his friends standing near the entrance, a short yellow bro and a big red brotha, laughing and poking each other as they pointed at the two of us. They weren't bad either, cut from the same angelic cloth that seemed to have favorably settled in that small, nondescript storefront in quaint little Julian. The heavy male pheromones instantly heated up the place to the point where the church ladies were beginning to primp and preen, chattering and clucking, trying to get some of that chocolate lust to flow their way. Even the Latino guy was doing more looking and crotch grabbing than sweeping, going so far as to bend over on some pretext and then crane his neck to make sure we were taking note of his special assets. There was so much wood going around you'd have thought it was a fucking forest.

My inquisitor, Gil, was a gunnery sergeant stationed just up the way at Miramar. His two companions, Bernie, the high-yellow cat, and Rufus, the handsome red dude, were drill instructors visiting from Camp Pendleton. Semper Fi, baby, Semper Phyne! We chatted amiably for a spell, getting the QT on what was what, even throwing the church ladies some love to keep them twittering all the way on the long bus ride home. The Marines were headed to a favorite swimming hole, and I told them about the hot springs, and as we exchanged more details, it became evident that we were all going more or less to the same place. It didn't take long for us to make it a joint expedition. We loaded up on sandwiches and apple pie, and gave the Latino guy a good long, last, lustful look. As we stepped out into the street heading to our cars, he came running after us and asked if he could tag along. It seems his shift had conveniently just ended. Yeah, right. I quickly offered him a ride in my car, to the good-natured jiving of my new comrades, who rolled their eyes, whooping and hollering, slapping each other on the back and reminding me to keep my eyes on the road and my hands on the wheel since the road ahead was steep and full of curves.

We caravanned out of Julian in two cars, the Marines in front, heading due east on Highway 78 toward Scissors Crossing and made a right turn onto forlorn Sweeny Pass Road. Juan said it was warm, which it was, in fact it was damned near scorching hot, and removed his shirt, giving me the pleasure of viewing the fine little beads of sweat rolling down his chiseled, bronze-colored chest and six-pack abs, several shades lighter than his face and arms, and totally hairless except for a thick trickle of black fur that ran from the center of his chest down into his pants. I could also see the outline of the thick bone he was sporting poking down the leg of his tight jeans. He looked at me with those silver eyes, smiling cagily, and reached over to feel my crotch as I tried to keep the car on the right side of the road. Juan was a wicked bugger, for sure, unzipping my shorts and pulling out my throbbing hard-on, stroking it and getting it all wet with juice before sucking the mess out of it.

With one hand on the wheel and the other down Juan's pants, fingering his hairy asshole, I was concentrating hard on driving right down the middle: of the lane, Juan's throat, and his butt. Of course, that was proving difficult since up ahead, Rufus and Bernie were taking turns mooning me, pressing their beautiful red and yellow globes up against the rear window and spreading their cheeks to flash me glimpses of their hot holes. I was on the verge of blowing a huge wad by the time we got to the turnoff, an unmarked and unnamed dirt track that crossed the road and went deep into the forbidding desert terrain. We drove just a short distance along the track, stopping at a steep, sandy rise just out of sight of the road. The Marines got out of their car and began getting out their gear. But Juan wasn't budging without tasting my load, and I was only too happy to indulge him. Seeing us still in the car, Bernie, Rufus, and Gil came to investigate the holdup and, seeing what was going down, whooped it up good as they stood on opposite sides of the car, leaning into the windows and leering with those big shit-eating grins to watch Juan finish me off.

They all had their dicks out, jacking away as they watched. The sight of Gil's uncut blue-black pipe, just beyond the reach of my mouth, and Bernie's big yellow stick poking inside the passenger window, and Rufus's thick red tube steak right alongside, and Juan's mammoth cocoa pinga jerking next to me, pushed me over the edge. I fired a bolt of thick jizz that had Juan choking as he tried to swallow it all. Gil popped a fat load that flew right at my face, landing mostly in my mouth. I loved his salty nut so much I pumped another big wad into Juan's throat even before he could finish the first. Bernie got off a load that landed on Juan's back and side, while Rufus blasted his clear across the car to hit me on the side of the head just as Juan shot a messy chunk all over the dashboard. That was just the warm-up. Once we got on the trail, we stripped naked and slapped ass all the way to the springs.

The 4WD track came to an abrupt end about two miles or so from where we parked the cars. Then it was a mile of scrambling across loose rocks on an unmarked, undulating trail to Vallecito Creek, and another mile along the creek to the secluded hot springs, a big, bowl-shaped pool hewn out of the rock and set in a ledge overlooking the creek and perfect for soaking, sunning, and sexing. In a precious sliver of shade on the edge of the pool, the five of us got into a multicolored daisy chain of sucking dick and eating ass. Besides the gentle bubbling of the springs that fed the pool and the soft gurgle of water spilling down the creek, the loud slurping and moaning of five horny dudes echoed off the little amphitheater of rocks that encircled us. I was working Gil's thick pipe for all I was worth, my jaws aching with the force of that foot-long joint banging the back of my throat. I felt Bernie's tongue greedily digging me a new asshole, while his hands jacked my fat eight-incher. Gil was enjoying Juan's tasty nine-inch chorizo while fingering his humpy butt. Meanwhile Rufus was pumping his thick seven-inch dick hard down Juan's hungry throat as he ate out Bernie's choice bootay.

The action shifted into overdrive when Juan squatted on Gil's dick, riding it up and down like one of those horses on a carousel pole. Watching Juan's cocoa cakes being reamed out by Gil's midnight blue–black meat was a sight to behold. It got Bernie so hot he stuffed his duo-toned eight-inch dick down Juan's throat and fucked his face in big, deep strokes that had his big yellow ass cheeks bouncing that voodoo rhythm. That's when Rufus and I made tracks to be the first to get into Bernie's badonkadonk highass. I'd have made it, but Rufus pushed me into the pool as we were getting to our feet, the bastard. I scrambled out of the superheated water and just rammed my stiff brown dick into Rufus's hard cheeks clear up to my balls and slapped the hell out of his butt as I dicked the brotha down something fierce. The moaning was awesome with all that backfield in motion. When we came, I know they must have heard it back down in Julian, 'cause it frightened every bird, bat, and beast within miles of that little canyon, causing them to scramble for dear life thinking they might be next.

We got really busy after that, slipping into one permutation of combinations after another, working every hole to within a fraction of its tolerances. It got so freaky that we didn't even notice when a group of would-be soakers stumbled upon our five-man dick train and then left just as fast as their legs could carry them. The only reason we knew they were there was because one of them dropped their rucksack in their haste to leave. While Juan was digging out Bernie's hole with his cocoa dick, I was banging on Juan's sloppy butt like a dog in heat, amazed at how tight he was despite taking almost three feet of dick up in there. His ass was so comfortable, cozy, warm, and inviting my joint set in for a good long stay. The deeper I fucked him, the better it felt, and I was more than a little jealous of Gil's big dick, knowing that he got some good stuff scraping the bottom of that honey pot of Mexican ass. Still, I drove my dick as far into him as I could, enjoying all the sweetness my randy bumblebee could collect.

My balls were on the verge of sliding into Juan's ass just as he came, sending a static charge of electricity up through my dick and into my ass. I never came so hard in my life; the way my body was shaking and carrying on, you'd have thought I was some old guy with the palsy. Juan's ass was so fine I didn't think anything could be better than that. But my eyes opened just in time to see Gil's coal black cheeks dancing as he came while piston-fucking Rufus into a dazed stupor, the drool flowing out of that boy's mouth as if Gil's juice had overfilled his hole. "You ain't had nutin' 'til you had mine," Gil had whispered into my ear back in the pie shop. Looking at those rock-solid cheeks, I got a sudden, voracious appetite for hot, sticky chocolate buns. I rolled out of the grip of Juan's hole with more than a little difficulty as he didn't seem to want to let go of my dick.

Gil was bent over, hands on his knees, breathing hard as he recovered from the pounding he had just given poor Rufus. His ass was shiny with sweat, looking like a piece of finely sculpted obsidian, reflecting the waning sunlight in bright glowing orbs on each cheek. I moved between his legs and pushed the blunt, thick head of my dick against his tight hole. It didn't take much pressure. Ali Baba had a harder time getting into his cave than my dick had invading Gil's hole. "Open Sesame, nigga!" Gil's ass was a smooth, silky tunnel of unearthly delights, sucking on my joint so soft and sweet it stiffened an extra three-quarters of an inch. In one gentle slide my dick was in deep, and Gil began rolling his hips and stroking on my jones in a lazy motion that was reminiscent of being gently rocked by a light Caribbean trade wind while swinging in a hammock. Ahhhhhh! I felt whatever tension was left in my body from fighting fish and sexing Charles just melt right out of my pores and fall like the sweat dripping off my brow to land in a cool puddle at my feet. This was some good ass, and Gil served it up right.

I reached around and held his solid body in my arms, caressing his thick nipples and pinching them until Gil was singing like a banshee. As his tits were being played, Gil's ass pulsated in fits and starts, sending spasms of ecstasy all up and down my dick, right into my spine, and making the top of my head tingle as if lightning was flashing just above me. I was losing all control; if you'd have asked me at that moment "What's your name?" I'd have drawn a total blank. The raw, primal spirits were leaping out of the marrow of my bones now. Obliterating any shred of civilized culture that I possessed. The beast in me pushed Gil down on his hands and knees, placed its hands on his back to arch his butt higher into the air, and then straddled him, just fucking the goddamn fucking holy shit out of his ass. The shock of my body slamming against his butt drove Gil's face right down into the dirt. He reached back and grabbed his butt, spreading his cheeks wider, screaming, just howling at the top of his lungs, "FUCK ME! DAMN IT! FUCK MY BLACK ASS, NIGGA! FUCK IT! FUCK IT! NIGGA! FUCK DIS SHIT!"

I didn't think I could fuck a man any harder than I was fucking Gil. But when Juan eased in behind me and shoved his fat prick up my ass, adding his weight to mine, Gil was jerking and screaming like something out of a horror movie, as if the devil himself were being reamed out of his ass and loving every deep thrust of dick sent his way. It was off the fucking chain! Juan was gripping me tight as he banged my ass in synch with my dicking of Gil, and the feeling of that big Mexican sausage scraping me out worked up a nut so big I could feel it clogging my balls. Bolts of pure energy penetrated every cell of our linked bodies, exchanging essences between us clear down to the level of our DNA. It was like being able to inhabit three bodies simultaneously, as if we had all merged into one giant mass of flesh and blood. While we were going at it, even Bernie and Rufus couldn't escape the sexual pull of our powerful black hole, and they plugged themselves into the melee too, with Bernie ramming his big yellow dick into Juan's ass and Rufus stuffing his red bone into Bernie's.

As the sun sank behind the mountains, plunging the pool into an ethereal gloaming, a supernova of come exploded, lighting up the canyon and sending the five of us sprawling into the pool and against the rocks in a deep satisfaction that left our balls shriveled, our dicks limp, and our asses beyond sore. We sat in the soothing warmth of the hot spring for a long time, until the stars and moon came out in a cacophony of splendor that rivaled the exquisite debauchery to which we had surrendered all hope. Only then did we finally break out our provisions and indulge in a well-earned feast by moonlight.

"So," Gil asked proudly, holding a half-eaten slice of pie in his hand and giving me that "What did I tell you?" look.

"Ummm," I said playfully as Juan came up beside me, toying with my dick under the water, "I'm not sure. I might need to have another taste to be absolutely certain." Juan nodded his head vigorously as Gil, giggling, slapped at the surface of the pool, sending cascades of hot water splashing all over me and Juan.

"Damn!" Rufus sighed, rousing Bernie from a light slumber. "Fasten your seatbelt, dude, it's going to be a bumpy night!"

Vale of Cashmir

What is a "hot ass"? A really *hot* piece of ass? I'm talking about the kind of ass that makes you forget your own name. What makes an ass that hot? I think it has something to do with the game you play to get it. You know the one, the game of infinite patience, bold daring, and cunning maneuver. A game of chance that requires skill to pursue your objective with solitary focus, undisturbed by minor sacrifices and unexpected reversals of fortune. It's the game you play where you hide your strengths in plain sight and your weaknesses are an open book. If you play the game and win, victory is sweet. If you lose, well, there's always next time. Either way, it makes the ass you hunger for, long for, lust for, that much more blistering when, finally, you can claim it as yours.

The drummers were down the hill, in their circle, pounding out tribal rhythms whose words had long ago been forgotten, back before there was even a memory of the homeland, but which nonetheless had the power to ignite that fragment of antiquity in our bones, whose resonance got the blood in our veins to boil with the familiar even still. The air was alive with the sounds of a lost diaspora. Gentle breezes carried the scent of frangipani, ginger, spice, and sweet girls gyrating to the steel pans, even though I was still some distance from the trailing lines of marchers celebrating their island heritages and shared experiences in the new world. Above me, with stern gazes, the Grand Army of the Republic, frozen for all time in triumphant procession, gave mute witness to the dizzying throngs milling about their feet, grilling plantains, roasting corn, frying acra, dusting salt on sweet-potato fries. Celebration and Triumph. Here was the crossroads of victory, and before me lay the field of battles yet to be fought. I was ready. I was ready to taste victory. I was ready for some hot ass.

As I entered the park, taking the overgrown wooded trail on the left, the other combatants were beginning to gather in preparation for the game. To look at them, you'd think the whole world was converging for this Olympian struggle to be waged, mano a mano, until only one stood victorious over the rest, broken and defeated, subjugated to the winner's capricious whims. There were old granddads, their white hair symbols of their survivorship through many such battles, who slipped away from their sons and daughters and grandbabies to get another fix, another jolt of adrenaline, that only playing the game can slake. Over there, some young thugs, passing around a blunt and a 40, steeling themselves for the trials to come and banking on their hard, lean bodies to pull them through if things went down. In front of me, on the right, some buppie cats, trying to look comfortable while being overdressed in Stacy Adams loafers and Dolce & Gabbana shirts, slumming on the down low and sipping courage from silver flasks. As I came to the steep slope that dropped down into the Vale, I took note of the motley crew, single and in small groupings, young, old, fat, thin, Dominican, Trinidadian, Honduran, Grenadian, Panamanian, Jamaican, Guyanese, Barbadian, Boricua,

Haitian, the great grandchildren of the Siboney, Arawak, and Carib, all the proud and fair specimens of the bounty of the Indies, and those tourists who longed to be there. I was ready. I could take them all.

The sun was slowly setting, not in much hurry to give the cover of darkness to the game. This was my favorite time of day, since it allowed me to see the setup of the board, to assess the character of the players, to look for signs that might indicate a line of weakness that could most profitably be exploited. As much as I enjoyed playing the game, if I could get the inevitable over with quickly, the longer I could savor my prize. The Vale was full tonight. The parade always brought out a big crowd. The players started to take their places. I saw him in the distance. Yeah . . . you, homes. You, G, standing in the back with your retainers beside you in sworn allegiance to protect their king. "I see you stand like greyhounds in the slips, straining upon the start."
PAWN TO QUEEN FOUR
"The game's afoot."
KNIGHT TO KING'S BISHOP THREE
"Cry 'Havoc!' and let slip the dogs of war."
The families, with their Labs carrying their own leashes and colicky babies in strollers, were unaware of the happenings on this field, being so far removed from their contrived domesticity.
PAWN TO QUEEN'S BISHOP FOUR
But sometimes, giving flimsy excuses about having to get milk for the baby, the young father loses his way amongst the gnarled trunks of stately oaks only to find himself here, again, just a bystander, sure.
PAWN TO KING'S KNIGHT THREE
The Gen-X brats playing Frisbee on the rolling lawn adjacent to the Vale claim not to know what goes on back here, except when they must chase an errant throw, which rolls to a stop at the

feet of some guy with a menacing demeanor, rough trade, just the way they like it.

KNIGHT TO QUEEN'S BISHOP THREE

Sometimes things get deadly in the Vale. But even the chalked outlines of recent casualties aren't enough to keep the true playas away from the game. They know the odds and accept the risks as the price one pays for the hope of victory.

BISHOP TO KING'S KNIGHT TWO

The opening maneuvers tell much about the strategy of the combatants. Who is looking for something, and who is looking to be found. What is for sale, and what is given freely.

PAWN TO KING FOUR

You learn to read the signs, because everyone here is signaling something, everyone, and you better learn quickly because there are consequences to be paid for misreading what is so clear to everyone else.

CASTLING

The Vale is no place for kids, and yet some do make their way into its midst, far too old at such tender ages to be entirely innocent of what awaits them there, as if deliberately chasing that which they know to be forbidden.

PAWN TO KING FIVE

But the game is like that, inviting those who know to enter into the labyrinth of their own desires to seek out the fleeting touch of one who will make them complete, for just that moment, forgetting the shame that comes later. There are no innocents here.

KNIGHT TO KING ONE

To read the strategy, you have to look into their eyes and see what lies beneath, only then will you know, only then can you be sure that they are in the game, only then can the truth, a bastard child if ever there was one, be known.

PAWN TO KING'S BISHOP FOUR

Leaning sexily against a tree trunk in studied nonchalance, fingers thrust into belt loops to hide your overconfidence. Gazing unsteadily from beneath a battered baseball cap slung too low on your shaved head—yo, G, you think I'm going to fall for that move?

PAWN TO QUEEN THREE

Fischer didn't, and he was one of the few who could play the King's Indian from the black side and wipe the field with his opponent. It's a classic game, G, and I've seen all that before. Come on; keep it interesting for me at least.

BISHOP TO KING THREE

The lines are forming as the pieces move into place; the field is getting crowded, and the darkness that was so long in coming has finally settled over the Vale, obscuring play, making it a game of shadows, which is fitting since so many men here would not be caught in the full light of day.

PAWN TO QUEEN'S BISHOP FOUR

The drums are silent now, but the pounding of our collective pulses more than makes up for their absence. The blood has picked up the beat, rekindled in its hunter's garb, smelling the scent of the prey and eager for the chase.

PAWN TO QUEEN'S BISHOP FIVE—TAKES PAWN

First blood. It won't be the last sacrifice. Before the night is over, the carnage will cover the field. By morning, only the discarded remains of Magnums and Rough Riders, stained underwear, roaches, empty bottles, nickel bags, and lost pride will give silent testimony to the fallen.

KNIGHT TO QUEEN'S BISHOP THREE

When a man has *that* hunger, when he needs what only another man can satisfy, he'll do anything, stop for nothing, to get it. That's the weakness that I like to exploit. If you want power over another man, the best advice I can give you is to control *your* desires, suppress *your* appetites, and then tease him with the very thing he can't, or won't, live without.

PAWN TO QUEEN SIX—TAKES PAWN
You feed him just enough of what you got that he gets that taste all down inside him. Then you stand back and let the poison do its work. In time, he'll be rolling on the ground at your feet, begging for the tender mercy of your dick like a bitch in heat, howling for that dick in your pants, his guts burning with a fire hotter than Hell, needing your fat prick to hose the nigga down.

PAWN TO QUEEN THREE—TAKES PAWN
In the Vale, a man learns to feed when the opportunity presents itself. A nigga on his knees is an easy mark, and once he's down, he won't come up. When the frenzy starts, not even a shark is safe from its own.

KNIGHT TO KING FOUR
Some heavy shit going down out here. Was that a knife? Fucking crackheads getting too frisky over there; be careful, bro. Damn, homes, how you gonna get back to the Bronx without your pants? Yeah, papi, suck the meat off that bone.

BISHOP TO KING'S BISHOP FOUR
Man, it's crazy out here now. Cats be humping and dawgs be pumping, shit be flying and homies be crying, jack. Dip my stick in this coochie over here, tag dat phatty over there. Yeah, homes, bust it good, bust it hard, bust it like you just don't care. Man's got to mark his turf or lose all title to his claim.

KNIGHT TO KING'S KNIGHT THREE
Now that the circuit of the upper course, the one with the scraggy hedges and abandoned ponds overrun with the masses in their ecstasies, has been run, and after passing through the lower course, with its manicured maze of gardens hiding unspeakable sins and restored fountains splashing psalms to drown out the grunts of the damned, the Vale descends into the lower depths, like Dante's Inferno.

BISHOP TO KING THREE
Down here, the rules get fuzzy, like the shadows lurking be-

hind the forms of men hiding in the deep growths. If you can't see in the darkness, then you shouldn't come down here. This is exclusive territory, boy; only the fittest survive in this man's jungle.

KNIGHT TO KING'S BISHOP THREE

There are snakes in the tall bush too, big snakes, anacondas. It's nothing but depraved shit in there. You can't see squat, but those slithering bastards can see your ass real good. Fuckin' rude Jamaican shit in there. If one gets you, the rest just huddle around, sniffing for scraps until there's nothing left worth bothering over.

QUEEN TO QUEEN'S BISHOP TWO

What da fuck!? You out o' yo cotton-pickin' mind, nigga!? You think you can take MY ass!? Okay, punk, let's see what you got. I'm going to back this ass so far up your fool self, I'll suck your face into my balls, jack, and you'll have to look out my dick like a telescope to see. Come on, nigga, is that the best you can do? You punkin' out on me? Shit! Just like you big-dicked fools, think you got it going on, but Daddy knows what you want and how to serve it up good. Get them legs up, punk; Daddy's going to drive this fat prick so deep inside your ass you'll have to blow your nose to take a shit!

QUEEN TO QUEEN'S KNIGHT ONE

At the bottom of a steep ravine that leads to the edges of the zoo, there's a quieter place for those needing a break from the frenzy. But don't get too comfortable; you're still in the Vale and all that that implies. And for God's sake, whatever you do, don't go in that tunnel at the edge of the slope unless you're packin'.

PAWN TO KING FOUR—TAKES PAWN

Yo', homes, got a light? Thanks. Yeah, this is some good shit. Want a toke? Naw, it's been unreal tonight, man. For real? You were in on that shit? Heh, heh, yeah, I busted a good one on that shorty too. You seen that high-yellow dude? If you want some good shit check that cat out, man. Damn, homes, this shit is making my joint scream. Can you help a brotha out? Ah, fuck, yeah, homes . . . just like that, yeah . . . take that dick . . . ah yeah, suck it, homes . . . suck it . . . oh yeah . . . that's it, yeah . . . oh fuck . . . oh fuck, yeah . . . I'm a bust it, homes . . . bust it good, yeah . . . yeah . . . oh shit, yeah, shit, mothafucka, shit. Whew, that was some good head, man, thanks. See ya round. Take care of yourself, yo? It's crazy out there.

PAWN TO KING'S BISHOP FIVE

Easy, easy, slow down, you're too big to take like that. What's that sound? What fool sticks a zoo in the middle of a park!? Oh, that's it, yeah, it feels good like that, yeah, real good. They got any lions or tigers or bears in there? Fuck, man, you fuck good. Hey, dawg, I don't think I can do that. No, dawg, one nigga at a time is all I can handle. Yo, dawg, I said . . .

PAWN TO KING FIVE

In the Vale, resistance is futile. After all, why else are you here if it wasn't to submit? Nobody asked you to come in here. There was no gun to your head when you took the turn down that path. If you wanted it nice and easy, you should have stayed up top. Down in here, this is where it gets real. No punks allowed. If you ain't got no protection, it's your own damn fault, nigga.

PAWN TO KING SIX—TAKES BISHOP

There is no wind, and even if there was, no leaves rattling in it could make that sound. That slappin', slippin', slidin', slammin' sound of niggas freakin'.

One feels so good you have to have another, and then another, and then another, until you become one of us, one of the denizens of the Vale. Some come here only after the parade, others once a week, regular, like church on Sunday, dick on Wednesday. Then there are those who are here every day. Those are the ones to watch out for. Those are the ones who have lost their souls, children of the darkness, legions of the damned, vampires of the dick.

There is no magic potion in your favorite botanica to protect you once you fall in with them.

PAWN TO KING'S BISHOP SIX—TAKES KNIGHT

Well, well, well, look what the cat dragged in! Fancy meeting you in a place like this. Come here often? Does she know? No, of course not, I got your back, jack. Uh, you do know it'll cost you, right? Uh, I'm not feeling you, bro. Uh, well, maybe we can work something out, then. Damn, nigga, why didn't you give me some of this before? Shit, this ass is phine, mothafucka! Yo, you know me better than that, bro, I told you I got your back. Hey, call me, I'd like to hit that again sometime. Naw, bro, I said I wouldn't, so I'm not going to do you like that. You going to call me, right?

PAWN TO KING'S BISHOP THREE—TAKES PAWN

Ah, there he is again, the guy from before, the one with the shaved head and lean abs slowly going soft, in the baggy jeans hung low enough to tease even the most hardened playa. Yeah, I know you see me too. Your boys look worried, G, and believe me they have reason to be concerned. The music has resumed, and the danse macabre is once again in full swing.

PAWN TO KING'S BISHOP FOUR

I am a relentless stalker. I can track my prey through water, mixed in with a herd, in dense underbrush, and without light. How do I accomplish this, you ask? It's the smell of fear. Each man's scent is unique, and I'm well attuned to distinguish it. Call it my peculiar gift. I've had my eye on you for a while, G, and now it's time to set the trap.

PAWN TO KING'S BISHOP FOUR

In a darkened clearing, they come face-to-face, unexpectedly, neither one of them willing to make the first move. A Mexican standoff? Their breathing is heavy, labored, expectant. If one goes for it, he better be quick, because you know the other is a fast draw. In the languid stillness buzzing with the sounds of a million insects lost in mating dances, you can feel the beads of sweat rolling down his brow, blurring his vision as it falls into his eyes, but he doesn't dare blink. The other's lips twitch as sweat drips from his fingertips, falling like gentle rain on the hard dirt, falling softly like the tears he dare not shed.

KNIGHT TO KING'S BISHOP THREE

Others, sensing the coming storm, begin to close in tightly around them, the better to see the action, feel the heat, maybe get in a lick or two themselves. No backing out now. The pent-up lust in the body of the crowd flows into the clearing, filling in the spaces between them, wrapping them in its menace, making them extensions of its wantonness.

BISHOP TO KING TWO

Circling like tigers in a cage, eyeing each other for just the right place to sink their claws so as to do maximum damage, trying to keep their flanks as far out of the other's reach as possible, baring their teeth, blowing stale breath dank from the rotted flesh of the previously unlucky as they roar their intimidations to rattle in the other's ears. The crowd presses tighter, more insistently, passions rising for the bloodletting to begin.

BLACK ROOK TO KING ONE

Suddenly, without warning, they leap simultaneously into the breach, fur flying, flesh ripping, the blood flowing like rivers. Here and there from along the edges of the crowd someone gets pulled into the melee, unexpectedly finding that its intensity is far more than they had hoped for, but now they're trapped in the twin jaws of a hellish fate, disemboweled and dismembered to the taunts and cheers of the gallery. It's raw, primal, feral, and beautiful in its way. But it isn't an orgy. Niggas don't do orgies. There are no orgies in the Vale.

KING TO KING'S BISHOP TWO

Now you move. Do you see it coming, G? No, I don't think so. Your posse gives you a sense of invincibility. That's why you feel you can taunt me with your fleeting smiles, teasing me with your ebony eyes as you dart behind the bulwark of their defenses. I want your ass, nigga, and no posse can save you.

ROOK TO KING THREE—TAKES PAWN

Even in the nebulous gloom of these forlorn reaches of the Vale, the yawning mouth of the Tunnel stands out in its inky desolation. Like a black hole, it lures objects into its grip, and once inside, the density of the wickedness therein snuffs out whatever pleadings they might have made. Standing on this side of the Tunnel, the stillness that ushers forth from it is oppressive and weighs upon one's body even before the pull of its gravity.

ROOK TO KING ONE

No one who has ever been inside the Tunnel has ever acknowledged it, leaving only a mystery about what takes place in there. If one is careful, and doesn't get too close, and stares into the void long enough, they say you can see things in there moving about, specters without form or substance committing acts of the gravest sin.

BLACK ROOK TO KING ONE

What da hell you lookin' at!? You like the way I'm dickin' this mothafucka's booty? You want some of this here? Yeah, nigga, this is some big meat here; you think you can handle all dat? This nigga didn't think he could either, but look at him now. Shit, he's so loose he'll have to stuff his drawers in his asshole to keep his shit from falling out. Yeah, stick your dick in his mouth; he likes to take it at both ends. This nigga can take some dick, can't he? Shit, homes, we got us a nigga on a dick spit, now! Heh, heh, yeah boy, reminds me of bar-b-cues back home in Leasburg, North Carolina. I think it's time to turn this meat, homes, so he gets done all over, heh, heh. Yo, I'm feeling him all right; the nigga's getting ready to bust a nut. Faster, homes, stuff it down his throat, yeah, that's it, get it in there good. Oh shit, I'm a bust it now, homes, let's fill this nigga up. Damn, that was some good shit, homes. You ready to take this soldier now? Yeah, spread them cheeks wide, homes, you got a real man now. Damn, homes, you got a tight ass! Shit, I haven't had a country ass this tight since I left Roxboro. Where you from, boy?

BISHOP TO KING'S BISHOP THREE

You sense it, don't you? Your posse builds a wall to protect their king. Tight formation, steady now, what's that sound? Sounds like a stampede! What? Over where? Who? Damn! Run, nigga! Pigs on horses coming down the ravine! Shit! Not that way, Smokey's on the ridge! Run! Faster! The Tunnel, G, the Tunnel! Hold up here, shorty! Damn, boy, they got a shitload of niggas tonight! They'll be gone now, got their quota. Fuck, that was close! Hey, where's your posse now, G?

ROOK TO KING SIX—TAKES BISHOP

Even on the threshold of its infinite darkness, there is a palpable chill that emanates from within its depths and clings to the body with such penetrating force that the fingertips are soon on the verge of numbness. It is as if your life is being drained from your body while you are conscious of the effect. As the dread encloses its grip around your heart, making it beat faster, harder, louder, the chill begins to work on your mind. It is not a question of whether anyone could hear you scream anymore, but rather, whether you could scream at all.

ROOK TO KING THREE—TAKES ROOK

The ground beneath your feet is broken, uneven, wet. You sink a few inches into the oozing muck, but before you can reverse your steps, you find yourself stuck. As you try to lift your foot, the muck threatens to pull your shoe off; what to do? Vaguely, you hear sounds in the void, muffled, first one, then another, not close, but not far away either. The slime oozes inside your shoes. It's cold, ice cold, and yet this is still the middle of summer. The panic rises in your chest and all you can focus on is not falling down, please God, don't let me fall down! Don't let me fall down, please, please, please don't let me fall.

ROOK TO KING SIX—TAKES ROOK

With piercing screeches, winged things brush past your ears from out of the depths, fluttering for the briefest of moments right in your face, startled by your presence and driving you blindly deeper into the void. Stumbling for traction in the muck, you flail helplessly at the legacy of images reflected in the shadows of your eyes. You hear them, not close, but they are not far away, either.

KING TO KING THREE—TAKES ROOK

Frightened and disoriented in the gloom, struggling to get your footing in the treacherous quicksand of mud and debris, blinded by the fear that surges from all your senses, you fail to see the beached remains of that tree, washed into the middle of the Tunnel, and you slam into it hard, G, knocking the wind out of you as your arms sink up to your elbows in the slime on one side of the trunk and your legs fall limp on the other.

QUEEN TO KING'S BISHOP FIVE—TAKES PAWN—CHECK

Umm, looks pretty bad, G, you spread-eagled on your belly like that, with that fine rump of yours up in the air like that, in this place where none but the damned can see. You're lucky I'm here, G, to save you from them. I'm not like the others, the ones so calloused by the vicissitudes of this life in the shadows as to become as stone, cold and heartless, without tenderness. But not me, G, I still have feelings, and I know how pitiful and vulnerable you feel. Here, let me help you, G. As long as I'm with you, the others won't dare come nearer. They know me. They know I won't allow them to.

WHITE CONCEDES

The muck holds your arms in a viselike grip, rendering you defenseless. Those baggy pants are quick to betray you now, G.

The soft flanks of your hairy thighs quiver beneath my fingertips. The furry bud of your moist hole is pliant and accommodating of my gentle probes. No need to worry, G, I'll take my time, I'm in no hurry. I want to savor this like a rare vintage port. Yeah, G, I know you want it, I can feel your whole body connecting to your hole and offering itself up to me, straining wide for me, gaping open for me. That's the way we are, G, you and me, lusting for the forbidden fruit, playas of the game, denizens of the Vale, the ones who have lost their souls, children of the darkness, legions of the damned, vampires of the dick.

Take it, G, take it all. . . . Take my dick, nigga.

Milking the Bull

He was what you call an "OG," a bad-ass mothafucka from the hood, with coal black skin, rat-tail dreads, and a very bad attitude. He used to boast about all the people he jacked up and how much heat he packed. In those days, he would have sooner cut off your dick than slit your throat if you so much as looked at him funny, in a disrespectful way. He was a big boi, six foot five and two hundred forty pounds of finely hewn muscle worked to a steel-hard sheen by many days and hours spent pumping iron in the yard of the Peter Pitchess Honor Ranch (a nice little vacation spot for bad boys who need a break from the usual jammin' and stylin'). He used to practice his moves by stompin' the Latino punks at the ranch, giving them a good taste of big, mean black dick up their butts. It's not that he was queer, mind you, just that a man gets horny in prison, and there aren't a lot of ways to release the tension.

I met him when he was just three days out of Pitchess. He was livin' large, hangin' wit da homeys, scoring bitches 'n' 'hos, smoking a little crack and the occasional blunt. Getting caught up with the 'hood after his six-year vacation. He was the stupid punk who accosted me in a darkened garage and had the nerve to try and steal my truck. He tried to hit me with a lead pipe, which I caught with one hand while swirling in close to his body to rip my steel-toed boots into his fucking balls. He dropped like a ton of bricks to the pavement, and that's when I decided to not only rearrange his face with that lead pipe, but to give the mutha-fucka a lesson in respect and discipline he would never forget.

I loaded his unconscious and bloody frame into the bed of my truck, chained him to the tie-down hooks, and threw a tarp over him so that his limp body wouldn't attract any unnecessary atten-tion during the trip out of town. I drove into the San Gabriel Mountains to a little spot just off Highway 138, near the Trappist monastery, not far from the Devil's Punchbowl. I had always liked this spot, being as it was between Heaven and Hell. It was iso-lated and secluded and was pretty rugged terrain, which made what I was about to do to that badass black boi in the back of my truck all the more interesting.

He was just barely regaining his senses when I pulled off the tarp. The whole left side of his face was bulging out, swollen and bloody. It looked pretty painful. I thought that at the very least, his jaw was probably broken and he might have had some damage to his teeth and gums. His left eye was nearly closed by the swelling. I took my knife and began to cut away his clothing. I made sure that he was aware of what I was doing, getting the knife blade right up to his skin and maybe nicking him from time to time. When the Bad Boi realized what I was doing, he made a feeble attempt to resist, but the chains and the pain of his jaw made him think better of his actions. As I cut, I took notice of his smooth black skin, with its almost iridescent shine. He was the color of coal, with the feel of ebony glass. His skin was cool to the touch. There was a depth and heaviness about him.

His dick was truly spectacular. Just what one would hope for in a big, black, mandingo slave. It was about six inches soft, with a purple-red dickhead half hidden beneath a thick fold of loose foreskin. His dick was smooth, with a number of small veins just barely visible on the surface. His balls were the size of a man's tightly clenched fist, almost as big as the balls of a bull. Bull balls. The Bull. That was going to be my nickname for this badass gangsta'. And his bull balls were going to play a most prominent role in the torture I was devising for him. With the sun beating down on his now naked body, the Bull got a most magnificent, foot-long boner. I think the warmth of the sun and the cold steel of the chains made something click inside his dumbass skull. At least, I was going to reinforce whatever it was that made him get hard at that moment, as he, now fully conscious, glared warily at me standing over him, staring at his dick, with my hunting knife gleaming in the noonday brilliance.

I like my bois to be smooth, with little to no body hair. But the Bull had a thick mat of fur below his waist. It started really at his navel and just ran out of control all over his pubic areas and legs. I told the Bull how I felt about such things, and he started to curse a blue streak at me. A sharp slap across the left side of his face quickly clammed him up. The rubber gag I fastened over his head made sure that he wouldn't try to speak again unless I desired him to. The gag also made sure that his mouth would be open to accept anything that I wanted to put there, like my nice bulging dick. I took the black daypack I keep behind the bench seat of the truck and started laying out its contents. I stripped down to my jock strap and prepared to get busy with the Bull.

First, I lathered up his ball sack and pubes with shaving crème. Then I took the sharpening stone and put a very fine edge on my hunting knife. Just to test the sharpness of the blade, I traced a few lines along the Bull's rib cage. A few strokes on the right side, a few strokes on the left. The Bull howled in pain. The small cuts just broke the surface of his skin, leaving beautiful crimson trails that mixed with the Bull's sudden, profuse sweat to make delicate patterns on his heaving sides. I proceeded to pull on his monster dick while placing the edge of the knife against his abdomen. The mat of fur easily gave way to that smooth black skin that I like so well. The only tricky part was the Bull's balls. Big round curves are tough to negotiate with six inches of case-hardened steel. The Bull probably thought I was going to castrate him, what with all the blood and the many cuts and nicks I made while trying to scrape the hair off his balls. Of course, it probably didn't help that the edge of the knife blade was dulled somewhat from shaving his Brillo-like hair.

When the last of the furry mat was removed, I took a short break to observe my handiwork. The sun was high in the sky by now, and the heat was oppressive. Despite everything, though, the Bull never lost his hard-on. I got a beer out of the cooler on the front seat and stood on the tailgate of the truck, looking down at the Bull's bloody, sweaty, crème-smeared body writhing at my feet. He would need to be cleaned up before I went any further with him, so I took out my own pretty impressive dick and started to piss all over the Bull. My hot urine acted like salt poured into the Bull's many cuts and nicks. Now I know all about the dangers of sharing bodily fluids, especially mixing blood and urine. But I knew my HIV status was negative and that the Bull was in no danger. For my part, I always play safely, and what I was about to do to the Bull next was as "safe" as anything.

I poured the last few drops of cold beer down the Bull's throat. He had worked up quite a lather around the gag, so I figured he must have been a little parched by the heat and the fear that must have been gripping him as my knife literally skinned him alive. The small cuts bled profusely, even in the heat, and I loved the look of the blood seeping along his ebony flanks. I attached the steel spreader bars to the Bull's ankles and thighs, making it impossible for him to close his legs. Then I carefully undid the chains on his feet to lift his legs back over his stomach and chest. I put a padded bar, which I had custom-made for just this sort of thing, under the Bull's lower back and attached it to the tie-down hooks over the wheel-wells. The result was a very pretty picture: the Bull's full, round ass was wide open and ready for business, with his legs comfortably out of the way and lots of support under him so he could accommodate the full weight of my average-sized frame leaning into him.

Nothing makes my dick harder than the thought of getting up to the elbows in a really hot asshole. The Bull's asshole had that squished-up, pinched, sucked-in look that only virgin asses have, that have never had as much as a finger in them, let alone a dick or a man's fist. The Bull's asshole was clenched so tight that it looked like a smooth button in the middle of his ass crack. This was going to be heavenly, and my jock strap was soaked with pre-come oozing from my rock-hard dick. Because my prick is pierced, trying to keep it restrained in that jock was really uncomfortable, so I just let my dick swing in the heat and glare of the sun. The warmth radiating off my stiff member and the sight of the Bull's asshole was too much for me, so I shot a thick load all over the Bull's legs and thighs. The heat of the sun made my surgical-steel piercings burn the delicate flesh of my frenum. The hotter the steel got, the harder my dick got and the more pre-come dripped from my piss slit.

Using some of my come juice, I started to feel up the Bull's asshole. I used a little spit and just kept massaging his crack. The heat of the day, which must have been over one hundred degrees in the shade—of which there was none—made the plastic bottle of lube soft and pliable. I could feel the heat of the liquid inside; what had been gel was by now as fluid as oil. I squirted a liberal amount of the hot lube all over the Bull's ass. It must have burned him a little, because he moaned and tried to buck out of the way of the stream. The lube sure was hot, so I can imagine how it seared the delicate flanks of the Bull's freshly skinned ass. With firm, circular movements of my thumb and fingers, the Bull's little asshole began to slowly give itself up to me. The little button of a hole started to look more and more like a nice chocolate donut, all slick and covered with dark icing and just a small pin-prick of a hole in the center. I worked up quite a sweat massaging the Bull's ass, but after a while I was able to get my finger inside him.

At first, the Bull's sphincter felt like it would just snap my finger off at the knuckle. But with more circular motion, his asshole began to warm up to my invading presence. His hole was on fire the whole time; the warmth of his guts was hotter than the air around us. I was mesmerized by the sight of that blacker-than-black asshole tightly gripping my brown-sugar–colored finger. I worked the Bull some more and was able to get two fingers in his butt. He began to moan softly then. Slowly, patiently, I kept up a firm pressure along the edges and rim of his asshole. Pushing and pulling, stretching and kneading, rhythmically timing each thrust of my fingers to coincide with his deep, labored breathing. As the Bull inhaled, I pushed aggressively against his asshole with now three fingers. When the Bull exhaled, I twisted my now four fingers counterclockwise out of his asshole. Inhale . . . I pushed five fingers into the Bull's ass. Exhale . . . I pulled my palm out of his ass. Inhale . . . I was up to my wrist in the Bull. Exhale . . . my fist churned against the inside of his hole, leaving only my fingertips to grip at the rim of his ass.

Between the Bull's dripping dick and my own wet willie, we had enough lube for an army of virgin assholes. With each breath the Bull took, my hand and forearm penetrated deeper inside him. Soon I was resting comfortably up to the middle of my forearm, deep in the fiery confines of a most splendid black ass. The deep purple-black skin, slick with sweat, pre-come, lube, and slime oozing from the Bull's ass, was so captivating against my lighter-hued skin. Small movements of my arm and fist made the Bull groan and bellow like a real bull in heat during mating season. His eyes were squeezed shut, the blood on his face had stopped flowing, and the cuts on his rib cage and body had clotted. The Bull's breathing came much slower now, and each inhale and exhale took like forever. Together, the Bull and I danced our ritualized mating, with slow, deep thrusts of my arm giving way to excruciatingly agonized withdrawals, resulting in guttural sounds from the Bull that were no longer human but which had long ago metamorphosed into the cry of bestial carnality.

The sun was low on the horizon, and the sky was red like blood; the heat was slowly dissipating, and the air grew thick with the buzz of insects. The pace of our dance grew more frenzied as the thrusts and withdrawals of my arm from deep inside the Bull got faster and faster. Through it all, the Bull's foot-long dick unflaggingly stood at attention, nestled against his chest, pointing downward into his still-swollen face. The lather around the gag in his mouth resembled that of a rabid animal, all frothy and foamy. My own dick made a solid slick of oily pre-come from the Bull's haunches clear down to the restraining bar under the small of his back. My head was reeling as if my brain and that of the senseless beast under me were connected through my arm.

I saw a bleak landscape of broken houses and shattered people. I saw a vision of a small black boy standing over the lifeless body of a once-pretty woman, mutilated by repeated blows from some blunt object, resting in an endless pool of blood. I realized that the beast beneath me had come from such a place and that this might have explained the brutality and violence with which it faced the world. I understood then that the Bull was as much victim as victimizer.

And in that instant of realization, a powerful wave of warmth sizzled under my skin, like a shot of electric current, making the hairs stand up on my arm. The wave started uncontrollable convulsions in my muscles, and the convulsions were transmitted to the Bull's welcoming asshole until, eventually, the Bull and I were connected as one, as wave after wave of spasms coursed between and through our conjoined bodies. I felt the rectal muscles of the Bull churn around my fist and arm, trying to eject them from their deep-seated place inside him. The Bull's whole body strained upward, pushing against the darkening sky; every muscle was working, and the chains that bound him creaked against the force being applied to them.

His powerful contractions squeezed tightly against my arm and were met with a like force emanating from deep within my own body. Together, we bucked and strained and moaned until a blinding and searing flash of heat swept over us, and we both came with such force that the Bull's come looked like a fountain of white cream washing over him and into his gagged mouth. My load came so hard that my legs buckled, and I slumped to my knees shooting spurts of silver bullets like the erotic equivalent of an AK-47. The sound we made must have been heard clear to Heaven and Hell, because all I can remember is how black the sky got and how the air was filled with a screaming cacophony of millions of bats, birds, and insects taking wing.

I left the Bull sleeping soundly beside a small stream. To this day, I will always carry with me the memory of the day I milked him dry.

Mastery

The Doorman

You had to be there. It was totally off the hook. Words can't really do justice to what happened. How can you possibly understand the impact of it all? The drama? The sheer sexiness of it? Without having been present at the time? Hell, I was there, and I've still got a boner because of it. Just thinking about it makes my dick wet. Yeah, man, it was hot! So fucking hot!

I'd say the guy was about five ten, more or less, and around one hundred eighty pounds, give or take. He was in really good shape. Nice-looking guy. He had that fine hair, thick and wavy, real nice. Black, which really set off his smooth café-au-lait complexion. Yeah, he was a hot dude. Puerto Rican. I think he was a lawyer or something; he wore a very expensive suit. I know because when he first came to the event, he had the jacket slung over his arm, and as he put it on at the door I saw the label, Brioni. He had on those new calfskin Ferragamos too, and a diamond-studded Cartier tank watch. He was sharp. And he smelled good; Paul Stuart, I think. Oh, and he had a really great smile. The kind of smile that could melt ice cubes in your drink and make you forget your own name. When he flashed those

pearly whites, all you could do was just smile back in total capti-
vation.

I think it was that smile that caught the black guy's attention.
He was clear across the room, by the stairs leading up to the VIP
mezzanine, but I know he saw the Puerto Rican dude flashing
that big smile as he entered the main floor. You know how those
big charity events are, everybody standing around, cocktail in
hand, listening to some tired-ass bore drone on about some bullshit but afraid to leave because they need something from the asshole and they don't want to risk offending him by walking away
for a more interesting conversation. The noise is just buzzing, and
then comes to a sudden pause as somebody new walks in and
everybody glances to see who it is in case they know them or want
to or think the new flavor might have something they want or has
more juice to facilitate their getting it than the bore they're with.
You know, the same rich-wannabe bullshit.

When the 'Rican guy walked in, the noise just came to a stop
and was silent for far longer than was polite as people stared at
him. That's when he flashed that big smile, as if to let folks know
it was okay if they admired his beauty, and the noise level picked
up again with a much higher buzz, like it was charged with some
kind of expectation of something more to come.

I couldn't leave my station for another couple of hours, but
from what I heard, the black guy had his eyes on the 'Rican dude
from the moment he walked in. I heard that the black guy had
these intense eyes too, and when he stared at you it felt like he was
seeing you stark naked with your shit hanging limp and looking
smaller than you knew it was. That black guy was scary, man, mad
crazy kind of scary, like at any minute he might put his arm out,
grab you around the shoulders, and slice your heart out with his
free hand while calmly telling you that you don't look too well.

I remember that black guy. When he came to the front door, it
was crowded, maybe a couple of hundred people all arriving fash-

ionably late and wanting to make their entrance with style, so people would notice them. I was manning the door and trying to get the high-rollers through the hoi polloi while keeping the madness manageable. You know those high-society types. Everybody standing on tiptoes trying to shout out who they are, as if that was going to get them to the front of the line so they could show off to everyone else how important they were. It was a tough job, man. I almost got physical with a couple of them. Oh, and the names they called me once they realized I was the only one standing between them and a boldface mention in tomorrow's *New York Times*. Society bitches have filthy mouths, man, just nasty, let me tell you!

Just as the crowd started to surge forward as if to rush the door, I noticed the whole energy of the scene change. From the rear of the crowd, it got awfully quiet and eerily still. The silence moved like a wave toward the front and through the middle of the pack; it looked like a bolt of lightning shot through the masses and parted them like the Red Sea. Folks jumped out of the way as if they had been hit by a Taser. Then I saw this figure dressed in black moving slowly down the aisle. As he got closer, I noticed it was a black guy. He was like Pharaoh passing through to his palace; he had such a regal bearing. He was unhurried and oblivious of all those around him. When he got to me, I did what everybody else had done; I looked down and turned my head away from him, as if it were a sin punishable by death to look the Living God in the face as he passed by.

All I saw of him up close was the trouser of one leg and a little of his boot. From what I saw, the black guy must have been dressed all in leather, man, and some really fine, hand-tooled leather at that. The workmanship just on that little sliver of trouser I saw was impeccable; intricate black stitching making an awesome pattern all over the pant. I could even smell the exotic aroma of the expensive leather as the black prince passed by. His boots were of the same fine grade of leather, and they were covered in the same pattern as his pants. He had a thin silver spur attached to his left heel. Yeah, that black guy was something else, all right.

The Bartender

I was serving drinks at the Cosmo Bar. We called it that because we served these really special Cosmopolitans that were very popular with the upper-crust society crowd. This tall black man, medium build, very muscular, you could tell even with his clothes on, dressed in the finest black leather I've ever seen, no jewelry, not even a watch, which was kind of odd, you know, since most men, even the most macho man who disdains flash, wear at least a watch. But then, come to think of it, the way he looked, time revolved around him rather than his being ruled by time, in which case a watch was meaningless. Anyway, this elegant black man comes to my station and asks for spring water, flat, no ice. I couldn't believe anyone would just want water, so I leaned over the bar and asked him to please repeat his order. That's when I looked at his face, to see his lips, so I could make sure I was getting his order right.

Whew! My God! What a face! And those eyes! He was gorgeous, just absolutely gorgeous! A dark caramel complexion, smooth, with a thick, black mustache dabbled with just enough silver hair to make it shine like obsidian. Thick black eyebrows framed his large, hazel-colored, almond-shaped eyes, whose hardness was softened by the long, delicate eyelashes that made them sensuous as well as ominous. When he looked at you, I swear, it was as if he was looking right through your skin and bones, into your very soul. My whole body just tingled from the heat of his gaze, as if at any minute I would just dissolve like melting ice right there behind the bar. I remembered that my hands were trembling so bad as I handed him his glass of water that I was afraid

I'd spill the whole thing. I wanted somehow to please him and to have him like me because for some reason I just felt that if he did-n't, I'd be sorely punished for my transgressions, and I'm not re-ally into that whole pain thing.

He seemed to have that same effect on everyone around him. People would just feel his presence coming toward them and they suddenly jumped out of his way or tried to serve him in some fashion—offering him anything they had, a napkin, a canapé, or a drink, whatever—just trying not to displease him in some way by their inattention to his needs or desires or wants, real or imag-ined. It was as though people wanted to gain some small gesture of his approval, a nod or bat of his eyelids, perhaps a smile, just to assure themselves of their worthiness to even be in his presence. I think that's what happened to the Latin man. He took one look at this imposing black man in black leather, and he just was a moth to a flame. But the funny thing was, the black man never seemed to take any notice of the Latin gentleman, no matter how hard he tried, which I think really got to him since, well, you know what happened to him! I mean, my God, to do that in front of all those people! Wow! I couldn't possibly imagine anything that would make me do that. But then again, that black man was just incred-ible! I guess, maybe even I'd have done that to be with him. Can you imagine what he must be like in bed? Yeah, maybe I would have done it too, just like that Latin gentleman.

The Waiter

It started in the men's room downstairs. I was taking a piss when this fine Puerto Rican dude comes in and steps up to the urinal on my right. I thought he was really hot and started to check him out as he took his dick out of his pants. He had a really nice, thick uncut dick with a big fat mushroom head. I guess I was staring, 'cause he turned just a bit so I could get a really good look at his meat, which made me glance up at him and see him grinning at me. Jesus, I nearly shot my load right then! But before things could go any further, the door opens again and this unbelievably sexy black guy comes in. When he walked up to the urinal next to the Puerto Rican guy, you could feel the energy in the whole room change. It took on a mad sexy vibe, like when an orgy hits its stride and people be bouncing off the walls an' shit.

Both the Puerto Rican dude and I turned our heads to follow the black guy. As he stopped in front of the urinal, he slowly unsnapped the fly of his leather pants, letting the echo of each "snap" fade away before he popped the next one. My dick was rock hard, and so was the Puerto Rican dude's. We stood there with our stiff dicks in our hands, panting in anticipation of what was going to come out of those tight leather pants. The black guy acted like he was ignoring us, but I knew he was aware of our rapt attention. I mean, the bathroom wasn't that big, and three guys in there pretty much filled it up. Even so, his seeming indifference to our stiff dicks just made the whole scene that much hotter. Finally, the last snap was undone, and the black guy reached inside and pulled out the hottest-looking dick I've ever seen. It was thicker than the Puerto Rican dude's, pierced all along the underside like it was riveted to his body, dark cinnamon colored, long, with prominent veins, and I just knew it tasted as sweet as it looked. He held it in the palm of his hand like he was displaying it for us, then he started to piss, a thick stream of light yellow fluid that smelled like vanilla. The Puerto Rican dude started to stroke his big dick as he watched the black guy piss.

Looking at all that hunky dark meat hanging big like that was just too much for me. I noisily shot my load into the urinal in front of the Puerto Rican guy, a good foot away from me, splashing some water out of the basin. The Puerto Rican dude and the black guy laughed good-naturedly and joked about tea-room sex not having changed much. That's when I noticed that the black guy's dick was rock hard and huge! A real monster dick snaking out of his pants. The Puerto Rican dude was looking at it too, never took his eyes off it. You could tell he wanted that dick bad, real bad! The black guy finished pissing and swiftly stuffed his big, thick bone back into his pants and left the bathroom, leaving both me and the Puerto Rican guy stunned by his sudden departure. The Puerto Rican guy quickly jammed his still-hard dick into his pants and hurried out to catch up with the black guy. I just stood there and jerked off a couple of times, playing the images of those two hot dicks over in my mind and imagining them fucking the hell out of my mouth and ass.

The DJ

From the booth, I could see everything that went down. I was spinning a mix of old school, hip-hop, and R&B, keeping it kinda mellow but still grooving for anyone who wanted to shake they moneymaker. Most folks just rocked back and forth where they stood. It wasn't late enough, and the alcohol hadn't loosened up their inhibitions, you know, 'cause white folks be all self-conscious about how crazy they look on the dance floor. Anyway, I saw the black guy come onto the main floor first; that cat must have had some serious mojo, man, 'cause the crowds just parted in front of him anywhere he went. Even from up in the booth I could tell he was hot. Those dark good looks and that leather outfit just lit up the room when he came in. He wasn't walking particularly fast, just deliberate, like each step was already well planned in advance. That guy moved like a cat, come to think of it, like a black leopard on the hunt, having already selected his prey and just waiting for the right moment to go in for the kill. He was awesome to watch, a real king surveying his kingdom.

The Latin guy came out next, darting about, stopping to stand on his tiptoes, looking out over the crowd, trying to find someone. He had that desperate look about him, like someone who's lost something really important and has to get it back or all hell will break loose. That dude must have caused at least two, maybe three servers to spill their drink trays, and I saw him run into at least a dozen more people, spilling their drinks and food, as he made his frantic search about the room. That's when I noticed that it seemed as though the black guy was kind of leading the Latin dude on some kind of chase, while also stalking him, you know?

It was as though the black guy was laying a trap for the Latin dude, staying just a bit ahead and out of reach. It seemed to be some kind of game, and I'd say it lasted for a couple of hours at least. I could tell 'cause by the time they got to the middle of the dance floor, there was a pretty healthy crowd of people shakin' it up real good. I figured I'd kind of stir things up a bit, so when they hit the middle of the floor I shined the big spotlight on them and cut the house lights, framing them in a circle of brilliant white light. It was eerie and sexy, the two of them stopped like that in their tracks, but I had no idea what would happen next.

When the spot hit them, the black guy stood stark still, intensely looking at the Latin guy, who was maybe a little blinded by the light, 'cause he stumbled into the black guy. BAM! The dude bounced off the black guy as if he had just hit a brick wall or something. That really stunned him! When he regained his footing, the Latin dude stopped and stared right back at the black guy. The spot looked like a boxing ring as the two dudes slowly circled each other, never breaking eye contact.

The Doorman

Man, it was like watching two pit bulls in a cage match. Those two looked right at each other; neither one said a word, but you could tell they were talking with their eyes. Then the black guy stopped and slowly crossed his arms in front of his chest.

The Bartender

The Latin gentleman furrowed his brow as if asking a question, when the black man suddenly folded his arms and stood rigid in the center of the spotlight. I saw his jaw drop and his mouth gape open when the black man unfolded his arms and slowly moved his hand down to his crotch and started stroking his groin.

The Waiter

I was only a few feet away when the hot black guy started to stroke himself. The image of that hot dick was still burning in my mind from the bathroom, so I got hard immediately. The Puerto Rican dude must have been thinking the same thing, 'cause his prick was practically pushing through his pants too!

The DJ

All of a sudden, the Latin dude takes off his coat and drops it to the floor. He undoes his tie and lets it slip on top of his coat. He unbuttons the top couple of buttons on his shirt and then slinks down to his knees in front of the black guy.

The Black Man in Black Leather

When I saw him I thought, now that's a very good-looking papi. But that's as far as it went with me. It wasn't until later, in the men's room, when I caught him showing his dick to the waiter at the urinals, that I got the notion that he might be fun to play with. He had a thick uncut dick: it looked to be a good nine to ten inches hard, with a fat mushroom head swelled to bursting. What attracted me most was his ass, though. The thin fine wool of his suit could barely contain that firm bubble butt. His ass cheeks were stretching the fabric so tight that I could read the name of his underwear off the waistband. As he flexed his butt when he shifted his weight from one foot to the other, all I could think of was that ass gripping my dick. That's when I decided to join the game. I took my fat dick out and let him get a real good look at what might be his if he played it right. I could tell by the way he started to breathe real shallowlike that he was hooked. I just had to reel him in, which I did after playing him a bit.

The Puerto Rican Guy

Even now, people will give me "that" look or, if they're bold, come up to me and ask, "How could you do that?" I always tell them that it was a small price to pay for the joy that has come into my life. They can't begin to imagine what he has done for me. I have never been more spiritually alive or sexually fulfilled than I am right now. If I hadn't done what I did, then I would never have known such total and complete peace of soul. Yeah, I did it, and I would do whatever he wanted me to do. He has made my life richer and more meaningful in ways you can't even begin to comprehend.

The DJ

The black guy just stands there stroking his crotch while the Latin dude gets on his hands and knees and licks the black guy's boots. The black guy pushes the dude off with a firm shove of his leg, knocking the Latin dude onto his butt. I don't know if they said anything; I couldn't see either one of them moving their lips.

The Bartender

The Latin gentleman looked so helpless and desperate after the black man knocked him to the ground. He seemed to be on the verge of tears almost, as if the black man's rejection of him was utterly devastating. He got up to his feet and then took off his shirt completely.

The Waiter

So the Latin guy is standing there without a shirt, and his muscular chest and tight abs are just perfect, shining in the glare of the spotlight. He had very little body hair, just that sexy trickle of black hair sprouting from around his pecs and curling down the center of his chest and abs to disappear into his pants. I love that! I call it the Glory Trail 'cause it always leads to something good!

The Doorman

The papi then takes off his pants and this skimpy silk thong that barely held his big dick and heavy balls. The cat is naked, stark naked in the middle of the room with thousands of people just staring at his hot naked body!

The Black Man in Black Leather

You have to realize that all men possess power. One man cannot take away another man's power, no matter how much force he uses. If I, as a master, have power over another, it is because the slave has voluntarily subjugated his power to mine. For him, it is a conscious act, an expression of his power to invest in me a superior position over him. It is a power that the slave exercises every moment, and at any time he could revoke the trust and become my equal again. But for now, he enjoys his station, and I go to great pains to ensure that he never tires of it.

The Puerto Rican Man

The prospect of losing him was just too unbearable. I knew that if I wanted him, I would have to show him my total devotion. I had to show him that I was willing to give him everything I had. That's why I did it. I wanted him so bad.

The DJ

So the Latin dude is butt nekkid in the middle of the floor, and the black guy begins to unsnap the fly of his leather pants. His dick is bulging against his pants leg, straining to get loose; all the while the black guy just stares at the Latin dude, daring him, you know. The Latin guy's eyes open wide, like he knows the ante has been raised and he's not sure he can meet the call. He kinda begs with his eyes, but the black guy just stares, impervious, slowly stroking the bulge in his pants.

The Doorman

Oh man, what happened next was off the hook! The papi, all naked, with that fat juicy caramel dick all hard, squats down, and . . . I still can't believe it, I just can't believe it!

The Waiter

I'm not one of those freaky guys into that far-out shit, but some of my friends are, and they always told me how sexy hot it is. But until I watched that Puerto Rican dude, I'd never seen a guy you know, like that. His ass was fine! And the sight of that hole like that, man, I got to tell you, it made me bust a nut good; hell, I could feel it oozing through my pants.

The Black Man in Black Leather

When a man honors you with the gift of himself—body, mind, heart, and soul—offers you his total being as the ultimate sacrament, then the relationship between you is infinitely greater than master and slave. You are interconnected at a level as deep as the cellular—it becomes a union of the spirit, and it must be taken with the utmost seriousness, since such a commitment is tantamount to a union with the divine.

The Puerto Rican Guy

A man like him is constantly being hit upon by guys offering him their bodies. He can pick and choose as he pleases, but I could tell he was very discriminating, a man who only wanted real challenges, real players who not only knew what he was about and what he was capable of doing but who were equally beyond puritanical conventions themselves . He is the type of man who begins at the edge where most people stop, spiritually and sexually. He is into conquering the unknown and the unknowable. If I wanted him to take me, I had to show him that I could reach into his world; that I wanted to be with him there; that my deepest yearnings were also his.

The Bartender

It was like a no-limit stud-poker match, each man upping the ante in response to the other's bets. With the Latin gentleman having placed his incredible wager on the table, the black man answered by opening the fly of his leather pants, pulling out his impressive pierced dick, thick and meaty, veins bulging, the head deep red from the force of his erection, looking as if it would burst it was so hard, a globule of sticky pre-come glistening at the tip of it, which he wiped with the thumb of his right hand, trailing a thin silvery strand from his slit as he brought his thumb to his lips and licked the come off it while staring the Latin gentleman straight in his eyes, taunting him as he ran his tongue seductively around the outside of his lips.

The Waiter

Everybody in that room got wet when the black dude unleashed that fucking dick and licked the come off it. I know those around me did, because I yanked my dick out of my pants too and busted a big ole nut, man! It was just too much for me; I would have exploded otherwise, like that rap artist next to me who was beating off while grabbing his crotch. But that was nothing compared to the Puerto Rican guy, who was dripping pre-come like a leaky faucet, creating a slimy puddle on the floor as he watched that black guy lick the come off his lips.

The Doorman

The papi had this wild, mad-dog look in his eyes, yo! When he saw that brother's meat, he nearly blew his own load. Instead, the cat got down on his hands and ... Shit, dawg, it was fuckin' freaky-deaky, man! Off the fuckin' hook!

The DJ

The whole crowd gasped as the Latin dude got down and did it. I was so into the scene that I didn't even notice that I was jerking off until I stood up to watch him do it and my balls slapped against the turntable, knocking off the music, so everybody could hear the Latin guy slurping and swallowing and shit. When he was done, he licked the whole floor around himself clean and then squatted on his hands and knees like an obedient puppy waiting for his master's command.

The Bartender

The black man walked slowly to the Latin man and gently grabbed him under his armpit and lifted him to his knees. He took his other hand and stroked the hair back from the Latin man's face, caressing his cheeks while looking deeply into his eyes.

The Waiter

Then the black guy grabs the Puerto Rican dude by the roots of his hair, shoves his dick into the dude's mouth, and fucks his face, driving his dick all the way down the dude's throat! You could see the guy's dick bulging in the base of the dude's neck! He must have fucked him like that, just drilling his mouth and throat, for at least fifteen or twenty minutes. All I know is I busted a couple of more nuts, between watching the two of them in the middle of the spotlight and the rapper next to me, who had dropped his pants and was whacking off his own impressive dick while sticking two fingers up his ass. I noticed at least five other guys spanking the monkey too, while their wives or girlfriends tried to hide their wet spots with their purses. Man, the whole place was on the verge of exploding into one hellacious orgy!

The Bartender

After what seemed like an eternity, the black man pulled his swollen dick from the Latin gentleman's mouth and gushed wave after wave of thick, creamy come all over the Latin gentleman's face and chest. As he did so, the crowd, which had been growing restless watching the proceedings, erupted. People were pulling their clothes off, other people's clothes off, and coupling like rabid dogs!

The DJ

When the brother blew his wad all over that Latino dude, I was right there with him, shooting shit all over the booth, man. I got naked, climbed down from the booth, grabbed this hot redheaded chick, and started to fuck her lights out. Just as my groove hit its stride, some white dude began poking at my asshole with his dick, and you know what? I didn't care! I just let him fuck my ass real good. Shit, I was probably fucking his wife anyway.

The Doorman

Yeah, it got mad fucking wild up in there, man; I know I got my rocks off enough to last me for the next year! By the time the cops came to break it up, the black guy and the Latino dude must have been long gone, because they weren't among those rounded up for indecent exposure and lewd conduct. I tell you what, though, if anybody ever asks me to work the door there again, I'd do it for free, just on the off chance that something like that would happen again.

Pursuit

He was a pretty boi.

Soft, smooth skin pulled tautly across a tightly muscled frame. He had an ass that begged for mercy and gave redemption to any who could make it there. His dark hair was full, long and unkempt, and kept falling into his eyes, which were dark brown, and into the corners of his moist, pouty lips, which were like two wet slices of sweet melon. He was the kind of boi who said "No" but desperately meant "Yes." I knew from the moment I saw him that I would have him, but none could truly possess him, for he was a wanderer and never stayed in one place long enough to be settled. Movement was his gift, and to watch his lithe young body glide across the terrain on beautifully proportioned legs, with just a hint of downy hair upon them, and to see that chest ripple with the movement of his arms, and especially to note how the little buds of flesh around his pointy, black nipples glowed with perspiration, was enough to make a man lose his soul.

However enjoyable his other attributes, it was the boi's ass that drove me to distraction and was my waking dream and my one and only desire. I became the Son of Satan just to have a moment with that boi's ass. My soul is forever damned, but the memory of the smell, the feel, the taste, the sound, and the sight of that boi swinging on my big fuckin' dick will soothe my tortured flesh for all eternity.

One morning, while running near the lake, I came across a group of bois. They looked magnificent in their young manhood. Agile, nimble, quick, and responsive, like young wild animals ready to run with their elder brethren. Since it was late June, they were just easing into a last season of freedom before work and adult responsibilities would wash away the remaining vestiges of boiishness and replace it with the steel of manhood. They were eager to prove themselves in the world, but they were also apprehensive, since these were sheltered bois, kept safe from life's vicissitudes. They ran like gazelles just out of my reach. I felt very much like the cunning beast chasing its prey on the open savannah.

Then I saw the boi.

His firm peach of an ass strained against the gauze-like fabric of his shorts. Wet from his sweat, the shorts rode high on his naked cheeks. I was mesmerized by the glimpse of thick black hair curling around his crack and spreading all over his sinewy café-au-lait-colored butt. I made my pact with the Devil the very instant his tight running shorts disappeared into the crack of his ass and totally exposed those full, round mounds.

The game is called Pursuit.

The object is to give the prey a head start of some distance and then for the hunter to chase after the prey until it is caught. It is a punishing game for the hunter at the beginning, since he must work twice as fast to close the distance to the prey. But over time, if the hunter is really good, his dogged persistence runs the prey to ground, and the dynamics of the game change as the prey tries desperately to avoid being caught. In the end, if the hunter is really good, the prey simply runs out of energy, having exhausted his muscles, his lungs, and his will to flee. Heaving and gasping for air, the prey just falls to the ground and begs for mercy. The boi was grabbing at the wall of an abandoned outhouse, slowly falling to his knees, when I calmly jogged up to him and gently ran my fingers through his dripping wet mane of hair.

Soft and silky. Jet black. Thick, full. I tightened my grip on his hair and jerked him to his feet. He was shocked and surprised, and the pain made him grab my hand in a vain attempt to ease my grip. The more he tried to resist, the greater the violence with which I shook his head by the roots of his hair. I twisted his face toward mine and stared into the terror-stricken eyes of my prize and kissed him until his trembling body was still, calm, at rest. His lips and tongue were not accustomed to the demands of a male lover. But I trained them, and I made them dance with eagerness and desire. By then, the terror was replaced with a hungry lustfulness. That's when I smacked him across the face, knocking him backward onto the ground. While he lay there, stunned, I ripped his shorts off and used them to tie his feet together. I took my T-shirt and tied his hands behind his back. Then I stuck my funky, sweat-stained running shorts in his mouth to gag him.

Everything happened fast from that point on. The boi was disoriented. I grabbed him by his heavy balls and dick and forced his head down into the dirt, thus forcing his fine ass up into the air. He had a real nice dick, uncut, thick, with a round head that looked like two pebbles stuck together. The slit was long, and I couldn't resist sliding my tongue deep into it. The boi's musty balls and tart pre-come filled my senses. Soon I was running my greedy tongue around his foreskin, making sure that not one drop of sweet boi-cheese was left. I scoured his dick and then sucked his balls, rolling them around in my mouth and spitting them out like the pits of avocadoes. The smell of his ass drew my tongue toward it in short lapping motions, cleaning each hair as I made my

272 / Forbidden Fruit

way toward that butt crack, slipping, slurping, and sliding into his fertile, tight, hard asshole.

He moaned and rolled his butt from side to side in slow grinding motions. It was a virgin ass, and his hole responded to the experienced touch of a Master. I kneaded his firm buns and slowly started to spank them, first the left cheek, then the right cheek. SLAP SLAP SLAP on the left. SLAP SLAP SLAP on the right. SLAP SLAP SLAP. SLAP SLAP SLAP. In rhythm to the beat of the desire burning in my loins. SLAP SLAP SLAP. SLAP SLAP SLAP. Gradually, I increased the force of the blows. **SLAP SLAP SLAP. SLAP SLAP SLAP.** Those fine café au lait cheeks turned to apple red, then to angry, bloody red, then the skin got very hot and hard, then pliant, and the boi tried to kick and scream and move his tender ass cheeks out of the way of the barrage of blows that landed with deadly accuracy on his tortured behind.

I forced the boi's bound arms up above his head, which helped to keep his face pressed firmly into the dirt and made his ass stick even further into the air, thus making his feeble attempts to protect his raw butt cheeks all the more pathetic. His boi-butt glowed in the morning air, with its soothing coolness causing a light steam to sleek off the boi's well-spanked buns. I spit on his cheeks to soothe them. I bathed them with my tongue and drove my tongue deep into his hole, chewing on it, forcing it to open and loosen its tight grip. The smell and feel of his asshole was beyond words. His musk was full upon my mouth, my nose, my face. I felt as if I could eat my way into his ass and never stop. Get my whole face into his ass, it was so good, and soon it was so ripe and willing, I could get anything I wanted into it. I started with my dick.

My dick is thick, cut and pierced, with a rod of stainless steel just under the head. Fully erect, it pulsates and bulges from its many veins. The thump-thump-thump of my dick against the hard walls of a willing asshole as it slides in and out drives most of my conquests wild with passion, since I tend to set a fairly constant, hypnotic motion. I set a pace so as to fuck for hours on end. I especially enjoy having my conquests beg me to fuck them faster, so they can piggishly shoot their loads. But I like to make them wait and beg and wait some more and beg and wait and beg some more, until they shoot their loads without even touching themselves, just letting their own body involuntarily give up their loads to me, give up their loads to my dick, ramming their assholes, slowly, grinding out their loads until I can't hold my own juice any longer, when I rip my dick out of their gaping holes and shoot my heavy load all over their slimy cheeks. I fucked the boi that way. His ass had never known how good a man's dick feels when it's deep inside, slowly grinding into his guts. By the time I was finished fucking him the first time, his asshole was so loose I could stick my fingers up his ass while still fucking him with my dick.

His ass felt so good. He wanted to feel a man inside him so bad that his little boi ass just opened up to me, begging me to go deeper. So I slowly slipped a finger, then two, then three, then my whole hand into his ass. I ran my fingers around the outside edges of his ass muscle. Massaging it and teasing it at the same time. Then I worked my wrist and soon my forearm inside him. I reamed his slimy asshole this way for some time, pushing in and drawing back, in . . . out . . . in . . . out, until the boi was moaning so loudly, even with his gag in place, that I thought he could be heard back to the main road. His eyes fluttered, his body heaved, as he went into convulsions of orgasm, shooting load after load of milky cream until his balls were empty. And still I worked his fine, hot ass, the cheeks still a deep purplish red from the spanking I had given him, and his asshole raw from the fucking and fisting I gave him. Then I fucked him some more and fisted him some more. The sun was well past its zenith by the time I finished with him, too tired to get a hard-on and my hands cramped from working him so.

He was a very good boi. He took everything his daddy gave him, and he never complained. I was impressed. So I untied him and gently massaged his limbs and laid him on his back. I kissed his face and then stood over him. As my piss washed over his body, he writhed in the hot yellow stream and covered himself in dirt and mud. I pissed for what seemed a long time, and when I finished, my boi raised himself up and sucked the last droplets from the slit of my dick. I tenderly held his head in my hands as I slowly shoved my dick down his throat. He sucked me until I came all over his face. I lifted him up and licked his face clean of my come, my piss, and the mud. We stood there, wrapped in each other's arms as the heat of the sun warmed our bodies and seared the memory of all that had happened forever into our souls.

Chat Room

It was late, probably after midnight, by the time I got home from the office. Every engagement always comes down to its "wake up and smell the coffee" moment, and this one had to be tonight. Feeling horny, like I always do after sticking it to some pompous corporate lawyer trying to show off for his client, I switched on the computer and checked my e-mail.

> Damn, baby, damn!!
> A hot and passionate puerto rican papi, 5'10, 29 and sexy is looking for horny brothers to bring his freak out. I have a deep and hungry throat for your throbbing dick. If you love to slam a big and hot ass until you bust a nut, then hit me back. Pound me, pump me and let me know who's my daddy. . . . If you enjoy digging out a wet, tight hole with your tool until I lose my mind, then hit me up. My birthday is coming up and I need some brothers in New York city to break me off a hard piece of chocolate. Make me your bitch.! Want to make you cum all over me let me feel your hot juice and want to sit on it till my legs are shaking! Cum on and let's do dah damn thing! . . .

It was an invitation I couldn't refuse, so I hit the papi back.

Freaky Blk Top lookin to scratch that itch

Yo, blkfistingtop here with a thick hard 8 to deep dick your azz until it's all sloppy and wet before I shove my fist down there and scratch that itch. Check my profile and send pics of that azz if interested.

I don't really get into the whole online cruising shit, too many games and not enough solid hooking up. When I get that urge, I want a hot, tight asshole sucking on my dick, not some endless e-mail string. So frankly, I didn't put too much hope in this dude either. I was already reaching for my address book to call up a reliable fuck buddy when my computer buzzed with an incoming e-mail message.

Love that dik, dawg! Damn you a phyne bro. Let's do
it, yo.
Carlito

Ah, what the hell, I thought; it was late and maybe a good jerk was all I was up for anyway. He attached some really hot pictures of his ass, face, and dick. He was as advertised, a hot, sexy papi with a butt that begged to be stuffed with dick for days. That alone was worth the effort so far; I could whack off to that pic all night, that dark cherry hole all opened up and ready for serious deep dicking. So I answered.

I want to fuck you for lunch. Meet me tomorrow around 1pm and I'll tear up that azz, boi.
Sir

Mmmm that sounds good, Sir, where do I meet you?
Carlito

*Midtown, there's a coffee place on 8th Avenue at 39th,
across from the bus terminal. I'll be upstairs, in the back, by
the bathroom, wearing a dark suit with a red tie.*

My booty will be clean and greased for you, Sir! I can't
wait to feel that big dick banging my hole.

*1pm Sharp! Don't be late; I want to have a nice long lunch
break!*

I pulled up his pics again and reached for the lube.

As the last bit of come oozed out of my dick, I drifted off to
sleep with dreams of Carlito's ass pressing against my crotch.

The next morning, back at the office, it was sheer hell. There
were more meetings with the lawyers and the bankers, arguing
over the fine points in the forbearance agreement. My assistants
were burning out from the pace, and I put a call into HQ to get
more replacements. I overheard my secretary ordering lunch, and
that's when I finally looked at my watch—twelve-fifteen. Damn!
It was almost Carlito-time! I told Cheryl that I was taking a late
lunch and then popped into the conference room to tell the
lawyers and bankers that I'd had enough of their bullshit and that
they had until four PM to put a final document on my desk. Then,
with a growing hard-on making a tent in my pants, I left the office
and grabbed a cab uptown to rendezvous with Carlito, if he actually showed.

At twelve-fifty, I walked into the coffee place; it was crowded
but beginning to thin after the noon rush. There were only a few

tables occupied upstairs, and downstairs was only moderately full. There was a really hot-looking mixed-race Vietnamese barista working the counter; he had great eyes, dark and sultry, with a terrific smile. We made idle chitchat as he took my order. Turns out his mother is half black, which accounted for his mocha complexion and beautiful features. I complimented him on his stunning good looks. He gave me a wide-grinned smile as his hand lingered in mine as he handed me my change, and there was definitely a strong spark between us. If Carlito was a no-show, it was clear this barista was more than willing to go for a spin on my very hungry dick. The barista gave me his number, and I promised to call him as I made my way upstairs.

Between sips of latte, I checked my watch; it was nearly one, the moment of truth. I hoped Carlito wasn't one of those typical chat-room fakes, giving good vibes over the net but not serious about actually hooking up. My cell phone rang; it was Cheryl trying to reach me. I hesitated for a moment then decided to answer; if Carlito did come, I wanted to appear to be the busy Master of the Universe that I am, not some desperately horny freak hanging out in coffee bars. Sure enough, just as I was finishing giving Cheryl some last-minute comments to relay to the lawyers, in comes this fine caramel-colored papi, pants hanging low off his hips, oversized wifebeater revealing sinewy arms covered in tats, do-rag pulled tight over his braids. He spotted me immediately and flashed a toothy smile, his gold caps sparkling in the lights. He looked almost exactly like his pictures, except he was naked in them. I could imagine that hard, skinny body under his baggy clothes; my dick was rock hard and leaking juice in anticipation of what was to come. I stood up so he could see how excited I was. His eyebrows arched upward, and by the way his pants poked out, I guess he was just as eager as I was. I motioned for him to head to the restroom, and as he brushed by me, he winked as his hand felt me up, firmly squeezing my dick and balls. After a quick glance around the room to make sure no one noticed what was about to go down, I headed for the restroom.

No sooner had the door closed behind me and I turned the lock than Carlito was on me like a bitch in heat. His hands were frantically pulling at my clothes, lips pressed to mine, tongue pushed deep into my mouth. He tasted sweet. He smelled like reefer. His skin was hot to my touch as I reached under his shirt and felt his nipples, small hard dark buds vibrating with desire. We were soon naked, and I was working my tongue all over his taut, thin frame, starting with those nipples. I held one tit in my teeth, swirling my tongue around the tip, while I pinched the other hard, making Carlito moan. His dick was rubbing up and down against my belly, dripping pre-come, as my dick slid between his legs, pressing up against his balls. The harder I bit his tit, the more juice he drizzled. Boys who do that have their assholes hardwired to their tits, so I knew that I could open and tighten this papi's ass just by working his nips the right way—soft, gentle pressure, his hole will open; hard twists, his ass will clamp shut like a vise.

To prove my hypothesis, I slid off his tits and ran my tongue down to his stiff dick and sucked him down to his balls. As I did so, I pushed a finger deep into his asshole, and with my free hand I started to play with his nipples again. His big uncut dick tasted salty, and the musty smell of his pubes and balls made my head swim. I was into this boy, and I wanted as much of him as I could get. As I sucked him and massaged his asshole, he was already on the verge of shooting a load down my throat. But when I started to tease those nipples, man! That boy's ass just started going wild, opening up so wide that it literally sucked in two more fingers, getting wetter as he rocked his butt to get more; then it shut so hard on my fingers I thought they were going to get broken. I eased off on his tits, softly playing them, and his hole released its grip as Carlito let out a long, deep moan.

"Fuck me, Daddy, fuck my ass," Carlito hoarsely whispered.

Still sucking on his dick, I pulled him down to the floor, onto his back, and pressed his legs hard against his chest. My dick was leaking so much that it lubed his hole as the fat head pressed up against it. I reached down and teased his nipple, and his asshole sucked my dick into him all the way to my balls. As the sudden sensation of being buried deep in his hole seared itself into my consciousness, Carlito busted the first of many nuts, shooting his load all over my chest and stomach as his superhot ass bit down on my dick. It took every ounce of concentration for me not to shoot too, but it seemed that Carlito's ass had other plans as it squeezed and stroked my dick from the base of my shaft to the tip of my head. I was loosing it fast, and after a few more deep pulls, sucking my balls into his hole, I exploded, squirting load after load into his hungry butt, almost passing out from the force of my eruption. We looked into each other's eyes after that, and it was as if we were both struck by a bolt of lightning. The mutual hunger that ignited into a firestorm between us made us mad crazy freaky. We fucked from one side of the bathroom to the other, up along the walls, bent over the sink, and seated on the toilet, with Carlito's asshole burning so hot it felt as if the steel rod piercing my dick was melting. I pumped his hole from every angle, and that boy just kept craving more. My balls burned from beating against his ass cheeks. His nipples were angry red buttons, raw from the biting, twisting, and rubbing. We were so into screwing that neither of us heard the knocking on the bathroom door. I was so busy wringing yet another serious load of come from his balls that I didn't hear the keys jangling in the lock or the door opening or the stealthy entrance of a silent voyeur to the hard, deep digging-out of Carlito's fine papi ass that I was engrossed in.

I'm not certain when it dawned on me that we weren't alone,

but since I was nearly ready to bust another load of come into that insatiable Boricua ass, I figured, What the hell? Let 'em look and see what a man-to-man ass-fucking really looks like. Just the idea of putting on a show for some unseen stranger in the same room made me pound Carlito's ass that much harder, doggie-style, bent way over his upraised butt so that each stroke of my shaft in and out of his fine ass was slow, deep, and long. Thinking about the view from behind us and what the stranger must be seeing drove me into an orgasmic frenzy, especially as Carlito shouted out, "Oh yeah, Daddy, fuck yo bitch!" I shot my load so hard I swear my balls collapsed from the effort. I was almost drained as I ground my hips into Carlito as he came again. I felt drops of hot, sticky come gush onto my ass, and I knew that our mysterious voyeur had really enjoyed the performance. I started to pull out of Carlito to see who the visitor was, but suddenly the intruder was jamming his fingers into my ass, using his own come to lubricate my hole.

Now, I'm not into flipping. I'm a hard total 110 percent top dawg. I fuck, okay? I don't get fucked. And now some punk was trying to do just that. In fact, before I could even turn around to confront him, the stranger was pushing his stiff prick into my hole. A fucking BIG prick at that! Maybe it was just the fact that I was so tired from the reaming I was giving Carlito, but I don't know how I took that huge dick up my ass. The stranger reached around and grabbed my pierced nipple as he started to get into his rhythm fucking my hole, which made my dick swell inside of Carlito, and before long the three of us were into a mad sexy sweat, fucking like junkyard dogs. That's when I caught a glimpse of the three of us, butt nekkid, with me sandwiched between a hot papi and that sexy Vietnamese barista. Damn! It was clear what part of him was black, as his thick ten-inch bone churned my guts. I shot my load first, backing down on the barista's dick so hard that he busted his nut in my ass with such force that Carlito felt it and shot his load too. Tran, the barista, was dazed, and that's when I made my move. The nigga was going to get it now, even if he did give a good fuck.

I ripped my dick out of Carlito's ass so hard that it made a loud POP when it was finally loose. I swirled around, pulling Tran's big fat dick from my dripping hole, grabbing him by the shaft and balls. He was one fine mothafuckin' boy, those black and Vietnamese genes mixing it up into the hottest package you could imagine. Smooth, hairless skin, six-pack abs, hard, sleek thighs, muscular chest, and well-defined arms. We exchanged a silent glance, but before he could regain his senses, I slammed his fat dick into Carlito's wide-open asshole and spread those fleshy mocha cheeks of Tran's as wide apart as my hands could hold them, forcing his clenched asshole to open. I spit onto his ass crack, rubbing my still-hard dick up and down as Tran squirmed. Then I rammed my dick deep into Tran's butt, making him yelp with pain.

"Now, mothafucka, I'm gonna pop that ass just like you popped mine!"

I reamed that tight brown Vietnamese ass, just ripped it open, I fucked that boy until my dick was raw. Carlito was also enjoying the fresh meat, moaning with every movement of Tran's meaty dick. As for Tran, if anyone could flip me, he'd be the one, since his ass was every bit as good as his dick, and I found myself wanting him every which way too. Our threesome action was just as intense as when Carlito and I were knocking it. The floor of the bathroom was so slippery from our sweat and come that none of us could stand up, so we just rolled into all kinds of nasty positions right there in the middle of the floor. When none of us could get it up anymore, we started this freaky fisting daisy chain, with Tran sticking his fist up my ass, me fisting Carlito's butt, and Carlito punch-fucking Tran's ass until the boy's eyes rolled so deep into his head I thought he'd faint. He didn't, though; he just channeled the deep pounding he was getting from Carlito into my ass, and soon all three of us were spinning our heads into alternative dimensions.

I came to and found both Tran and Carlito, facedown, out cold, legs sprawled apart, buttholes just gaping open like the mouths of twin caves. I got up onto unsteady legs, trying to keep my balance on the slippery floor, and stood over the both of them, slowly rubbing my raw, red, swollen dick until I could feel the piss working its way down my shaft. I let loose a stream of dark yellow urine, aiming at both their assholes, filling each up, then just pissing all over their still bodies. My balls were beyond blue; each step I took was unbelievably painful. My guts hurt from being tossed around by Tran's huge dick, Tran's hand and arm, and then Carlito's arm. I made my way to the toilet and sat down heavily on it, praying that nothing would fall out. After I got myself together a bit more, I looked around the room for my clothes. Dressing, I checked my watch: three fifty-five PM, I was going to be late.

The elevator stopped at my floor, and thankfully no one saw me get off or saw the way I hobbled to my office, bent over like a man dying from a stomach wound in some old Western. It was four-fifty PM. Crosstown traffic had been murder. My phone was flashing angrily, seventy-eight messages, and the flickering red light only intensified the dizziness and nausea I was feeling.

"Whoa! What happened to you, buddy?" Dale blurted out as he passed by my open door. He popped his head inside. "Mean run-in with some Chinese food?"

"Naw, Thai and Puerto Rican."

"Oh, that's a tough combo. Well, you didn't miss anything; they're still at it. Should I tell them you're back?"

"No, in a minute, I want to hit the head first. "

Dale mercifully left, and I dragged myself to the men's room and splashed cold water on my face to revive myself. As I dried off, I took inventory in the mirror. Not too bad: no unexplainable stains, no noticeable marks. But I knew it was going to be a very long time before I got over this lunchtime encounter. As I walked to the conference room, my fingers ran over the piece of paper in my pocket with Tran's number. Yeah, a very long time indeed.

Epilogue: The Interview

What's that smell?

I love the smell of Crisco in the morning. It brings pleasant memories of tight butts discovering they have fewer limits than they imagined.

Why do you do what you do?

Because it makes me feel alive; because it gives me power; because I am very good at it; because it makes my dick hard.

Don't you feel like a traitor to the race?

No, sugar, I'm not betraying anything. I'm doing my part as one of the Talented Tenth, helping our entrepreneurs, financing our businesses, supporting our artistic expression, helping brothas under stress to relieve some of that tension they're under. Don't you feel relaxed after all that good sexing we've been having?

But, you're same-gender loving. Don't you think it's your duty as an educated, professionally employed, upper-middle-class, high-income black male to marry an eligible black woman?

I'm a faggot, okay? Queer, Gay, Bent, or, as my mother used to say, speaking about others, Funny. I don't buy that politically correct, *same-gender loving* bullshit. And I'm not DL, down low or any of that other shit. I fuck men, okay? And I love fucking 'em.

Okay, you're gay. And as such, you're reducing the eligible pool of accomplished black males who could marry educated sistahs. Don't you think black women should be able to marry cats like you inside of the race?

Girlfriends can do whatever they want; they're liberated. They can follow their pleasure just like I follow mine. But is it my responsibility to single-handedly, or in this case, single-dickedly, make up for the choices that other brothas have made?

That sounds like blaming the victim.

That's tired PC bullshit. A man is only a victim if he chooses to be. Otherwise, he is the captain of his fate, and whatever comes his way, the power resides in his hands to make the most of it, even lemonade out of lemons if that's what's called for.

Exactly! That's why fine, upwardly mobile black men like you have to step up and look out for the race. Get married, procreate, make stable families, keep moving our children forward. Don't you agree?

Everybody has a part to play in the great drama of life. My role is to open the way for faggots of color to take ownership of their lives and revel in the eroticism and sexuality and sensuality and glory of loving a man; to give us triple outcasts—cast out of our homes, cast out of our churches, cast out of our races—a space to gather our power and bring the mothafucking house down, to Burn it all, baby, Burn it down! To bring about the final revolution in the collective consciousness that will ultimately enable everybody, Black, White, Brown, Yellow, you name it, to see that

God made us all in his image, every one of us, and He did not make mistakes with any of us. That is the profound truth of this millennium, and it must be learned and incorporated into all of our actions, every moment of our existence.

So you're saying that gay men of color are the key to revealing the mystery of the ages?

I'm saying that strong, positive, conscious, determined gay men OF COLOR are the key to society's collective salvation. When society at large can love gay men of color, openly, as much as those wide-screen TVs and *Girls Gone Wild* tapes and fast-food and PlayStations, then there is hope for its ability to sustain itself.

Well, they say the Roman Empire fell because of its fall into depravity, debauchery, and buggery.

Honey lamb, just shut your mouth and back that ass up on Daddy's phat dick. I feel another reaming coming on, and your butt is making me hungry.

Ummm, can we do it in the sling? I'd love to have your dick in me when I'm in the sling!

See there? That's why you my boo! Come on, boy, Daddy's gonna dick you down good!